THE Storm THAT SHOOK THE World

THE Storm THAT SHOOK THE World

—— A NOVEL ——

WALTER SOELLNER

New York

THE Storm THAT SHOOK THE World

Published in New York, New York, by Morgan James Publishing. Morgan James and The Entrepreneurial Publisher are trademarks of Morgan James, LLC. www.MorganJamesPublishing.com

The Morgan James Speakers Group can bring authors to your live event. For more information or to book an event visit The Morgan James Speakers Group at www.TheMorganJamesSpeakersGroup.com.

Shelfie

A **free** eBook edition is available with the purchase of this print book.

CLEARLY PRINT YOUR NAME ABOVE IN UPPER CASE

Instructions to claim your free eBook edition:
1. Download the Shelfie app for Android or iOS
2. Write your name in **UPPER CASE** above
3. Use the Shelfie app to submit a photo
4. Download your eBook to any device

ISBN 978-1-63047-863-6 paperback
ISBN 978-1-63047-864-3 eBook
ISBN 978-1-63047-865-0 hardcover
Library of Congress Control Number:
2015917799

Cover Design by:
Rachel Lopez
www.r2cdesign.com

Interior Design by:
Bonnie Bushman
The Whole Caboodle Graphic Design

In an effort to support local communities and raise awareness and funds, Morgan James Publishing donates a percentage of all book sales for the life of each book to Habitat for Humanity Peninsula and Greater Williamsburg.

Get involved today, visit
www.MorganJamesBuilds.com

Habitat
for Humanity®
Peninsula and
Greater Williamsburg
Building Partner

Jesus met Levi and said to him, follow me and
I will call you Mathew. (In German, Mathew is Mathais.)

Dedication

To Sandra York Soellner, my lovely and loving wife:
charming, kind, patient, forgiving, and smart.
She who senses the rightness of things:
words, sentences, stories, people.

Europe and Africa, 1914

The Levi Estate in Bavaria, Germany, 1909

Table of Contents

Note: For your pleasure, I have included preview chapters of
Book III in the Kalvarianhof Series entitled ***The Long Way Home***

Kingdom of Bavaria

Acknowledgments

Thank you to my friends and family, who have, over the past eight years, assisted, consulted, proofread, and edited this second in a series of four books tracing the lives of Markus Mathais and Solomon Levi.

I especially want to thank my wife, Sandra, for endless hours assisting with conceptual ideas, actual proofreading of text, and the computer applications necessary to bring book two to its present form.

High on the list of dedicated assistants are George and Gilda Forrester, who patiently read various iterations of the book two manuscript, dotting i's and crossing t's at every stage.

Thank you, Eve and Ken Reid, another pair of minds of true value, who contributed insightful margin notes throughout.

My daughter, Anna Soellner, for her ongoing support in keeping my spirits from flagging and encouraging me onward over the long writing process, thank you.

Edward Rooks, talented artist and designer who created maps and transformed photos and drawings into true works of art for publication, many thanks.

Thank you Kristi Conley, for your artistic skills with the cover design.

There are unnamed friends and colleagues who have encouraged, supported, and inspired me in this wonderful endeavor, warm thoughts and many thanks.

Kaiser Wilhelm II
King of Prussia and Emperor of Germany

—— CHAPTER 1 ——

Imperial Germany, Autumn 1909

ailing south from the city of Bremerhaven, a major port for Imperial Germany, in a reverse route Markus had traveled seven years earlier, the young Imperial German officer leaned on the familiar railing of a naval cruiser and watched the coast of France slip by.

The SMS *Konigsberg*, loaded to the gunwales with supplies for Germany's four African colonies, plowed through late September swells, bringing troops, military supplies, settlers, food, and beer—lots of good German beer—to the thirsty colonials in Africa.

Markus Mathias, newly minted lieutenant of His Majesty, the German Emperor, King of Prussia, William II, was bound for the Imperial German colony of South West Africa. This was Markus's third trip to this wild and primitive land on the south west coast of the Dark Continent. He enjoyed his first trip with his friend Levi in 1898 as teenagers on an adventurous holiday. His second trip, Christmas of 1900, was the coaling stop on the return of his military unit after the Boxer Rebellion in China.

Now, in the autumn of 1909, this third journey was to be the start of a new life after the tragedy of his lost love with Levi's sister, Ilsa. Yes, they agreed, both teary-eyed, that it could never be—a Jewish girl and a Catholic man. Catholic Bavaria in general and their social and professional circles were not ready to accept a union so mixed, no matter how true the love. And, of course, the families would have had none of it—if they had known.

So Markus, now twenty-seven, found himself alone on a long and important military mission, and for the first time, without his close friend Levi.

I've always relied on Levi to give me good advice and encouragement, and he had a way of tempering my more reckless impulses. This trip is different; I'll be alone and with some serious responsibilities. He thought of these things as he jostled other soldiers crowding the railing on a sunny, blustery day off the coast of France.

"Well, young man, what do you think of our ship? It's one of your navy's finest, I imagine." The speaker was a stout man with a quick smile, speaking in heavily accented German and wearing a perfectly tailored civilian suit. Markus turned to respond to the hearty questioner.

"*Ja*, it is a fine ship, and fast, but these cruisers are being superseded by a new class of heavier more advanced design and with better armor." Markus hesitated. "And who, sir, do I have the pleasure of addressing?"

"Warner Lange, Professor Warner Lange"—he cleared his throat—"from California."

They both blinked in the gusty wind. "And I see you are a lieutenant—and with lightning bolts on your epaulets. You must be in some kind of communications outfit?" He looked expectantly at Markus, waiting for an answer.

"Yes, sir, that's correct." Markus stood erect, clicked his heels, and said, "Lieutenant Markus Mathias, electrical unit officer of the First Bavarian Army Corps for Lower Bavaria, with headquarters in Munich, currently assigned special duty to the Kaiser's colony in South West Africa." They nodded to each other in mutual recognition.

"So, Professor Lange, what brings a professor from far-off America— California, you say—aboard a German cruiser heading for Africa?" It was an intriguing question, and Markus focused intently on the American.

"I have been invited by your government to assist in the upgrade and testing of the long-range wireless telegraph installation in your South West Africa colony. So we are headed to the same destination. How interesting."

They both eyed each other with growing professional interest. "And you, Lieutenant, what is your purpose in this long sea voyage to the southern hemisphere?"

"It appears we are both going to the same facility. I am bringing our latest wireless equipment for installation."

There was a long pause as the two men, pressed momentarily against the railing, let other passengers through the crowded deck.

Markus continued, "You say you are from California? I just read about Marconi's radio broadcast from some little town over there. Very impressive!" He grinned and shook his head slightly before adding, "And exciting for the future of direct-spoken wireless communication."

They both smiled broadly, with the knowledge that it was, indeed, the future direction in their field.

"Well—Markus, is it? Markus, I've just come from that little town; it's San José . . . San José, California, and I was with my friend and colleague Gugliermo Marconi when he made that transmission. A wonderful scientific event! We were both teaching at the college there until he left to develop his business interests."

Lange stared out to sea. Markus, so impressed with the stranger he had just met, thought, *He's a friend and colleague of Marconi, and apparently, he participated in the first voice radio broadcast ever!* Markus didn't know quite what to say.

Warner Lange solved that by offering, "Lieutenant, would you join me and my family for dinner at our table this evening? Say, seven o'clock? We're in the first class dinning salon. We can continue our conversation over a nice meal."

"It would be my honor and pleasure, Professor Lange."

With that, Warner Lange took his leave with a tip of his hat and disappeared into the crowd on deck.

Dinner was served separately in a dining salon reserved for civilian passengers and high-ranking officers. It was a plush, ornate room, with deep carpet, curtains on the windows and the dinnerware had the ship's own motif, with SMS *Konigsberg* prominent on each plate and bowl. Markus felt a bit on display as he walked upright through the tables of military and civilians.

Most officers who looked up immediately fixed their eyes on the two Iron Crosses on his uniform, earned by his daring actions in China.

He spotted Lange across the room at a round table for six. Two naval officers were already seated with the Langes. As he approached, Warner's eyes lit up, and he rose slightly as he greeted his new acquaintance.

"Lieutenant Mathias, glad you could join us. Dear, this is Markus Mathias, Bavarian lieutenant assigned to the same project I will be working on." All eyes were on Mrs. Dorothy Lange, a strikingly beautiful, willowy woman of about forty.

Next, Lange introduced his daughter, who was sitting with her back to Markus. He stepped to her side as she offered her hand as her mother had done. Diana Lange smiled but said nothing as the two naval officers rose from the table.

Lieutenant, this is Captain Spencer, the chief medical officer on board and Captain Becker, the purser. Markus saluted and received salutes and greetings in return.

Dinner was served and pleasant conversation was had around the table. Professor Lange inquired, "What can we expect when we get to port in Africa?"

The two naval officers each commented that he had been to other German colonies, but not to German South West Africa.

"And you, Lieutenant, have any ideas?"

"*Ja*, well, this will be my third visit to this colony."

Thus began a series of lively questions from all around the table; most were taken aback that such a young officer could have visited this far-distant and impoverished corner of the world twice all ready.

Questions about South West Africa led to the *whys* and *wherefores,* which led to Markus's experiences in China and finally to how he managed to receive two Iron Crosses, one of the most prestigious honors in the German military.

The conversation was brisk and entertaining and progressed long after most guests had left the dining lounge.

Finally, Mrs. Lange suggested it was time to retire. Everyone agreed, with chairs pushed away and cloth napkins dropped onto the table. Parting words were exchanged and everyone headed toward their rooms. Warner caught the cuff of Markus's uniform. "Shall we retire to the bar for a final toast to our joint venture?"

German South West Africa

—— CHAPTER 2 ——

Swakopmund and Windhoek, German South West Africa

arkus was surprised to see how much progress had been made in developing the port and town as the SMS *Konigsberg* eased into a berth at Swakopmund. The railroad to the capital, Windhoek, had been completed and expanded to other parts of the colony.

Over twelve thousand German missionaries and immigrant farmers flowed into the back country fifty miles beyond the desert terrain of the coast for free land, and in the process, transplanted German culture to the wilds of Africa.

There was the usual excitement and confusion of disembarkation, with piles of civilian luggage next to tons of government equipment. Warner Lange, followed by his family, managed to spot Markus and exchange lodging addresses.

"We are staying here in Swakopmund for a few days to see the sights and get our land legs before moving on to the capitol next week. And you?" Lange was practically shouting because of the stiff wind howling around the superstructure of the ship.

Markus replied in kind, "I'm off by rail to the military base at Windhoek tomorrow morning. I'll be bunking here on the ship this evening, although I thought I would walk the town to see what's new. Can I help you with the luggage?"

"No, no, Lieutenant, but we are staying at that new hotel over there, the Bismarck. It's the building with the ladders leaning against it. Join us for dinner if you like, about seven."

"That would be delightful, Professor. I'll see you then." He did a half-salute, with a smile to the two ladies, and said, "Ladies," and left. Dorothy Lange, in her gracious and subtle way, said to her husband, after Markus left, ""You seem especially taken by that young officer, dear. Could our daughter have anything to do with your interest in him?" Fortunately, Diana was peering over the side of the ship, watching all the activities.

"Now, Dorothy, the man's in my same field of work and very bright—and you saw his two Iron Crosses. They don't give out those honors except for exceptional reasons. He wouldn't be a bad match for Diana." He hesitated and took his wife's arm, turning her slightly. "Look at her, so lovely and smart. She's got a head on her shoulders, that girl, but she's already twenty-two!"

"Twenty-one, dear, twenty-one."

"Yes, for another eight weeks!"

"But a foreigner? You can't be serious. And we know nothing of his family."

"He's German. You can't beat that for a foreigner. They're some of the smartest people on the planet. Look how many successful Germans there are back home."

"That's my point, dear. They're back home." She finally added, "And there's that Andrew Hopkins. I'm told he's going into his father's business in San Francisco."

"Really?"

"Railroads and banking."

"Are you sure about that?"

"Yes, dear."

Markus arrived at the Bismarck and found his way to the dining room while sniffing the fresh paint in the lobby. Black servers, obviously well trained by the hotel staff and impeccably attired with white gloves, were busy serving guests.

He came up behind the professor and faced the two women across the table. "Greetings again, Mrs. Lange and Diana. I hope you are well settled here in this lovely hotel." He did a quick sweep of his arm around the dining room.

"Professor." Markus nodded his head to him.

"Yes, Lieutenant, welcome to our little home away from home—very nice quarters." Lange picked up the menus. "Now, let's see what they serve in one of the Kaiser's colonies, shall we?"

As everyone studied the menus, Markus related, "The last time I was here in Swakopmund was Christmas 1900 on the way home from China. Governor Theodor Leutwein gave us a wonderful New Year's Eve party just down the street at Government House. The food and music and dancing were excellent. Everyone had a grand time!"

"You mean there were ladies to dance with here in 1900?" Diana asked.

Markus delighted in answering the Lange's lovely young daughter. "Why, yes, there were, but not enough of them." The Langes burst out laughing in unison. Flustered, Markus quickly added, "What I meant to say was that I was on a troop ship, so there were a lot of men and they all wanted to dance, so the ladies were really put upon to dance most every dance."

He regained his composure and smiled broadly before adding, "My good friend Levi, whom I served with in China, was also with me. Our ship stopped in Uruguay, and we met a very nice family whose daughter, Katherina, was on her way to Berlin with her aunt for her studies. She danced and danced, and it was all great fun. Levi actually married her several years later. They recently had a pretty little girl." Warner Lange looked across to his wife who exchanged *the look*.

Markus was staring at the center of the table in a fixed way, lingering in his private thoughts. Diana looked at her mother. Finally, Dorothy looked intently at Warner. He caught the unspoken signal.

"Yes, well, an interesting story and nice to hear everyone had such a splendid time. And your friend, Levi, is it? You must be very happy for him and his family."

Markus snapped back to the here and now. "Yes, it's a wonderful family. They deserve all the happiness in the world."

"So, let's order!" Lange said with a flourish. "I could eat a longhorn!" The two women laughed while Markus looked puzzled.

Diana spoke up, "A longhorn is a cow, well, actually a steer, and most of them are wild! You will find them in the West . . . of America. They have big, long horns, each one this long!" She stretched out her arms full length, almost reaching from her mother's shoulder to Markus.

"That must be some animal. I'll have to come to California and see one someday."

Mrs. Lange said, "Diana, put down your arms!"

"I was only showing Herr Lieutenant, I mean, Lieutenant Mathias, how big they were." Diana blushed in embarrassment.

"Frau Lange, your daughter has really quite a wide reach. Those cattle must truly have big horns." Everyone chuckled as dinner arrived.

CHAPTER 3

The Ranch, the Hunter, and the Huntress

T he next few weeks found Markus settling into his quarters in Windhoek, getting acquainted with the existing military staff of the wireless station, and uncrating the delicate wireless equipment. The Langes also found their accommodations in Windhoek, and Warner and Markus began their collaborative efforts of installing and testing the new equipment Markus had brought from Germany. Governor Leutwein expressed great interest in the wireless station and its vital military and commercial value by staying in close consultation with Lieutenant Mathias and Professor Lange.

At one of the frequent, long lunches held by the governor to discuss progress and technical problems of the wireless, several leading businessmen also attended. One of them was a large landowner, rancher, and early settler in the South West Africa colony named Tomas Conrad. After one of the luncheons, Herr Conrad invited the Langes and Markus out to his ranch for several days of relaxation and hunting.

The sprawling Conrad holdings encompassed several thousand acres of grasslands, salt pans, upland forest, a few year-round springs, and during the dry season, dry river beds. With several blacks in his employ, Conrad and his seven children lived as isolated, landed gentry. Conrad was one of the lucky ones, or rather, he got in early, got good land, and diversified his enterprises. Some of his fellow German farmers and ranchers weren't so fortunate.

"We raise cattle, some sheep, and the orchards do quite well for us. The railroad makes it easy to transport our meat, fruit, and livestock." Conrad was obviously proud of his accomplishments and his family.

"We've started doing a bit of mineral exploration up along the escapement."

As the four guests settled into overstuffed, slip-covered couches in the parlor of the ranch house, Tomas proceeded to introduce his seven offspring who had filed in. They were lined up as in a military formation but with bright smiles for their visitors.

"My oldest, Wolfgang, now twenty-six; Arnold, next, twenty-five; Humboldt, twenty- four; Helena, twenty-two; the twins, Michael and Norbert, nineteen; and our little angel, Christina, eighteen." Everyone exchanged greetings before several of the Tomas boys excused themselves.

"Always lots to do around here," Arnold said, staring at Diana as he took his leave. The two daughters stayed and were delighted to talk with another young woman. After many questions about ranch life, Tomas said, "Petre, our houseman, will show you to your rooms. We dine at seven and retire early, as we will head out just after sunrise tomorrow. The wagons, guns, and equipment will leave at five, and your horses will be saddled by six. It should be good hunting."

Talk at breakfast was all about the hunt. Wolfgang began, "We will be after antelope today, several types actually, but we may see elephants, zebras, giraffes, and hyenas—lots of hyenas. If we're lucky, we may spot a desert rhino, the black one . . . That would be a bit of luck."

Michael added, "With real luck, we may spot *die strandwolf*. Now that would be something!" He concluded with a grin.

"At least we won't have to worry about the Nile crocodiles; we aren't going as far as the river today." He chuckled at his own joke.

Warner spoke up, "You have crocs here? In America, we have alligators, thousands of them, but not in California!" Everyone thought that was funny.

"*Ja,* I know about your alligators," Conrad said, looking across the table at Warner.

"But these Nile crocs are something else again. They get to eighteen feet or more, live for seven or eight decades, are surprisingly fast over open land, and are man eaters. We always stay clear of them when we're down by the river. They take cattle, sheep, antelope . . . anything that goes near the river." Michael looked serious and sounded serious. "All the animals out here are dangerous in one way or another, including the wild dogs. We had a visitor to the ranch once who went out early one morning. He saw a wild dog and decided to feed it a breakfast roll. He came back with a bad bite on his hand . . . very lucky there weren't several other dogs. They would have taken him down, gone for the throat; that would have been the end of it . . . And I won't even mention the snakes!"

"Now, now, let's not scare our guests. No one in the family has had a bad experience with snakes," Conrad added

"What about Mobuto? He—," Arnold spoke up but was interrupted by his father, who gave him an exasperated look.

"He wasn't part of the family," Conrad said.

After a morning blessing recited by a very devout Helena, the breakfast table was abuzz with chatter about the animals. The hungry hunters devoured fresh-baked Kaiser rolls with honey and butter, African coffee, and an assortment of fresh fruit and sausages.

"Everyone finished? Good. Let's saddle up," said Tomas.

The Langes and Markus were fascinated by the topography of the ranch—so different from California or Bavaria.

"You warned us it would be very warm out here in open land. You're right," Lange said, as he used his riding crop to swat off a horsefly on the mane of his mount.

They had been riding for over an hour, away from the tall trees and cool shade surrounding the ranch house. Markus was glad he now wore the cowboy-style hat with one side pinned up that the German army had issued to its African troops. The wide brim all around kept the blazing sun off his neck and out of his eyes. Better to see the lovely Helena, with her silver crucifix rising and falling with the rising and falling bounce of her white blouse.

Their horses trotted through the vast grass lands that swept to the distant, shimmering, blue-gray hills miles distant. Diana, obviously an expert rider like her mother, rode on the other side of Helena. The entire Conrad and Warner families, and Markus, were riding out, but only several were actually to hunt. The rest would stay in the day camp already set up for them before dawn.

Tomas and Warner lead the twelve riders, along with three black rifle bearers. The tracker was several hundred yards ahead of them. Tomas made sure all were kept far behind the tracker. He pulled back on his rains and brought his horse to a stop. The others caught up and also halted.

"From here on, I must ask you all to refrain from talking," Tomas cautioned. "Our tracker has signaled that he found traces of game nearby." On signal, the rifle bearers quietly rode up, slid out of their saddles, and distributed a half dozen rifles out of large saddle bags: one to each of the lead riders and one to Helena.

"They're loaded, but no rounds are in the chamber," Tomas said quietly. The metallic click and counter click sounded six times simultaneously as each hunter opened and closed the bolt, sliding a round into firing position. Markus held his rifle across his lap behind the saddle pummel, as did most others.

"So, Helena, you're to be a hunter today also?" Markus asked, smiling.

"Of course! Why not? I often hunt with Papa and my brothers. It's fun. I like to get out into the open country and see what surprises God has for me today." With that, Helena spurred her horse forward and joined her father.

Most of the hunting party without rifles broke off and headed to the camp. The hunters walked their horses quietly for several hundred feet through high grass interspersed with thorny bushes twelve feet tall.

While khaki-colored dust was everywhere, there were patches of dark, almost black, spiky leaves on the bushes and faint traces of a lighter green at the base of the straw-like grass. All around were shades of tan, brown, gray, and black. Only the cool blue sky broke the deathlike colors of the arid landscape before them.

Tomas raised his hand and all stopped in their tracks. He did a hand signal, twirling his finger held out to his side, then raised it to his lips for silence. Everyone knew the hand signal meant, "dismount." The rifle bearers came up, without making the slightest sound and took the reins of the horses.

The six hunters with both hands on their rifles cautiously moved forward toward the tracker, trying carefully to avoid stepping on dry sticks and other debris.

Without turning around, Conrad brought his left hand directly out from his shoulder and rapidly spread his fingers out twice. Everyone stopped in his tracks and remained motionless. Each stood like a statue for at least three minutes when the tracker, in the line of sight of them all, raised his hand slowly and signaled three times with his hand and pointed off to the left.

Fifteen, everyone thought. By rotating his wrist, he communicated for the six hunters to come forward into a firing line. The group had been briefed that when the tracker found antelope, each hunter was to pick out one as a target but not shoot until Tomas fired the first shot.

The party members in camp heard the crack of rifle fire: ten, eleven, thirteen shots in all. Flocks of birds flapped into the air near the fallen antelope. The crashing of thorn bushes and branches was heard as the rest of the frightened animals sprinted, in great leaps, for their lives.

"How many did we knock down?" Warner practically shouted as the group moved forward. One of the antelope lay on the ground but still kicked its legs in an effort to get up. The tracker, with a quick shot, dispatched the wounded animal.

"Looks like we have seven fine kills," Tomas declared as the others walked around, prodding and poking and debating who shot which antelope.

"This one's mine!" several said.

"How many shots did you get off?" asked Warner.

"One," Markus replied.

"One? Only one?"

"It's all I needed."

"But didn't you try for a second kill? I mean, there were a whole herd of them!"

"It wasn't my intent to shoot the whole herd," Markus said, as he examined the chamber of his rifle.

"Breaches open, everyone!" Tomas ordered the safety procedure, and added with a big smile, "Time for lunch!"

Back at the ranch house, after a lunch at the day camp, a late dinner was prepared that included antelope steaks, roast antelope, and a wonderful, cream-based antelope stew. Following the leisurely meal with tales of past hunts and famous African hunters, everyone strolled into the parlor for a surprise Tomas was eager to share.

"This just arrived on the same ship our guests sailed on, the *Konigsberg*," he said, primarily addressing his family. Tomas walked to a small table and dramatically pulled a cloth away, revealing a beautifully finished wooden box.

"It's a gramophone! See here," he opened the lid. "I ordered several dozen of these musical cylinders. Helena and Christina selected the musical pieces. Shall we try it?"

As the Edison gramophone was cranked and a cylinder recording of Brahms piano lullabies wafted through the parlor, Michael asked Diana if she would like to go for a stroll in the garden, just outside the double doors of the parlor. Several others joined them, including Markus, Wolfgang, and Helena.

"The last time I was here, the Boer War was still being fought. Of course, that was nine years ago. I'm interested to hear what impact the war had on your family and the ranch," Markus directed his comment to Wolfgang, with Helena listening.

"Yes, well, actually, it had a positive effect," Wolfgang began. "Both the British and the Boers purchased our crops: beef, sheep, and of course, timber after the war. We had a lot of sympathy for the Boers's cause, actually. After all, they were ranchers and farmers like ourselves. As soon as gold was discovered in the Boer territories, the British jumped in to take control of as much land as they could . . . and to expand their empire."

Markus listened intently as Wolfgang went on, "Of course, the Boers weren't blameless. Up until around 1900 they still supported slavery!"

A calm silence enveloped the threesome as they looked at the dazzling night sky, blazing with a million stars against coal-black infinity.

Finally, Wolfgang added, "But we get along with our British neighbors all right. They're good customers!" A little laugh and smiles warmed the star-studded heaven gazers.

"This is one of my favorite times. I mean, at night, like this," Helena spoke to no one in particular. "I often stroll in the evening, after dark. It's like I feel closer to God when I am alone and it's quiet, with the vast heavens above." She was looking up at the shimmering sky.

Markus paused and lingered, looking at her staring up, her head back and the faint light from indoors just lighting her white neck and the side of her face. Wolfgang again broke the silence. "Helena already has a reserved seat in heaven . . . if she can get one of those for her devotion. A good Catholic she is, always in church and always praying for everyone in the family!"

"Don't mock me, Brother. God can hear every word you say." With that, she turned and walked off.

"I'm sorry, Sister. I was just making a joke for our guests!"

There was an awkward moment, and then Markus offered, "Maybe I'll join her for a few minutes." With that, he turned and stepped lively in the direction Helena had taken. The young woman stopped by a small grove of fruit trees her father had planted.

"May I join you, Fräulein Conrad?" Markus spoke softly.

"Oh, I thought I was alone."

"I'll leave if you like."

"No, no. Stay if you wish." She paused "My brother . . . it's disrespectful how he talks. I don't have any unrealistic expectations about his beliefs, but he shouldn't have—"

"Of course he shouldn't have! It was just an inappropriate attempt at humor. I think he was trying to entertain his guest."

"Yes, well, it wasn't the first time."

They were both silent for a few moments before Markus said, "I think I know how you feel . . . I mean, about God . . . and religion." A few moments of silence passed as Helena turned slightly toward him.

"Back home in Bavaria, we—I mean, my mother and sister and I—go to church every Sunday . . . to the Mariankirche in Munich. It's a big, beautiful church with a wonderful organ."

She turned more toward him. "We don't have a big church like that, like the ones in Germany, but we do have a good choir, and an organ. I'm in the choir."

She was looking at him. "If you like, you can join us next Sunday. We go to the later Mass, the High Mass, at ten. It takes us a while to get into town."

"Fine then, I'll meet you at the church. Which one is it?"

"It's the only Roman Catholic church in Windhoek, Saint Joseph's. The other church is Lutheran, and there is a Dutch Reformed congregation, but they don't have a church."

They walked on awhile when Markus spoke again, "I'm glad it's to be a High Mass. I love the pageantry of the music and candles and bells and the processional. It's all so beautiful—and the incense . . . I like that, too." They were both smiling.

"Maybe we should turn back," she said, touching his arm.

"Must we? This is a piece of heaven you have here, all to yourself."

"It's for everyone. All one has to do is look up to the heavens."

Markus could not resist himself. He raised his hand to her cheek and gently turned her head to his. He leaned in a bit closer to her and looked into her eyes.

"Lieutenant, you are too forward!" As his dropped his hand, "I am so sorry, Fräulein. I didn't mean to offend you. It's just such a beautiful night and such a beautiful place.

"Just because you've been to China and in the army and all those places, and medals and such, don't think you can, you can…"

"I said I'm sorry, and I am sorry, truly."

They were silent again, standing there in the dark. He with a passion built up over months, she with mixed emotions, but with a warm stirring. "May I still meet you at church this Sunday?"

"Of course, of course, you can." She had involuntarily touched his arm. Again, stillness, a beautiful stillness, with energy in the air between them that they both felt separately.

Finally Markus spoke, "Do you have a favorite star, somewhere up there?"

"Why, yes, it's at the tail end of Cassiopeia. See? Up there, near that bright one." She was pointing. He pointed, too.

"No, no, you're too far over to the left . . . This way. See where I'm pointing? Below that fuzzy bunch of little stars, see?"

"Which fuzzy bunch of little stars? There are dozens of fuzzy bunches of little stars!" They both broke out in laughter, and it took several minutes to recover.

"Oh, you are such a slow learner," she said, in a feigned exasperation. "Now, let me show you exactly where my star is. Now, point up where I am pointing. Now, sight straight up your arm and off your finger . . . Keep it straight! Fine." She walked around him to his upraised arm.

"No, no, don't move. Now a little over that way." She was close behind him and raised her arm to his, gripping his wrist and moving his arm a bit down and to the right.

"Now, do you see my star?"

"Oh, *that* bunch of little, fuzzy stars!"

"Now, don't you get started again," she scolded him with a smile. "It's just there!" She squeezed his arm for effect. "Do you see it now?"

After a moment's pause, he replied in a soft, quiet voice, "Yes, yes, I see it, and it's beautiful . . . very beautiful."

They hung there in silence, in the dark, not moving, with only a million stars glowing down on them for light. She could smell him, his manly smell, and it stirred her. Her hand was still on the back of his wrist, and being so close to his back, she could feel his body rise and fall with each breath.

He realized her hesitation, her silence, her hand still on his wrist. He slowly lowered his arm, turned toward her and in a husky whisper,

"Beautiful, it is truly beautiful."

Her arm came down with his, and they stood there, close together, she was not looking up but staring almost through him in the dark. This time she could feel his hand slowly raising, coming between them, just brushing the front of her blouse as it touched her chin. He lowered his head slightly as he raised her chin. Their lips barely touched. Each could hear, —feel the other breathing. He moved his lips away an inch, perfectly still.

Then he moved gently in again. She was rigid, but he could hear her breathing. His hands slid around to her back and pressed her to him. Each was swimming in emotion. He could feel her voluptuous body against him, and he was very aroused. His hand slid lower down her back and pressed her to him. This was too much for her, and she broke off from their embrace.

"No, no, you mustn't. I must go!"

With that, he released her as she moved swiftly down the dark, well-worn path.

"Gute nacht," he said.

St. Joseph's Roman Catholic Church, Windhoek

—— CHAPTER 4 ——

A Note Not of Caution

It was a small church, but built of solid, rough-cut blocks of stone mortised together, like many of the buildings in Windhoek. There was a single bell tower, in a style that resembled medieval structures, with elements of Gothic architecture. On this morning, the sun slanted through the stained glass windows, creating what the monks used to call "divine light." The atmosphere had a mystical, artificial illumination that made the congregation feel as if they were halfway to heaven.

After meeting Tomas Conrad, several of his sons, Christiana, and Helena earlier, Markus sat, stood, and knelt with the group six rows from the alter. Helena left them to join the choir for the service. It was the first time Markus had seen her since the morning after the kiss, when everyone had a noisy breakfast before he and the Langes boarded the surrey for the ride back to Windhoek. He had no chance to talk privately with her then.

All the Conrads went to communion except Wolfgang and Markus, who had not been to confession since before leaving Munich. In his adult life, he tried to make it a point to attend Mass on Sunday, but Markus did not subscribe to the church rule that it was a sin to miss.

Now he found himself enjoying the familiar rituals of the Latin Mass: the organ music reverberating off the stone walls, the drone of many voices reciting the familiar prayers, the candles and incense and the bells.

After Mass, the family lingered outside the church, greeting neighbors and passing the latest news and gossip.

"We're having lunch at the hotel where the Langes are staying. Why don't you join us, Markus? I'd like to hear more about China and that wireless tower you're building," Wolfgang offered.

"*Ja, danke.* Your father has already invited me." He just finished accepting the invitation when Helena walked out of the rectory. She stepped into the bright sunlight from the dark shadows of the stone church and presented a dazzling vision. Her full-length, lavender dress flared from her tiny waist, and the lace parasol matching her dress was held just above a wide-brimmed hat. Markus could not take his eyes off her, and she noticed. Wolfgang did, too. She smiled gaily as she seemed to float up to her family, where everyone engaged in light conversation.

"I saw you sneeze just at that part you say you don't like singing," Christiana laughed. "Did you do that on purpose?"

"No, I did not!" Helena replied to her younger sister. "Frau Dietrich was wearing that awful perfume again. Next Sunday, I'm standing at the other end of the line!" Everyone enjoyed the exchange between the two girls.

Finally, Tomas suggested, "Let's walk down to the hotel for lunch. Shall we?"

It was often the custom of the Conrad family to have their midday meal at the hotel after church. The host seated them at their usual, long table, with Helena and Markus across from each other. They smiled and talked through the lively chatter and the final goodbyes as the Conrad family headed back to the ranch.

During the luncheon, Markus excused himself for a moment, enough time to write a brief note to Helena: Meet me at Dimplemeyer's Dry Goods Wednesday. Noon. –M

He managed to pass the note to her. She had a chance to read it, and she replied silently with a smile.

———

"The Kaiser doesn't supply his army officers with their dry goods needs?"

He heard her voice before he saw her among the tall stacks of an amazing assortment of farm, ranch, and household goods. She added, "Are you going to buy one of those camel saddles? They're quite comfortable, I hear." They both laughed before Markus could say anything.

"Grüß Gott!" he smiled. "Any problem getting into town? I mean, alone, without your brothers and such?"

"No, no. I'm a big girl now, and this isn't Munich or Berlin, with its restrictions for women alone in public. Besides, I usually come into town on Wednesdays to go to confession. It's when Father Lorraine, our French priest, is in town." She paused, then added, "We country girls are pretty independent . . . in some ways."

"Yes, I'm sure you are. *Ja*, so, do you have something important to confess?" He looked at her mischievously.

"Don't you know, sir, it's not polite to ask a girl her sins?" They both enjoyed the banter, back and forth, as they strolled among the aisles of iron skillets and bolts of cloth.

"Good day, Fräulein Conrad," a familiar voice said.

"And to you, Frau Hofstein. How is your family?"

"Well, very well, and yours?"

"All are just fine, Frau Hofstein. By the way, this is Lieutenant Mathias, a friend of the family. Lieutenant Mathias, this is Frau Hofstein, the proprietress here. I see you have new merchandise in. How interesting!"

All through this exchange, Frau Hofstein stared at Helena's companion. Finally, a customer summoned her away.

"Shall we walk about awhile?" Markus asked.

"Yes, let's do. I'll need a few moments in the church between two and three."

"Of course."

As they stepped along the wooden planks that made up the town walkways, Helena squeezed Markus's arm gently and asked, "Are you going to invite me to lunch? If you are, I know of a nice Dutch café that has tasty crepes."

"Crepes sound perfect. I've only had a few rolls and coffee this morning, about seven." She took his arm, opened her parasol, and they were off to lunch.

Blue and white porcelain plates with windmills and sailing ships hung in profusion on the walls of the little café. There were five tables with blue and white checkered tablecloths, but they chose one of the two booths, further back. Beer, bread, cheese, and cold cuts came to the table, with jam-filled crepes promised for dessert. Their conversation, animated fun for both, involved reciting their life stories to each other—with certain gaps in Markus's recent history. The time flew by until Helena glanced at the pendant watch pinned to her dress.

"Oh, I have just time enough to get to church, Markus. Let's hurry!" Two dozen school children were kneeling in the front pews, watched over by several nuns, as Helena made her way down the side aisle, followed by Markus. She slid into a pew and knelt across from the confessional door. A dozen adults were also waiting their turn with the priest.

"Are you going to have your confession heard?" she whispered. The thought had crossed Markus's mind, but he hadn't decided until she asked. He was surprised by Helena's devotion to the church and had thought about it earlier. He decided he liked that about her. He liked her virtuousness, rural earthiness, and independence—and her charming elegance and raw beauty. He couldn't look her way without stirred feelings.

As the weeks went by, Markus was invited to the ranch twice more, taking stolen kisses in the shadows. He also managed to meet Helena several times a month on Wednesdays, usually at the Dutch café. Christmas was approaching and Markus, alone in his officers' quarters, thought many times about Ilsa and the painful love they had shared. He knew he had strong feelings for Helena, but it was hard for him to separate his sexual desires from a more deeply felt emotion. Her body, smile, and laugh—that simmering passion just below the surface, held in check by a genuine sense of propriety, caused Markus conflicted feelings toward her.

He also thought back to his China days with Li Ling. How perfectly lovely it had been The two of them, innocent in their love, had not realized the forces outside her father's walls would forever separate them.

Now here I am, he thought, just three months into my military assignment in Africa, and I find myself captivated by another woman. I must go slowly with this. I can't let my desire to make love to her fog my judgment. What am I getting into here? I go back to Germany in nine months! Would she go? Do I want her to go? We would have to be married. Would she marry me? I think so, but who knows?

Do I want that? I wanted that with Li Ling and with Ilsa, but do I want that now? And what would her family say? Do they know I'm meeting her? They must see there is a strong attraction between us . . . That's for sure. I wonder what Tomas thinks of me. I know he likes me, but would he want me as a member of the family? Or what would he think of a man who might—would—take his daughter away to Germany . . . thousands of miles away? And her brothers? OK, Wolfgang and I get along fine, but the others not so much yet. They're busy with their own interests.

The sister, I hardly talk to . . . except hello and goodbye. Her mother is gone. How much does Helena fill that spot, she being the only grown woman in the house? Who knows? Every time I see her, I want her. I'd better take care of that part of it myself. I can't be so sexed up all the time when I'm around her. I might do something stupid. That's not what I want either.

German East African Line

—— CHAPTER 5 ——

Thoughts

C hristmas 1910 passed and the spring and summer of 1911 flowed by, seemingly as brief as a desert stream in a rare storm. The seasons dissolved into a blur of work, trips to the coast, inspection tours of telegraph lines and equipment, hunting safaris, and of course, visits to the ranch.

Markus and Helena had become somewhat of an informal couple within the family and their small circle of friends. But Markus had also been invited to Professor Lange's for dinners and went on several walks with his daughter, Diana. She was beautiful and vivacious and seemed interested in him.

There's something about the quality of Americans, Markus thought. *They're fascinating and much more informal in their habits. They speak out directly on every subject that comes up. These women, at least these two American women, Diana and her mother, are both bright and beautiful.*

He thought back to China and vaguely remembered some of the American missionary women. They too had some of these same outgoing qualities.

Diana is surely fun to be with, but Helena holds a special charm. Is it that we've kissed, and I've felt her body close to mine? I know she is, or could be, a passionate lover.

It's something I have to think about. We're not engaged, but I'm not a free man either.

It's gone further than I thought I wanted it to. I probably shouldn't be seeing Diana so much, giving her the impression I'm available. With Helena, our relationship has become much closer, more passionate, too. I can't keep my hands off her when we're alone, and she doesn't seem to mind . . . up to a point. Her self-imposed abstinence and virtuous discipline has seen to that!

Markus felt tension and frustration boiling up in him as he thought of these two women.

Lieutenant Mathias's commanding officer gave outstanding service reports to Markus and suggested he extend his military service an additional year. Helena asked repeatedly, "What are you going to do?"

He managed to sidestep definitive answers, but knew he couldn't—shouldn't—put off an honest reply much longer.

He really wanted to go home and see his mother and sister and Levi. In many ways, he wanted to be in Germany again, but he also knew he would miss Helena.

Would Tomas Conrad permit his daughter to visit Germany with me without being married? Natürlich nicht. Was für ein dummer Gedanke!

And now his commanding officer offered him an increase in rank and pay and a two-month furlough to visit his family if he would extend one more year.

He loved military life, at least the way he was living it. He had wonderful officers' quarters, and the officers' club was small but nice. There were smart military men all around and lots of freedom within his duties.

And Africa—what a grand and beautiful and exotic land! There was a spiritual quality to the vastness, the unspoiled landscapes that stretched to the horizon, as if handed down from the Garden of Eden. Helena would like that thought. He smiled to himself.

The decision was finally made. Helena insisted on seeing Markus off at the chilly, windy port at Swakopmund. The Deutsche Ost Afrika Linie ship was scheduled to depart for the long voyage home to Germany, weighed anchor October 10, 1911. Wolfgang, Arnold, Michael, and Christiana also came dockside to wish him off.

"Please give my greetings to your mother and sister and your friend Levi you spoke so much about. They will all be happy to see you and hear about your success here in Africa and your higher rank. I'll miss you . . . especially at Midnight Mass this Christmas." It was an awkward, emotional moment for Helena and Markus.

Wolfgang sensed it and made a point of leaving the two alone at the bottom of the gangplank. Arnold, Michael, and Christiana were enjoying the hustle and bustle of the ships and people—so different from life at the ranch.

"Markus, two months seems a long time, but when you come back, I will be so pleased." She looked away a moment. She told herself she would not lose her composure, but it was very difficult.

She had never in her twenty-three years met a man like Markus. She had other suitors and even a kiss or two but never experienced the feelings she felt for this soldier now leaving for his homeland, thousands of miles away. She knew she loved him. She felt he loved her, too. But she knew there was something holding him back, something in his past, possibly, that he did not, would not, reveal to her.

Does he have a girl back home? she wondered. I'll probably never know.

Helena had made a pledge to herself, not to push him, not to give herself to him as she longed to do. She would wait for him to come back to her. She would pray to a merciful God to give him to her. She asked God to do this one thing, as she had never asked for anything before. Now they stood on a windy, cold dock, she holding his two hands in her two hands close to her chest. She looked down at them, then up at him, expectantly, as the ship's horn bellowed across the harbor.

"I will miss you, Helena. I will—"

"Just say you'll be back, Markus. That's all I need . . . Say you will be back."

"Of course I'll be back, of course." They were close together, their heads almost touching. He moved his hand up and touched her chin. Their lips came together gently, then with a passion emerging from a sense of loss and separation.

He brushed a long streaking tear from her cheek as the ship's officer shouted, "Last call! All ashore that's going ashore."

He approached the young couple. "Gang plank's coming down in two minutes, sir."

"Thank you." Markus pulled away, then pulled her close and kissed her again.

"I—" He touched her lips with his finger, interrupting her. She whispered the rest to herself. She released him.

He turned to go, then turned back and said, "Yes, I know." Just as he turned to leave, she saw a tear at the corner of his eye. It gave her, for a moment, a sense of misgiving.

Wolfgang ran up just as Markus stepped onto the gangplank. He slapped Markus on the back, wished him safe voyage, then pulled him close in and said, "She'll be waiting for you, Markus. We'll all be waiting for you!" With that, he gave a hearty laugh and released his sister's one true love.

—— CHAPTER 6 ——

Advice from Home

L ook at you, dear Markus, so tanned and fit!" Katherina gushed as Markus's mother and sister, Anji, welcomed him home at the Munich train station. Levi held back just long enough for Frau Mathias to have a moment with her son. Then he too hugged his dear friend in an embrace that lasted several moments as the two exchanged greetings.

"And you have an increase in rank, I see, Captain! What have you been up to down there?" Everyone laughed. "What? No new medals? *Ha!*"

"No, they don't give medals for just doing your job." He looked at them. "It's a long way home . . . and so good to see you all again. Oh, and this must be little Rebecca. How you have grown in one year!"

"Yes, it has been a full year since you left, but now you're home with us again. What fun we'll have, just like old times!" Katherina exclaimed.

Everyone crowded around the new arrival as his mother pronounced, "We're all going home to a nice dinner, to a welcome home dinner for my son!"

Levi had his own shiny, black Benz automobile, and they crowded in, bundled to stay warm on the short but blustery drive to Frau Mathias's apartment in Munich.

"So few suitcases?" his sister Anji commented. "When you came home from China, you had so much, so many crates. Did you bring us a present, Markus dear?"

Markus's mother, Fanny, spoke up, but with a smile, "That's not polite, Anji—even if it is your brother."

"No, no, Mama, it's all right . . . and yes, Anji, I have something very special for you, but you must wait. Several trunks will be delivered from the station tomorrow."

It was a short drive from the train station to the Mathias apartment near the Englischer Garten through the bustling city of Munich.

"There seem to be so many more automobiles on the streets than last year when I left. They outnumber carriages and wagons."

"Yes, and I want to learn to drive an automobile, too!" Anji exclaimed, peering out at the busy streets.

"You? Drive a Benz like this?" Levi said in a slightly mocking tone.

"Well, no, not one of these big ones. More like one of those little ones—like that one!" She pointed at a much smaller, red vehicle zipping by on the snow-covered boulevard.

"Oh, that's an electrical auto. You could handle one of those!" Levi conceded. Everyone laughed.

Through the long, happy, homecoming meal, Markus sidestepped questions about his future plans with vague comments about his profession. Levi and Katherina were the only ones to pick up on his evasiveness, but they didn't say anything at the time.

For the next week, Markus was busy reporting to headquarters on the progress and technical problems in constructing one of the most advanced wireless communication systems possible in the German South West Africa colony. Visiting friends and army buddies from the China campaign and spending wonderful moments with his mother and Anji consumed most of his free time. He was simply enjoying being home.

The Levis invited him out to Kalvarianhof several times for lunch or dinner, with walks in the snowy woods and lanes. The elder Levis, happy to welcome him back, told him their daughter Ilsa was expected home from Berlin in a few days. Hearing this heightened his expectations of seeing his former, secret love.

How will I—we—react? he thought.

Levi and Katherina gave Markus time to come around to what his plans really were.

"We sensed your hesitation to talk about the future, Markus," Levi said, as they strolled through the crunchy November woods surrounding Kalvarianhof.

"*Ja,* I'm a bit undecided about my future. You know they gave me rank and a raise and this two-month furlough, so you know I have to do something for that . . . which was to extend my duties for another year at the wireless station."

"Yes, I thought it was something like that. Remember Günther and Heiner? They did the same after China. Of course, they didn't go to university and become officers. You must really like the army life and Africa and your electrical engineering project down there."

"*Ja,* of course I—" Markus's arm went up almost in front of Levi's eyes as he pointed. A deer with six prongs stood forty feet away. It spotted them and bounded off.

"Oh, my father and I still hunt these woods," Levi replied. "Not so much anymore, but we do get out some."

They continued their walk on the wooded road as the late-afternoon, golden rays streamed through breaks in the tall pines.

"Well, there's a complication," Markus began. "There always is, right? It's not really a complication exactly. You see, I've met this girl . . . charming, beautiful, a wonderful woman, truly. We've become very close. But I'm not sure what to do."

There was momentary silence between them.

"Let's head back the long way, around behind the barns," Levi suggested, helping to break the silence.

"You know, Levi, since Ilsa—and before that Li Ling—I'm not so sure of myself when it comes to women." He bent over and picked up a thin branch and began casually breaking off short pieces and throwing them away.

"Do you love her?"

"Yes, yes, I think so."

"Did you . . . you know, sleep with her?"

"No, no. She's very religious. I mean, that's not the reason. I maybe could have, but you see, I want to go slowly this time. I mean, she's really . . . I just couldn't do that to her if it wasn't . . . you understand, a real commitment. And I was, well, *am* still not sure I want that level of commitment."

"*Ja*, I see what you mean . . . and she is in Africa!"

"Yes, Africa. It does complicate things. So what do you think I should do? Any advice?"

"Of course that's got to be your decision, but I would say, since we talked earlier about Ilsa and you having totally different lives now, if you love her, this Helena you said her name is, I mean really loved her..." Levi didn't finish the sentence. It didn't need saying.

"Yes, you're right. Thanks. Good advice—just like old times." They both smiled as Levi rested his hand on Markus shoulder. They passed out of the woods and crossed the meadow to the house as darkness closed in.

That evening, Katherina asked, as they curled up under the big feather bed with little Rebecca between them, "Do you think he's going to marry her? And Africa . . . would he stay down there? It just seems strange to think of him so far away forever. Remember when we walked the dunes and looked at the stars; it really was beautiful." She was smiling. Their baby gurgled, and Katherina gave her the nipple.

"You won't be doing this for very much longer, my little one," she whispered as she adjusted herself and the baby.

"How much longer will you be nursing her, my love?"

"Another month or two. Did you know, Husband, that I can't get pregnant while I'm nursing? Did you know that?" There was a mischievous smile on her face.

"Really?" he said in mock surprise. "Well, now."

"Wait, wait . . . She isn't quite done."

———

The weeks slipped by quickly for Markus and his friends, but the five of them—Anji, Markus, Katherina, Levi, and Ilsa—managed outings frequently. Ilsa and

Markus had a guarded first encounter when she arrived home, but after a long conversation covering each other's past year, they seemed detached emotionally. All seemed well.

Late November found four of the five spending a wintry day in Munich as the Christmas Market opened. Ilsa was home baking her favorite *stollen*, stuffed with walnuts, raisins, and dried fruit. The four saw big snowflakes falling as they sat in a warm *Biergarten,* chatting and munching Nuremberger brats and beer and reading the latest news.

"Snow seems light this year. You'll just miss skiing, Markus," his sister commented.

"Yes, and no skiing in the colonies . . . well, except on Kilimanjaro in East Africa. That is, if you can hike that far up with your skis strapped to your back!" he responded.

"It truly must be beautiful, Africa, with all those wild animals and primitive people," Anji mused.

Markus turned to his sister and admonished lightly, "I've found most of the blacks are gentle and, in their way, intelligent . . . It's a different world than what we know here. You'll have to visit Africa to really understand."

"Yes, of course, Brother." She looked at her three companions. "The three of you have been to Africa. How unusual, don't you think? I mean three in our little group." Anji gazed out the window of the café at people bundled against the cold, scurrying by "It will be Christmas soon. Why do you have to go back to Africa, Markus? Mama and I want you home. You could get a job here. I'm sure of it."

Her brother looked up from his paper, and across to his sister. He said gently, "Of course I could, Anji, but I'm in the army, doing some very important work. It's only one more year. Then I'll be home." He was trying to be sympathetic to her. He knew how emotionally dependent she was on him since Papa died. He knew she truly missed him, what with only Mama at home.

"You said that last time. You said, 'I'll only be gone a year.' Now it's two years! Are you ever really going to come home?"

Katherina looked across at Levi after that comment. Levi looked up at her, too.

"What? I saw you two looking at each other . . . with that kind of look, that stare," Anji sat up stiffly in her chair. "You know something. What is it?" She looked at her brother. He was hiding behind his newspaper. She abruptly reached over and pulled the paper down. "Markus, I know something's up. What is it?" There was a long silence. She could read her brother like a book.

"What?" Markus shook the paper free and raised it again.

"I know! You've got a lady friend in Africa. Correct? Am I right?" There was a long pause. "Is she black?" Another pause. "She's black, isn't she . . . and you don't want to bring her home because Mama would have a heart attack!"

Levi and Katherina burst out in convulsions of laughter. Even Markus couldn't hold back. He too exploded with a roar, crumpling the paper in his lap. Between gulps of air and gasps, with tears in his eyes, he said, "Well, Sister, you're half right!" And with that, the three of them burst again into hilarity. People at other tables looked over with grins on their faces, wondering what was so funny.

"You have a girlfriend! So that's it! Why didn't you tell me? That's wonderful!" She looked around, caught the humor of it all, and joined in laughing. With Markus's "secret" out in the open, they all had many questions about the mysterious woman: her looks, her family, her personality, and so on. And the big question was, of course, how serious is he about her and will she come to Germany or will he stay in German South West Africa?

"I'm not sure . . . I'm not sure about anything." With more beers all around, the rest of the lazy afternoon was spent in warm, intimate coziness, listening to all the details.

After a French lithograph of the Colonial Empires, 1898:
England, Germany, Russia, France, and Japan (Missing
Spain, Portugal, and the Ottoman Empire)

—— CHAPTER 7 ——

Storm Warnings

T he crumpled newspaper that slid to the floor in that charming café
that day, in December 1911, also presented a warm rosy picture of life
in Munich and in Germany as 1912 approached. Good news, at least
on the paper's front pages, distracted readers from the back pages, where news
stories and articles of a different kind could be found. Over the last several years,

events in seemingly obscure locations and backwater countries caused growing unease among more astute readers.

The world's empires—Germany, France, Austro-Hungary, Russia, Great Britain, Japan, and the Ottoman Empire—with their vast colonies, were all aggressively jockeying for advantage in securing foreign lands to add to their various colonies. Most disputes, while settled peacefully, caused social and political tensions.

Many of these events appeared in the headlines for a day or two and were though of by the general public, if thought of at all, as isolated aberrations from a generally peaceful Europe. Over the past half dozen years, headlines read:

1905: "Russian Revolution Crushed by Czar's Loyal Troops"
1905: "Russian Battleship Potemkin Mutiny; All Officers Killed by Sailors"
1905: "Jews Massacred in Odessa, Russia"
1906: "World's Largest Battleship, the British Dreadnought, Launched"
1906: "Germany, Austria-Hungary, and Italy Form Triple Alliance"
1906: "German Navy Launches First U-Boat Submarine"
1907: "Bulgarian Prince Ferdinand Crushes 10,000-Peasant Revolt"
1907: "Kaiser Buys Count Zeppelin's Dirigible for German Army"
1908: "King Carlos of Portugal and Crown Prince Assassinated"
1908: "Serbia Threatens War over Austrian Annexation of Bosnia"
1908: "Germany Pledges Support of Austria's Actions in Balkans"
1909: "Austria Considering War with Serbia"
1909: "Russia Invades Persia"
1909: "Lord Northeliffe: Germany Preparing for War with Britain"
1909: "France Creates Colonial Armies in Case of European Conflict"
1910: "France: Mandatory Military Training"
1910: "Imperial Russia Annexes Finnish Duchy"
1910: "Imperial Japan Invades, Annexes Korea"
1910: "Kaiser and Czar Agree: Germany Gets Baghdad Railroad Deal"
1910: "Czar Gets Free Hand in Persia"
1910: "Palestine Arab Uprising Crushed by Ottoman Troops"
1911: "German Reichstag Increases Army by 500,000 Troops"

1911: "Britain Declares: No Support for France in Case of War"
1911: "Russian Premier Stolypin Assassinated"

Like the crumpled paper under foot, these headlines and articles slipped from memory, as each new addition of these newspapers quickly became so much litter. Markus spent his last afternoon with Levi, after saying his farewells to Mama, Anji, and his friends in Munich. Before Levi was to drive Markus to the village train station, they again walked the woods at Kalvarianhof, like many times in their youth. The two tramped noisily through the high, frosty grass.

"Have you decided about Helena?" Levi inquired as they both braced against the cold December wind.

"No, not really. I'll just let things unfold when I get back to Windhoek . . . see how Helena feels about me, truly, and me her." They both pulled their collars up against the icy wind.

"I didn't tell you earlier," Markus began, "but there is another woman, an American, whose family is very friendly toward me. I've been invited to dinner and such with them. She's very nice, a real beauty, but—"

Levi cut him off. "Another woman?" Levi stopped in the crunchy snow, turning toward his friend. "You never said anything about another woman. Are you really seeing two women at the same time?"

Before Markus could reply, Levi continued, "*Mein Gott*, you'd better be careful. You could lose your commission if a scandal—"

"No, no. It's nothing like that at all. Diana's dad, Professor Lange—Diana, that's the American's name—her dad is working at the wireless station with me. Really fine fellow. They are such a nice family, so I see him almost every day. We both live in Windhoek, so we dine together on occasion, me and his family. I've only been out and about with Diana five or six times, all very proper. But she is a vivacious girl, beautiful and, well, a lot of fun." The two fell into silence.

Then Levi continued exploring this new revelation: "Five or six times? Here at home, that's practically saying she's spoken for! Does Helena know?"

After an awkward pause, Levi pressed on, "You dine with a family with a single daughter, beautiful, as you say, in that little town of Windhoek?" Levi took his hat off and brushed his hand through his hair. "Markus, my friend, this has all the makings of a sad—and possibly scandalous—nightmare for you. Haven't you learned anything?"

"Yes, I know. Don't you think I know that? But, you see, I don't know what I want. I mean, I'm not sure I want to make a commitment to, to just one girl."

"Well, you better! You must make a decision. It's not fair to either of those women, is it? Is it?"

"*Ja*, no, you're right. I mean, I know you're right."

"Markus, I know you've had some disappointments with women, with Li Ling and my sister, Ilsa, but those relationships are in the past. You have to let your doubts go, but learn from them. Don't let those sad episodes in your life cripple your future. You only have your future, your career, and your happiness. Remember, you're not in the South Pacific anymore. You're not a young lancer. You're an officer." Levi turned and continued walking. "That's all the advice I can give you except to remind you, you must do what's right. Make a decision, and be honest with those women. That's all I can say." With that, they headed back toward the manor house, both now shrouded in an uneasy silence.

Katherina and Ilsa and the senior Levis bid farewell to their lifelong friend, as Levi loaded Markus's suitcase into the Benz. The little group waved goodbye as Otto said, "Your express train leaves at five, so you have plenty of time to get to the station."

Levi and Markus both enjoyed the drive along the forest lane, this time slow and steady on the snowy road. Their lighthearted chat after their sober walk in the woods brought the two men close again, like the old days.

"You wouldn't believe how Windhoek has grown since you were there. Did I tell you they even have three aeroplanes at our installation?"

"And you took one of them up, didn't you?" Levi grinned.

"*Natürlich*. They were surprised at my flying ability and aeronautical knowledge, especially in repairing those engines. It wasn't long before they let me fly. And, I did fly all three at one time or another. It was great fun to see the African countryside and magnificent herds of animals from the air. Levi, you should come back to Africa sometime . . . and bring Katherina."

"I'm quite happy here, but who knows? Someday it would be nice to do a grand tour of our colonies in Africa." They ended their time together on a warm, brotherly note.

"I'll be back in ten months or so."

"Well, don't forget to write and let us know how it all works out for you. Good Luck!"

With that, Markus threw his suitcase through the open wooden door into his first class train compartment and gave a wave to Levi. He was gone in a cloud of steam and gray coal smoke, headed north to the Port of Kiel and the light battle cruiser SMS *Dresden*.

German South West Africa

—— CHAPTER 8 ——

Passion and Regret

T he SMS *Dresden* was three days late steaming into Swakopmund Harbor, German South West Africa, because of winter storms at sea. Captain Mathias had a long time to think about his life and his future on the voyage south. It was Wednesday, December 21, 1911, and Markus was eager to get back up to Windhoek, his job at the station, and of course, Helena.

He sent a telegram ahead, stating his train's arrival time, and she was at the station, with Wolfgang, Humboldt, and her sister, Christiana. Markus was laden down with Christmas presents, gifts for both the Conrad family, all of them, and for the Lange family, too. One trunk was completely packed with presents.

They all gave him hugs, and Helena gripped his arm tightly as they rode in an open carriage to his military headquarters. The two young women wore long, white, summer dresses, with tight waists and lace around the bodice. They both carried open parasols. It was a balmy seventy-six degrees in the bright sun. It was a pleasing shock for Markus, with such a contrast to the howling winds and cold of Munich in December and the storms at sea. Here, below the equator, spring and summer lay ahead.

"I must report in, but I should be free this weekend," he announced to everyone in the carriage. "It's so good to be back!"

As the others chatted, Markus turned his head toward Helena and whispered, "Did you really think I might not come back?" She looked at him with a smile, squeezed his arm, and said nothing for a moment.

"I prayed for you . . . for your safe return," she said, not looking at him. "Will you be coming out to the ranch for the weekend?"

"*Ja,* I do so want to greet your father and everyone." This time Helena looked Markus in the eyes and smiled. They both felt a strong desire to kiss, but held back, knowing that Christiana was watching them.

Earlier Christiana had elbowed Humboldt and nodded her head toward the couple. Wolfgang looked at her and said quietly, "Behave yourself," and then engaged her in lively distractions.

Professor Lange met Markus on Thursday afternoon at the wireless station. The two were genuinely glad to see each other and to be able to talk the talk of their profession.

"Won't you join us for dinner? The family will be most happy to see you again."

Mrs. Dorothy Lange was elegant and lovely as always, and Diana, in a pink, flowery dress was as beautiful as a fairytale princess.

Over dinner in their spacious apartment in the Bismarck Hotel, Markus said, "I told my friends in Munich about my American friends from the California Wild West and about your longhorn animals. They said we should get some for the Munich zoo!" This made the three Californians laugh to tears, thinking of their cattle in a German zoo.

"Shall we go for a stroll after dinner?" the professor suggested. "They have just finished the park—little trees and nice flower beds and all such. When it grows up, it will be a fine addition."

"Oh, let's do!" Diana exclaimed. "Mother? Markus?" It was agreed, and in no time, the four were out the door, headed for the newest addition to Windhoek.

"Markus," Warner began, "did I tell you I had one of the antelope racks from the hunt mounted . . . head and all? Fine trophy. I'll show it to you when I get it back."

"Splendid, sir. I'd like to see it and maybe mount one for myself soon." They walked the sweeping, stone-lined paths recently planted with a profusion of native, flowering plants.

"I need a rest," Warner declared as he sat down on one of the wooden park benches. Dorothy followed suit, saying, "I believe I'll join you, dear."

The young couple stopped and Markus offered, "Would you like to go back to the hotel, Professor?"

"No, no. Dorothy and I will just sit here awhile. You two go on. Enjoy yourselves. If we're not here when you get back, we'll be home."

As the two started out, Warner added, "There's a café just on the corner there. Maybe you know it, Markus. Great Viennese pastries. Diana, if you do go in, bring me several of those long, twisty ones with the cream inside . . . great for breakfast."

"Yes, Father." With that, they were off down the curving path and were soon obscured by the bushy ferns and other plantings.

"It's good to see him back. What do you think?" Warner asked.

"I think you think too much of him, dear. I've seen Markus in the company of that young woman from the ranch, Helena." Dorothy thought a moment and continued, "I just don't want Diana getting too involved. I don't want to see her hurt." She sighed.

"You know she likes him."

"Yes, well, of course she likes him. He's a fine young man."

Warner turned and looked down the path, then turned back. "As for that other woman, of course Captain Mathias would be social with the Conrads. There's not that much to do out here in Africa. It's not like San Francisco . . . well, before it burned down after the earthquake, but you know what I mean."

Strolling along the poorly lit path, Diana began, "It's nice to have you back, Markus. My father enjoys working with you on those wireless projects." They were not touching at first, but Diana slipped off a cobblestone and collapsed to one side. Markus lunged for her and grabbed her arm as she was halfway down, pulling her upright.

"Oh, my! Thank you! I almost fell. This part of the path is so uneven," she exclaimed, taking his arm firmly.

"Are you all right?" he asked. They had turned toward each other, still very close.

"Yes, yes . . . I believe so," she replied, looking up at him in the dim light. "Good thing you caught me, or I would have gone right into the bushes." They were both smiling. "You would have had to come in after me!"

"It would have been my pleasure." They both had a little laugh over that potentiality, and Markus added, "Let's go to that café your father was talking about." She took his arm as they made their way to the brightly lit café, buzzing with others out for the evening. After coffee and the purchase of her father's treats, the two resumed their walk, but this time down side streets, the long way round back to her hotel. It was much darker, with fewer people about. Diana held Markus's arm.

"I hope we can do this again soon, Markus. It was such a lovely evening."

He hesitated, "Yes, it is, and you, Fräulein Lange, are so lovely in that pretty dress."

She stopped and turned in closer to him. "Really? Do you like me in this dress?" She looked down at her front, then up at him.

She was beautiful, and he thought, *She wants to be kissed.* But, before he could finish the thought, their lips met. She melted into his arms, and he could feel her body pressing against him. She lingered in the embrace, and he was moved by her body close to his and by the night and by her lips.

He surrendered to the impulse and allowed his hand to circle around her and press her to him. She let out a tiny sound as her arms went around his neck. He was sure she could feel his desire, but she didn't pull back from his pressing hands. Against his instinct, he finally broke off the kiss and loosened his hug. She slowly lowered her arms in a moment of awkward silence between them.

"I'm sorry. I shouldn't have done that," he blurted out. "We should be going."

"No, no, it wasn't you . . . your fault, I mean. We, I mean, I . . . it was just a lovely moment. I hope you thought so, too," she said with a touch of embarrassment in her voice. He didn't respond, but turned, took her arm by the elbow, and continued their walk. They turned the corner into a small square with a double row of trees and park benches. A small fountain gurgled in the dark shadows off the path.

"Isn't that a pleasant sound?" she said, griping his upper arm.

"Where is it, the fountain?" They stopped a moment to listen for the direction of the water. It was almost pitch dark, and Markus broke away and took several steps, stopping by a tree as he listened. Oh, it's a water trough for horses!"

They both laughed. He came back to where Diana was sitting on a nearby park bench. He sat down beside her, raised his arm and pointed into the night. "It's over there somewhere," he said. She raised her hand and slowly pressed his arm down, turning into him.

This time, though still gentle, it was a more passionate kiss. Shrouded in the darkness of night, with not a soul to be seen, amidst the splashing of the water, the two enjoyed each other's touch and kisses. His hand traced down her arm to her breast and his fingers closed around it. She did not resist. Their lips parted slightly as their tongues touched.

His hand pulled slowly, effortlessly revealing a smooth, soft shoulder and chest. He kissed her there. She held his head to her, not thinking, only feeling the sweet pleasure of it all. Up to her lips again, as they were both enveloped in the moment, his hand went to her knee, to her inner thigh. She leaned into him and kissed his neck.

"We must be going," she whispered.

"Yes, of course." They walked in silence most of the way back. Nothing had to be said.

As they approached the lobby of the hotel, she asked, "When will I see you again?"

"Soon," he replied. "I'll have to check my work schedule." She wanted to kiss him good night, but even she knew it couldn't happen there.

"You can drop me off here in the lobby. No need to go up. I'll see you soon." She smiled and whispered, "Good night."

He looked at Diana, this lushly beautiful young woman before him.

She would be any man's dream, he thought.

"Good night, then." They exchanged smiles, and he turned and left.

He was hardly out the doors of the hotel when he started a monologue with himself: What were you thinking? Stupid, stupid! You weren't thinking at all. Your loins were doing all the thinking. But she is damned beautiful, and she loved it. You damn fool. You are not in love with her, and you know it. Helena means so much more to you, and you know that too. You've really done it now. What is Diana to think? She probably thinks we're practically engaged. Verdammt! Will she tell her mother? You're really up to your neck in it this time. How could you be so dumb! Levi was right—two women at the same time is just asking for a scandal. Jesus, now what am I going to do? What if the two of them get together at the ranch?

Markus walked fast toward his quarters, his hands clutching and unclutching into fists at his sides. He shook his head in anger at himself.

For a few moments of passion, I've created a real mess for myself; that's for sure!

───── CHAPTER 9 ─────

Conflicted

Markus was due at the ranch Saturday morning and arrived by horseback, having rented a horse from one of the town stables. The whole Conrad family was there for the noonday dinner, with Helena looking stunning in a frilly, yellow dress that almost swept the floor when she walked. Everyone was eager to see the German officer again and had many questions about events in Germany and the political happenings in Europe.

The meal stretched into the late afternoon and finally moved to the parlor's settees and couches. Markus enjoyed the large, warm, friendly family but could not shake an uneasiness in the pit of his stomach every time Diana's image flashed through his mind.

Finally, the two of them, Helena and Markus, were able to take a walk down to the stables and to be alone. As soon as they had passed through the barn's Dutch door and were out of sight of the house, Helena stopped and turned into Markus. She looking up into his eyes and whispered, "I missed you."

They easily slipped into a long, wonderful kiss and held each other close. He thought to himself, *She means so much to me. I've got to make this right somehow.*

"I thought of you often while I was back home." They smiled at each other.

"Will I see you this Wednesday in town at the café?" she asked.

"I'm afraid not. I have to ride out to several problem areas. We're installing new relay devices to get stronger signals. It's important." He hesitated and added, "I'll be gone ten days or so."

"Ten days? You must leave so soon? You just got back from your furlough."

She gripped his arm as they strolled down the center aisle of the long stable, looking at the horses in the box stalls. "I love the smell of horses," she said casually.

"Me too. I suppose that's why I was a lancer when I first enlisted. They're such beautiful animals . . . and intelligent."

"Well, you may be riding camels here in Africa if you have to go into the really arid parts of the country." They both found that amusing. The two of them walked out the far end of the stable and along a covered walkway to the open door of the tack room.

"I received a new saddle from father last Christmas. Would you like to see it?"

They stepped into the plank-floored room, and she struck a match to light the lantern. More than a dozen saddles on racks and assorted tack hung off posts on the walls. "There," she said.

"So, no side saddle for you, Fräulein Conrad?" he said with a light laugh.

"No, no. I'm a country girl. If I'm to keep up with my brothers, I have to ride like them."

"Can you keep up?" He was looking at her lovely, tanned face while waiting for her reply.

"Yes, I can, mostly." She was pensive for a moment and added, "And I can keep up with the women too." She was looking at him, and he could not escape the double meaning of her comment.

She moved to him, and they were together again in a kiss that had meaning beyond the passion of the moment that swept over them. The raw, physical desire, which had been building in both since being alone, was suddenly interrupted by Sambolo, the teenage stable boy, leading a horse to the coral. They broke off in time to see him disappear behind the stables. They turned back and looked at each other, desire in their eyes.

Helena stepped to an inner door and passed through. Markus followed. It was a feed storage room, with table-height bins for oats and other grains. A mound of freshly cut hay was in one corner. Helena walked to the center of the dimly lit room. Markus stood in the doorway, silhouetted by the lantern light. She turned toward him.

"I love you, Markus," she said in a soft voice. He stood there, looking at her, this wonderful woman before him. There was silence. She slowly raised her arms and crossed them in front of her. Her hands touched her shoulders. She gently slipped the edges of her dress off her shoulders. Her skin was a pale white—an ever so lovely white in contrast to her tanned face and neck. She hesitated a moment and slowly eased her dress down, revealing her chest and the top of her breasts.

"No! Helena, stop!" Markus burst out. "No, please. I won't have you. You don't have to do this for me . . . as much as I desire you." He moved swiftly to her and held her upper arms gently. There were tears in her eyes.

"I love you," she whispered through her tears.

"I know . . . I know. I love you, too." He repeated in a gentle voice, "I love you, too." They kissed again, a long, soft wonderful kiss that stirred their passions. Both were breathing rapidly as they held each other in a delirious embrace.

Moments later, interrupted again, this time by the banging of a box stall door slamming shut, Sambolo came around the corner with a saddle in his arms. He was startled to see a man deep in the shadows of the feed room.

"Oh, sorry, sir, I'll just leave this and come back later." With that, he was gone. Helena had a chance to pull up her dress over her shoulders and compose herself. The two of then walked out into the cool evening air.

"Do you really love me?" she asked quietly as they headed for a row of shade trees along the ridge of the ravine.

"Yes, my dear, but . . . but there are things you don't know, things you don't know about me. I'm afraid . . . That is, I'm not sure."

"Not sure. Not sure of what? What things?" She stopped and turned to look at him. "Do you have a wife or a fiancé in Germany?" She waited expectantly, with a worried quiver to her lips.

"No, no, it's not that. It's not that at all." He was silent for a moment. "I don't have anyone in Germany." He stopped talking and thought about what he just said: *That's not actually true. Ilsa might still love me, probably still loves me. And I—I don't know whether I still love her or not. It doesn't really make any difference any more. But how could I have gotten involved with Diana? How stupid of me!*

"Markus?" Helena was looking at him intently. "Markus, you don't have to tell me everything about your past. I believe you are an honorable man. I believe you would not hurt me intentionally. You say you love me. I believe you. I can wait until you sort out whatever is troubling you. But if it helps, if I can help you, you can trust me too."

CHAPTER 10

Two Notes, Two Women

Markus managed to avoid Diana the few remaining days until he left on his required excursion. He did see Professor Lange and asked him to deliver a note to his daughter from him, stating he had a required trip for the next ten days and would contact her when he got back.

The excursion proved to be grueling but fascinating as the wireless party made their way by saddled camel, crossing changing landscapes and catching glimpses of wildlife, some he had never seen before. At the end of the two-week trip, he found himself back at his billets with a bundle of mail from home, tied with a string, waiting. There were also two local envelopes, both by feminine but different hands. He skipped the mail boat delivery bundle and took up his letter opener, slicing through the stiff fold.

The first note was from Helena:

Dearest Markus,
I hope you had a successful trip to fulfill your duties.
My father and I invite you to the ranch for the weekend next.

Professor Lange and his family are also invited. I await your visit.
God bless, with love, Helena

The Langes are coming too? Cold sweat beaded on his forehead. How am I going to explain this, deal with this? The two of them will surely talk, and for sure, they'll talk about me. This other one must be from Diana. Let's see what she has to say.

He tore open the envelope with certain trepidation and turned over the card to read it:

Dear Markus,
I'm sorry I missed seeing you before you left on your trip.
Daddy gave me your note. I must see you right away.
Meet me at the Dutch café this Thursday, one past noon.
Affectionately, Diana

He walked briskly from his military post, making his way toward the Dutch café. He had rehearsed several versions of an explanation—all seemed totally inadequate, even ridiculous.

Why this urgent meeting? The tone of her note was strange, kind of abrupt. Maybe she's mad at me, or worse, totally in love with me and will demand, no, expect, some kind of commitment—even a proposal. Jesus, I don't feel like going into that café. What am I going to tell her? But here you are, Markus, so in you go.

He stepped in and went to a familiar booth in the back and realized he was the first to arrive.

"I need a beer," he mumbled. "Waiter, one liter, please." He had drained half the stein when he spotted her outside the café, talking with another young woman. Her companion departed, and Diana turned and came through the door. *She is as beautiful as beauty can be*, he thought as she approached.

As he got up, he said, "Hello, Diana. You look as lovely as ever."

She approached and returned the compliment with a half-smile as he took her hand.

"I'm just having a stein. Would you like one?"

"Yes, a half would be fine."

"Waiter, half a stein for the lady." They were sitting across from each other in the half-empty café.

"Would you like to order now for lunch?"

"Markus, dear, I can't stay for lunch . . . I'm sorry."

"Oh, I'm sorry, too. Something important?"

"Well, yes." Diana glanced at the other patrons across the room. "You see, I have something very difficult to tell you. You know I care for you. I think you are a wonderful man, dear Markus. I don't know how to begin, so I'll just start."

Markus could see how distressed Diana was, with her eyes darting away from his gaze and with her fidgeting behavior. He was surprised, perplexed, and completely taken aback as she struggled through the recitation of her unfolding circumstances. He sat in silence, listening.

"You see, you are a very attractive man, and that evening was so much fun . . . I feel I led you to believe . . . or I should say, I thought we . . . that is, it was wonderful being with you then. But, you see, while you were gone on that military assignment of yours for two weeks . . . you see, the mail boat came and—" Her face was flushed, and she was gesticulating, her hands moving in front of her.

"Well, I should start at the beginning. You see, back in California, before I came out here, I had . . . there was this man. Our families were, are, close. He and I . . . I thought I loved him, but he didn't seem to love me, so I came to Africa with my parents. But now, from the mail boat, I received a letter from him. He says he misses me and is offering me a proposal of marriage, which is what I wanted before I left." She paused. "You see, Markus, I still love him, and I want to go home." Tears were streaming down her cheeks as she lowered her head and dabbed her face with her white-gloved hand. Several patrons looked intently at the couple. "I am so sorry, Markus. I have done you a grave—"

"No, no, no," Markus interrupted as he handed her his handkerchief. Thoughts flew through his mind: This is a godsend. It is more than a godsend. Thank you, Jesus, Mary and Joseph. I can't believe it.

"Are you sure that's what you want?" he said softly. "And is it truly clear in his—your gentleman's—letter that he is proposing marriage?"

"Yes, yes! Both my parents read and reread the letter. They're so happy too."

"Then I'm happy too—for all of you."

She looked up, examining his expression. "You're not angry or disappointed? I thought—"

"Of course I'm disappointed, Diana! You're such a beautiful woman and fun and interesting to be with. Of course, I had hoped we could have developed a much closer relationship." They were leaning in toward each other across the table, and he was holding her hands. The same patrons kept glancing over to the couple. The cook and the waiter, with big smiles on their faces, were also keen on observing these two young people, obviously lovers.

"But, you know, Diana, I think it is probably best for both of us, really. My life is pretty much unsettled right now." There was a noticeable uplift in his voice. "I didn't tell you this before, and I suppose I should have. But back in Germany, I had a relationship with a wonderful woman that didn't work out. It's why I came to Africa, really . . . almost just like you." They both laughed at this astonishing coincidence as Diana blew her nose.

"So, you see, it might be best for me to be alone for a while, to sort things out . . . in my head I mean. Maybe it was meant to be, to end this way . . . on a happy note with your pending engagement. What do you think?"

"Yes, yes, I'm sure you are right, Markus. Oh, thank you. I was so worried about telling you. Thank you for taking this all so well . . . and I'm sorry your affair in Germany didn't have a—well, didn't work out."

"So, we're friends still?" he asked.

"Yes, of course, we will always be friends, Markus."

"Well, congratulations!" He leaned across the table and kissed her on the cheek.

Diana smiled broadly and brushed a loose hair with her hand. There was a long silence after that. They both were drained emotionally.

"Well, I must be going," she said at last. "My friend is waiting for me back at the hotel."

"Shall I accompany you there?"

"No, that's not necessary. It's just a short walk."

"Right then. Oh, I understand I'll be seeing you and your parents at the Conrad ranch this Saturday and Sunday."

"Yes, of course. Until then." She got up, raised her hand in a little wave, and was gone.

Markus was beside himself with relief and had a joyful bounce to his gait as he hurried back to the wireless station. *This must be Divine Providence interceding on my behalf,* he thought. And he half believed it. But he soon developed an uneasy feeling about the two families meeting at the ranch, or more specifically, the two young women.

Their conversation still could cause him embarrassment, or Helena could be too affectionate in front of Diana. *She would pick up on that right away,* he thought.

Well, he continued in his mind, *Whatever happens, at least there won't be a scandal.*

All went famously well at the weekend gathering, with Diana's parents announcing proudly the pending engagement of their daughter to a man from a fine San Francisco family and, Diana and her mother would be leaving on the next available ship for home. Warner Lange would stay on for a short time to finish his contract.

Markus and Helena had a chance to slip away on horseback for an evening ride, to a secluded spot on the ranch. In tall grass under the trees, their passion again swept over them like windblown ocean waves. Both bodies surrendered to kisses and caresses.

"Oh, my dearest," she whispered as his hand traced back and forth across her body. And she moved with his every move until they finally lay quiet in the grass in each other's arms, still clothed but in disarray.

"I'm so happy, Markus, darling. I know you wanted to . . . to make love . . . completely, as I did. But you resisted what I could not have resisted. Thank you for loving me that much. I will give myself to you completely, Markus, when we are one."

"Yes, my dear Helena, and it will be—"

"I know, I know," she stopped him as they came together again in a long, lingering kiss.

CHAPTER 11

Best-Laid Plans

A mere two weeks later, Diana and her mother were packed and ready for the long sea voyage. Warner had arranged an unusual passage. The usual route was to take a German steamer back to Germany, on to New York, and finally, a four-day train trip across the country to San José, California.

By special permission of the German Consulate in Windhoek and with the co-operation of the British Consulate in Walis Bay, a small British territory on the coast, the two women instead planned to take a British ship from Walis Bay to British South Georgia in the South Atlantic, then on to the Falkland Islands, another British possession off the coast of Argentina.

There the two ladies would book passage on an American or Chilean vessel that would take them around Cape Horn into the Pacific and due north all the way to California. It would save the women at least a week's travel time if they made timely connections. Several of Lange's American colleagues in Africa were also returning with them.

Three days before the homeward-bound group was to leave, Warner Lange and Markus were in the small military compound that housed the wireless station. It included an electrical assembly and repair building, a barracks, and other support facilities. When not on inspection tours or meetings, the two of them spent most of their time in the small assembly building, testing electrical components.

"Where did you get your hands on these French, experimental, R-type vacuum tubes?" Warner asked in surprise when Markus opened the newly arrived box. "These were being developed in America . . . very private, secret stuff."

"*Ja*, well, we have our ways, Professor." Markus paused in his work and glanced up with a slightly embarrassed but proud look on his face. "You're an American scientist. You see how many Europeans are working in the United States. Take the Austrian Robert Van Liebon, a great electrical engineer. We just installed his electron beam telephone relays on our equipment, thanks to his work in America. We get much stronger signals now."

"I can see that. Are you going to tell me where the next box is coming from?" Warner was looking at Markus and grinning. "I hope it's not from my lab in San José!" They both chuckled, but the message was obvious.

"And what ideas from here are you going to take home with you, Professor?"

"That, my boy, is a state secret!" They both burst into hearty laughter.

"It's time for lunch!" Warner proclaimed. "I promised the ladies I'd be back to the hotel by noon. Come along; we'll dine together." They each grabbed their coat and headed out into the noonday sun.

"Ah, that sun feels good. These stone buildings stay cool all day."

As they strolled along the plank walkway, Warner continued his questioning: "How are those triodes in the amplifiers holding up?"

He didn't get an answer, however, as Dorothy and Diana burst out of a shop directly in front of them.

"Oh, darling, I just found the perfect shawl for back home . . . not too thick and heavy but just right to keep the evening chill out." Dorothy had spoken before she spotted Markus.

"Markus, so good to see you. Are you joining us for lunch?"

Several days later and a day before their ship was to leave, Dorothy and Diana had finished the last of their packing and were directing the servants to transport the luggage to the docks. As the last steamer trunk and pieces of luggage were loaded onto the dray in front of the hotel, an assistant to Professor Lange ran up, gasping and out of breath: "Professor Lange had an accident or something. They've taken him to the hospital!"

"Oh, dear, what happened? What happened? Is he hurt? We must go at once!" Dorothy Lange grabbed her daughter's hand and climbed aboard the half-loaded dray.

"Take us to the hospital!" she ordered the black teamster.

"Forget the rest of the luggage for now; we'll get it later. Hurry!"

Warner Lange was lying on his back under a white hospital sheet in the emergency ward, with a cloth screen drawn halfway around his bed. Markus was by his side, talking quietly to him. A nun in a white habit and apron was holding a damp, folded cloth to the professor's forehead.

Mrs. Lange and her daughter burst through the glass-paneled doors at the far end of the ward. Dorothy scanned the room as she thundered across the wooden floor toward her husband. A frightened look was on her face, and Diana's cheeks were streaked with tears.

"Warner, Warner, my dearest, are you all right? What happened?" Warner raised his right hand a few inches off the sheet as the white-clad Catholic nun stepped forward and raised a single finger to her lips in a sign of silence.

She spoke in a quiet voice, "Your husband has had a heart attack and must remain still . . . and quiet. He must not exert himself in any way right now. His friend here, the soldier, may be able to answer your questions." The nun returned to her care giving.

Dorothy and Diana crowded in close to the bed and were looking intently at Warner's face.

"It's not bad; I'll be fine in a few days," Warner spoke in a tired voice.

"Professor Lange, you must not talk!" ordered the nun. "I must ask you all to leave now, for the good of the patient," she said in a stern but understanding voice.

"Just another moment, please, Nurse," Dorothy pleaded.

"Just another moment then," the nun answered, "but the rest of you must leave now."

Markus got up, looked at Diana's anguished expression, and took her by the arm as they walked slowly down the long room toward the glass doors.

"Oh, what am I to do? Daddy looks so pale. That's not like him. Will he be OK?" She was looking sideways at Markus as they stepped into the hall. He turned to her, and she folded into his arms.

It was a long evening and night for the two women and for Markus, who stayed by their side and held hands with both of them. The doctor had been by several times, with updates on the professor's condition, reassuring them that with plenty of bed rest, the prognosis was good for a stabilized recovery. He suggested there was nothing they could do at this time and that they should go home and get some rest.

"You can return tomorrow morning at eleven, after my rounds, and I'll give you Professor Lange's latest condition." The doctor continued, looking at Markus, "His wife and daughter can visit for fifteen minutes, but with no emotional outbursts. The patient must remain absolutely quiet. His heart needs to rest and heal." With that, he nodded to the two ladies and left.

"I think it best you two go back to the hotel as the doctor suggests. I'll escort you." It was past midnight when the three of them arrived at the spacious suite at the Bismarck Hotel. Mrs. Lange invited Markus in, even at that late hour, to hear the details of the events of the day. Diana appeared completely exhausted, and with a teary good night, she excused herself. Dorothy and the young soldier sat down together on a couch in the elegant parlor.

"What exactly happened to my husband today? Were you with him? Were you two at the electrical building?"

Markus explained how they were at their usual duties at the wireless station and suddenly Warner felt faint and collapsed. He was semiconscious and complaining of pain in his chest. Several workers loaded him into a cart and took him to the hospital.

"I'm so sorry your husband has this difficulty. The doctor seems assured that Warner will recover shortly." They were turned in toward each other. Markus saw the stress and fear in Mrs. Lange, and he tried to comfort her with reassuring words. He took her hand and told her that her husband was in good hands.

"But what am I going to do? Our ship leaves in two days . . . Now it's just a day and a half. I can't leave Warner now. He needs me here." The trail of a tear traced down the edge of Dorothy's face. "This is such an important time for Diana. It should be a happy time for her . . . and now this." She hung her head and brushed an annoying tear streak away.

Dorothy continued, "Her chance at happiness is with a fine, young man in San Francisco. She must pursue this marriage opportunity she so desires, but—"

Markus cut in. "Possibly she could go ahead, travel with Professor Lange's associates back to California. You and the professor could follow in a few weeks when he is better. What do you think?"

She looked up and said, "I don't know what to think . . . Diana traveling all alone—well, not exactly all alone, but I should be with her . . . but, I should also be with my husband." Another tiny rivulet of moisture ended at the side of her jaw and fell onto her dress.

"I wish there was more I could do for you, Mrs. Lange. Perhaps it's best that you get some sleep."

"Yes, yes, of course. And you must be exhausted too."

"Then I'll say good night."

They both stood up. She took his two hands and squeezed them. "Thank you for your caring and concern. Good night."

Markus turned to leave, adding, "I'll see you at the hospital tomorrow."

The next day consisted of a fifteen minute visit by the two women to Warner's bedside, with Markus a few feet away. The doctor had given Warner a sedative, so only a few words were whispered by the patient, with a nun standing as a guard over him. "He must sleep. He must rest while his heart heals," she said.

Later that day, in the dining room of the hotel, Diana agreed to leave the next day with the others, expecting her mother and father to follow as soon as possible. Markus had to get back to his wireless duties but agreed to meet again the next day at the hospital.

Twenty hours later, the two women were again at the bedside. In an emotional farewell, Diana kissed her father, bid him a speedy recovery, and was finally shooed away by a sympathetic but rule-abiding nun.

As she left, her father said in a whisper, "Your mother and I will see you married soon, my dear."

The following morning, Diana, Markus, Mrs. Lange, and Diana's traveling companions were in the train station lobby when several of the Conrad family arrived.

Having finally heard from Markus of Professor Lange's illness and knowing Diana was to leave, they hurried to Windhoek to see her off and extend sympathies.

Markus had a chance to converse with Diana out of earshot of the others. He handed her a small bundle three inches high, wrapped in a native, printed cloth.

"It's a small ceramic bottle made by the Herero blacks who live in the northeast of the colony, up by Rhodesia. They're known for their beautiful pottery. It's for you to remember the happy, beautiful times you had here. I put some African soil in it and sealed up the top with candle wax."

She smiled at him, looking directly into his eyes. "I will always remember you, your kindness to my father . . . and to mother and me. I wish you all the happiness you can find, Markus. You are a fine man, a gentleman . . . and if I may add, I know you will find someone someday who will make you wonderfully happy."

The others crowded around as happens when someone is leaving, her mother giving Diana last minute instructions and hugs and tears and promising to bring her daddy to California soon. The Conrads, including Helena, who was observing the departure, hurried forward as Diana leaned out the train window.

Helena called, "Here is a small bouquet of wild flowers from the ranch. Have a save trip and Godspeed! Press one of the flowers in your Bible. It will always remind you of your friends in Africa."

With that, Diana was gone, heading for the coast and the long trip home.

"She meant something to you, didn't she?" Helena asked without a hint of anger or jealousy.

"I mean, I saw how she looked at you . . . that knowing, familiar look of someone who cares about you, who knows you. It's all right, Markus. I know life can be complicated and—"

"I love you, Helena, more than anything."

———

Markus and Helena were at the ranch the weekend after Diana departed and had strolled out among the trees near the ravine. The last light of a setting sun lit just the top branches in a brilliant, golden glow.

He pointed up and started, "How fleeting that beauty is. Look how it changes colors almost every moment." They gazed up into the gently swaying tree tops.

"Life is like that," he continued, "beautiful, fleeting moments that—"

Helena stopped him with a slight squeeze of his arm. She looked at him for a long time after he spoke. Her lips quivered, and her eyes misted over. They stepped forward into each other's arms in a gentle embrace, a loving hug devoid of overt passion. It was a surrender into beauty and serenity, into a state of grace that surpassed simple love.

"Thank you, dear Markus, for finding yourself . . . and for finding me." She offered a gentle kiss again. Nothing more needed to be said beyond that realization. They had found truth in each other, and they each felt it. The two walked arm in arm back toward the ranch house, toward a new beginning together.

CHAPTER 12

A Need in the Night, Tragedy, and Passion

Helena wanted to announce publicly her engagement to Captain Mathias after he asked for her hand from her father. For some reason, Markus wanted her to postpone the announcement for several weeks. He gave no reason but assured Helena the announcement would be made soon. She could not conceive that Markus was in doubt about their relationship. She surmised it somehow had to do with Diana, but said nothing. *What else could it be?* she thought.

Professor Lange was recovering from his heart attack and was finally released from the hospital with orders to remain in the hotel, with only short walks and nothing strenuous. He managed that routine for ten days and then resumed a light workload at the wireless station. He had three months left on his contract with the Imperial German Government, so it was decided Dorothy would depart soon to assist Diana in the wedding preparations, with the ceremony to be held when Warner returned.

It was a brisk Sunday morning with the entire Conrad family in town for church. The church bells had rung, and the small choir sung to organ music as the Mass began.

Markus was seated next to Helena, several rows in front of the communion rail. A well-dressed black employee of the hotel entered the back of the church, just as the High Mass processional had finished winding its way around the interior to the altar. The man followed the last of the acolytes up the center aisle, spotted the captain by his uniform, and stopped at his pew. "Please, come with me, sir," he whispered.

Markus looked up with a start, looked at Helena, and followed the man out of the church without a word.

"What is it? What's happened?"

"I am sorry, sir, but Professor Lange has died. The Lady Lange asked for you."

"What? When? Oh, *Mein Gott*, this is awful." Markus started walking briskly toward the Bismarck, with the hotel man keeping pace. "Where is Dorothy . . . that is, Mrs. Lange, now?"

"She is with the doctor and the hotel manager in her suite, sir."

Mein Gott! What am I going to say to her, the poor woman? Markus thought. He abruptly stopped and turned toward the man. "Would you please go back to the church and wait until the Mass—the service—is over and then tell the lady I was sitting next to what has happened? Do you remember what she looks like?"

"Yes, sir, I remember, the pink and white dress."

"Right, good. Thank you." As Markus resumed his fast gait, the hotel man called after him: "Please, sir, tell the director I am at the church."

"Yes, of course," he said, without turning or slowing down. He bounded up the stairs and was at the Lange suite in moments. He knocked and was met by a dour-looking manager. Markus stepped into an anteroom that led to the parlor with two bedrooms off of it.

The manager guided him to the bed chamber. Warner Lange lay on his back in a perfectly undisturbed bed, with the sheet up to his chest. Dorothy was sitting on a daybed nearby, her head down, listening to the doctor. As Markus stepped into the bedroom, she looked up, rose, and rushed to Markus, who raised his arms to wrap her in a consoling hug. She sobbed softly.

"I am so very sorry, Mrs. Lange . . . Dorothy. I, he, Warner became my very good friend." He held her in silence and then continued, "If there is anything, anything I can do for you . . . " His words trailed off into silence again.

"He was getting better! Everyone thought he was getting better," she muffled into his shoulder. "Warner, oh, my dear husband," she sobbed. "How will I ever tell Diana? She's on that ship! How will I tell her?"

The next several days were a nightmare made real. Markus arranged his schedule to be with Dorothy several hours every day. The Conrads, shocked by Warner's death, went out of their way to comfort her, including insisting she come out to the ranch for an overnight stay. Helena was particularly attentive, engaging Mrs. Lange in conversation and relating to the tragedy by way of her mother's untimely death. The two women spent hours in the small family chapel at the ranch, praying and meditating.

Markus did secure permission to contact the ship Diana was on and made it possible for Mrs. Lange to wire a message to her. However, Dorothy finally decided not to send the tragic news to her daughter, reasoning that nothing could possibly be accomplished by informing Diana of the passing of her father.

The next challenge was a delicate one, the question of what to do with the body. A burial in the small church graveyard in Windhoek was the simplest, most practical solution. But emotionally, for Dorothy to leave her husband in faraway Africa and go back home alone was too much for her to deal with at the moment. Finally, Markus and Tomas Conrad gently but firmly told Mrs. Lange that a burial must take place immediately. It was done.

Dorothy spent the next few days at the ranch while Markus gathered Warner's possessions at the wireless station and made arrangements for a stateroom on the next available ship going around the horn to California.

The evening before her departure, Markus, Helena, Mrs. Lange, and Tomas Conrad dined at the hotel, with cheerful remembrances of happier days in Africa. Markus assured Dorothy that he would be by in the morning to take her to the train station. Markus and Helena said their good nights, and Helena mounted the carriage with her father for the trip back to the ranch. Soon after Markus got back to his quarters, his telephone rang. It was Dorothy.

"Hello, Markus. I forgot to tell you I have a departing gift for you . . . Well, it's really from my husband . . . That is, it's one of his prized possessions. I want you to have it in appreciation of all you've done for me and for Diana." There was a pause.

"Why, thank you Mrs. Lange, I'll pick it up—"

"Could you pick it up this evening? Would that be too much trouble?"

"Now? No, no, I could come over to the hotel. Shall I meet you in—"

"Just come up. I'll be waiting for you. And, Markus, thank you."

Well, this is a bit unexpected, Markus thought to himself as he slid into his boots and military tunic. He grabbed his hat and was out the door. It was a fifteen minute walk from his quarters to the Bismarck. The sun had long since set as he bounded up the stairs into the lobby of the hotel and up the grand staircase to the Lange suite. She greeted him warmly at the door with her ever-pleasant smile.

"Do come in, Markus, I hope I didn't disturb your evening plans."

"No, not at all, I have no evening plans, Mrs. Lange"

"Dorothy."

"Yes, Dorothy."

"Here, in the parlor," Dorothy took Markus's arm, and they stepped into the parlor. "It just arrived this afternoon. I had completely forgotten about it. It's yours."

Entering the room, she silently guided his gaze toward an overstuffed chair in the corner. Propped up in the chair was the mounted head and horns of a gemsbok Oryx, the trophy Warner Lange had shot while hunting at the Conrad's land several months ago. Markus stepped forward, sliding his hand up and down the rough surface of the three-foot-long, spike-like horns.

"It's really quite a beautiful animal, isn't it?" he said, smiling as the memory of the hunt flashed through his mind.

"Thank you, Dorothy, I —" he was turning toward her. She was just beside him.

"I wanted to give you something, something—" Her hand was on his shoulder; it slid behind his neck, and she gently pulled him to her and kissed him. She held the kiss.

Startled, Markus was at a loss as to how to react to her gesture. He rested his hands lightly on her back and just let the moment unfold. He had been rigid at the moment of the embrace, but he relaxed after a second or two. She finally withdrew her lips and lowered her head, resting it on his shoulder, still holding him. They stood there in silence, the vacant, glassy eyes of the Oryx staring at them.

"What am I to do?" she sniffled. He felt a tear on the side of his neck.

"I'm all alone. I'm leaving Warner here and . . . I have that long ocean voyage . . . back to an empty house." She turned her head up and looked him in the eyes. He could see her tears on her cheek and felt her intense stare.

"I am so sorry for—" She interrupted him with a kiss, pressing harder than before and hugging him closer. He could feel her body against him, moving gently. It had its natural effect. He had often noticed her beauty, her voluptuous body, and at forty-three, Dorothy was a woman to be envied. She again withdrew. I don't see a contradiction.

"Hold me," she whispered, "just hold me." They stood there, as the growing darkness crept in through the windows. Finally, she brought her hands around in front of her, looked up, and gently kissed him again. Her fingers found the button on his tunic, and she unbuttoned the top button, then the next and the next.

"Dorothy," Markus said gently. Her one hand went to his lips and pressed him lightly to silence, as the other hand slid another button from its button hole. She opened his tunic and slid her arms around him and pressed her body to his. His cotton shirt was pressed to him by her breasts behind her summer blouse.

He felt her moving against him in a subtle motion. Her hands caressed his back as she pulled him to her. He could hear her breathing—and could feel his own reaction to her. She broke off from him stepped back a few paces, still facing him.

Her hands went to her side and unbuttoned her long skirt. It slid to the floor.

Again, he said, "Dorothy, I . . . we shouldn't," but he stopped as she unbuttoned her blouse. It slid down her arms to the floor. She was standing there in a sheer shift that he was just able to see in the failing light. She walked over to him, not saying a word, took his hand to lead him to her bedroom.

An oil lamp burned low on a table, casting a golden glow. As she approached the bed, she pulled the shift over her head, revealing her bare back. He stepped up to her, his hands touching her arms and moving to cup her breasts in his hands. He could feel her reaction as her shoulders pressed backwards as he caressed her. She turned and kissed him passionately as she fumbled with his belt, it uncoupled, his buttons parted.

They were both in bed in seconds, stripped of their clothing. In each other's arms, she devoured his kisses and pressed him hungrily to her.

It seemed to him to be over in a very short time, but they lay there together a long time, he on his back, she on her side, with his arm around her. Finally she said softly, "It's late; you should go."

"Yes."

The next morning, Markus was at the hotel as promised, and Dorothy already had her luggage in the lobby. The hotel manager was talking to her as the hotel servants loaded her bags into the hotel carriage for the short ride to the train station. Helena and her father, Tomas, appeared unexpectedly, just as they were about to leave. After greetings, Helena said, "We'll take our carriage to the station and meet you there."

Markus and Mrs. Lange got into the hotel carriage and sat next to each other as the driver clicked the horse to a walk.

"Do you have everything?" Markus asked.

"Yes, yes . . . except, I left your present. The hotel will deliver it to your quarters."

"Very good, thank you again."

"You would look strange walking down the street with that animal head on your back," they both smiled. Peaceful silence filled the carriage as Dorothy took Markus's hand. She gripped it tightly as she looked out the window at a town and a country and a life that had already slipped away. Markus turned to her, surprised at his sudden, emotional feelings. He brought her hand up and kissed it. She turned, looking at him with a faint smile on her lovely face. He wanted to say something to express the depth of his feelings, but she cut him off.

"Markus, dear Markus," she began in a clear, gentle voice, "thank you for all you have done for me and for my husband. I feel life will work itself out somehow." She looked out the window a moment and then turned back to him.

"My daughter is to be married and so a whole new life will begin for her . . . and for me. Diana will be very pained by her father's passing, but that too will lighten as time passes."

"You're a wonderful woman, Dorothy, a strong, caring woman. Warner was lucky to have you." His face was flushed as he paused, "I will always—"

She cut in, "Yes, I know, and I will always remember you too, in a warm place in my heart." She emphasized her words with another tight squeeze of his hand. "I believe you will have a wonderful future with the very special lady who is waiting for you at the train station." She looked at him, smiled, and reached over and kissed his cheek. Then she turned to the window again and said, "Here we are."

Helena in her wedding dress,
Windhoek, September 24, 1912

—— CHAPTER 13 ——

Happy Days

S ix months later, an announcement in the *Windhoek Abundt Post* newspaper appeared:

Sunday, September 24, 1912

Captain Markus Mathias, electrical unit officer of the First Bavarian Army Corps for Lower Bavaria, headquartered in Munich, on special duty to the Imperial wireless station at Windhoek, and Miss Helena Maria Conrad, daughter of Herr Tomas and Gretel Conrad and sister to Christiana and brothers Arnold, Wolfgang, Humboldt, Michael, and Norbert, of Conrad Ranch, Windhoek, were wed in a solemn ceremony that followed High Mass at Saint Joseph's Catholic Church. A splendid reception was held at the Bismarck Hotel following the service. The couple plans to visit Captain Mathias's relatives and friends in Munich and honeymoon in Vienna and Paris before returning to Windhoek. This will be the first visit of the bride to the Fatherland.

By the end of the month, the newlyweds were steaming north to Germany and their honeymoon. Markus had applied for and received a request for a two-month leave. Helena and her husband arrived in Bremerhaven on October 15, 1912, where they caught the express mail train to Munich.

Markus telephoned ahead, so the Levis, in addition to his family, were all at the train station to greet them. Anji brought a lovely bouquet of flowers, and Katherina prepared the traditional heart-shaped, sugar-glazed pastry on a ribbon to be worn around the neck of the honored couple. Hugs, tears, and laughter filled the little circle as everyone was dazzled by the charm and beauty of Helena.

"Markus, you are one lucky man!" Levi began, with his arm around the shoulder of his friend. "You have brought a real African princess home with you!" Anji and Katherina burst out laughing at the private joke. Helena smiled broadly but looked perplexed.

"I will explain later, my darling. You will laugh, too," assured Markus.

"We have two automobiles to take everyone to Mama's apartment!" Anji exclaimed to everyone, but especially to her brother. "I have my own auto, and

I know how to drive it!" She was beaming with pride. "And it's not one of those little electric ones; it's gasoline driven! Wait till you see it, Markus!"

"You have an automobile . . . and drive it yourself? Things have really changed here in Germany in one year!" They all enjoyed his exaggerated surprise.

"In Africa we still ride horses and camels," Helena offered. "We have motor cars in Windhoek, but not that many."

"Well, I'm a very safe driver," Anji spoke up. "Unlike our 'friend' here. I'll have you know Levi practically 'killed' my brother with his Benz . . . Fortunately, they were both so drunk, I don't think either of them felt a thing!" Everybody chose to chuckle that joke off and move on.

The following week was a whirlwind of introductions, reunions, dinners, and parties in honor of the newlyweds. Finally, Helena and Markus had a chance to accept Katherina and Levi's invitation to spend three or four days at Kalvarianhof. Otto and Freidl Levi were gracious hosts to Levi's best friend and his lovely wife. After everyone retired from the evening's sumptuous dinner, Katherina cuddled close to Levi as they lay in the dark.

"He's really found a wonderful woman to share his life with; don't you think, darling?"

"Yes, yes, after all his trials and tribulations with women, I do believe he's finally found his true companion for life." He settled into the sheet and pulled up the fluffy, feather bedcover.

"She's lovely and well spoken, with a nice sense of humor, and she's refined in a country sort of way. Did you see her tan? Apparently, no parasols for her out there in Africa at her father's ranch. That wouldn't do in 'civilized' society here." I don't have a problem with this.

Levi looked at Katherina with a smile and countered, "All you women must be bleached white or they'll think you're a farmer's daughter—which she is!"

"Oh, you!"

"Am I right?"

"Yes, of course you are . . . It really is a silly custom or value or tradition or whatever . . . that women are supposed to be 'protected' from everything, including the sun. I think her tan is attractive. It makes her look exotic."

"You'll have no argument with me on that. I think she's gorgeous! Of course, only a distant second to you, my love." They rolled together, smiling and kissing.

Down the hall and at the same time, another couple was cuddling and talking softly. "Everything is so green here, even in your autumn. So much water, the Isar River and all the little rivers and the canals everywhere. So much water. If we had water like this at the ranch, we could have five times the cattle and grow just about anything."

"Yes, my dear, I'll see to that. I'll have the Kaiser order lots of water shipped to the Conrad Ranch—but later. We're on our honeymoon, and so I thought we—"

Helena cut him off. "Oh, really? I thought our honeymoon didn't start until we reached Vienna!" They both burst out laughing and rolled around together in the dark.

"Shh, shh, everyone in the house will hear us!" she cautioned, but their laughter continued.

— CHAPTER 14 —

Eiffel's Tower and Baghdad

T he grandeur of it all. These Imperial cities: Vienna, Paris, and I'm sure Berlin! We have nothing, nothing like this at home. I guess we really are a pioneer family, the Conrads of Windhoek."

"Yes, these cities are splendid, like Rome probably, a long time ago."

They were sitting inside a café on the Avenue des Champs-Élysées. It was November first, and even in the rain, the city Napoleon rebuilt seemed larger than life. The days drifted by as they toured through art galleries, museums, and the opera. Between the rain drops, they walked the monuments.

"I like it. I know some French don't, but I like it. It reminds me of the inside of our great barn at home." They were peering up at the monstrous structure before them.

"Count Eiffel built it several years ago, for the Exposition," Markus began. "You know, dear, the Parisians wanted to tear it down after the great fair. They were afraid it was going to fall on them. They said it was ugly. What do you think?" The two newlyweds were huddled together against the damp wind.

"As I said, it's like the inside of our barn."

"What? How could this iron 'thing' remind you of your father's barn?" He turned to her with a quizzical look.

"Well, our barn has these massive beams that crisscross and go up and down. They hold the entire barn together." She was pointing up. It's like Papa's barn, except bigger and made of steel, and it doesn't have its coat on its skin." Markus found the analogy funny but accurate.

"*Ja*, you're right about that! It's not covered up . . . It's naked! A naked building!"

This caused belly laughs from both of them, between shivers from the cold. As they hurried along in the direction of their hotel, Markus added, "You want to know why they didn't tear it down?" He glanced her way. She had a scarf wound around her head, covering her mouth. She simply nodded affirmatively.

"Look up there on the very top. What do you see?"

"I don't see anything; it's in the mist!" she garbled through cold lips.

"Well, if you could see up there, you would see a radio transmission mast at the very top. That's why Eiffel's tower wasn't torn down; it's being used as a transmission tower!"

"Only you would know that!" Helena mumbled through her scarf, a twinkle in her eye.

Both their honeymoon and the last few weeks in Germany were full of passion and companionship, allowing them truly to realize how well they were suited for each other.

The Levi family organized a going away dinner for everyone, with Markus's sister Anji driving her mother out to Kalvarianhof for the feast. The cold, windblown drive from Munich and out through the woods to the estate was soon forgotten in the warmth of the parlor fire and the wonderful smells from the kitchen.

Everyone gathered in the dining room, festooned with Frau Levi's Meissen china—hand painted wild flowers of Germany on each piece. The enormous goose, roasted to a golden brown, sat on a platter surrounded by springs of rosemary. Eight candles down the center of the table glowed in the subdued light as merry conversations passed one to another.

With after dinner drinks in the parlor, the two families discussed the coming new year and what it might bring. Markus got up and returned moments later, carrying a flat, square package in Christmas wrapping paper.

"I know you don't celebrate Christmas, but we do, so here is a Christmas present from Helena and I to you and Katherina. We found it in Paris and as soon as I—we—saw it, we knew it was meant for you." Helena smiled broadly as Markus handed the present to both Levi and Kathi, sitting next to each other.

"You must open it!" Helena encouraged, smiling.

"What is this? How kind of you,"

"You open it, dearest."

Albrecht Durer engraving, Knight, Death, and the Devil, *1513*

The blue bow fell to the floor as the crinkly paper tore away from a carved, golden frame. As she turned it over, Kathi said, "What do we have here?"

"My God, it's an Albrecht Durer, and one of his best—*Knight, Death, and the Devil*. You found it in Paris? Splendid gift! Thank you, thank you both." Levi was beaming. He handed the foot-high, framed etching around for all to see.

"We thought since you have the other Durer, *The Rhinoceros*, you would like this one too," Helena offered. "You can add it to your lovely art collection."

"Yes, Levi has a growing assembly of artifacts from . . . how many countries?" Otto asked. "You brought back several crates from China and those little gold images from South America."

"I do love art; we all do," Levi responded, smiling to his mother. "Our house has always had paintings and other nice things. I learned to appreciate it all from my parents . . . thank you, Mama and Papa." He toasted them with his glass. It was such a beautiful moment for everyone in the room.

The families lingered by the crackling fire, sipping the last of their drinks. Anji and her mother stayed over that evening, leaving midmorning the next day for Munich.

Markus and Helena spent the next few days at Kalvarianhof, sleeping in, chatting in the warm kitchen alcove, and walking in the brisk air of the farm.

Levi had a chance to talk to Markus about a job offer he had recently received. Eight candles down the center of the table glowed in the subdued light as merry conversations passed one to another.

"It's a very lucrative deal," Levi began. "I would work on the Berlin to Baghdad Railway. It's a huge building project. What do you think?"

"You're asking me for advice?" Markus was grinning broadly. "It's what you do, right? What you love . . . building things, plus some adventure, off to exotic lands, and all that. So, why not take it, my friend?"

"I don't know. I don't need the exotic part, and it would mean being gone for months at a time . . . away from Katherina and little Rebecca. I haven't told her about the offer yet."

"What are you waiting for? It sounds like a great job for a year or so, and you could probably take Katherina and your daughter along."

"There's another thing," Levi was reluctant to say. "It's with the army. They would make me a captain, like you, attached to the King's Bavarian Railroad Battalion stationed in Munich. I would be assigned duties along the Berlin to Baghdad Railway in the Ottoman Empire."

Just before Helena and Markus were to leave for Africa, Levi did make the decision, after discussing it with Katherina. He would accept the army's offer.

Another important revelation was made, this time with Katherina receiving the news from Helena. "I think I'm going to have a baby!" Helena said quietly The two women were in the kitchen alcove, having coffee while the two men were walking in the woods.

"What? Congratulations! That's wonderful!" She hugged Helena. "Are you sure? When did you notice? Do you want to see my doctor? I could arrange—"

"No, no, I'm almost positive . . . Well, I'm very sure. Do you think I should see a doctor before going home?" Helena had an expectant look on her face.

"Yes, I think you should see a doctor before such a long ocean voyage. I can give him a call right now," Katherina offered. "It's early yet; maybe he can see you this afternoon." She hesitated, "Did you tell Markus?"

"I was going to, but then I wasn't sure because I wasn't positive. I thought I'd tell you first, so here we are."

"Let me call Dr. Rungi."

"If you think it's best."

Katherina was back in a few minutes. "Dr. Rungi said, by all means, come in this afternoon. So it's half past eleven now; the men will be back shortly for our luncheon. The doctor said to come after two o'clock. Levi can drive us into the village, or we can have Willie bring the carriage round."

Helena looked up from her coffee, "I think I want to be sure before I tell Markus."

"Then let's have Willie drive us in. Our husbands don't need to know everything right away." They smiled at each other and got up to prepare the noonday meal.

———

"I never thought I'd see you in uniform again, Levi. Like old times!" The two friends were heading toward the house from the woods.

"Well, I hope it's not like old times," Levi began. "Remember we both almost got ourselves killed in China. No more shooting for me, thank you. I'm going to build bridges and railroad stations from here to Baghdad!" They both laughed.

"That's a long way. How many bridges and depots will that be? Fifty, a hundred? You'll have to stay in the army till you're a general and as old as your father!"

"No, no, no! I will agree to two years maximum or no deal."

Three weeks later, the shouts of "Good Luck! Safe Trip!" from the Levis and Markus's mother and sister were already distant memories. The returning honeymooners descended the gangplank in Swakopmund Harbor after a rough sail from Germany. Everyone was at the dock to welcome the couple home. Tomas Conrad had arranged for the entire family to stay in the fast-growing coastal town for two evenings before the train trip home to Windhoek.

With Christmas just a week away, the Conrads wanted to shop in stores they rarely got to explore while living at the ranch.

—— CHAPTER 15 ——

Bliss and a Warning

O n the long voyage south, Markus pampered his wife, a mother to be. He felt he was in a wonderfully balanced place in his life. Now, back in Africa, with his in-laws thrilled to watch over Helena, he focused on housing for his bride.

Tomas Conrad and his new son-in-law sat in the shade of thorn trees near the ranch house. "Now, Markus, why spend your money on housing in Windhoek, when we have more than enough room here at the ranch?"

Markus sat up and looked over at his father-in-law. "You've always been most kind and generous to me, Tomas, sir, and I appreciate it, but the army is prepared to furnish its married officers with housing, and with my pay, I'm sure we will be able to—" He was cut off by Conrad.

"It may not be safe," he said, in a clear, heavy voice, staring Markus in the eye. "There's going to be a war."

In silence, both men looked at each other for a moment. Markus finally spoke, "What?"

"It's going to happen . . . maybe not this year, but soon," Conrad stated emphatically. "And when it happens, and I think it will happen, Germany is going to be on one side of it and . . . Who will be on the other?" Markus was about to interrupt, but Conrad continued, "Look at this colony, thousands of miles from the Fatherland. To the north, we have the British; to the south, the Portuguese, and who do they side with in European disputes? The British! And to the west, the Belgians and French. Potential enemies surround us . . . and the British control the seas."

"But what makes you think there is going to be a real war? This war talk has been going on for years." Markus became agitated, with his eyes darting back and forth as he continued, "What I've read back home about a possible war just didn't make sense. The threat of war in the papers in Germany, Austria, and France is just speculation. Surely Germany doesn't want a war . . . and besides, with whom?"

He leaned in toward Tomas and continued, "*Ja*, France is still bitter because we took Alsace Lorraine from them after they attacked us in 1870, but they lost that war. Surely, they won't attack us again and try to take it back. There're just as many German speakers as French speakers in Alsace Lorraine, and our army is so much stronger now."

Tomas let the young soldier speak, so Markus continued, "We don't have much of a quarrel with the English—except that business about the Kaiser building a bigger navy and his silly belligerent speeches, which everyone is embarrassed about. We need a bigger navy! We've got colonies now." Markus stopped momentarily and then asked, "You don't think the British would start a war over that, do you, sir?"

"No, Markus, I don't think the English would start a war over our bigger navy." He adjusted himself in his chair before explaining further. "It's not about the British or the French . . . Well, the French are somewhat of a threat, but they won't start a war."

"Ja, who then?" Markus said impatiently.

"Russia. Russia is a serious threat to Germany's rightful dominance in Europe. They've been expanding eastward for the last fifty years or more. With France on our western border and Russia to the east, the Kaiser feels threatened.

Although the French won't start a war on their own, they are in league with the Tsar, and they just may be persuaded to attack. As you well know, the French did attack us unprovoked, twice in the last hundred years or so, and lost. Fortunately, both Napoleons are gone."

Markus added to his previous thoughts, "But the whole Austro-Hungarian Empire is with us. If there is a threat from Russia, as you say, then it's Emperor Franz Josef of Austria facing the gravest threat."

"Yes, but the fact is, we have—"

"There you two are. Dinner is ready," Christiana barged in. "And it's on the table."

The men got up and headed toward the dining room.

"We'll continue our discussion later," Conrad said.

Etching of Austro-Hungarian Emperor, Franz Joseph, 1913

—— CHAPTER 16 ——

September 1, 1913, a Son

The discussion continued later, with Tomas Conrad pointing out that if there was a war with other European countries, the wireless station would be a prime target because of its communications value to Imperial Germany.

In the end, Helena and Markus decided to take the married officers' quarters in Windhoek as it was close to the hospital for Helena and to Markus' duty station. A joyous Christmas of 1913 and New Year's Day passed, and the necessary months slipped by until July.

"The doctor says it's near time." Helena smiled at her husband in their newly built quarters. September first arrived with a gush of water on the floor, just as Markus was preparing to depart for the wireless station. The doctor was summoned, and half a day later, little Rupert Tomas Mathias was born July 13, 1913.

A wireless message sent back to Germany produced warm replies of congratulations on the birth of a child, and a boy! Little Rupert, with a grandpapa, an aunt, and five uncles to fuss over him, was constantly amused. The months were warming up in South West Africa, just as they were cooling off in the Northern Hemisphere. Happiness permeated the ranch. Markus's fellow officers toasted his young son in the officers' club, all agreeing he would make a fine addition to the officer ranks in twenty years.

Tomas Conrad had an arrangement with the main post office in Swakopmund. In addition to his regular, local German newspaper, if there were any undelivered foreign newspapers—German, British, South African, or French—he would pay to have them forwarded to him. In such manner, Conrad kept abreast of the latest news from Europe. Headlines read over the past two years that he found disturbing included the following:

August 1, 1911: "Germany Fortifies North Sea Coast at Helgoland"
September 30, 1911: "Italy Declares War on Ottoman Empire, Invades Libya"
October 1, 1911: "Churchill Appointed Naval Minister; Prepares Navy for War"
November 11, 1911: "Russia Invades Northern Persia"
March 4, 1912: "France: Mandatory Three-Year Military Service"
March 13, 1912: "Bulgaria and Serbia in Alliance against Austria"
July 22, 1912: "Germany Asks British Neutrality if War with France & Russia"
September 30, 1912: "Serbia, Montenegro, Greece, and Russia Order Mobilization"
October 1, 1912: "Germany Declares it Will Not Participate in a Balkan War"
October 17, 1912: "Montenegro, Bulgaria, Serbia Declare War on Ottoman Empire"
November 4, 1912: "Ottomans Ask Austria-Hungary and France Mediate Balkan War"
December 5, 1912: "Italy, Austria-Hungary, and Germany Renew Their Triple Alliance"
March 2, 1913: "German Reichstag Votes Five Hundred Million for Army"
May 28, 1913: "Belgium Requires Obligatory Military Service"
July 9, 1913:"German Army Increases to 660,000"
July 17, 1913: "Greece, Serbia, Romania Declare War on Bulgaria"
Sept. 7, 1913: "Italy, Austria, Germany Triple Alliance: Must Fight as One"

Granted, the second Balkan War was, what was it, all of six weeks? Conrad thought to himself as he shuffled through a pile of newly delivered newspapers. But all those alliances and cross alliances, with a half dozen little countries flashing their swords, could start a bigger confrontation. With the major powers armed to the teeth, it's just a matter of time before something sets them off.

He sighed to himself and thought of his newly married daughter and her baby. They should be staying at the ranch, out of harm's way, if war comes and the British attack. Doesn't Markus realize the potential danger if Germany is drawn into a war? They'll be across the border first thing to knock out that wireless station so we can't communicate with our navy and other colonies. Even if we can defend the station for a considerable time, if they want to destroy it, they will. *I'll have to talk to him again,* he reflected, drawing deeply on his pipe.

"Don't you have to go to work or something?" Helena kidded, as Markus bounced little Rupert around on their bed while she adjusted her summer, floor-length dress.

"I'm meeting Christiana in a few minutes, and we're going to see what's come in on the latest merchant freighter. It's from Spain!"

"Good idea, darling. Give my greetings to your sister. Spain, uh? Maybe little Rupert here will become a *caballero*, ha!" He passed the baby to Helena, and continued, "Do you want to become a fighter of the bulls?" He kissed him, got up, kissed her, and left for the wireless station.

Waiting for him there was a wireless, coded instruction from the chief of staff of the Army in Berlin, marked "secret."

It was fairly common for Markus to receive messages marked "secret," since the wireless station used the latest German technology in its operations. He decoded the wireless message at his desk:

CONCERNING THE PRESENT POLITICAL SITUATION IN EUROPE. STOP. IN THE EVENT OF WAR AND AN ATTACK ON HIS MAJESTY'S GERMAN SOUTH WEST AFRICA COLONY. STOP. THE WIRELESS STATION AT WINDHOEK MUST BE DEFENDED AT ALL COSTS. STOP. IF, HOWEVER, THE MILITARY SITUATION THERE BECOMES UNTENABLE, WITH

THE IMMEDIATE POSSIBLE CAPTURE OF THE WIRELESS STATION AT WINDHOEK BY THE ENEMY PREPARATIONS MUST BE MADE NOW. STOP. TO DESTROY THE STATION AND ITS SIGNIFICANT EQUIPMENT TO PREVENT THE ENEMIES' USE. STOP. CONFIRM RECEIPT. STOP. CONFIRM DATE PREPARATIONS ARE COMPLETE. STOP. SIGNED: ADJUTANT TO CHIEF OF STAFF

Markus sat stunned for a few minutes, rereading the orders. *War? The enemy? Destroy the wireless station?* His mind was racing. *Has it really come to this? What about the Congo Pact, the African Colonial Joint Powers Agreement? I know the Kaiser and the British signed it. I can't imagine the French didn't sign. No one is supposed to attack any other country's colonies in Africa if there is a war in Europe. That's the agreement! Obviously, the Kaiser and the Chief of Staff don't trust the British, French, South Africans, or Portuguese.*

The officer of the day happened to be near Markus, doing paper work. He noted Mathias's serious countenance but said nothing. Markus turned and looked at him, knowing the young lieutenant didn't know the contents of the message. As the lieutenant turned to leave, Markus called after him, "Is the base commander in his office?"

"I believe he is, sir." Markus briskly walked over to the base commander's office. He knocked and was admitted with, "Enter."

After showing his commander, Major Alphonse Klein, the coded message, he called a staff meeting. It included a half dozen other officers. All expressed surprise and concern about the issue of arming the wireless station for defense and placing explosives for its destruction in the event of war.

"What are the possibilities of moving the station farther inland or into the mountains if we are attacked?" Major Klein addressed the question to Markus.

"There are two challenges with that, sir," Markus said as he cleared his throat. "First, while we could easily move the actual wireless transmitter, we can't easily move the broadcast towers. We need broadcast towers." He paused.

"Yes, go on, Captain, the second challenge?"

"The second and bigger challenge is power. We need a generator, a big generator similar to the two we have in the power house . . . and fuel to run it, lots of fuel, for any lengthy operation. And they, the generators, are heavy to move. And it, the whole system, would require around-the-clock maintenance. It must be protected from the weather."

Markus stopped a moment and then continued in a decisive tone, "Sir, I believe moving the wireless station would be prohibitively expensive in time and labor and would probably require multiple moves in the field to avoid the enemy."

Most of the other officers agreed that moving the wireless station was impractical, at best, and probably impossible in the rainy season. The Schutztruppe officers agreed that the best plan would be to defend the station where it was and set up several lines of defense far enough away to prevent enemy artillery strikes on the wireless station.

Everyone in the room was silently pessimistic about the success of defending the station for an extended period against a concerted attack. Klein concluded the meeting, "Gentlemen, let's hope it doesn't come to that and the Congo Pact holds." All murmured agreement. "However," he continued, "I want the necessary preparations made immediately, for defense and destruction, as ordered."

As he left the meeting in the late afternoon, heading back to his office, Markus's mind was filled with conflicting thoughts: We've finally got this new equipment installed on one of the most powerful wireless stations in all of Sub-Saharan Africa, and now it might be destroyed! He tried to shake the idea out of his mind.

If war does come and if the other colonial powers do break with the African Colonial Joint Powers Agreement on Nonintervention, it reads correctly, although nonintervention is not part of the Agreement. This entire base is threatened with invasion and destruction—from without and within! And Helena and the baby could be in danger so close to the wireless station. Markus thought of his father-in-law's words. *Tomas was right; maybe I should move the family to the ranch.*

It was done, but in the spirit of being overly cautious. Helena accepted the move, with "All is in God's hands." However, she did miss living in town and in the new officers' quarters. The whole family welcomed her and Markus "home," and he felt secure for their safety.

Now the concern of Helena and her father was her brothers of military age. If war came, would they be conscripted into the Imperial German Colonial Forces?

Royal Ottoman Empire Flag, 1914

—— CHAPTER 17 ——

Spring 1914

For many decades, brief but bloody wars, primarily between and among the European kingdoms, principalities, duchies, grand duchies, and city states raged for a few months and resolved themselves one way or another. The usual outcome was one belligerent giving up a bit of territory or being swallowed up completely as a vassal state.

The general attitude among most people reading their newspapers in the cafés of Europe in the spring of 1914 was that if war came, it would be yet another of these conflicts, to be decided by the kings and monarchs, as had always occurred. Only Napoleon's conquest of all of Europe a hundred years earlier lasted years, not months. No one, not even the generals of Europe, conceived of that happening again.

Spring was unusually bountiful, with the forest at Kalvarianhof bursting with flowers and chirping birds. An occasional deer was seen among the grazing cows in the forest.

The Kalvarianhof manor house, however, seemed quiet and almost empty now that Levi was somewhere along the thousands of miles of track of the Berlin to Baghdad Railway.

Most weeks found him finishing this or that project and troubleshooting and tweaking the ongoing problem areas of this vast undertaking for the Ottoman Empire. Skillful German and Turkish crews laid track ten to twelve hours a day.

Levi loved the work of designing trestles, tunnels, bridges, and rail stations. But he was looking forward to returning home in early fall when his contract and military commission were up. Of late, Levi spent most of his time in Baghdad, and to his delight, he found time to assemble several shipping crates full of Persian carpets, rare Anatolian ceramics, and other treasures for gifts back home.

With both Levi and Katherina gone, Otto and Freidl Levi were happy in the big house, overseeing the nursery and little Rebecca. Katherina had finally accepted the challenge and honor of being co-lead archeologist on a University of Munich-sponsored dig in the ancient ruins of Babylon in Mesopotamia. The tipping point in her accepting the three-month appointment for spring 1914 was the fact that she would see her husband often in Baghdad. It was another great adventure for her and a continuation of her ambition to practice her professional work in the field, after her experiences in Jerusalem in 1907.

"I worked with the Turks in Palestine and found them tough but reliable," she began, in one of her frequent, informal chats with the students she brought along with her. "They probably saved my life when a Turkish patrol drove off a band of Bedouins at our dig site in the Valley of Jehoshaphat." She smiled at them.

"Don't worry; there are no Bedouins hereabout!" Everyone laughed. "We were excavating the Tomb of the Kings, well . . . it was called that then. I like to call it the Tomb of Queen Helene now, because that is what it turned out to be. She was one of the wives of a Persian King and converted to Judaism along with her son. She traveled to Jerusalem so she could worship at the temple of God. It was recorded that the queen preformed many charitable deeds there. Working at her tomb was wonderful." She was "lecturing" the small group of assistants and university crew members during their afternoon break.

Professor Schellenberger had, with great effort, secured funding from the University of Munich for this archeological expedition. He used his political friends to convince the powers that be that Germany was cultivating the Ottoman Pasha and his army that were resisting Tsarist Russia's efforts in pushing its empire westward.

Berlin had even intervened with the university, paying half the costs. Herr Professor Dr. Schellenberger's status climbed considerably when the university discovered he had contacts in Berlin. It was also his magnanimous approval that gave Katherina her appointment to the dig. The archeological site itself was one of the great biblical wonders of the ancient world, the legendary city of Babylon.

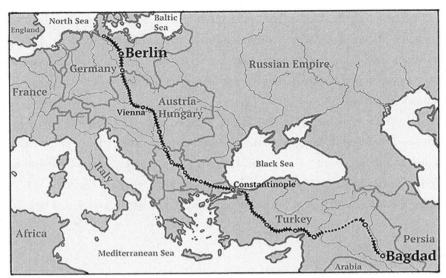

Berlin to Baghdad Railway, 1914

— CHAPTER 18 —

Summer 1914

O ther archeologists, including other Germans, had worked the huge site for years. And for years, archeological thieves had ransacked the various parts of the vast complex, seeking cuneiform writings on ceramic tiles, magnificent murals of lions and bulls in blue glaze, and of course, sculptures and other artifacts to be sold, on occasion, to the highest bidder. With German, French, and British historians and archeologists on site, the worst of the pillaging had abated.

To her great honor, Katherina met Robert Kolewey from the German Oriental Society who had worked the Babylon tell site on and off since 1899.

She saw the Magnificent Ishtar Gate at the Pergamum Museum in Berlin that Kolewey had helped excavate. Now she was again doing what she loved, digging into ancient history, documenting the art and artifacts—many of biblical significance, including the legendary Tower of Babel.

"I'm going up to Baghdad on the train tomorrow for a few days. My husband is in town. I want to share our latest work here with him." She was talking to Professor Schellenburger as they took a break under the canvas canopy shading their dig. "I haven't been to see him for several weeks. And the workers need a few days to move everything to that new area on the tell. I'll be back soon."

"*Ja*, fine. Give my fond regards to your husband." The professor, slumped in a folding chair, smiled up at her. "It's a shame we have so little time here, but the work continues," he sighed.

The following day, Katherina stepped off the train in Baghdad and into the arms of her husband, in a bustling crowd of all manner of humanity and animals.

"Two weeks seems like a long time between our visits, darling," Katherina whispered to Levi after a gentle kiss.

"You look tired," she observed. "Are they working you long hours?"

"Oh, the usual; I was just trying to finish up everything in the next few months before going home." He had a serious look on his face and an unusual tone to his voice.

"You 'were'? What does that mean, darling?" She had taken his arm after he picked up her satchel.

"I have something to tell you, my love. Let's have coffee in the station restaurant." They made their way through the crowd of long-robed Arabs, Turks in traditional costume, Ottoman soldiers, and an assortment of Europeans. They found a small table and sat down. She pulled in her long skirts so as not to block the aisle in the packed establishment.

"What is it, Levi? You look concerned. Did something happen?"

"No, no nothing like that. But it is a disruption to our current situation." The waiter brought two small cups of Turkish coffee and slid them onto the little table. Katherina and Levi's heads were almost touching as they leaned in toward each other.

"I have been 'requested' to take on an emergency assignment. My commander promised it would not affect my discharge date from the army the first of October."

"What is the assignment, darling? Is it here in Baghdad?"

Levi looked at his wife and reluctantly said, "I wish it were." He knew she would be very disappointed and concerned. And it would permanently end their rendezvous every two weeks or so.

"I have been 'asked' to take the most rapid means of transport to a place called Tabora. A rail bridge collapsed on their main line, their only line actually, and unfortunately, it killed the only two bridge engineers in the country."

"Where? Is that close by?" Katherina was quick with more questions. "There're lots of railroad engineers all along this new route. Why you? And where is this Tabora?"

He took her hands into his.

"It's in Africa, German East Africa—at our colony there. It's the only rail line that connects the eastern and western parts of the country. It needs to be rebuilt right away."

"Africa! You're going to Africa? From here?" Katherina was visibly upset.

"But why you? There must be somebody in the whole of Africa who can fix the bridge!"

"I'm sorry, darling. I really don't have any choice. I don't want to go either, but I'm an officer in army engineers." He turned his hands up in an expression of hopelessness. "I've been told that the job could be done in a month."

"Africa!" Katherina was looking off in the void, her mind racing at the implications of this news.

"When do you leave? And how do you get to East Africa from Baghdad?"

"My commander is still working that out, but he wants me to leave as soon as possible . . . in a few days I suspect." Levi could see a tear forming in the corner of Katherina's eye. It finally spilled over and trickled down her cheek.

"I don't want you to go," she said softly, holding his hands tightly.

"I don't want to go either. It will only be for a month or so, and I suspect I'll be shipped directly home from there for my discharge. I'm really going to miss our little get-togethers here, my love." He kissed her hands and reminded her, "You have your work here, and we'll both be home before the snow falls."

She looked at him with a sorrowful expression and almost whined, "But that's months away."

"Yes, I know." They both sat there in silence for a long time. Finally, he said, "Let's go to the hotel, shall we?"

Katherina stayed on in Baghdad until Levi's orders came down with his transit plans. She had telegraphed Professor Schellenberger of the situation and indicated she would return shortly to the dig. Levi turned over to others his workload on the Berlin to Baghdad Railway and was free to spend his last few days in Baghdad with his wife.

They lay under a thin sheet in the canopied bed after making love in Levi's spacious hotel room. The two had whiled away their time together, browsing the stalls and open-air markets that had served the locals for perhaps three thousand years. Now on the eve of Levi's departure, both just wanted to be alone together.

Both felt an uneasiness in Levi's unexpected assignment in far-off Africa. At least in Baghdad, one could now take the train almost all the way to Berlin. It didn't seem so far from home.

"You'll be going home in less than a month, my love," Levi murmured. "Give Rebecca a big kiss from her papa." The thought brought smiles.

"Of course, dearest." She turned in to him, to his nude body, and slid her leg over, covering his abdomen.

With his arm around her neck, he pulled her lips to his, as he continued, "She's growing every day . . . she is a little miracle, isn't she? I do so look forward to the three of us being together again in a month or so." Levi was randomly stroking her shoulder and back.

"I've enjoyed this time in Baghdad. What an exotic city—it actually reminds me of some places in China—the open air markets, the smells, the chattering in foreign tongues. But I'm very ready to go home." He exhaled heavily.

"One more project and it's back to civilian life!"

"Yes, darling, it's what I most want too," Katherina whispered as they both drifted off to sleep and to their separate dreams.

"June fifteenth, my departure date for home! It's coming up, and I do have a lot to do at the dig," Katherina said as Levi watched her get dressed. She only had on a sheer slip, and as she moved around their bedroom, he could see her body dip and sway. The baby had not affected her figure at all as far as Levi was concerned. She stirred him every time he saw her like this.

"Dr. Schellenberger is staying on for a few weeks to lecture at the university here," she said casually, "and at the invitation of the Sultan, no less. He's very happy about it." She turned around.

"And what are you staring at, sir?" She had a big smile on her face. "Or more importantly, what are you thinking about?" She gave her body a little shake, knowing her breasts would move and bounce. They both started laughing.

"Come here, you!" he said in exaggerated boldness. "We're in Baghdad, so you have to be my harem slave girl!"

"Oh, really, mister Grand Poobah?" She came by the bed, and he reached out and grabbed her hand and pulled her onto the bed. His hands slid up under her slip.

"Now I've gotcha!" And they rolled over and over, laughing and kissing with mock escape attempts, until they were both aroused to a passionate pitch. She pushed him back onto his back and straddled him.

"Now I've got you, mister!" She pulled her slip over her head and leaned forward, kissing him. She swayed back and forth against his chest.

It was noon the next day, and his time had come to depart. She was there to see him off in front of the hotel. It was a short, sweet parting after the morning spent in each other's arms. What needed to be said had been said. His last words to her as he stepped onto the running board of the car and adjusted his dust goggles were, "I'll telegraph you, my love, as soon as I get to Dar-es-Salaam. Love and kisses to Rebecca."

The German consulate in Baghdad assigned Levi a Benz automobile and driver to motor down along the Tigris River to where it flowed into the Euphrates and on to Kuwait City on the Persian Gulf.

She stood there, stoic, watching the swirl of dust form a tan cloud behind the open-air car. He turned around in his seat and waved to her as the earth cloud finally obscured their view of each other. She stayed transfixed, staring down the road and thinking how much she loved him.

German East Africa

—— CHAPTER 19 ——

News from Home

T he telegram arrived eight days later. It was delivered to the hotel and a messenger came out to the dig to hand it personally to Katherina. She carefully opened the yellow telegram envelope.

12 JUNE 1914. STOP. DEAR KATHERINA. STOP. ARRIVED SAFELY DAR ES SALAAM. STOP. SAW PROJECT PLANS. STOP. BIG JOB. STOP. TRAIN TO TABORA TOMORROW. STOP. HOME IN TWO MONTHS. STOP. HAVE SAFE TRIP HOME. STOP. LOVE LEVI STOP

She shaded her eyes and reread the telegram and then stuck it into her skirt pocket. She had expected the message from her husband any day as she knew the sailing schedule of the supply ship Levi was on. It sailed from Kuwait through the Persian Gulf and into the Gulf of Oman and then into the Arabian Sea. It headed South West into the Indian Ocean and passed British Oman, the Italian Colony of Somaliland, British East Africa, and finally arrived at German

East Africa. His ship docked in the ancient Arab port of Dar es Salaam, an ancient trading post for ivory, exotic animals, and slaves bound for Middle Eastern depots. She was happy to have his safe arrival confirmed, as half-forgotten memories of her South Atlantic crossing and the iceberg incident came back to her with a shudder.

Back inside the staff tent at the dig site, Katherina waited for her lunch to be delivered to table by their Turkish camp cook. She had a chance to read the latest newspapers from Berlin. With the Berlin to Baghdad Railway almost complete, news and newspapers traveled long distances in just a few short days, even to the tell in Babylon.

As she skimmed various stories and assorted advertisements, including the latest summer fashions, she was enjoying the physical connection, the newspaper, to home. "Kaiser Sends First Wireless Message to President Wilson in America," she read. It made her think of their dear friends Markus and his wife Helena in German South West Africa. I wonder if he will ever move back home, she thought. I hope they will someday.

"German Prince de Wied, Crowned King of Albania," she read. *Interesting, and what's this?* "Germany and Britain Agree to Divide Portugal's African Possessions." *How can they do that?* As she continued to read, Professor Schellenberger entered the tent and slapped his hat against his pants, creating a cloud of dust.

"I wish you wouldn't do that, dear Professor, there's enough dust on our lunch already." She smiled, and he took note of it.

"Sorry, Sorry. Ah, newspapers from home?"

"Yes, and always it's full of triumph and tragedy. What do you make of all these articles like this one?"

She read aloud: "'War Talk Grows: Russia to Quadruple Army,' and this other one: 'Albania Threatens War with Greece.' What does this all mean? Is it a threat to Germany?" She had put aside the paper and looked intently at her companion.

The professor sat down in a folding camp chair just as the cook brought in several platters of food, including one with thin slices of sausage swimming in a vinegar brine. Two types of bread were already on the table, caraway seed rye and dark pumpernickel, freshly baked in camp. The crock of butter had a small, domed fly screen over it. Beer poured into clear glass steins by the cook's helper attracted the two hungry archeologists.

"Ah, *ja*," he sighed, "Thank you." He nodded to the helper. "It never ends. Here we are excavating a magnificent civilization, that even after almost three thousand years we still learn about in school: Babylon. What happened? Why is it just a pile of ruins we dig through?" He stopped a moment, lost in thought.

"War, wasn't it? It's always war that brings a civilization down to rubble. Well, except for a very few: Pompeii, from a volcano, or that earthquake in America a few years ago; the whole city burned up. But even those didn't destroy a whole civilization, only cities. War is what destroys civilizations."

"Yes, but what about Albania and Russia and Greece and all this talk of a war in Europe?" sShe stopped serving herself, still holding the bread basket. "Why could there be a war? . . . Or I should ask, why *would* there be a war? And with Germany involved? I don't understand it!" Exasperation was evident in Katherina's voice.

"I understand your concern. Why do neighbors fight? Why do husbands and wives fight, sometimes leading to tragedy? Oftentimes, no one remembers exactly what the disagreement was in the first place! Countries are a lot like neighbors. They become jealous or envious or fearful, and that starts it off." He stopped to stuff a fork full of potato salad into his mouth.

"He's good, this cook, German trained. Did you try the potato salad? *Ja*, the Fatherland!" Schellenberger began again, "Bismarck had the right idea in several areas years ago. He unified Germany; he was against having colonies, and he developed a powerful army. But then our Kaiser dismissed Bismarck and rushed to acquire colonies." He took a long draft of beer and wiped his face.

"So now we need a big navy to service our colonies," He shrugged. "You know how the British sing, 'Hail Britannia, Britannia rules the waves'? They've ruled the oceans since the first Napoleon. And they don't like anyone building a big navy because it threatens their dominance. So now the Kaiser is building a big navy."

Schellenberger shook his head before adding, "And that's just one little piece of the puzzle that has all of Europe on edge. I could go on, but you don't want to hear another history lecture from me! Let's finish our lunch so I can read the papers and have my nap."

"I won't interfere with your nap, Professor, if you promise to continue your 'lecture' at dinner!"

"You, young lady, are beginning to sound like my wife!" They both tried to laugh with their mouths full of food.

Serbian Royal Crown

—— CHAPTER 20 ——

If Only a Third Crown

Captain Mathias was not as lucky in German South West Africa as his best friend's wife, Katherina. There were no rail lines from Germany to South West Africa. When he got newspapers, they were usually a month old or more—even the British ones he occasionally got from the British Cape Colony in South Africa or even, more rarely, from the Portuguese West Africa colony to the north. Most of his news came over the wireless station in Windhoek. It was limited but current.

His big advantage: he got to read the wireless messages first as they came in. Markus was at his usual duties in the wireless building, working on a schematic for the installation of the latest vacuum tubes just delivered by ship. The duty officer came running out of the receiver room with a message, not encoded, from the War Department in Berlin. Markus sat at his desk and swiveled around in his chair at the sound of the steel-studded boots clicking rapidly on the long, wood floor.

"What do you have, Sergeant?"

"Bad news, sir." Markus rose from the chair and reached for the type-written message.

TO: MILITARY COMMANDER, GERMAN SOUTH WEST AFRICA: 28 JUNE, 1914. STOP.
THIS AFTERNOON ARCHDUKE FRANZ FERDINAND, HEIR TO THE THRONE OF AUSTRIA-HUNGARY, AND HIS WIFE, THE DUCHESS OF HOHENBERG, IN THE CITY OF SARAJEVO, BOSNIA, BY A SERBIAN NATIONALIST. STOP. KAISER WILHELM HAS RETURNED TO BERLIN TO MONITOR THE CRISIS. STOP. EMPEROR FRANZ JOSEPH OF AUSTRIA-HUNGARY STATED THIS EVENING THERE ARE INDICATIONS THE ASSASSINS ARE PART OF A POLITICAL CONSPIRACY ORGANIZED BY SERBIA. STOP. IMPLEMENT ORDER NUMBER 1177. STOP. SIGNED, GENERAL, CHIEF OF STAFF, BERLIN

"Sergeant, take this immediately to the commander," Markus urged as he literally pushed the message into the hand of the duty officer. "That will be all." The sergeant saluted and left the room as Markus slumped back into his chair, his mind racing.

Those Austrians! They should have given the Serbs a third crown! The Austro-Hungary Empire already has two crowns; what's one more? They talked about it, about offering Serbia a crown, a kingdom, within the empire. It probably would have relieved the anger of the Slavs, their feelings of being discriminated against. Now we have this assassination! Damn fools, they should have given them the crown!

Imperial Austro-Hungarian Crest

—— CHAPTER 21 ——

Meanwhile at Kalvarianhof

Katherina arrived back in Berlin on June 23 and visited her parents and brothers in Potsdam for three days before taking the overnight train to Munich and then the local out to the village. Otto, Freidl, Ilsa, with Rebecca in her arms, and Willie were waiting at the little train station. Willie had learned to operate the Benz and drove for the elderly couple, since Otto's eyesight was in decline.

"Oh, how wonderful it is to be home again!" Katherina bubbled while nuzzling her baby. "How you have grown!" she purred. "I have so much to tell you all. It was a wonderful dig. We found some very interesting artifacts. Levi should be back to Baghdad from Africa in a few weeks . . . or a month at most. Everything has been so hectic."

"*Ja* and you can sleep in your own bed again!" Freidl offered warmly, to the amusement of all. Willie took the suitcases and loaded them into the Benz.

"It's good to see you again, Willie. How is everything at the farm?"

"Very good, Frau Katherina. Everything is going well at Kalvarianhof."

"Oh, Willie. There are several big crates from Levi to be picked up on the loading dock. But you'll need one of the farm wagons."

"I'll do that right after I get you home."

Freidl had the cook prepare a lovely lunch with fresh spring flowers that Otto and Willie had picked that morning on the table. Katherina spent the afternoon luxuriating with little Rebecca and the family. Anji and Markus's mother were invited for dinner and to stay the night.

It was a wonderful evening for the two families, almost like old times. It would be one of the last evenings, for years to come, of pure joy and happiness for them, unencumbered by the intrusions of an unknown, harsh, and deadly world.

The afternoon of June 28 was mild and sunny. The Mathias women sat in the parlor, enjoying late afternoon coffee and cake with Freidl, Katherina, Rebecca, and Otto. They were preparing to leave for the station and home when Otto got up from his comfortable seat to answer the telephone.

"Hello, hello. *Ja*. Fritz. Hello. What? *Mein Gott*. No! When? Both of them? *Mein Gott!* This is very bad news . . . Fritz, Fritz, are you sure?"

The five women could not help overhearing Otto's agitated conversation. Freidl and Katherina got up from the couch and moved toward the front entry hall where Otto had slumped into the chair next to the telephone.

"What? What is it?" Freidl had her hand on her throat. "Is it Levi? What's happened?" She reached for his arm. "Otto, what's happened?"

"Fritz, hang on for a moment," Otto said as he met his wife's questions.

Otto looked up at his wife and exclaimed, "The Arch Duke of Austria and his wife have been shot!"

Obvious relief appeared on Freidl's face. "Who? Which duke and his wife? What happened, Otto?" Otto put his hand over the telephone mouthpiece, "I'll tell you in a moment. Fritz, I must go now, but thanks for letting me know—*ja, ja. Auf wiedersehen*."

By this time Ilsa, Anji, and her mother had joined the group in the hallway.

"*Mein Gott*—" Otto began, looking up at the ladies. "The Archduke and his wife, Sophie—she's from Hohenberg—were assassinated this afternoon. He's the heir to the Austro-Hungarian throne! Somewhere in Bosnia, I think he said. Let's go back to the parlor."

Freidl was thoughtful for a moment. "Oh, that poor man, Franz Joseph. To lose his son . . . you know he's quite an old man now. Otto, how long has he been on the Austrian throne?" Freidl asked.

"Oh, for decades and decades," he responded, dismissing the importance of the question. "The serious issue, besides these two ghastly murders, is what will the Austrians do in retaliation for this crime?"

"Who would do such a thing?" Frau Mathias asked. All were looking one to another.

Anji spoke up, "Mama, I've read in the papers how the Slavic peoples in the Austro-Hungarian Empire have been agitating for fair treatment, and they are really frustrated by the lack of any relief. I read that Serbia is frightfully angry at the Austrian Empire. I would not be surprised if Serbs were behind this in some way."

The morning edition of the newspapers came on the early train from Munich. They were delivered by ten, along with the morning mail, to Kalvarianhof by the postman on his bicycle. He also brought out the afternoon addition, along with the afternoon mail, at about four. Otto and the rest of the household were up and waiting when they heard the postman's bell ring. Katherina was the first to the door and stepped out as the postman's bicycle slid to a stop. Everyone was out and gathered around as the big, black leather bag was opened and letters were shuffled through and the two newspapers handed over.

"Morning Herr Levi, ladies. Everyone's been out waiting for the news this morning. It's bad news; that's for sure. Well, I'm off." With that, he peddled in an arc and headed down the dirt road toward town.

"What does it say? What's the news?" someone asked. Anji and Frau Mathias stayed another night as the discussion of the previous evening had grown late. Both mothers were concerned about their respective sons.

Frau Mathias offered, "I'm just grateful our two men are far away in Africa and not involved in all this talk of war in Europe."

Otto didn't say anything but caught the eye of Katherina. They exchanged a knowing look. Anji and Ilsa picked up on the eye contact too. Anji was about to speak, when Katherina, with the subtlest shake of her head, stopped her.

Everyone returned to the house and congregated around the table in the kitchen alcove to read the papers.

A while later, Otto said, "I'm ready for a walk in the woods. Who's going to join me?" The three young women immediately agreed to go.

"Do you want to go for a walk in the woods, Mama?" Anji asked.

Frau Mathias looked over to Freidl and asked, "Do you want to go?"

Freidl wrinkled her noise and shook her head. "No, but you go with the girls. I'm happy right here."

"I'll stay with Freidl. We'll go another time. And pick some flowers to take home, Anji, my dear. It will be nice to have some fresh wild flowers on the table."

They were out the door in a moment and across the meadow, following the cow path into the woods. Anji was waiting for someone to say something. It was as if no one really wanted to speak, to start a conversation about something that was fraught with fear and danger and uncertainty. Finally, she could wait no longer and ventured to ask a weighty question: "Why didn't you want me to speak up back there, Kathi?"

The women walked on either side of Otto. He spoke up, "Katherina didn't want any of us to challenge your mother's idea, Anji. She believes that the men are safe somehow, isolated from anything that happens in Europe. Why upset her unnecessarily?"

"You mean Markus and Levi could be involved if something happens here?" Ilsa asked.

"If there is a war and it involves Germany, then, yes, they probably will be involved . . . somehow," Otto said. "Remember, they're both in the army. And war is about more than winning. It's about land and grabbing more land. The colonies, our colonies, are vastly rich."

———

"If ever there was a month that should have been relived and altered, July, 1914, was it," Otto mumbled quietly as he sunk into the overstuffed sofa in the music room upstairs at Kalvarianhof.

"What was that, dear?" Freidl asked, not looking up from her darning.

"Just reading page after page of terrible news."

"Are you going to fill me in? You know I never seem to have my glasses when I want to read the newspaper," she remarked, then paused. "Although I'm not sure I want to read of this dreadful war that just started." She bit off the end of the thread. "There, that button should stay on for a while. I don't understand how you can pop your buttons all the time." She dug into her darning basket and pulled out a sock.

"Well, at least you seem to catch most of them." She stopped and looked over to her husband. He looked back.

"All right, I'll fill you in," he said. "They published a chronology of the last six—no, eight weeks. Let's see. It goes from the Archduke's death on June 28, through all of July, till today." He stopped a moment to focus.

"Ach! The Japanese just declared war on Germany today!"

"What?" she exclaimed.

"It's right here, '23 August, Tokyo, Japan Declares War on Germany.' They want Tsingtao and the whole of our Chinese colony! Most of this you've heard me read to you earlier, so I'll just skim through it." He stopped to clear his throat and read the summary of events to his wife:

Austria prepares to invade Serbia; Serbia rejects Austrian demands; Russia declares it will protect Serbia; Austrian Empire declares war on Serbia; Russia mobilizes one million two hundred thousand troops; Belgium King Albert I mobilizes army; Germany declares war on Russia; Russia invades Germany; Germany invades France, Luxembourg, Switzerland; Germany declares war on France; German ally Italy declares neutrality; Germany invades Belgium; England declares war on Germany; United States declares neutrality and offers mediation; Austria declares war on Russia; Serbia declares war on Germany; France invades Alsace; France and England declare war on Austria-Hungary; British Expeditionary Force lands in France; Germans capture Brussels.

He paused to catch his breath. "Do you want me to go on?"

"No, no, for heaven's sake. I've heard enough of declaring this and declaring that. Isn't there some good news in that paper you read from front to back?"

"*Ja*, well, no, but I must tell you one other news item . . . because you'll find out soon enough yourself. France and England invaded our colony in Togo."

There was silence between them for a few moments. She sat up and put her darning down. Finally she asked, "What does it mean, Otto?"

"It means, my dear, that the Congo Pact has been violated. It has not held. It also means that this European war is spreading to Africa, just as it has spread to China."

Another long pause. "Levi!" she cried.

"Yes?"

Freidl got up from her chair and came across the room and sat close to Otto on the sofa. He put his arm around her as she wept silently.

Kalvarianhof, Summer, 1914

—— CHAPTER 22 ——

Dashed Hope and Life in the Undercroft

Of course, Anji, Ilsa, and Katherina had heard of the British and French invasion of the German Colony of Togo in Africa and understood its implications for Markus in German South West Africa and Levi in German East Africa. The three women were, of course, deeply concerned about their men. They were, therefore, elated by the latest news.

The women were shopping, having a late lunch in Munich at Dolmaiers, near the Marienplatz, when a newsboy passed selling the afternoon edition.

"Here, boy, I'll take one," Katherina said, digging for the five *pfennig* in her change purse. She studiously scanned the lead articles while the others chatted. Kathi sat up with a start, griping the newspaper tightly. "Oh, listen! This is wonderful news!"

She read aloud: "September 17, 1914, Berlin: 'Germany Asks United States to Elicit Terms for Peace'! It is rumored the Kaiser has ordered the Foreign Office to approach President Wilson to elicit terms for peace from England, France, and Russia."

Anji's and Ilsa's eyes widened, with both talking at once. "This is wonderful news! The war will be over soon! Levi and Markus can come home. Will the American President do that, mediate a peace agreement? Will the British and the Tsar and the French go along with it? What about the Belgians?" They peppered Katherina with questions, with excitement in their voices.

"We must ask Papa!" Ilsa exclaimed.

For the next several weeks, everyone in the Levi and Mathias households eagerly awaited the morning newspaper for announcements of a negotiation agreement. When nothing appeared in the morning paper, the same anticipation applied to the afternoon paper.

"Why doesn't the Kaiser say something . . . or President Wilson? Surely everyone wants this war to end," Ilsa said in exasperation, with anxiety in her voice. "Why don't we hear something?"

When the three women got a chance to ask Otto Levi earlier, he answered, "These negotiations usually take a long time . . . a week, maybe months. Wilson knows that these European wars usually last a few months, at best. He may be pressing Britain, Russia, and France, but he may also figure the war will end of its own accord. Or, perhaps, one or more of these nations aren't interested in ending it without concessions that the Kaiser will not agree to. It's complicated, and it's all speculation at this point."

Life went on at Kalvarianhof and with the Mathias family in Munich. Anji and her mother looked down onto the park, from behind the lace curtains of their spacious, second-floor apartment as young men, raw recruits, drilled awkwardly.

"They're so enthusiastic about joining the army. Don't they realize they could get killed? Mama, look at how excited they are. They seem to love the idea of war. If Markus was here, he could tell them what it's really like in battle . . . those stories he told about China. It's a good thing we didn't know, *ja*, Mama . . . I mean, about China."

Frau Mathias moved closer to her daughter and put her arm around her waist as they both watched and listened to the drums and the shouted commands.

"I'm so worried about dear Markus and his wife," Frau Mathias began. "What's going to happen to them way out there in Africa? I wish he would have brought her home."

"But Mama, Helena and Markus moved to the family ranch, and it's far out in the country. Remember his telegram? There certainly won't be any danger way out there even . . . if there is any fighting at all around Windhoek. Let's hope that before those boys in the park are trained," she nodded toward the window, "the war will be over."

The Levi family continued doing their daily tasks while hoping for a swift end to the conflict. Frau Levi and Ilsa were in the vast, lower level of Kalvarianhof, the undercroft, or basement, of the old estate. It was a musty, dark, cavernous space with massive stone supports for the building above. After three hundred years, old furniture and a few trunks with remnants of past lives were all that remained of the original monk's forest cloister.

It was early October and the two women, along with Freidl's cook, busied themselves with the seasonal work of putting up an array of homegrown provisions, meant to be consumed during the long, winter months. Willie was helping, too, by bringing baskets of onions, potatoes, carrots, apples, beetroots, and cabbages down the stairs from the kitchen garden and orchard.

The women, long trained in how to store various fruits and vegetables for maximum preservation, were sorting the foodstuffs. Onions were bunched and hung from hooks to be kept cool and dry; potatoes were put in dry bins and covered to prevent frost; two varieties of apples were placed in layered straw on deep, wooden trays; no two should ever touch. Oranges and lemons from Italy, bought cheap at the height of the season, could be preserved for surprisingly long periods when the women kept them dry and away from circulating air. "Look at all the leftovers from bygone years," Freidl commented with a nostalgic air. "See, on these shelves over here, soap! We used to make our own soap. I remember my mama saying, 'Don't use it till it's as hard as a brick!'"

A smile was on her face. "Oh, and here are candles; look, dozens of them. These are really old. When I was a young girl, we were always using them . . . till we got gas lighting, and then later, Otto put in electric wires." She stopped and stood there a moment, lost in her own thoughts. "How times have changed," she said as she returned to sorting.

—— CHAPTER 23 ——

Meanwhile in German South West Africa: September, 1914

Half a world away, in the German colony of South West Africa, Captain Markus Mathias was momentarily startled to hear gun fire. He recognized the rapid, sporadic bam, bam, bam of "fire-at-will" shooting. It instantly reminded him of the battles he fought during the Boxer Rebellion in China fourteen years earlier. He reined in his mount and used hand signals to bring his small unit to a halt.

"Dismount!" He had come in recent days to the southernmost reaches of the German colony on one of his periodic inspection tours of the telegraph system that connected the vast colonial land. These communication links were even more vital now that the European war had spread to Africa.

Since war had been declared a month ago, Captain Mathias was assigned a camel-mounted, armed escort of six Schutztruppen for his inspection tours. These black troops were originally trained for policing the colony, but now they assumed more wide-ranging military duties under the command of white officers. Markus adapted quickly to camel riding, the only sure means of rapid travel in the vast Namibian and Kalahari Deserts and the arid waste lands that constituted a significant portion of the colony.

The war in Africa became a reality for Markus on this day. They had just crested a high, rock-strewn, scrub-covered hill and could clearly see the action below.

"Keep the camels below the ridge line," As he stepped off his mount, he slid his rifle out of its saddle-mounted holster, as did his six escorts. Two of the black troops tended the camels while Markus led the others back up to the ridge line.

As he surveyed the landscape below with his binoculars, he spoke almost to himself: "It's Commander Franke's forces engaging the enemy! The South Africans have crossed the Orange River into our territory! Have a look, Corporal."

Markus handed the binoculars to Corporal Ubangi, his highest ranking Schutztruppen. He pointed toward the edge of the fierce fighting. "See the flag?"

Ubangi hesitated a moment and replied, "Yes, Captain, but it appears the South Africans are tremendously outnumbered." He handed the glasses back. Markus stared intensely through the magnifying lens.

"There is no way the—" Markus stopped short. "Look!" he pointed. "Part of the enemy forces, those horse-mounted troops! How many? Count them, Corporal!"

There was a tense pause.

"I count about twenty riders, but there's so much smoke and dust down there, it's hard to tell, sir." He handed the binoculars back to Markus.

"They're disengaging from the battle and heading toward that gap in the hills off to our right! We can cut them off if we hurry."

Markus was already up and heading for the camels when Ubangi spoke up: "We're only six, Captain."

"Yes, but they don't know that! Mount up!"

The gap in the hills was narrow, with space for maybe three horses abreast.

Markus arrived in time to quickly survey the pass, hide the camels, send four of his men to the far slope of the narrow canyon, and position himself and two others opposite.

"On my signal, my shot, each of you choose a target and fire two shots. Then stop firing. We on this side will bring down the lead horses. Collectively, we should drop at least the first several riders. Then let's see what happens. If we scare them enough, they may surrender. If not, we continue the fight. We have the advantage of surprise, and look, the sun will be in their eyes."

It wasn't long before the Germans heard galloping hoof beats thundering toward them. The path through the hills was not straight, so Markus and his men could not see the oncoming enemy. The sound of the horses on the hard pack, with rocks and stones being kicked up, reverberated in the narrow canyon.

In a blur of sweating horses and khaki uniforms, the retreating soldiers rounded the curved path into a hail of rifle fire. Pandemonium! The front two horses, shot out from under their riders, pitched forward, only to be trampled or rolled on by several additional horses that tripped on the downed animals and men. An additional half dozen riders, horses rearing, slid out of their saddles.

Blood from the two lead soldiers, hit by the fusillade of fire, sprayed back into the faces of the following troops. Shouts and screams of fear and of the wounded mingled with the neighing of crippled and dying horses; it created a sense of panic. There was little room for the South African soldiers to turn their mounts around, becoming perfect targets for the Germans.

Fortunately, for this unfortunate enemy, the German native troops were highly disciplined and obeyed Captain Mathias's exact orders. Only one soldier fired three shots, not the two Markus had commanded.

As soon as his troops stopped firing and before their adversaries had a chance to return fire, Markus shouted in English, "Cease firing! Cease firing! Surrender now or die; surrender now or die!"

In the loudest voice he could command, he again shouted a cease fire and followed that with, "Throw down your weapons, now!" Among the moans and groans of man and beast, the clatter of rifles hitting the rock-strewn pathway could be heard.

Again in English,

"Dismount and hands up. Do it now, or die!" The shaken soldiers, having moments earlier retreated from a losing battle by the Orange River and now ambushed in a narrow canyon with a half dozen of their companions wounded or dead, put their hands in the air.

"Soldiers, line up away from your mounts, hands in the air. Corporal, have your men collect the weapons and horses and guard the prisoners." Markus walked down near the line of beaten men, still carrying his rifle.

"Who is your commanding officer here?" he asked.

A British sergeant spoke up: "He's dead by the looks of it." He pointed to a limp form half-buried under a dead horse. "So is the second, you got him right in the chest . . . a good man he was."

The number of able-bodied prisoners numbered eleven. There were six wounded and five dead.

"Soldiers," Markus began again, "you will be properly cared for as our prisoners; however, if you try to escape, you will be shot. I need you to care for your wounded." Several of the South Africans turned, hesitated a moment, then rushed to the aid of their fallen comrades, assisting them as best they could.

"Corporal, place two of your men on each of the slopes above the prisoners and one at either end. Give the prisoners water and our medical supplies. I'm going to scout the battle by the river and see if we can join our forces there. It sounds like the firing has died down. I'll be back soon." With that, Markus mounted his camel and headed in the direction from which the South Africans fled.

As Markus approached the site of the battle along the Orange River, he was surprised to see a mass of soldiers sitting in a tightly packed group, their weapons piled off to the side. Obviously, these men were prisoners. They numbered at least a hundred. There were also many dead and wounded. He rode up to a group of officers and reported the fact of his recent scrimmage and that he too had prisoners.

Commander Frank spoke up, "Good Work, Captain . . . ?"

"Mathias, sir."

"Yes, Captain Mathias. I'll have several of my men bring your prisoners and their wounded here. We'll march them up country to our garrison."

"Yes, sir," Markus took a long drink from his canteen. "How many crossed the border and attacked us, sir?"

"That's the strange thing," Commander Franke replied. "Several prisoners said their unit has about three hundred rifles. That's an astonishingly small number, and as far as we can tell, they didn't even have a supply train big enough to carry enough ammunition for this sort of operation. I have over a thousand men here right now, and that number is considered small for our mission to intercept any cross-border incursions by the enemy. This defeat suggests to me the gross incompetence of the South Africans—or whoever is in command down there." He paused and surveyed the disheartened enemy before him.

"An invasion force of three hundred was doomed to failure before they crossed the river. They don't seem to have learned anything from their Boer War." He shook his head. "I can only surmise that this was supposed to be some sort of diversion for a much stronger attack, possibly on the coast. I've already ordered telegraphs sent to our ports at Lüderitz, Swakopmund, and to Windhoek, alerting them of this attack."

Commander Frank was about to light a cigarette when Markus offered him one of his. "They're Turkish, sir. The best smoke I've ever had, and this is my last pack . . . My friend sent them to me from Baghdad." All three lit up and sat easy in their saddles, watching the wounded being cared for.

"By the way, Captain, thank you for keeping the communication system in good working order. It's our vital link."

"Thank you, sir. It's why I accepted my commission in the army. I came here to build an updated wireless station in Windhoek and improve the telegraph service."

The commander finished his smoke.

"Sergeant, take a scouting party across the river. Make sure there're no enemy troops nearby. But do not engage the enemy. We don't want to give the South Africans a reason to attack again." As the sergeant rode off, Commander Franke turned to Mathias: "You shouldn't be in these battles. You're far too valuable an officer to be in the line of fire."

He looked intently at Markus for the first time and saw the double Iron Cross ribbons on his uniform. "How did you earn those, Captain?"

"China, sir."

Commander Franke turned his horse's head and spurred his mount into a walk. As he left, he nodded toward Mathias, "I'll have to hear the story behind those sometime."

A week later, Markus was back at the ranch on a short break from assisting with the mobilization of the German population for the defense of the colony. He rode up to the ranch house and handed the reins of his horse to Sambolo, while Helena hurried out to meet him.

"Oh, dearest, I'm so glad you're back," she said breathlessly. "There's been talk in town of an invasion. And have you heard? They want two of my brothers to enlist!"

He opened his arms and hugged her. "Yes, my love, I was at the Orange River during the attempted invasion. Actually, it was a pretty pathetic display of soldiering. Commander Franke defeated them in no time . . . had them outnumbered three to one." As they walked toward the house,

"I'm sorry, but most young men of military age are being called up."

"At least you're safe for now, thank the Lord," she said. "Come in. I just put Rupert down to nap. I'll fix you something to eat . . . We're all waiting to hear what's going to happen."

Mounted Soldiers of German South West Africa

—— CHAPTER 24 ——

Meanwhile in German East Africa: July 7, 1914

From Dar es Salaam, capitol of German East Africa, the train from the coast of the Indian Ocean chugged inland. Through the train window, Captain Levi viewed startling herds of African animals. He was on his way to Tabora, site of the collapsed bridge.

He enjoyed the ocean passage from Kuwait to German East Africa and now was eager to get a firsthand look at the damage. The train churned out black smoke as it left the coastal mangroves and jungle behind. The rattling cars passed miles of grasslands studded with huge, thick-trunked trees, crowned with wide, dark-green canopies.

Tabora was a sleepy, dusty little market town like thousands of others in Africa. The train station was the most significant feature besides the open-air market of farm produce and handwoven textiles, wooden implements, and practical pottery.

Meeting Levi at the station was an overweight railroad man in civilian clothes by the name of Horst Dorfmann. His blue eyes were set deep in his red, puffy face. Ringlets of sweat coursed down to a very damp shirt that absorbed every drop.

"Greetings, Captain Le… Levi, so glad you finally arrived. I've been sent out to pick-pick you up. You only have the-the one grip?"

"No, they're unloading a field trunk with my things. Thank you. How far is the damaged bridge?" Levi scanned the scene before him and realized how primitive the African colony was, at least based on what he had seen so far.

"We'll take the wa-wagon," Horst stuttered as he picked up Levi's grip.

"It's a two-two hour ride out to the site. They've set up a temporary work camp there, but we'll stay in town tonight and get a-an early start in the morning. There's no hotel here, so you'll sta-stay at Schragers's. He's a local land owner . . . Has a ni-nice place. He and his wa-wife."

It was a nice place, surprisingly nice, Levi thought as he was warmly greeted by the middle-aged couple. Joseph Schrager wore a light-colored summer suit, and his wife, Mina, filled out a white, floor-length, lacy dress that revealed a Rubenesque woman with a quick smile.

"Welcome, Captain. All the way from Baghdad . . . How interesting," she said.

"Yes, greetings," offered Joseph as he ushered Levi onto a polished wood floor in a beautiful sitting room.

"Rashid, please bring our guest a beer and one for me also. Dear?"

"Yes."

"Three, Rashid."

Levi eyed the servant.

"He's from India. There're many Indians and Arabs here in this part of Africa. Did you know that, Captain?"

"No, I did not. Well, with a capitol named Dar-es-Salaam, I knew there would probably be Arabs," The beer was brought in on a silver tray with what proved to be freshly baked pretzels.

"You seem to have all the comforts of home," Levi offered while sinking his teeth into an inch-thick, salt-encrusted pretzel the size of his hand.

"Yes, with the ranch and my local business, we're doing fine. In a few years, this colony will be known across Africa for its riches."

"What is your business, Herr Schrager?"

"*Ja*, I have several interests; the ranch, of course, ivory and hides, but mostly I supply labor to the government, mostly porters. If you want to go somewhere that is not near this railroad, you need porters, lots of them, sometimes hundreds. No roads, you see. And pack animals usually don't last long . . . Diseases kill them off, mostly from the tsetse fly."

"Joseph," Mina interrupted. "Levi? Yes, Levi may want to freshen up a bit before dinner. Shouldn't Rashid show our guest to his room?"

"Of course, of course. Captain?"

"Yes, that would be nice, but I do have one question, if I may." Levi looked at his host and continued, "What do you know of the rail trestle collapse?"

The couple looked at each other and held the look a long moment.

"It burned."

"It burned?"

"Yes, it burned," Joseph stated emphatically. "Or I should say, it was burned."

Levi sat up and his eyes widened. "What do you mean, it *was burned*?"

"I mean, it was burned, and on purpose, by . . . by—"

"Now, Joseph, you don't know for sure."

"I damn well do know for sure! I just don't have any proof. It was those stinking Hadzas, that's who it was . . . And they made a real mess of it. And killed how many? Eleven, right? Eleven, counting that man who just died from his injuries. They're murderers; that's what!"

Joseph had worked himself up to the boiling point and could not stop. "We should send Vorbeck out to hunt them all down and shoot 'em."

"Joseph, please!" Mina looked embarrassed.

"All right, all right, but I know they did it because the whites are moving into their traditional roaming lands and pushing them out. So they burned the trestle, thinking that's going to stop the whites from seizing more land."

"Well, you're probably right about that," Mina said in a conciliatory tone.

Levi jumped in, "Who are these Hadzas?"

Mina took the question while her husband was lost in his angry thoughts. "They are probably one of the most primitive people on earth—or at least in the colony. They are hunter gatherers, like their ancestors way back in the Stone Age. They travel in small family groups of a dozen or so. They dig roots, hunt mostly small game, pick berries, have almost no possessions, wear almost no clothing, and sit around most of the time singing and chatting away in their primitive language. They don't seem to have any real leadership in their groups. They just appear to agree on what to do by looks and gestures."

She stopped, knowing by Levi's intense stare that she had his full attention. Levi was impressed by this knowledgeable and very articulate woman before him.

"Oh, one other thing, they boil down a certain plant sap. The paste that remains is used to make a deadly poison for their arrows to kill their prey."

Later in his room, Levi lay awake half the night, turning over in his mind the implications of what he had heard about the trestle sabotage and the Hadza people who might have done it—and their poisonous arrows.

He turned over his thoughts in his head: The trestle burning and train wreck means intense heat and violence to the rails, he thought. That would certainly have bent them, twisted them into scrap metal. Where are the replacements, and how long will it take to get them to the site? Maybe the rails are there already? That would be a stroke of good luck.

He continued turning over in his mind other implications. The tracks were laid on a curved trestle, so the rails aren't straight . . .

As he drifted off to sleep, his final thoughts concluded that the "bridge repair job" was turning into a major engineering project.

It was a two-hour wagon ride out to the deep ravine where the wooden trestle once stood. After an early morning breakfast of hard boiled eggs, freshly baked rolls, honey, and coffee with the Schragers, Levi was content to be on his way.

There were two dozen native workers and a dozen whites working the site.

Most of the damaged trestle had been removed—as well as many of the damaged rails. An elaborate hoist system was under construction to bring the engine and tender back up onto the tracks. The three wooden passenger coaches, consumed in the fire, had only their trucks and steel undercarriage still visible.

Horst Dorfmann pulled on the reins to bring the wagon to a halt. "This is Captain Sol-Solomon Levi, sir." he said haltingly. He addressed a German officer-of-train, Lieutenant Andre Rosenbloom.

"Ah, finally, the bridge engineer! Welcome, Captain Levi. As you see, we've been clearing the site for you . . . salvaging what we felt was still of use." He pointed to piles of railroad ties, rails, and lumber not burned in the fire. "You, of course, will make the final judgment as to what is still useable. Have you any questions, Captain?"

After saluting the lieutenant, Levi asked a pressing question: "Yes, when can we expect replacement rails and the lumber for the new trestle?"

"Ah, the most important question first, sir. The lumber is being shipped from the coast as we speak. As a matter of fact, some of it came in on the train you arrived on. The rails are a bit problematic, shall we say. We will have to survey the inventory along the line. You will have to build your trestle based on what rails are available in country. We've already started the search."

"Very good, Lieutenant. Another question: What about the Hadzas, the ones that burned—sabotaged—the line?"

"Ah, the Hadzas. Yes, they roam this part of the colony. And yes, they are angry about being pushed further afield, but there is no proof they started the fire. It could have been British saboteurs, what with all the war talk . . . or an accident . . . The train's embers could have started a fire in the ravine . . . Fires along the tracks are not infrequent."

"So the Hadzas probably aren't responsible?"

"Captain, sir, the Hadzas are a primitive people, but they are not stupid. They would gain nothing from burning one trestle." He paused and added, "Shall we inspect the site now, sir?"

Levi spent the next ten days in the ravine and the surrounding approaches, figuring the fastest way to build a new trestle, hoping they would soon find the necessary rails. Late one afternoon, back in Tabora, he visited the local military base, such as it was, a very spartan unit of several officers, several dozen soldiers, and a contingent of native Schutztruppen. It did have, however, a telegraph station.

Levi sent a telegram to Katherina and included a brief greeting to his parents. His message was short and to the point: project delay, more later, etc., was all he could offer with his greetings. Even so, he felt better having sent Katherina the message. As an afterthought, Levi decided to send his friend Markus a telegram also, wishing him well and including his mailing address.

The telegraph operator, a corporal, said, "Sir, we estimate your message to Germany will take a full day or more, depending on the atmospheric conditions and the traffic. Lately, the weather has disrupted our wireless transmissions most every day. No predicting it, sir. Your other telegram should arrive at Windhoek in several hours, at most."

"Thank you, Corporal." Levi walked back to the Schragers and dinner. Light talk and a glass of port offered by Joseph brought the evening to an early close.

Tuesday, August 4, 1914, found Levi attending a small afternoon lawn party that Mina and Joseph had prepared for a dozen friends. Most conversations debated the chance of war and its effect on the African colonies.

"We do have the Congo Pact," someone offered. "It should insulate us from the European conflict if war does come to Europe."

Levi, only half-listening, was lost in his own thoughts. He had tried everything to speed up the reconstruction of the rail bridge and had made steady progress.

Another week or so, and it will be finished, he thought to himself as he drained off a stein of beer. He had already discussed his pending departure with his commander, contingent on a final inspection of the finished trestle. The overall military commanding officer of the German East African Protectorate was Lieutenant-Colonel Paul von Lettow Vorbeck. He and Levi had several long discussions after realizing they both had been in China at the same time during the Boxer Rebellion.

"Yes, I've approved your transit and separation papers. You have a choice: take one of our supply ships from Dar es Salaam to Bremerhaven, a three week trip, or take a ship back the way you came to Kuwait and from there take a train from Baghdad to Munich. What do you think, Captain?"

"I prefer the train from Baghdad, sir. I can look over my work on that railroad again."

They both smiled before Vorbeck added a cautionary note: "If there is a war soon, the Kaiser quite probably will be in the thick of it. If that happens, you may wish you were back in Africa!"

They both had a good laugh at that, downplaying the all-too-real tensions in Europe. Vorbeck concluded, "Finish your bridge, and you'll be on the next ship home. You've earned it."

Joseph Schrager approached the two military men with Rashid close behind, carrying a tray of half-liter beer mugs.

"I hope you gentlemen are enjoying yourselves . . . Care for another beer?" All three men took a stein off the tray.

"*Prost!*" saluted Vorbeck, and they all had a hearty drink.

"It's cordial of you and Frau Schrager to open your home like this. It appears to be the social center of Tabora," Levi offered with a grin.

"Why, thank you, Captain. I, that is, we, enjoy entertaining, and I always learn something new at our gatherings . . . and of course, we enjoy the company."

Rashid disappeared into the house, but he reappeared several moments later, carrying a yellow envelope. He walked briskly up to Schrager and said, "A message for you, sir, and a gentleman waits in the front hall." Schrager hesitated a moment, looking first at the unopened telegram and then to the house.

He began walking briskly toward the house, followed by Vorbeck and Levi. His hands tore open the yellow envelope as he entered the front entry hall.

"Who is it? Oh, Lancaster! What are you doing here?" He stared at the big man in dusty, brown boots and clothes to match. Vorbeck and Levi stood to the side, eyeing the newcomer.

Joseph hesitated, turning reluctantly to the two soldiers "This is Sidney Lancaster, my ivory hunter. He's excellent at bringing down big game. He hunts here and up in British country, north of Kilimanjaro." He shifted to the hunter. "Sidney, this is Lieutenant-Colonel...." He finished the hurried introductions, "You're two weeks early." Schrager's eyes looked back and forth between the three men.

"I've brought another load in. Yes, old man, a bit early, but I probably won't be hunting up north for a while. Seems the Brits are securing their border." He eyed the two Germans in uniform as he spoke. "I'll have to go farther east, up near Ikoma. The herds have started migrating in that direction anyway. Take more time, cost you more money, Joseph."

"Yes, well, let's discuss that tomorrow. About ten?"

Lancaster acknowledged the time, nodded, and left.

"He's been a hunter for me for several years . . . Always comes back from his expeditions with quality kills, but I never know when he'll turn up." Joseph eyed his two guests.

"Now, let's see what have we here."

Schrager slipped the thin sheet from the envelope. His eyes darted across the lines once, then a second time. He held the fragile paper in his two hands a long moment, looked up, staring into his own world, and without saying a word or moving more than his arm, he laid the telegram face down on the hall table.

"Germany declared war on Russia," he stated. "August first.." He turned, "Excuse me, gentlemen, I have to catch Lancaster." With that, he scurried out the front door. Lieutenant-Colonel Vorbeck looked at Levi and held the stare a moment. Then he stepped to the hall table and turned over the telegram. He quietly read it aloud:

HERR SCHRAGER. STOP. GERMANY DECLARED WAR ON RUSSIA. STOP. FRANCE. STOP. ENGLAND. STOP. BELGIUM. STOP. CEASE ALL SHIPMENTS UNTIL FURTHER NOTICE. STOP. LATEST PAYMENT TO YOUR ACCOUNT LLOYD'S LONDON. STOP. SIGNED BOND STREET IMPORTS. STOP.

Vorbeck half-whispered to Levi, "I must leave immediately for headquarters." With that, the two soldiers left the house, "I'm afraid you'll miss your boat, Captain. The sea lanes will be dangerous now, although we do have the SMS

Konigsberg here at Dar es Salaam. It's up the coast or in the Atlantic that the British navy is most dangerous. And if I know the British, they'll attack us as soon as they can, probably along the coast. We have a lot of work to do before that happens."

Oh mein Gott, I can't believe this—I'm supposed to be on a boat for home in two weeks! The thoughts and the implications of war spun around in Levi's head as the two military men made their way to the Tabora railroad station. The colonel was talking, but Levi was only half-listening.

"As commander of defenses for this colony, I've got to get to the coast, set up defenses . . . and you have to get that damned bridge finished. We'll need to move supplies and men, and quickly if the war spreads to Africa . . . and I am sure it will. There's too much land, wealth, and prestige at stake."

"Yes, sir. Good luck, Colonel," Levi responded as Vorbeck boarded the eastbound train.

Levi left the station, walked to the military base in Tabora, secured a horse from the stables, and rode out to the almost-completed trestle. He pushed his mount in the late afternoon sun and arrived in little over an hour. His sweaty horse breathed hard through a mouth dripping with foam. Lieutenant Rosenbloom was still on site. Levi informed him that war had been declared and added, "Mount guards out here from now on. We don't want more mysterious fires. I want this trestle finished and serviceable in three days. We will concentrate on the main supports . . . Leave the guard rails and shoring up of the embankments until after we finish the essentials. I want rail stock rolling along those tracks in three days. We'll add more workers, work from sun up until dark. Arrange it, Rosenbloom."

"Yes sir, Captain!"

Something bothered Levi all afternoon, but he couldn't place it. As he walked beneath the trestle at the bottom of the ravine, it struck him. "Lloyd's of London?" he said out loud. "Why would Schrager have an account at an English bank and not at, say, Bank of Berlin?"

Late that evening, Levi was back at his room at the Schragers's house, exhausted. He sat on the edge of his bed, pulling off his boots, when he heard a commotion in the front hall. Levi walked to his door, opened it enough to hear

Lieutenant Rosenbloom's voice, with Frau Schrager saying, "He just retired for the evening, but I can give him a message in the—"

"No, no, that won't do. I need—"

"What is it, Lieutenant?" Levi stepped out into the hall with one boot on.

"Captain, I need to speak to you immediately . . . in private!"

"Come in, come in, Lieutenant." Rosenbloom made haste for Levi's room, leaving Mina Schrager standing in the front hall, perplexed.

As soon as the door closed behind them, Rosenbloom spat out his message: "Trouble . . . big trouble tonight, Captain. Horst Dorfmann is dead! And the guards shot and killed that Indian Rashid. He was caught with a can of kerosene. He tried to run away, and they shot him!"

Levi was taken aback. "What?! How did Dorfmann die?" Levi grabbed Rosenbloom's arm.

"The guards found him at the bottom of the ravine . . . too dark to tell how he died."

"All right, Lieutenant. Now I want you to go to the military post and bring back three armed guards—not the Schutztruppen. They have to be white. Herr Schrager has some questions to answer. And hurry back! Come directly to me."

"Yes, sir." Andre Rosenbloom, sweat dripping from his chin, did a half-hearted salute, spun around, and was out the door.

As he left, Levi added, "Silence is the word, Lieutenant. Don't tell anyone what happened."

As soon as Rosenbloom left, Levi went to his satchel in the armoire and retrieved his revolver, belt, and holster. *What to do next?* he thought, as he slipped on his other boot and strapped the weapon in place. Mina must be wondering what's going on. I'd better give her an explanation.

As Levi opened his door, he heard agitated voices in the hall. Mina's frightened demands could be heard and in reply, a yes. Schrager's voice!

Levi instinctively unsnapped his holster cover as he called out, "Joseph, I need to talk to you."

They were forty feet apart as Levi stepped into the long hallway. The light was dim, with only the front hall illuminated. Joseph and Mina were close together, with Joseph holding his wife, both hands around her upper arms.

"Quiet down! I can explain!" he had just said to her in a stern voice.

When he heard Levi's voice, he released Mina and pushed her aside, peering down the darkened hallway.

Levi repeated himself in a commanding voice, "I need to talk to you . . . about tonight."

Within seconds, deafening blasts of sound, smoke and flashes of light lit up the front hallway as Schrager repeatedly pulled the trigger on his gun. Mina shrieked in panic, spun around in front of Joseph, her arms in the air, as her husband continued shooting down the hall.

Mina was thrown back by the force of the shot that tore through her as she spun directly in front of Joseph's weapon. Levi felt his left foot flung back as he pulled his revolver out, just as Mina crumpled to the floor.

Levi had a clear shot, as Joseph was momentarily distracted by his unintended victim. Levi took it. With instinctive skill developed over years of shooting, he squeezed off one shot at a time. Three cartridge shells bounced onto the floor as he slumped against the wall.

It was over in seconds. Only the moans of Mina Schrager could be heard in the silent house.

The tremendous thunder of the gunshots roused several of the townspeople and brought the contingent of guards running for the house. Lieutenant Rosenbloom barged through the front door, followed by three enlisted men. They confronted a blue mist of acidic gun smoke hanging over a blood-splattered hall, with two bodies lying before them.

"Captain, Captain!" Rosenbloom shouted frantically.

"Here, here, down the hall," Levi responded as he pulled himself up the wall.

"You're injured, sir. Are there other enemy about?"

"Not that I know of. Have your men check the grounds and search the house. An English hunter named Sidney Lancaster may be part of this, so be alert."

The lieutenant ordered his men to their tasks and then turned to Levi: "Are you shot in the leg, sir?"

"No. I caught a bullet in the boot . . . It didn't touch me, but it sprained my ankle."

Levi was looking down the hall at the couple on the floor. Mina moaned and stirred a little. "Help her, Lieutenant; she's still alive!"

—— CHAPTER 25 ——

Close to Heaven

T he reality of the European war came to South West Africa with the abortive South African/British attack across the Orange River. Simultaneously, in German East Africa, following the second attempt at the destruction of the Tabora rail bridge and the slaying of the traitor Joseph Schrager and his Indian servant Rashid, Colonel von Vorbeck intensified his preparations for war. He knew it would soon descend on the German East Africa colony.

Captain Levi sent what turned out to be his last telegram to his wife Katherina, from East Africa to Bavaria, before the vital relay wireless station in German Togo was overrun by a combined force of British and French. That station had a strong wireless for all German African colonies, as well as communications with German shipping in the South Atlantic. With the fall of German Togo on August 25, 1914, the German African colonies ceased to have direct wireless communication with Berlin and the Fatherland.

Markus knew well the precarious position the Kaiser's colonies were in. There was no joyous excitement with the outbreak of the war as had been demonstrated in the German, French, and British cities of Europe. Only resignation and a sense of duty prevailed in the town squares and enlistment offices of the German colonies.

Markus spent most of his time at the Windhoek wireless station intercepting British, French, Belgian, and Portuguese wireless messages; most were not encoded. It was a great source of news on the war in Europe, and he found the news appalling.

Even if the enemy, all of them, were exaggerating, the battles and casualty numbers were staggering and hard to believe. Thousands killed, even tens of thousands killed, in one battle after another.

With the ranch nearby, most nights he was able to sleep with his wife in his own bed, a luxury afforded few other soldiers. Markus trained several assistants to continue the intercepts around the clock, making his nightly departures possible.

One evening, in the front parlor at the ranch, with his wife absent, Markus said, "Helena needn't hear the harsh details of the war; it will only upset her." He spoke to his father-in-law, Tomas, and two of her brothers, Norbert and Michael.

"I'm reminded of my army buddies during the China campaign. My friend Levi, of course, and Heiner, Günther, and Captain Mayerling . . . They must be in the thick of it—except Levi." He hesitated a moment and went on, "I got a telegram from him a week or so ago. The wireless is still broadcasting between us, but of course, he can't say much on account of the censors and enemy intercepts . . . just that he is all right."

"Good, good," Tomas offered. "It's a terrible thing, this war." He hesitated and continued, "And now with Wolfgang and Arnold called up . . . " Emotion was rising in his voice. "I don't want any Conrads killed for some God-forsaken European war!"

Helena entered the room carrying Rupert as Markus finished his thoughts: "The British and South Africans have their hands full with the threat of a Boer uprising; I think everyone's safe for the moment."

"What? What is it, dear?" Helena asked.

"Just more talk of politics and the war."

"Well, come to bed now. It's late."

She never ceased to beguile her husband. He was always ready to sweep her up into his arms, and she was almost always ready to surrender to his embraces.

Rupert was put down in his crib and after a few sniffles, drifted off to sleep. Markus was already in his nightshirt, propped up in bed when Helena came out of the dressing room in her floor-length, lacy white nightgown.

"You look lovely, my dear. I love it when your hair is up like that."

She came to her side of the bed and slipped in. "You do, do you?" and she shook her head.

"Do you like this?" She pulled pins out of her stacked hair, and it fell down onto her shoulders.

"Yes, I do . . . and especially when your lovely hair is resting on your lovely, bare shoulders." They both chuckled. He reached over to her and tugged at the ribbon closure of her nightgown. Freed from the tie, he was able to slowly pull the lacy collar open and off her right shoulder.

"See how pretty your hair is against your skin?" he whispered. They both smiled in that knowing way.

"Well, I like my hair best when it's on *your* shoulder . . . or your chest. What do you think of that, mister ribbon puller?"

"I have a string that could be pulled," and as he said that teasingly—he twirled the end of the string of his night shirt.

In a moment, she pulled his night shirt over his head as he smiled at her. She swept her head back and forth, forcing her long hair to trace across his chest and shoulders. Their lovemaking was luscious and languid. They lingered in suspended pleasure and finally slipped into that moment that became a singular bond.

After a time, he said, "We are so fortunate, in all this turmoil, that we have such a life as this."

She turned. "And I am so blessed you came from so far away and found me here in Africa. God is good. He will watch over us. He will see us all through this if it is his wish: you, darling, Rupert, Papa, and my brothers."

"And Christiana?"

"Oh, heavens, God always favors Christiana!" They both smiled at that and soon faded into their separate dreams.

In German South West Africa, after the complete defeat on the Orange River, the South Africans were slow to mount a second attack. They finally did plan an invasion; this time, from the sea at the small port town of Lüderitz. Through German spies, intercepted wireless messages, and Boer sympathizers, the German Command found out about the attack before it happened.

Unlike the South Africans, the Germans had three aeroplanes at their disposal in South West Africa. They were used for observing enemy movements and, on occasion, came under rifle fire from the ground. One such incident happened just before the invasion. A young German pilot was wounded, but managed to bring his Otto Pusher biplane back with only bullet holes in the wings of the frail craft. These were patched with cloth and glue, and the craft was ready to fly its important missions again. However, the only other pilot was laid up with malaria.

"Captain Mathias," began von Heydebreck, the commander of military forces in the colony, "your military record indicates you are a pilot with professional knowledge of aeroplanes. There are only two other men in this colony with such skills and experience; both are laid up with injuries or illness. We need to know what our enemies are doing beyond our normal resources for such information. Flying scout missions over the enemy is what's needed." He paused to size up Captain Mathias.

"Governor Seitz and I formally request that you volunteer for this special duty. Of course, you are not obliged to take on this dangerous mission, but it's a vital one in defense of the entire colony. You are privy to the knowledge that the South Africans are planning an invasion along the coast. We must know when and where. If you could—"

"I'll do it. I'll take on the mission, sir." Markus paused. "And I apologize for interrupting, Commander."

Von Heydebreck, taken aback for a moment at this forthright enthusiasm by Mathias, said, "Fine, fine, Captain. The Kaiser would be proud."

"Thank you, sir." Markus's mind was already elsewhere—in the vast blue of the endless sky.

To get back behind the controls of an aeroplane, up there, as close to heaven as I'll ever get, he thought! He could not contain a grin at the idea.

But back at the ranch, he faced questions. "Dearest, you volunteered for what kind of duty?" Helena asked, not fully understanding the nature and danger of her husband's announcement.

"Where can you fly to from here, and why would you want to fly there anyway?" They had just sat down to a late dinner at the ranch, with Tomas and Christiana and Michael. The other boys were either in military training or in bed.

"I'm the only one in the colony who is available and knows how to guide an aeroplane in flight. As I said, dear, the other two pilots are laid up in hospital."

Tomas spoke up, "*Ja*, one has malaria and the other one?"

"He was injured," Markus said, hoping that would end the inquiry into the second pilot.

"I hear he was shot while flying over enemy troops," Tomas continued.

"Yes, but only slightly . . . He will make a full recovery." Markus looked to Helena in expectation.

"Shot . . . while driving that aeroplane! Shot while up in the air?" Her voice raised in apprehension. "Why would you volunteer for such dangerous duty? Wasn't that battle you were in down on the Orange River enough?"

"Helena, dear, first of all, it wasn't a battle, at least not my part. And second, I could not refuse my commanding officer, especially under these circumstances."

He looked to Tomas for support. Tomas Conrad was reluctant but finally said, "Markus is right. You can't refuse a request like that in time of war."

"Well, I wish . . . I wish this war had never happened! My two brothers are in the army, and now you are going off to fly that silly aeroplane . . . And for what? What are you going to do up there?" She had worked herself up emotionally.

Markus reached over to comfort her, saying, "I'm only going to do some scouting . . . for British ships, along the coast. I promise to stay far away from them and way up so they can't see me . . . and I'll fly so the sun is in their eyes. You know, dear, aeroplanes don't hold very much fuel, so I can't stay up long, and when I bring it back, the mechanics have to work on the engines, and that sometimes takes days. So, you see, I won't really be doing that much flying anyway." After that long, preposterous story, Markus eased back and glanced at Tomas.

Conrad was wiggling in his seat, not knowing if he should be grim or grinning. He looked to Helena to see if she actually believed her husband's story.

Then Helena looked to her father, "What do you think, Papa?"

Tomas, put on the spot, but in the interests of his daughter's peace of mind, said, "That's pretty much what Markus will be doing . . . It's pretty light work." He then turned to Christiana and Michael: "Clear the table. Come along; help clean up."

"If you are in the right, then God will protect you. Isn't that right, dear?"

"Yes, my darling."

The next day, Markus took the train from Windhoek to Lüderitz on the coast.

His first priority was to inspect the aircraft and become familiar with its many idiosyncrasies. The mechanics knew most of them, and the two other pilots knew the rest. Markus visited both pilots in the hospital.

The malaria-ridden pilot was weak but well on the mend. The pilot who was shot while flying had a bullet wound that entered the side of his hip, traveled up his body, and broke four ribs. Every breath he took was painful. Both men managed to give Markus valuable tips on maneuverability, quirky landing attributes, and the dangerous fact of the perpetually leaking fuel tank, caused by intense vibrations of the engine in the fragile craft. They also warned of very difficult wind conditions along the coast and over the water, depending on time of day and weather and because of the winds from the inland deserts. Markus thanked them each with a bottle of Jägermeister Schnapps.

After leaving the hospital, he went directly to the airfield and took one of the aeroplanes up for a test flight before reporting to Commander von Heydebreck.

Captain Mathias was immediately assigned the task of scouting the ocean and inland from the coast for a few miles and from Lüderitz, south, as far as his fuel would allow for a round trip. He looked for any signs of an enemy landing or preparations for one along the desolate coast.

It was a perfect day for flying, light wind and clear sky. As Markus skimmed out over the choppy blue waters, he marveled at the sea life, so completely different from flying in Bavaria. Dark shadows in the sea were huge schools of fish. He saw porpoises and several whales, to his amazement. He'd seen these creatures before, but from shipboard. From the air, it was different. There was a primeval purity to it all. *Like being a part of nature, like a bird looking down*, he thought.

Kabam! His daydreaming in the sky came to an abrupt end when a cannon shell burst several hundred yards above and to his front.

"Jesus Christ! What the hell?" he shouted in alarm. He felt the shock wave and felt his aeroplane shudder as black chunks of shrapnel radiated out from the burst.

A second later, he heard a frightful sound, a sound he had heard described to him by other pilots who had survived crashes. It was a sound he had hoped never to hear: the simple "ping" of a wing guide wire snapping. He looked to his left and saw the guide wire slapping the wing in the wind.

He was two thousand feet off the ocean's surface, and as he circled around, he saw a ship, its black, oily smoke trailing behind it. Two white puffs of smoke appeared amid ships. He knew instinctively those were two more cannon rounds fired at him. He banked his craft sharply, forgetting for a second about the snapped wire. His left wing began to shudder. He knew the wing could simply fold up.

Markus knew he had to fly with the least amount of stress on the wing, and at the same time, escape the blasts from the enemy. Looking back for the first time, he noticed a group of ships, five or six, heading north.

"Invasion!" he shouted, as two more shells burst behind him. He knew he could easily outrun the ships but not the speed of their shells. He flew a straight course for the coast, losing altitude as he went and watching both the crippled wing and the ships behind him.

He was finally out of range of the guns, so he slowed the aeroplane, gliding gently down, riding the thermal currents of hot air from the desert. *If only I had a wireless up here*, he thought to himself as he spotted the airfield in the far distance. *I've got to work on that.*

CHAPTER 26

A Matter of Unique Skills

The South Africans planned the invasion of the German Colony with the backing of the British navy. What Captain Mathias saw on his flight south along the coast was that invasion fleet.

Not surprisingly, little effort was made by Commander von Heydebreck to defend the port at Lüderitz. The German defense plan was to fall back toward the interior and force the invaders to deal with the harsh coastal conditions and the forty to sixty miles of desert from the coast inland. He told Markus: "You are ordered to evacuate the two aeroplanes from Lüderitz inland, east up the railroad to the town of Aus."

Markus piloted the first one and returned by train for the second. He kept the second craft closer to the enemy, so he could continue his scouting mission. Flying directly west along the rail line, Markus saw his fellow soldiers busy tearing up the track as they retreated.

The rails were put into great stacks of firewood that were set ablaze, which caused the rails to bend and warp into useless shapes. Markus flew through the gray smoke over no man's land. As he approached the British and South African lines, he observed the enemy rebuilding the same tracks. Fortunately, their progress was slow for lack of useable rails, giving the Germans much-needed time to organize their defenses.

The coastal desert region offered nothing to feed the large contingent of horses, oxen, and camels required to move and provision the invading army. Cavalry horses often sank up to their stirrups in places where the winds and time had ground the sand into fine powder. Even water for the livestock was very scarce and often had to be brought in by wagon from distant wells. Weeks went by with only small military actions, but the South Africans made relentless progress up the rail line.

On November 12, disaster struck when the German colony lost her military commander, General von Heydebreck, killed in battle from a rifle grenade. In addition, the war footing for the colony had brought acute food shortages to both the military and civilian populations. The governor began confiscating all food stuffs, including cattle, and began rationing all goods.

Markus was able to communicate by telegraph with his family, and after the sick pilot, Schleiffer, returned to duty, Markus was reassigned to his original duties at the wireless station. It was with a sense of both foreboding and relief that he rode the train north to Windhoek. He knew the colony could not hold out indefinitely against the South Africans, the British, and the Portuguese to the north.

Helena met Markus with open arms at the train station. After their warm greeting, she related her own worries: "And they want to press into service boys of even a younger age. That means Humboldt could be called . . . And they impounded most all the cattle. Fortunately, a few strays were not with the herd." There was true anxiety in her voice. "Wolfgang and Arnold are fighting over near Swakopmund! Did you hear?"

They were standing on the station platform, close together, jostled by the crowds of soldiers and their families and piles of military equipment heading east toward the coast and the invaders.

"Yes, I know, dear. It's the wireless station here in Windhoek that they're after. It's our only link to the other colonies. They're determined to knock it out."

They both looked around at the confusion among the din of clanking equipment and swirls of dust.

"I've brought you a horse. It's faster than the carriage . . . They took most of the horses, too." Helena squeezed his arm and laid her head on his shoulder for a moment, as the young couple made their way through the crowd.

"The new Commander, Franke, is calling up all able-bodied men here in town . . . and the little news we hear from Europe is dreadful. They say tens of thousands of soldiers have already died on both sides. Did you know we are fighting in France and Belgium? I just can't believe it. Why are we in France and Belgium? I can't believe this is happening!" Dust on her cheeks soaked up her tears leaving trails.

"It's so good to have you home again; thank God," she whispered as they broke off and mounted their horses.

Markus reported to Commander Franke and assumed control of the wireless station again, spending most of his time trying to communicate with the other colonies and also intercepting enemy signals. He was surprised and very disturbed when, again, he was given a special assignment that would utilize his special skills.

It was daring and dangerous, and he was very reluctant to tell Helena until the last minute, with the hope he would not have to do it. The orders were top secret and came directly from Berlin on one of its last communications before the relay station in Cameroon was destroyed by the British invasion of that German colony.

He returned to the ranch very late in the evening on the day he received his special orders. Helena had retired, but Tomas Conrad waited up for him as he was wont to do.

"You look very tired, Markus. Come; sit; have a drink with me." They both sank into the familiar, overstuffed sofa. It was a dark night and the oil lamps in the large parlor gave a golden, yellow glow to their faces. Markus slumped down, propped his black boots on an ottoman, and unsnapped the collar buttons on his tunic. Tomas's black houseman, Petre, brought each a shot of schnapps and a cool beer from the root cellar.

"Thank you, Petre."

"Tomas, sir," Markus heard the tiredness in his own voice. "I have something to tell you . . . in the strictest confidence. I don't want Helena to know anything about this, unless it happens."

"It sounds very serious. Are you sure you want to tell me?"

Markus sat up, turned to his father-in-law and began, "You know that it is only a matter of time until Windhoek is occupied. We have too few men and munitions, and the South Africans have vast military resources. Commander Franke is going to move the army north and east and take the cattle with him. You should be safe out here on the ranch, but the town is in danger of artillery attack, and of course, the wireless station will be destroyed by us before they get here." He paused and looked at Conrad.

Tomas leaned forward to reply, "Yes, I have heard rumors of all that in *der biergarten* in town. But I have a feeling that isn't what you wanted to tell me."

Markus and Tomas edged even closer to each other.

"What is it?" he asked. Tomas could see his son-in-law struggling with inner turmoil. Finally, Markus said, "We received an order from Berlin. That is, I received an order from Berlin."

Tomas's eyes widened and interrupted Markus, "You? You yourself, personally, received an order from Berlin? Why would the Grand High Command in Berlin give you, a captain way out here in Africa, an order?" He waited for an answer.

"It's because of my unique set of skills. That's the only reason, of course."

"*Ja*, so you're an expert electrical engineer, and you know how to operate an aeroplane. What is this special order, if I may ask?"

"I have to leave . . . with one of the aircraft . . . and with some of the wireless equipment. But only if—when—the enemy reaches Windhoek."

"Ahh, so you're going up north with the army and setting up your wireless somewhere up there. Is that it?" Conrad didn't wait for an answer but continued, "Well, I imagine it's to be expected. You're in the army, and you must go where it goes. *Ja*, my boy?"

Markus looked at the aging man next to him, feeling a love and a sorrow for him and his boys and daughters and for what they were going through.

"I wish it were that simple, my dear Tomas. You have been like a father to me. I've had such a wonderful life here with Helena and your family."

"Had?"

Markus hesitated and then said what he didn't want to reveal. "I have been ordered to leave the colony."

"What? Leave the colony?" Conrad sat up straight on the edge of his seat.

"How? None of the ports are open; the British control the seas; the South Africans are across the Orange River to the south," he stammered and got up, standing, facing down at Markus. "And the Portuguese are to the north." He thought for a moment. "Not the Kalahari! Nobody goes west into the Kalahari Desert!" There was a worrisome look on his face.

"No, Tomas, none of those." Markus paused. "I have been ordered to take the newest wireless equipment we have and fly it to our colony in East Africa and set up a more powerful transmitter there."

"What? That's crazy! No one has ever tried to fly across Africa! That's hundreds of miles full of danger . . . mountains, jungles . . . It's full of danger. Where will you refuel? You have no maps . . . Nobody has any maps. How can you carry all that equipment in that little machine?" The questions came pouring out as the old man gesticulated, arms flying, and hands animated.

"Please, sir, keep your voice down, or you'll wake Helena. The equipment isn't that heavy, it's only—"

"You'll never make it! It's a suicide mission; that's what it is. I should talk to Commander Franke!"

"No! I could be shot for revealing a top-secret order from High Command." Markus had shouted out his objection; even he was surprised at his forceful retort.

"Yes, yes, of course. I won't breathe a word of this to anyone," Tomas backtracked hastily. "I'm sorry, Markus. It just sounds so impossible and over enemy territory!"

"Well, that's one good thing. It may be enemy territory officially, but there will probably be no troops anywhere along the route. It's about as deep as deepest Africa gets." Markus was lying, of course. He had already examined what primitive maps there were for the central part of Africa he was to traverse. He knew the only way he could get all the way across the desert, jungle, grasslands, and savannah was to steal gasoline from the only sources there were: British,

South African, Boer, and Portuguese military facilities. And that was assuming they would have aeroplanes or, more likely, automobiles that needed gasoline.

"When are you expecting to leave?" Conrad hesitated a moment and noted, "You can't fly in the rain . . . some of that country gets . . . It's a whole different climate and the topography . . . There are mountains . . . You've got to carry a gun, the animals . . ."

He trailed off into silence and the silence endured as the two men sat there, lost in their own thoughts. He got up and refilled the schnapps glasses. Finally, he spoke in a more calm and reasoned voice: "My boy, that's one hell of an assignment they've given you. When are you going to tell Helena?"

Markus looked at Tomas and saw, for the first time, weariness in his slumped shoulders and concerned look.

"Not right away, but soon. Commander Franke is leaving it up to me to decide the exact date, but probably within two weeks. We're modifying the aeroplane, stripping it of weight, adding more fuel tanks. I'll be doing a lot of night flying when the moon's up. It's surprising what you can see on the ground just from moonlight," he half smiled.

Markus motioned to Conrad, "Come sit down with me, sir, here." He scooted over on the sofa, and Tomas sat down. "Herr Conrad, I want you to do something for me," Markus began. "I want you to take care of my wife and son while I'm gone. I know, of course, you will, as you love your daughter and grandchild as much as I. But, I mean, if things get bad when they come . . . if you hear about unruly South African soldiers or their native *askari*. If you hear anything, I want you to take Helena and Rupert to that cabin back in the hills, just to be safe . . . and leave her a gun. It's just that I've seen soldiers, our own too, in war in China, take advantage of civilian women and I—"

"Of course, of course, I and my boys will do what's necessary. Nothing is going to happen." He stifled a sniffle.

"I'm sure it won't. I'm just being extra cautious."

Later, as Markus slipped into bed beside a sleeping Helena, he thought, Mein Gott, what a mess this is. This war is not like in China where I only had to worry about myself. Now my world is completely different. I'm leaving Helena and Rupert and the Conrads for who knows how long . . . and in danger.

Two weeks stretched to four as the aircraft modifications needed more tests on the ground and in the air. Markus thought to himself, I've never seen an aeroplane like this, but it seems to handle fairly well so far.

Meanwhile, scant intelligence coming from the east of the colony on terrain and the enemy, had to be gathered clandestinely and transmitted back to Windhoek for him.

Helena was naturally very upset and fearful upon hearing Markus's new orders.

"But why can't one of the other two pilots go instead of you?" she asked as she, baby Rupert, and Markus lay together on the canopied bed. The evening air, breezing through the open doors from the outside garden, scented their room with African hibiscus.

"They've both recovered, and both of them are unmarried. Surely your commander could arrange some—"

Her husband cut her off gently. "As I told you earlier, my dearest, I'm the only one who knows the wireless equipment. It's too complicated to give instructions to someone. I'm needed to reconfigure the equipment in East Africa."

She knew all this, of course, but emotionally, Helena didn't want to accept it. "Oh, when will this terrible war be over?" she began again. It was the ultimate recurring question, on a million lips on three continents. "I pray every day that God will intervene. Surely he hears my prayers." She looked into Markus's eyes for an answer.

"Of course, of course he does, my dearest, but as you know, God works in ways we may not—we cannot—understand."

Markus felt a degree of guilt in his words, as he had struggled for a long time with the question of God's intent and even his ability to intervene in human affairs. He did think—feel—there had to be something, or someone, up there: Catholic God, a supernatural being, some power above all mankind— but answering prayers? Somehow, it just didn't make sense. He remembered his school years back in Bavaria, playing soccer, when the team coach would have the parish priest come out to the field. The team would pray to win the next game. How could God help one team over another? It seemed impossible, even immoral in some way.

But Markus's first concern was the well-being of his family and supporting Helena's beliefs was a part of that, so he did it.

Knowing her husband would be leaving soon and would be gone for a considerable time, she clung to him at every opportunity, particularly as his visits home to the ranch became less and less frequent. It had become common for Markus to bunk in the officers' quarters most nights in recent weeks.

The enemy made slow but steady progress in pushing back the German defenders deeper and deeper toward the interior and Windhoek. It was obvious to Tomas and his daughter that the time of Markus's departure was approaching.

"They say the Kaiser has approached the Russian Tsar and the British King with peace feelers. They say it's only weeks before the shooting stops. Isn't that wonderful news, darling?" Helena whispered enthusiastically. The couple lay in their bed, having put Rupert in his crib and doused the lights for an early bedtime.

The ranch house was quiet, with only Tomas, Christiana, and the two youngest boys at home. Helena had exhibited great mood swings in the weeks following her awareness of his impending departure. This night she was high with optimism.

"When peace comes, we'll be able to go to Germany and show your mother and sister and all your friends our baby. It will be a grand trip! Won't it be wonderful, darling?"

"Yes, of course, dearest. We'll have a wonderful visit." It was all he could do to continue the false hope of a quick end to the fighting. He loved her so much, and she seemed so fragile, so delicate and vulnerable, even though he knew deep down she was a tough, strong woman. In her heightened mood, she was also more desirable than ever, he thought. He rolled onto his side as she did the same to meet him. They were in a different world together, far from war and fear and separation.

He rose over her, and she pulled him into her. It was their way of saying goodbye and I love you, with an unspoken promise: you must return, and you must be here when I get back.

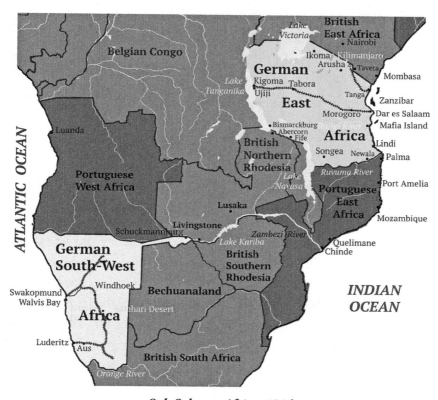

Sub-Saharan Africa, 1914

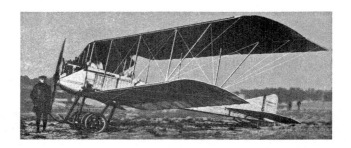

—— CHAPTER 27 ——

Death at Dawn

The mechanics worked on not one, but two aircraft; one was a backup for Captain Mathias's secret mission. With a final departure date eminent and a rough map drawn, final preparations were made. The first and easiest leg of the journey was to fly both planes to the farthest northeast corner of the colony. This would be the jumping off point into and over enemy territory. Siegfried Schleifler the young flyer recently recovered from a bullet wound, was chosen to fly the backup plane to Schuckmannsburg, the most eastern village in the colony.

In the early morning stillness, at the improvised airstrip on the cavalry parade grounds in Windhoek, all was ready. Tomas Conrad escorted Helena, carrying Rupert, through the dust, toward a cluster of a dozen officers and several mechanics. Markus' family were the only civilians near the two, strange-looking aeroplanes.

Guards were posted around the field, with only a few early rising soldiers looking on.

Markus stepped away from his commanding officer to his waiting family. "It's time for me to fly, Helena, my dearest. Take good care of Rupert. I'll be home as soon as I can." He also spoke a few words to Tomas as he hugged his wife. Michael, Christiana, and Norbert, as well as Petre, also bid him farewell.

As prearranged, Tomas guided his family back to their carriage at the edge of the airfield. After a few short words with the officers, Markus and Siegfried climbed into the cramped, single-seat cockpits of their biplanes, adjusted their goggles, and waited for the mechanics to rotate the propeller of each aircraft into the start position. The two inflated rubber wheels under each aircraft were pressed into the hard pack of the parade field from the weight of the extra fuel stored in sealed cans in the fuselages.

Markus adjusted the revolver in its holster at his hip as he settled into his seat while turning to look at the limp windsock.

There will be no lift assist from that wind, he thought. He turned back forward, nodded to his mechanic, and gripped the stick as the propeller was forcefully pulled down. The engine roared into life as Markus adjusted the choke and the throttle. Four soldiers, gripping the wings, held back the machine as it strained to move forward. Markus looked first at the men holding the left wing and then to the men on the right. Two others were gripping the tail. He increased the fuel flow to the engine. Blue exhaust smoke blasted from the exhaust pipes and swirled into the calm air. He gave a last look to the distant carriage, waved his hand, and signaled the soldiers to release his aeroplane.

The ungainly craft leaped from the hands of the six soldiers, and with the throttle wide open, the heavy ship lumbered across the dry grass. As it picked up speed, the biplane fishtailed wildly back and forth before bumping momentarily into the air, coming down hard on the rubber wheels. Several bumps later and far down the field, the craft appeared to leap off the ground and was finally airborne.

Markus circled back around the field, while Siegfried followed the same ignition procedures as his six soldiers held back his rumbling aeroplane. He too signaled the six for release, and like Markus's craft, Siegfried's was slow to gain speed. With fuel pouring into the engine, it finally had the necessary lift and speed to rise into the still air. His engine sputtered several times and descended to the grassy air strip, with a hard bounce that brought it again into the air.

Markus flew to the far end of the parade grounds and part of the town while watching Seigfried's ship gain speed midway down the field. From his vantage point, he saw the biplane first fishtail and then take the expected bounce or two before lifting off. Markus leaned over the edge of his cockpit wall and could see Helena and the family waving to him.

He noticed they all stopped waving and turned to look down field. Siegfried's aircraft had sputtered again, descended to a hard bounce, and popped the inflated tire on the left side and collapsed the landing struts. On the next bounce, the deflated tire and rim plowed a deep gash in the earth, causing the heavy biplane to pivot left. Siegfried gave a hard right rudder, but it was not enough to correct the flight path. When finally the wheel, rim, and strut pulled free of the earth, the ship was virtually sideways, heading down field and loosing what little altitude it had.

Markus switched sides and was quick enough to see his friend's aircraft in its precarious position. An instant later, the tip of the lower wing on the right side of the backup ship gouged into the ground, causing the biplane to flip to the earth on its back in a rolling crash of exploding gas cans and flying pieces of wing and dust. Markus couldn't hear Helena's shriek or the involuntary gasps from the cluster of officers on the ground, but his mind raced to a horrible realization: Siegfried couldn't possibly have survived that.

"*Verdammt!* Damn it all to hell!" he shouted over the roar of his engine. He again circled back around the field, this time slowing as much as he could, coming in very low. Helena and Conrad were still standing in the same spot, her head on her father's shoulder. When they all heard his engine, they looked up in time to see him clearly as he waved and blew a kiss as his biplane roared by only thirty feet off the ground. As he passed over the mangled wreck, several soldiers were trying to beat out the towering flames with their military tunics. There was no fire brigade at the erstwhile airfield. The last Helena saw of her husband was the tiny speck of his aeroplane disappearing into the rising cloud from the burning gasoline northeast of the cavalry parade grounds.

It was roughly six hundred miles between the capitol of German South West Africa, Windhoek, and its furthermost northeastern outpost of Schuckmannsburg. This tiny settlement was essentially a military outpost to establish a German presence in the most desolate, god-forsaken eastern reach of the colony. Swampy during the rainy season, with swarms of hard-biting flies; in the dry season, it was intensely hot with swirling, powdery sand.

With the arrival by oxcart of barrels of gasoline and cans of oil, both highly unusual products for a region with no automobiles and no gasoline-consuming engines of any kind, speculation was rife among the few inhabitants in the area. No one at the military outpost knew of the mission except the commander, a young lieutenant. All he knew was to expect an aeroplane at any time and to immediately clear a landing strip of certain dimensions. He and his small garrison of six *askari* troops, and an additional white sergeant, had been waiting weeks for the wonder of the skies to arrive.

None of the *askari* native soldiers had ever seen a flying machine, and the lieutenant had only observed the more primitive aircraft in popular flying circus demonstrations back home in East Prussia. The few local inhabitants saw or heard about the cleared airstrip, causing gossip and speculation.

During Markus's flight from Windhoek, after witnessing the blazing tragedy, the aviator had time to reflect on the death of Siegfried: He was an accomplished pilot and friend, thought Markus. We should have waited for better wind, better lift . . . It was overloaded; we—I—should have calculated more closely on maximum cargo weight. What a loss! And with Helena and Tomas there . . . Jesus, she's going to be extra worried after seeing that. I never should have let Tomas bring her to the airfield . . . but nothing I can do about that now. I'll send a wireless to her soon as I land in Schuckmannsburg . . . let her know I'm all right. Christ! I shouldn't have let her come. I've got to write to Siegfried's family before I leave the colony . . . try to get it home on a neutral ship, maybe through the Portuguese.

Two landings were made at prearranged fuel depots along the six hundred-mile route to the eastern-most corner of the colony. Both were bumpy but uneventful. He refueled and was on his way.

For extended periods of time in flight, Markus escaped the bounds of earth and its troubles. He reveled in the beauty of the endless sky, the views to the distant horizons, and the comforting drone of the engine. He had an extraordinary view, looking down on the German colony. He flew across the northern edge of the endless sands of the Kalahari Desert. He spotted rhinos and gazelles in the parched grasslands and thorn thickets of the savannah. Nearing the Kubango River and the great marshes of the Okovango, Markus saw the black backs of hippos, mostly submerged, sunning themselves in the rare water source.

He landed just before dusk at Schuckmannsburg on May 11, 1915. Two days later, Saturday, May 13, the tiny outpost of Schuckmannsburg received the last wireless transmission from Windhoek, transmitted to all receivers in the colony and in German East Africa. Imperial German naval vessels in both the South Atlantic and the Indian Ocean also picked up the message. British, Belgian, South African, French, and Portuguese colonials received the transmission, too:

TO ALL IMPERIAL GERMAN RECEIVERS. STOP. BRITISH AND SOUTH AFRICANS ON OUTSKIRTS OF WINDHOEK. STOP. THIS WIRELESS STATION IS SIGNING OFF. STOP. GOOD LUCK AND GODSPEED. STOP. SIGNED CAPTAIN FRANKE, COMMANDER, GERMAN SOUTH WEST AFRICA. STOP.

Markus, standing next to the primitive outpost building, read the message a second time. He knew the prearranged plan, the destruction of the wireless station, his wireless station. He felt anger, frustration, and determination. "I'm getting this equipment to East Africa, so help me God!" he said to no one.

"What? What was that, sir?" one of the *askari* asked respectfully. He was one of the two guards assigned to the aeroplane.

"Oh, I was just talking to myself. You speak very good German, soldier. Where did you learn it?"

"The mission school at the orphanage, sir. I was taught by the Lutherans after my parents died in the Kalahari. We're Herero, my little sister and me." He looked down and away.

Jesus, Markus thought to himself, *he's still loyal to us after we massacred his people.*

"Very good, soldier, very good." It was all he could say.

Markus rested and spent the next day servicing his aircraft. He knew he must immediately leave the occupied colony before the tiny hamlet was overrun. The next morning, with fresh food and water and all the fuel he felt he could safely carry, Markus waited patiently for the wind to pick up.

A small crowd had gathered. Pretty much everyone for miles around came to see the strange flying contraption. There was a festive mood as the forty-some people huddled together, chatting and pointing and swigging beer in the early morning light. Pipe and cigar smoke hung in a thin, white cloud over their heads.

With the first roar of the engine and the resulting blast of oily, blue smoke, the crowd jumped back and let out a collective cheer. Many in the crowd had never heard a gasoline engine before, let alone seen a flying machine. None in the crowd knew of the pending danger of a severely overloaded aeroplane. Only Captain Mathias had visions of a deadly fireball etched in his mind and flashes of a smiling, laughing, young Siegfried, now consumed by those flames. He practiced earlier with the four *askari* on how to hold the plane so that there was no danger to them from the noise and smoke.

"It's just like the herds of animals thundering across the veld during the migrations," he said in a reassuring voice. With a final look, first left then right, and a quick salute to the young lieutenant commanding the post, Markus gave the signal and the four *askari* let loose their grip.

With a good headwind, his heavy craft lifted briskly into the blue sky. He circled once to see the landscape features and then headed due east across the Zambezi River. British Southern Rhodesia lay beneath him.

His intent was to follow the Zambezi to Lake Kariba and follow it east toward Portuguese East Africa, declared neutral in the war. Markus's final destination was, of course, far-off German East Africa, now over seven hundred miles away—if traveled in a straight flight. But following the Zambezi, his only "map," Markus figured the trip at one thousand miles. His immediate challenge was to bypass the village of Livingstone, a mere thirty or so miles ahead on the Zambezi. Locals who had traded there informed him of a British garrison, but none had seen or heard of any aircraft thereabouts.

Markus took the precaution earlier to paint out the German markings on the underside of his wings. The Iron Cross insignia could have easily been spotted from the ground among those few inhabited places he intended to fly over.

It was not long before he was spotted. Livingstone was a river town, a village really, but a fair-sized one. Markus had no knowledge of any inhabited locations along his route, so he felt the simplest solution was just to barrel on through, following his flight path. Few, if anyone, on the ground would have time to react if they saw him at all, he reasoned, thought, even if they determined he was German. He figured, if they saw him, they would think he was British. Unfortunately, he had not correctly anticipated their heightened state of alert and the British wireless communications.

He approached the garrison town of Livingstone from the west, saw mainly native huts on the outskirts, and was surprised to see a British native contingent of provisional police, their *askari*, drilling in the village square. Heads turned as he skimmed past. His last visual was to see several white officers running to a nearby building.

I wonder if the British have any aircraft in Northern Rhodesia, he thought. *I'd bet a barrel of beer they don't. We only have—had—three, with only two airworthy, till Siegfried's crash . . . and now there isn't a flyable aeroplane in our entire colony.*

Cruising east above the Zambezi, Markus could just make out Lake Kariba simmering in the midmorning sun. He checked his gas gauge and started looking for a place to put her down. The southern end of the Muchinga Mountains was discernible to the northeast as he approached the western end of the lake. Its southern shore seemed flat and sandy in places, with much more green vegetation, trees, brush, and patches of forest inland.

He cut the throttle and the roar of the engine faded to a purr as he glided low over the water. Flocks of birds, millions of them, rose from the water in great clouds of flapping wings, honking and crying as they clustered in flight, moving as of one living organism. Markus was mesmerized by their beauty.

He found a strip of beach that looked promising, circled back around, and came in for a perfect landing on the sand. With one-quarter of his fuel weight burned, the aircraft was easier to handle. He carried extra cans equivalent to two complete refuels. The aeroplane came to a halt, and he cut the engine. His ears rang from hours of engine noise and blowing wind. Silence was a welcome relief.

Standing up in the cockpit, he stretched, pulled off his goggles and leather flying helmet, rubbed his eyes, and scratched his head vigorously with both hands.

Stepping off the wing, he hit the dry sand and thought, *Ja, good enough.* He looked inland from the beach, scanning the brush and tree line, and then looked out across the lake. The flocks of birds were returning, settling into islands of white and gray feathers, preening themselves in a way that seemed almost vain. He smiled to himself.

Markus walked around his craft, looking here and there, checking the important wires and parts, but mostly enjoying being upright and on the ground. It wasn't long before they found him, as he knew they would. Swarms of Anopheles mosquitoes swirled around as he turned up his collar and wrapped a scarf around his head and face. He went to work pulling a heavy can of gasoline out of the fuselage and carefully pouring the precious liquid into the tank. Two cans did it.

He was about to pitch the cans off to the side when he detected movement a hundred feet off the beach in the shadows. His hand moved to his revolver.

He waited. Sounds! More movement. He stared intently—white! Is that a uniform, a shield? He waited. Several small trees seemed to bend toward the lake.

Elephants! First, a bull with white tusks swayed into view. It stared at the aeroplane, snorted, flapped its ears, and stepped to the water's edge. Several more elephants followed. *Must be the females,* Markus thought. *And a young one, almost invisible on the opposite side of its mother.* Soon they were all in the water, rolling over, spouting water from their trunks, and enjoying themselves, with only the bull keeping an eye on the intruder.

This is all very interesting, thought Markus, *but I've got a schedule to keep, and you are in my way.* There was nothing he could do, of course. Any one of the beasts could end his mission with a few swings of a trunk, even the little one.

Markus decided to climb back into the cockpit, to help avoid the mosquitoes, and he could have a roll or two, some cheese, and a beer. He settled in, munching his meal and watching the elephants. With a full stomach, the beer, and the heat, he dozed off in no time. His head rested on the edge of the fuselage as he snored peacefully.

Sometime later, as he stirred, he sensed something. An uneasy feeling crept into his gut. He opened his eyes and scanned the lake shore. The elephants were gone.

As he turned to look back down the beach, a mouthful of jagged teeth flashed before his eyes as his head wrenched violently to the side. Howling, gnawing, snapping jaws were all around him. Fortunately, he had put his leather helmet back on before he ate to help ward off the mosquitoes. It was ripped off his head along with a small patch of hair. Instinctively, he grabbed for his revolver, pulled it from its holster, and fired directly through the wall of the fuselage. A death howl rang out.

He spun around as he raised his arm in a defensive position above his head, just in time to have it slam into the side of the head of a jackal that had leaped the seven feet up to his open cockpit.

"Jesus!" he yelled as he fired again. The beast fell backward onto another just below. Two more were on the lower wing, the nearest crouched, ready to spring. Markus raised his revolver, aimed, and fired. The nearest jackal fell backward from the force of the bullet slamming into its body. The second one leaped off the wing but was not quick enough to avoid a bullet into its hip. A slow death awaited him—if his fellow jackals didn't tear him to pieces first.

"Christ all mighty! Where did they come from?" he gasped. "That was a hell of a scare!" He laughed it off nervously, as he tenderly touched his head wound. It's stopped bleeding; that's good. Ja, so Markus, time to get out of here!

He stepped out of the cockpit, onto the wing, revolver in hand. He looked around, then reached back into the cockpit to the control panel, flipped the ignition switch, and pulled out the choke. He hopped to the ground and quickly walked around the wing, cautiously kicking the body of the nearest animal, and bent down to retrieve his helmet.

He turned, reached up, rotated the propeller into the proper start position, and forcefully pulled down. Thankfully, the engine started on the first pull. He quickly ran back around and climbed in just as the engine sputtered. He stabbed at the choke, pushing it all the way in. The sound of the engine evened out.

Before he landed, Markus had specifically selected a landing site with plenty of length for takeoff. Now he opened the throttle full and the whirling blades pulled the craft forward. He was airborne in less than a minute. *That was a close call,* he thought to himself as he circled back around the landing site in time to see a dozen red-skinned buzzards circling lower and lower toward the kills. The four dead jackals lay where they fell, with three new arrivals sniffing the carcasses.

"You're welcome to them!" he shouted and laughed as he flew northeast down the lake.

Kreigskarte von Deutch-Sudwestafrica, 1904

—— CHAPTER 28 ——

Friendly Encounter, Holes in the Sky

The most up-to-date maps that Lieutenant Mathias had available to him were created in 1904 because of the uprising of the Herero and other native tribes. The German colonial troops had virtually no reliable maps before then. Charts that showed more than settlement names, locations and roads, ports and railroads, were nonexistent.

Comprehensive "war maps," as they were called, produced in record time, showed detailed topographic features. Knowledge of mountain ranges, swamps, deserts, water holes and wells, rivers, and many other vital bits of military information, including passes through mountains, was vitally important. Markus had these. Unfortunately, they were only good while he was over the German colony.

Now, over Southern Rhodesia, he had nothing. And the same would be true when he crossed the frontier into Portuguese East Africa. Following the Zambezi River was a sure way of knowing where he was. He knew that if he just followed the river, it would flow into Portuguese territory—and hopefully to safety and help on his way to German East Africa.

The last information the commander in Windhoek received was that the King of Portugal, while officially an ally of Great Britain, endorsed the Cairo Code of non-hostility between colonies, for neutrality in Africa. Markus hoped that agreement held and that Portuguese East Africa would remain neutral.

Markus traveled about a hundred miles down the lake. He watched thunderstorms over the Muchinga Mountains off to his left and felt the air temperature change. He simply enjoyed the sense of safety, far above and away from snapping jaws and the other dangers he left behind.

Wait till I get to East Africa and tell Levi about that last experience, thought Markus, a grin on his face. He'll think I made it up! We'll have so much to talk about. It was easy for any pilot to daydream on long flights, and Markus was as susceptible as any. His plane drifted down in altitude so that it was about six hundred feet off the surface of the lake, but it was right on course. Markus peered over the edge of the fuselage and saw several native fishermen below. It was a tranquil scene. His eyes followed the edge of the lake northeastward and saw several boats, three or four, in a line in the far distance. They appeared to be crossing the lake.

He knew that north of the end of the lake was Lusaka, a substantial village and regional trading and market town. He also knew it was about forty-five miles distant, a considerable way in a region with virtually no roads. The easiest way to cross-country travel was to follow animal tracks, many quite wide, made over hundreds of years.

Markus had seen many of these trails from the air. *Traders on the way to market*, he thought.

The white puffs did not register for several seconds. The sounds were absorbed by the vastness around them. But he did hear the distinct sound of bullets zipping by him and knew immediately the "traders" were British or South African military.

"*Verdammt!*" he exclaimed as he banked his aircraft sharply, made a complete U-turn, and then another, so as to put himself back on route but way to the east of the hostile boats. He could see them still shooting by the puffs of smoke, but he knew he was far out of range of their guns.

"How in hell did they know I was coming and that I was German?" he said to himself, as he squirmed in his seat a moment. *They must have sent word from the village ahead to Lusaka. Or maybe when they overran Windhoek, someone tipped them off, or maybe it was at Schuckmannsburg. Well, it doesn't really matter now; I'm out of range.*

He flew on, following the river and knew he'd better find a place to set down for a refueling soon. As he progressed east, the countryside became much more lush and green. *This terrain is so different from the ranch and most of our western colony,* he thought. *I wonder why Conrad chose such a barren landscape to raise his family. He could have homesteaded in a much more hospitable place. Mysteries.*

He located a long strip of beach and set the aeroplane down after circling around the spot, checking the landscape for any signs of humans. *There are going to be animals,* he thought, as his aircraft glided to another smooth landing.

As he turned off the engine, he decided to make camp here for the night. He reloaded his revolver as he stood on the wing. His eyes surveyed the area, up and down the beach. *Let's build a fire,* he thought to himself, *a big fire.* During the hour he spent gathering wood to last the night, he decided actually to build two fires near his aeroplane: one on each side, with him sleeping under the wing with his revolver out and ready.

He purposely cut some green wood that burns slowly and creates a lot of smoke. *Best to keep the bugs away and probably certain animals,* he speculated.

Markus got a light tarp out of the fuselage, along with half a hard Thüringer Rostbratwurst sausage, more rolls, cheese, a large tin cup, and a pouch of ground coffee. He walked to the edge of the water, scooped up water, and looked down the beach.

"Ah—trouble," he said aloud. Fifty yards down on the water's edge, a group of little animals were drinking as half a dozen more emerged in the descending darkness. "Monkeys . . . or baboons, probably."

Mathias family members, particularly on his mother's side, had the habit of talking out loud when alone. He had picked up the habit or trait or whatever it was. Levi walked in on him innumerable times and asked who he was talking to. It always led to a laugh.

"The fire should keep them at a distance, the little buggers." Near his foot was a thick branch, half-submerged in the water. He reached down, grabbed it, and dragged it back to his campfires. "More smoke!" he grunted as he pushed the wet end into the fire nearest his "guests."

Settling in with his helmet on, stretched out under his tarps, clutching his Thüringer in one hand and his hot coffee in the other, Mathias felt secure. He also had his revolver lying next to his head. He stoked the fires, and for now, there was not a mosquito in sight. His half-eaten Thüringer rolled out of his hand as he slipped off to sleep.

The coolness and silence of early dawn found the airman up and brewing more coffee. The monkeys were all about, but none came close enough to be hit with another rock. that Markus had bounced off the shoulder of one daring critter. After munching half of his remaining supply of rolls and more cheese, the electrical unit officer of the First Bavarian Army Corps, headquartered in Munich, on special assignment to the Imperial wireless station in Windhoek, German South West Africa—now blown up—decided to relieve himself.

He had to admit the monkeys were cute little creatures, so he spontaneously lecture them in a serious military tone: "One of the first procedures a soldier learns, when in the field and no latrines are dug, is how to relieve himself. Taking a piss is no problem." Markus proceeded to demonstrate to his attentive audience, of fifteen or so monkeys, the proper way to take a dump in the field.

"First of all, comrades, you always take your gun along." He scanned his audience. They were all attentive.

"Next, you squat down, making sure your britches are out of the way so you don't shit on your pants." He performed this maneuver for his guests' edification.

"When finished, comrades," he explained, "you never leave your business behind for your fellow soldiers to step in, or all hell breaks loose." He got up, pulled up his trousers, but just to his knees, and kicked sand over the steaming pile. Only half-upright, he continued his lecture.

"A soldier should not be tempted to wipe his ass with any of a variety of leaves and grasses unknown to him." He stared at the monkeys. They were all staring back, and probably thinking he left them a present—at least that's what Markus thought they were thinking.

"Several of these unknown leaves and grasses have either stickers on them or give a terrible rash just where you don't want one." Markus was having fun and suppressing a laugh at his own performance.

"You, in the back, pay attention!" One of the monkeys in the front actually turned around and looked back. Markus burst out laughing as he staggered over to the edge of the water. He hunched down again, with his backside facing the lake.

"Very important, men. Don't do this where you go to get your coffee water." He washed himself in the lake. Several monkeys came down to the shore, reached their hands in, scooped up water, and drank.

"I thought I told you not to do that!" he yelled as he fell over, laughing hysterically.

With all his gear stowed in preparation for takeoff, Markus checked the gasoline level with a stick, knowing he had to refuel.

"Less than a quarter tank, just as I thought." He threw away the stick, stuck himself halfway into the fuselage, and reached for the two remaining cans of gas.

Expecting the heavy weight of a full can of gasoline, Markus fell backward, dragging a hollow-sounding can out with him.

"Holy Christ, what happened?" The can was almost empty. He quickly examined the sides and saw a bullet hole a few inches above the bottom on one side and a higher hole on the far side.

"Jesus!" He sloshed the can to get a sense of how much gasoline was left. "Maybe one-tenth of a can."

He jumped back onto the wing and dove deep into the fuselage, reaching for the last can. He got his hand on it and gave it a tug. It had weight, but as he tipped it to slide it forward to get it out, gasoline poured out of a hole three quarters of the way from the bottom. "*Verdammt!*"

He gently slid the can and pulled it out. After examining the hole and looking at the other can he realized, "That bullet went through both cans! *Verdammt!* That's half my remaining fuel gone." After refueling with his diminished supply of gasoline, he lowered a stick into the tank.

"Three-quarters of a tank, max. I better start looking for a place to 'borrow' some gasoline. Which way to go? With what fuel I've got, I'm pretty sure I can make it to neutral Portuguese East African territory, but that part of their colony is probably almost completely uninhabited."

He kicked sand into the fire as he continued his one-sided conversation: "I could fly over Lusaka, see if there's any evidence of automobiles. I can't imagine there would be any aeroplanes there. I wonder what Levi would recommend; he always gave me good advice . . . Right, that's in the wrong direction, and there aren't even any roads, so why would there be any gasoline? It's east to the Portuguese then!" It was as if Levi was there with him for a moment. Markus smiled at the thought.

As before, he prepped the controls, pulled down on the propeller, hopped aboard, and was off into the rising sun. As his aircraft rose into the beautiful morning sky, he saw, far off on the horizon, dark storm clouds directly ahead.

The rainy season, he thought. *I've never flown in the rain. It's not recommended.* He laughed to himself. *I've got a feeling I'll still have fuel when that storm overtakes me. First time for everything.*

Markus had no way of knowing when he would cross into the relative safety of neutral Portuguese territory, or even if the Portuguese were still neutral, but he did know that he only had several hours of flying time left before his craft would be on the ground. He flew at moderate speed to conserve fuel. He tried to find wind currents he could use to propel him along. Dark clouds were dead ahead.

The BaTonga People

—— CHAPTER 29 ——

Darkness Descends

Just keep it steady. Keep going, my little flying wireless. He knew he was low, very low, on fuel, and now, with the pelting rain and winds, it was hard even to keep a steady course. His goggles steamed up on the inside, with rivulets of rain on the outside. He had to bring his compass almost up to his eyes to see the needle.

Clouds hugged the smooth hilltops and rose from the great savannah he was passing over, so it was hard to see the ground. "I may run dry any time . . . I've got to stay low to see a landing site."

His engine sputtered several times, drenched by the deluge. Each time, he thought, *That's it. I've got to put her down. I'm losing altitude.* But each time, the engine kicked in, and his aircraft rose again.

Now the sputters continued in a steady staccato. He could visualize the last of the gasoline sloshing around in the tank every time the aeroplane bumped or swayed in the turbulent air. *I've got a minute or two left,* he told himself. Through driving rain, he strained to see the ground—what vegetation, what surface, what open area?

He didn't know what hit him until much later. The BaTonga found him, only because their hunting party was camped nearby. Rain poured out of thundering clouds, following flashes of lightning. Markus dangled in the air from the wreckage of "the big bird of the sky" as his rescuers called the tangled and broken aeroplane.

One of the hunters had just moved his shield to a better position to deflect the rain when he saw the huge "beast." He let out an alarm cry, and the others looked to where he was pointing with his spear, just as the dark shadow against the sky slammed into the upper trunk and branches of a tree. With no gasoline, there was no fire, but even in the storm, the BaTongans heard the crash.

They looked at each other, conversing briefly, then got to their feet in the pouring rain and cautiously crept toward the strange apparition. The seven hunters spread out as they approached the strange scene. Markus was unconscious, hanging upside down out of the shattered fuselage. One wing was pointing straight up with the stump of a branch punched through it. The other, broken in many pieces, lay scattered in a small debris field, including the engine, still steaming in the pelting rain.

The BaTonga hunters stood in silence for a few moments. Several approached the steaming engine and poked it with their spears. They returned to the group, conversed again, and then looked up at Markus. Finally they laid down their spears and shields and built a human pyramid, three men high, to reach the lowest branches. From there, two of the hunters climbed nimbly up to the white man.

They lifted his head gently and did other things to determine if he was still alive. One of them called down to the others for further discussion. Five of the warriors took off their long, woven, robe-like blankets that encircled their bodies.

They tied them together and to the end of a spear and threw it up to the wreckage. They extracted Markus's body carefully from his precarious position and skillfully lowered him to the ground.

Several days passed before Markus opened his eyes slightly. Everything was a painful blur. Every time he breathed, he felt the worst of it, with aching shoulder and thumb. Mercifully, when he closed his eyes, he slipped into a numbing sleep.

When he finally woke again, he could smell wood smoke and human smells. He felt a hand behind his neck that gently lifted his head, and he sensed a bowl of water pressed against his lips. He drank eagerly, slurping the liquid down his dry throat, while staring at two beautifully formed black breasts hanging over him. They were oiled and gleaming in the dim light, and many colorful necklaces swayed with her every movement. Because it was so striking, a large pendant stood out. It was of a fierce-looking, dragon-like snake carved from bone or ivory. He wondered what it meant.

He was in a hut, he realized, but had no sense of time. He heard voices, but it pained him to move even a little. He lay still, listening to a strange language, not like the Herero or other tribes he was familiar with. A woman's voice, and then a man's, spoke softly, in a hush. He turned his head; they saw him move. She came closer and said something. He just stared at her, and after a moment, she reached her hand to his eyes and brushed them closed.

The rainy season was in full force. Water pounded down on the shelter, but he was dry. Markus still had no sense of time, but he felt he must have been in the hut for a very long while because his beard had several weeks' growth. He surmised he must have been given something to be able to sleep for such long periods, awake only to eat and drink. He noticed the branches tied firmly to his right leg, from his hip to his ankle.

I must have broken my leg, too. He sensed, during those several weeks of semi-consciousness, that he had been visited many times. *Probably the whole village saw me at least once*, he thought, with a slight inward smile. He was sure he was starting to think clearly again as he tried to reconstruct his last minutes in the air. *Well, I obviously crashed. I wonder how it happened. And my aeroplane and the wireless parts?*

A day came with a break in the rains; the sun shone brightly. He had been up a few times to hobble around the small hut, but this was his first time to venture out.

Several young boys apparently had been assigned to him, so he used them, one on each side, as crutches, with his hands on their shoulders and the woman behind him, with her hands on his back and shoulder. He still had short splints on his leg.

The sun was intense as he shuffled out into its brightness. It blinded him for a moment. He heard the laughter of little voices. As his eyes adjusted, he saw a village of a dozen or so huts in a *kraal*, made up of upright limbs and branches for walls and thatched roofs. Kids ran in circles around him and reached out to touch him. The two boys supporting him felt proud of their special duties.

Markus recognized several hunters who had visited his hut. They came up to him with two other of their fellows. They also were wearing the strange pendant he had seen earlier on thongs around their necks. One of the strangers surprised Markus when he spoke in broken German.

"*Guten Tag*, German soldier. I portage for *askari* German," he said with a broad smile. "I portage . . . make German silver." He produced from his leather pouch seven Imperial German silver marks. Probably a month's wages for a porter, Markus surmised.

"Very good. Yes, very good," he replied as he exaggerated his interest in the money in the extended black hand.

"BaTonga mens carry Germany man from tree . . . Big boom; bird fall down; you sleep long time."

"So, you're telling me your people rescued me . . . from a tree?"

"Storm toss big bird in tree."

"Will you ask them to take me to the tree?" The porter had trouble understanding the question, but after changing a few words and speaking more slowly, Markus got his idea across. The translator relayed the request to the other two men, and they enthusiastically agreed.

"Hunters say sleep till half-moon; long walk tree." Markus calculated that meant about two weeks of rest before departing. He didn't want to wait but knew he needed more time to heal his leg.

"Good, very good . . . Thank you." The black men were about to leave when Markus asked, "Why do the BaTonga people wear that pendant around their necks?" He pointed to the nearest example.

The translator smiled, "BaTonga peoples believe in Nyaminyami, river monster. Many peoples wear Nyaminyami so no eat BaTonga peoples!"

Two weeks had passed with heavy rains and a few sunny days. Living with the BaTonga was a profound experience for Markus—unlike living with Le Ling and her father Wan Ling in China, who were educated, highly refined, and had a living standard approximately the same as in Europe.

The BaTonga were basically simple fishermen and hunter gatherers living near the Zambezi River, probably no different from people of five or ten thousand years earlier.

Markus realized these people, of such primitive means, were as kind and gentle and loving with one another as any people he had ever met. As he got to know them and watch them each day, he perceived a beauty in them, unique to his experience.

The children were playfully happy; the men had beautiful bodies and carried themselves with dignity in their fishing canoes and on their hunting parties. The young women were fetching and had a raw sensuality.

The woman—her name, he found out, was Sisibeco—who nursed his wounds and cared for his needs was particularly attractive. He lay there in the dark on his mat, through the long, lonely nights, and fantasized about making love to her. He thought about the morality of his erotic dreams. Was it some kind of betrayal of Helena? He finally decided to blank that question out of his mind, unresolved.

—— CHAPTER 30 ——

January 1915, Nyaminyami

M arkus estimated it was sometime in early January 1915. He couldn't be sure, but he looked to the moon for guidance as the ancients did. "Yes," he said to himself, "it must be early January."

The day finally arrived for him to search for his wrecked aircraft. *I'm not leaving the village for good, only going out to retrieve what I can from the crash site,* he thought. He knew he was still too weak to trek alone across the unknown Africa that lay ahead of him.

"I feel good," he mumbled to himself as he limped along, two hunter guides ahead of him and two behind. He still had pain in his leg, but his chest was not bothering him anymore.

"If I don't overdo it, my leg will heal correctly."

It was a long walk, with a half dozen stops he knew his guides didn't need. Before they arrived at the wreck, he could see it way off on a rise in the land. One wing was pointing straight up, the fuselage upside down in the tree and badly crumpled.

"Good God! I survived that?" he said aloud. "I hope the radio parts are still undamaged somewhere in there." His BaTonga guides ignored his comments.

A mixed herd of zebras, wildebeest, and four kinds of antelope grazed on new grass among the scattered trees near the aeroplane. A leopard leaped down from a nearby tree and slinked away in no hurry. When his four guides arrived, they sat down and waited. Markus walked around the tree, looking up, inspecting his erstwhile transportation.

"Christ, I was lucky to survive this."

The German *askari* porter was one of his guides, so Markus asked if there was a way to bring down whatever was still in the aircraft. This took a lot of explaining and gesticulating and a drawing in the dirt. The translator finally understood and told the three other men. Two of them shimmied up the tree trunk in surprising fashion and were at the wreck in moments. They rocked the fuselage back and forth. Parts of debris fell off.

"No, no, don't rock it!" Markus shouted. "Just bring down what's inside." He gestured to the translator to repeat the command, which he did, and the two tree climbers gave a mighty shove that brought the entire wreck plunging to earth.

"Christ, all mighty! I said just the contents!"

He hurried over to the pile of what was left of his aeroplane and pulled away the fabric, wires, and broken wooden struts. There in the remains was his knapsack. He pulled it out gently and heard glass tinkling inside. He pulled out the wooden box from the knapsack. His hands trembled a bit as he pried it open.

The wood shavings were packed tightly around vacuum tubes and other electronic parts. He slowly removed the stuffing and laid the wireless parts on the flattened knapsack. Only one tube was broken.

"Thank God! I'll bet they'll have this type of tube at the East African transmitter. What luck, only one loss!" He was grinning from ear to ear and the four black men joined in with smiles on their faces.

The next few days Markus spent in the village of the BaTonga, resting after the long trek back from the wreck. He cleaned the wireless parts, his binoculars, and his revolver and repacked them in his knapsack. He had also retrieved his map and hat from the wreckage and leisurely spent his time organizing his gear.

Early one morning as Markus prepared for his final departure, Sisibeco hurried into the hut with the translator guide.

"White soldiers found big bird tree," he began. "Them tracking toward village. Come village, high sun. BaTonga mans watching soldiers." Markus thanked his friend, the black translator, nodding his head to him.

Now Markus had to decide: hide somewhere in the village or head out quickly and cover any traces of his presence? He knew the soldiers would have expert native hunters, capable of detecting the slightest impressions made by a human in the wild. He thought for a few moments. He knew he was ready. He knew he had to take his chances in the bush.

He turned to his translator and said, "Please tell Sisibeco," he gestured toward the woman, "I must leave at once. Please tell her that."

The interpreter nodded, turned to Sisibeco, and relayed the message. He looked at the German and then at her, and he left them alone in the hut.

Markus took a few steps toward her, realizing how much she had done for him over the many weeks of his recovery. Seeing her here in the shadows of the hut, in all her naked beauty—the rich, brown skin oiled to a shiny sheen, the dark eyes, full lips, and pulled-back hair—he wanted to pull her into his arms and feel her body against his. She understood his look and waited for him.

Finally, he took her hands in his; she tried gently to pull away. He lifted her hands, palms up, and gazed into her eyes for a long moment. Slowly, he bent down and kissed each one. He lingered a moment with her hands in his, then released them.

Their eyes were fixed on each other as she raised her left hand and placed it on his shoulder. Whatever it was she whispered in her unknown native tongue, he felt the profound meaning of it. She reached behind her neck and lifted the leather thong holding the Nyaminyami amulet that dangled between her breasts. She placed it around his neck without saying a word and backed away. Finally, Markus picked up his knapsack with its precious contents and left the hut.

He felt he would never see Sisibeco again, but he knew she would remain forever in those deep recesses of his mind where his most private, precious memories lay.

After several days heading approximately due east through Portuguese East Africa, limping along, still feeling a twinge once in a while, he stopped for most of a day to rest. Sisibeco packed him smoked fish and smoked meat, possibly kudu, a deer-like creature.

He followed the river, actually walking close to the shore, in the water, to cover his tracks. He knew it was extremely dangerous, with crocodiles, thousands of them, feasting on anything that entered their world. And there was the rest of the wild carnivores, also needing the river to drink. Most times his hand rested on the butt of his revolver, and at other times, his hand had gone up inside his shirt to the Nyaminyami carving. Sisibeco had given him her good luck talisman, and he felt he surely needed it there along the river.

Those first few days were nerve racking, stressful, and exhausting; he was always watching the shore ahead and the shadows in the water, always keeping an eye inland and behind him. Nights were especially bad as many predators hunted after sundown. He finally determined his safest bet was in a tree, or between two or three fires on the ground as he did earlier. Markus was concerned about the smoke from his fires being seen by enemy patrols, but he chanced it.

One evening, as always, he had lots of time to reflect, and he thought about his life and how it had unfolded, growing up with Levi and the two families in the little village in Bavaria. What a wonderful youth I had, roaming the lands and woods around Kalvarianhof and hunting and the girls in the village, he smiled to himself. Joining the army—that was something! The uniform and adventures and travel and the medals and China! What an experience that was, fighting the Boxers and loving Li Ling . . . I really loved her. I wonder where she is now? And those other women, those Samoans in the forest!

He smiled to himself and shook his head as he threw more wood on the fire and continued reminiscing: *Ilsa, innocent, passionate Ilsa—and what a body—I loved her, too.* He got up and stretched, looked around, checked the fires and his wood supply, and settled back down. *Religion, how cruel to keep us apart!* He felt a pang of regret as he thought of her.

Diana Lange, well, that was nothing really, but her mother, Dorothy Lange, that was . . . What was that? After her daughter left and her husband died . . . she needed someone, for just that one night. I never would have approached her, but I was there.

The night sounds—birds, animals, and insects—disturbed and distracted Markus's sleep until he grew accustomed to them.

What a mysterious, exotic place, this Africa! It's like nothing else, both cruel and beautiful. Ah, beauty. He smiled broadly. *And Helena, my lovely, precious Helena, what are you doing tonight? Should I have left, taking on this mission? I could have refused, made up some excuse, but here I am . . . and you're there, darling, with little Rupert. My boy, how you must be growing. This damned war! It better get over quickly before I get myself killed.*

Late in the afternoon of the next day, Markus approached a fishing village. He studied it from a distance. He'd been thinking about the idea of entering it for some time.

"This may be my opportunity," he whispered to himself. He waited until dark, skirted the village inland, and came out down river of the *kraal*. He snuck back up stream until he found what he was looking for, a canoe with a paddle. He easily slipped it into the river and was off. Markus had been studying the river and particularly the crocs. Most of them stayed pretty close to shore where their prey was. He headed farther out.

"I might do what we did in China, sail all the way to the coast!" He smiled at that as he recalled the time when he and Sun Yet Sen commandeered the Imperial Chinese Navy mail boat and sailed away to freedom. *Ha! That might work again!*

There was netting in the canoe, so Markus was able to hook up a drag net with branches as he flowed with the current. There was almost always something in the net when he stopped. He most often had fish roasted on a stick, but one evening, he found a piece of thin slate rock and heated it up and more or less fried his filets.

The Zambezi got wider and wider as it coursed now southeast toward the Indian Ocean. He had no way of knowing how close he was to the ocean, but he figured at least another two hundred miles, a staggering distance to paddle a dugout canoe.

"If the plane just hadn't crashed . . . I should have put her down earlier . . . Well, I was pretty much out of gasoline anyway. Don't beat yourself up about it now."

After a few more days of traveling down river, often at night in bright moonlight, he saw another village ahead. It was late evening, very quiet except for the bugs buzzing and the bats and birds chasing them. He slowed, letting the gentle current carry him along. *Should I lay low and pass as I've done several times before? Or should I land, skirt the village, and steal a boat on the other side? What would Levi do?* He pulled on the paddle and headed into foliage along the shore.

Grabbing his gear, he headed inland very quietly, watching for both humans and animals. As he made his way round, Markus was surprised to see military tents at the far edge of the village. *Tents*! He studied them for a time, quietly swatting flies as best he could.

He moved to a different location to have a better look and was again surprised. This time, it was horses. It appeared there were two dozen or so in a corral made of piles of thorn bushes to keep predators out. He knew instinctively that there had to be guards around the camp.

Looks like Portuguese; must be. I would love to be back in a saddle again. Let's see what I can do about that. He knew guards, being guards, get bored and sleepy and inattentive, especially at night. He knew he had the advantage, assuming there was only one guard. If they doubled the guard, the game was probably up. He edged closer to the horse enclosure, trying not to startle them. They could smell him, and he hoped they would accept the smell of a human without too much alarm.

He heard a smack! A slap. *Guard and bug*, he thought. Markus slipped out of his knapsack and took his revolver out of its holster. In the dark, it appeared the guard was wearing an *askari* uniform. *He's black, much more aware of his surroundings, and probably very fit*, he figured.

As he approached the shadowy figure, he realized the guard was very short—a young kid, probably. He came up on him, and the child-guard turned and stared at Markus.

He thinks I'm Portuguese! Markus touched the brim of his hat as a greeting. *I can pull this off.* He held up two fingers and pointed to the horses. The boy spoke in a native dialect. Markus put his hand over his own mouth, indicating silence and made a sweeping gesture with his other hand, ordering the makeshift gate opened. The boy complied.

Markus walked past a row of saddles on a large log and slowly moved in among the horses. He selected two, went back to get two bridles and a lead rope, and returned to the mounts. The boy, seeing the man select two horses, picked up one of the military saddles and approached Markus. Markus took the saddle from the boy and cinched it up on the first horse. He walked the horses to the gate where the boy stood with a second saddle.

"*Nein.*" Markus said, and then he realized he had spoken German! He stared at the boy for a moment, but there was no reaction from him. Markus gestured toward the gate, and the boy opened it. He walked the horses out as quietly as possible, and the boy closed the gate. Just before Markus turned to leave, he dug into his pocket and retrieved a one-half mark silver coin he knew he had. He handed it to the boy. The child-guard held it in his hand and raised it up to his eyes to see it better in the moon light. A broad smile appeared on his face. He again spoke in his native tongue. Markus made the sign for silence and left to retrieve his knapsack.

He walked the horses quite a ways down a path, leading away from the village, toward the coast. With one foot in a stirrup, he swung himself up and onto the horse. Markus felt so good he chuckled to himself. Even the smell of the horses energized him as he sat tall in the military saddle.

Traveling alone, through most anywhere in Africa, he knew, was always a dangerous undertaking. The BaTonga people would never venture out far alone.

He had to remain constantly on alert, as there were so many animals everywhere, which meant there were predators everywhere. A pride of lions could easily overpower one man with two horses.

The countryside was lush and beautiful, and after a few days of switching the saddle between his two horses, Markus felt he was making good headway. The chance of Portuguese soldiers from the camp overtaking him was very small.

Markus risked detection on account of the noise when he shot a large bird, probably a hornbill. It was similar to the ones Helena hunted at the ranch. After reloading, he counted eleven more bullets left for his revolver. "It's enough for hunting," he noted to himself.

He roasted the fowl and feasted on it for several days as he made his way through hills to lower elevations and the savannah. Tall trees, tall grass, and thorn bushes, fifteen feet high, were spread out across the plain in front of him. The rains continued on and off as he followed his compass, bearing due east. He had not seen or found traces of any other humans, Portuguese or native, since stealing the horses. The land was pristine, without the slightest mark of man.

—— CHAPTER 31 ——

From Terror Above

T he day began with a drizzle that continued as he rode at a walk, so the horses could go all day. He had heard that a man could actually outrun a horse over the long haul, but he didn't know whether it was true. At this point, he was inclined to believe it.

"Early afternoon, time for the last of the hornbill." He had been talking to the horses for days. He reined them in under one of the larger trees, with its spreading branches forming a canopy like an umbrella. He sat quietly in the saddle for a few moments, surveying the landscape around him.

The first thing he remembered after the attack was feeling like his head was being ripped off his shoulders. He had heard the gunshot. He had heard both horses whinny and found himself on the ground. His hands were up to his face and covered in blood. His revolver, still in one hand, was also covered in blood. He could only see out of one eye.

"*Gott allmächtig*, what happened?" he spattered through the blood running down to his chin. Then, a flash of memory, a picture came to his mind. The spare horse, terrified, with a spotted leopard on its back, kicking wildly and galloping off with the leopard's claws raking its back and the cat's mighty jaws sinking into its withers.

Markus sat there for a long time, stupefied. Finally, he staggered up and leaned against the tree. Both horses were gone. He felt pain. He gently touched the slash marks across his face.

"It must have come down on me out of the tree. Thank God in heaven it chose to go after one of the horses, or I'd be half-eaten by now," he said. His face ached and was swelling up fast. He wiped the coagulated blood out of one eye and was grateful that he could see with it.

His knapsack was still on his back, but the canteen and water gourds were strapped to his saddle. He unslung his pack and rummaged for a cloth to wipe and bandage his face.

"Can I track the horse? It probably hasn't gone very far . . . They usually don't."

He walked slowly over to a large puddle and washed his face, wincing as he did it. Markus managed to get a smoky fire going under the big tree and sat there eating the last of the big bird. It was late afternoon when he fell asleep, dreaming bad dreams and then a good dream of his wife and little Rupert, with his happy smile and lovely hair and soft body.

He heard the sound before he opened his eyes, a low, growling sound. He opened the least-swollen eye as his hand closed around the grip of his revolver in his lap. Two striped hyenas were staring at him from the other side of the burned-down fire. With their ugly heads low to the ground, their tongues were hanging out as they sized him up.

Markus raised his revolver slowly as he stared down the barrel into the eyes of the nearest beast. The animal crumpled and rolled backward as the sound wave of the single shot blasted the ears of the other. After a few twitches, the animal laid dead still. The other was gone. Markus grinned through a pained face and said, "Thank you, Jesus; here's dinner!"

Most people who had never been to Africa—and that would have been most people—thought of Africa as a quiet place, with grand vistas of undeveloped land, or trackless jungle, of deserts stretching to the horizon. It was often, however, a noisy place, especially at night.

After gathering a large pile of kindling and building two fires, Markus was exhausted, but he continued to prepare a spit to roast his kill. In the background, he heard elephants trumpet and lions roar.

With a full belly, Markus felt a little better. He decided he was too weak to look for the horse that evening; it was too dangerous, but if it survived the night, he might find it in the morning. In the meantime, Markus dried the skin of the hyena and made a carrying bag for the meat he was cooking. He made a last-minute decision to burn off the hair on the hide to get rid of the bugs. With a stick, he dragged the skin through the fire, hearing the bugs pop. Back and forth, he pulled the hide until it was bare of hair but still pliable.

He built a third fire, knowing that creatures in the dark could smell his blood. He knew he needed sleep, so he built three fires with heavy, green branches to smoke and smolder all night. Even with a light drizzle, the fires flared up occasionally, lighting up his camp and reflecting off several pairs of eyes watching from the dark.

Morning came, and Markus was up feeding his fires. He wasn't going to take any unnecessary chances. After relieving himself, he gathered enough water to fill his tin cup. He dumped in a small measure of his precious coffee grounds. He seldom threw away the grounds. Either he drank them down or dumped them back into his cloth coffee pouch. He gathered the meat he had hung over the fire the night before to smoke and placed it in the leather bag he made. Roasted meat also went in. Markus was a bit clumsy with the bandage on part of his face and tied around his head, but he managed to press his hat down firmly. The pain had greatly subsided, and with a good night's sleep, he was ready to look for his horse.

Markus abandoned camp and started tracking the horses. *Which set of prints to follow?* After a short distance, he detected blood on the ground. *Wrong horse.* He backtracked and took up the trail of the second horse. It led quite a ways in an almost straight line.

Oh no, he thought as he looked up into the sky ahead. Sure enough, a flock of black-winged, red-headed birds surrounded the carcass. With such a thick gathering, Markus couldn't be sure it was his horse. He watched them from a distance and finally his suspicions were confirmed. One of the large birds took off, carrying in its beak a section of leather bridle.

"That's just great!" He actually knew the chances of a domesticated horse surviving alone at night were not good. It would be an easy target for a half dozen predators.

"Thanks for carrying me this far," he said as he turned his attention to his compass. As an ex-lancer back in China, he remembered how horses had saved his life more than once—he really meant the thanks.

I know there's a village on the coast, due east of the lakes. That'll be my goal.

Markus set out to find the old Arab slave port of Quelimane, now a Portuguese possession. He vaguely remembered hearing about German farmers settling in Portuguese East Africa, inland from the coast, harvesting sisal for rope.

That would be a stroke of luck to make contact with them.

Royal Portuguese Crest

—— CHAPTER 32 ——

General Albuquerque

The Portuguese patrol came upon him several days later, attracted by the smoke from his fires. He was still asleep when his foot was kicked. He woke with a start, his hand grasping his revolver.

"No, no, German. Neighbor, friends," the soldier said in broken German. He had a smile on his shaggy face, as did the other six Portuguese troopers. Markus struggled to get up; his whole body ached from the crash injuries, animal attacks, and hard trekking over land for many weeks. A hand extended to him and pulled him up.

"Where you going, German? What you doing out here? Very dangerous, one man alone."

Markus thought quickly and decided to tell the truth. "I'm walking to German East Africa to visit my friend and rejoin my unit."

"Where you come from, German?" the Portuguese soldier asked.

"I came from German South West Africa—by aeroplane—but it crashed way back there." He pointed west. "About a month or so back west."

There was rapid discussion among the seven Portuguese soldiers. Finally, the leader turned to Markus. He looked at him a long time, up and down. His gaze lingered on the deep scratches on his face. He noticed Markus was favoring one leg. He saw a small patch of hair missing from Markus's head and noticed the crude animal sack with the half-rotten meat inside. Markus was a terrible sight, with months of beard growth.

"My companions," he gestured with his thumb, "they think you crazy. No aeroplane in Africa. You desert German Army, *correto*? Ha!" He laughed, the others, not understanding any of the conversation, laughed too.

"OK, German, we take you with us." The Portuguese soldiers were riding horses, and Markus was helped up onto the supply horse.

No saddle, but at least I can ride. They headed east toward the coast and, he assumed, toward their detachment. He was happy to be back on a horse—even though he wasn't in a saddle. The soldier who spoke some German often rode beside him, so Markus had a chance to hear fragments of war news—old news, but news nonetheless.

"Big battle in France—British, Belgian, all fight German. German fight Russian, too. Portuguese no fight, stay alive . . . ha, ha."

"But what about here in Africa—in East Africa?" Markus obviously knew of the fighting in South West Africa. "Is there any fighting in East Africa?"

"Yes," said the soldier. "British soldiers like fight. All time." It was a long, hard ride, maybe twelve or thirteen hours, to reach the small Portuguese garrison post. Markus figured they wanted to bring back their prize and so did not make it a two-day trip. It was early evening when the eight riders passed through the rickety gates of the walled enclosure that was the base. One of the riders had gone ahead and informed the commander of their coming.

The party reined in their horses and slid out of their saddles, bone tired. Markus was helped down and, after knocking mud off his boots, ushered into the commander's office. It had started raining again. He pulled himself together as best he could and saluted the captain of the fifty-man garrison.

"Lieutenant Markus Mathias, electrical unit officer of the First Bavarian Army Corps, assigned to the Imperial German wireless station in Windhoek, German South West Africa, sir." He knew he sounded bone-weary tired.

Commander Joaquim Augusto Mouzinho de Albuquerque, in a perfectly pressed and bemedaled uniform, returned the salute as several other officers stood by.

Commander Albuquerque looked at the bedraggled soldier before him, shook his head slightly, and motioned for a chair. Someone brought a chair, and Markus gratefully slumped into it.

"Wine," ordered the commander. He sat down behind a beautifully carved desk that seemed out of place in the otherwise spartan surroundings. He conferred quietly with one of his subordinates and waited for the wine to be poured. He motioned for Markus to take the tall glass of red liquid. They toasted each other silently and took long drinks.

"I have heard fragments of your story, Captain Mathias. Now share with me the details of your," he hesitated, "your adventures." He spoke in perfect German.

Markus was impressed and began to spell out his story, leaving out the main objective of his mission delivering advanced wireless parts to German East Africa.

After Markus finished, he was asked several innocuous questions, especially about the aeroplane, with the commander looking skeptical of what he heard.

"I've heard there are several aeroplanes in the British East African colony, way up north, and the South Africans may have one or two down south. I have not heard of any in the German colonies." Markus remained silent.

The general spoke "As we are not at war with Germany, you will be treated as our guest. For now, Captain, we have a room for you and temporary clothing. If you will leave your uniform with the orderly, it will be cleaned and mended and will be ready for you in the morning. You may dine with the officers this evening, or you may wish to rest. Please ignore the guard outside your door. It is standard procedure. You may walk around the garrison as you wish. However, as you know, it is dangerous outside the gates at night." With that, the commander stood up. Markus stood up, returned the commander's salute, and was escorted to his room.

On the way there, he asked the orderly, who spoke a bit of German, about the commander. "He has a familiar name . . . but the Joaquim de Albuquerque

I've read about committed suicide . . . and some say he was murdered back in Portugal. Is your commander related to the man I speak of?"

The orderly stopped and looked both ways up and down the hall, then whispered, "It's him. The Commandante is the same man!" Again, he looked both directions. "But say nothing!"

"He's still alive! But what is he doing here? Why can't anyone talk about it?"

"It's a long story, *senior*—sir. He has many enemies. That is why he is in this distant post, out here at the end of the world. He was a great man, but . . ." the orderly trailed off as others approached.

"Here is your room, sir," he said stiffly. The orderly waited for Markus to undress, then gathered his clothes, pointed out the soap and washstand, and left.

Markus looked at the straight razor, cup, and brush and thought, *Later,* and instead started a basin bath. He ate all the bread and butter and smoked ham on the tray and drank half a bottle of the wine before falling into the luxury of sheets and a pillow. It had been almost three months since he had felt the coolness of a pillow. But sleep eluded him for a short time as he speculated on the reasons for the strange story.

"So your objective is to travel on to German East Africa?" General Albuquerque asked over a midday meal with the German and other officers.

"As you know, while we Portuguese are allies of the British, we are remaining neutral in the European war and also here in Africa. The fight is of no concern to us at the moment." He was looking at Markus while Markus was eyeing him. The commander glanced at several of his officers and continued:

"Some officers in Portugal and here in Africa would like to get into this fight for the glory of it, but our king—and I—prefer to watch and see what unfolds."

"A wise choice, Commander. I've seen war in China; it's not glorious. It's dirty, bloody, deadly, and frightening."

Several of the officers at the table sneered, with a smile of contempt on their faces. Markus ignored them except to say, "It's not like fighting primitive tribes here in Africa." He hesitated a moment. "What would be the best way to get up north to German territory, sir?"

Albuquerque looked at his officers and then at Markus before speaking: "I've been to Dar es Salaam, an old city but interesting for its mix of Arab, African, and Germans. I would take a coaster from Quelimane—that's a two day ride from here—and then sail the five hundred miles north to the Ruvuma River. It's the frontier between our two colonies. Depending on the winds and weather, you should get there in about five or six days. But if you are going to attempt it, you had better move along quickly."

"And why is that, sir?"

"Because, my young German officer, our king may be changing his mind about remaining neutral."

Markus, looking startled asked, "Why is that, sir?"

The general half-smiled and appeared resigned to the inevitable. "Because the British have offered Portugal a large piece of your colony. If we break our neutrality pledge, join their war effort, and, if we win the war, we extend our border north."

Silence fell across the officers' dining table. The general looked off into the distance and drank his wine. The other officers stared, like wolves, at the German.

Markus sat quietly thinking, *What would Levi do?*

"Sir, would you lend me a horse and directions to the coast? I'll find a boat north. I'll send payment for the horse when I get to German East Africa."

He waited for a reply. The other officers, at first, looked startled at the audacious request, then laughed and shook their heads.

Commander Albuquerque raised his hand slightly, and the room quieted down. They all stared at him. "May I remind you, gentlemen, that we are still in a state of neutrality with the Empire of Germany and with all the other belligerents? Therefore, we will continue normal relations as before the war."

He looked over to Markus. "Captain Mathias, you may join the supply train to the coast leaving in two days. You can ride on one of the wagons. Is there any discussion on the matter?"

Without hesitating, the commander said, "Fine," pushed his chair away from the table, and got up.

Everyone also got up.

"Dismissed," he commanded, leaving the room.

Markus arrived a week later at the Portuguese coastal town of Quelimane. Several German businessmen had shops or trading concerns there, and Markus soon was sitting in the back room of Herr Leopold's shipping company, quaffing a warm beer.

"So the Portuguese let Germans settle here and have farms and businesses," Markus observed. "Pretty good of them."

"*Ja*, well, they tax us enough for the privilege, and besides, they wanted to open up the country to make something of it, so they invited us in." Leopold took a deep draw on his pipe. "So you want to go up north, do you?" He got up and pulled a dusty shade down to block the afternoon light. "You could wait for one of the coastal freighters . . . a couple of weeks, I imagine, or you could hire one of the Arab sailing scows, but they're slow."

The two men sat there in silence for a few minutes, then Herr Leopold added, "Or you could try to intercept the *Konigsberg* off the coast. She passes by on occasion, but now with the war, we don't see much of her. She's probably out chasing British ships! Ha."

They both smiled as Markus expressed immediate interest, "The *Konigsberg*? Here?"

"*Ja*, SMS *Konigsberg*, the Kaiser's light cruiser." He paused a moment. "They call it a light cruiser, but she's the biggest German ship in the Indian Ocean, I'll wager. She sails out of Dar es Salaam. That is, she did till the war started. Now, who knows?" He took another deep draw in his pipe.

"How would I do that? Intercept the ship, as you said? How could I contact her?"

"You could try our wireless. It's pretty weak, but we manage to reach Dar es Salaam when the weather cooperates. She might pick up our signal."

"You have a wireless? Wonderful! I didn't know you had one. Can I see the equipment?"

"As a matter of fact, the wireless is upstairs in my office." He gestured toward the narrow wooden staircase. Markus was out of his chair before Herr Leopold had put down his stein and pushed himself away from his workbench.

It was, indeed, old equipment and probably weak, but it appeared to be in working order. Markus reverently bent over the machine. A bicycle generator was wired up to it.

"It doesn't get much use; I wire ships on occasion." Leopold sat down in front of the dusty apparatus and flipped a switch. A small, red light faintly glowed.

"I'll get a boy up here to pedal the generator," the tradesman said. He got up, went to the open window, leaned out, and shouted, "Luanga! Up here, now!"

In no time, the young, black thirteen-year-old was pedaling away at breakneck speed, with a big smile on his face. "Make plenty 'lectric! Ha!" he laughed.

"I've got business to attend to, so I leave you to see what you can do," Leopold said as Markus slipped into the chair.

"Thank you, sir," Markus replied smartly.

"You can slow down now, boy . . . Just keep a steady pace,." Markus closely examined the wireless, turning it around for a closer inspection. He swung his ever-present knapsack off his shoulder and pulled out several parts. In a short time, he had the transmitter functioning far beyond its previous strength. He began an open transmission to the German colony, hoping there was someone other than the British listening. He identified himself and stated he was heading north soon.

How to speak and not reveal my mission? thought Markus, knowing anyone could pick up his transmission.

Just then Leopold bounded up the stairs with a much-dog-eared notebook in his hand. "Here. This may be of use. It's kind of a code book—well, not really a code book so much as some substitute names we gave ships and certain cargos we didn't want *others* to know about." He emphasized 'others'.

"I believe the *Konigsberg* is in there . . . not sure." It didn't take Mathias long to find the entry: "Kberg = SeaSearcher." He began transmitting that call sign requesting a rendezvous off Quelimane.

Markus was surprised how strong the signal was from the SMS *Konigsberg* and how quickly she replied.

"She must be very close," he said to himself, out loud. Markus sent the following wireless:

SEASEARCHER NEED IMMEDIATE TRANSPORT TO G.E.A. STOP. FROM QUELIMANE. STOP. TIME, DATE, LOCATION. . STOP. SIGNED SAINT HILDEGARD VON BINGIN

Leopold had given Markus his wireless name, known to most German traders along the coast and probably by the Imperial German Navy in the Indian Ocean, but probably not by the British navy. A short time later, Markus received a cryptic reply:

SAINT HILDEGARD VON BINGIN. STOP. COORDINATES 18 DEGREES 6 MINUTES. STOP. 37 DEGREES 2 MINUTES E. STOP. 3-13-15. STOP. 2200 HOURS. STOP. SIGNED SEASEARCHER

The location was one mile off the coast of Quelimane and in three days. "This is such good news, Leopold, my friend. Such good news . . . thank you."

"Well then, this calls for a celebration. How about a bottle of schnapps at a nearby café?"

Settling in at the Rosalinda Café, Markus offered, "A toast to the Kaiser's navy!"

"Not so loud. Remember this is 'Portuguese' East Africa, not German East Africa," Leopold hastened to warn Markus.

"They tolerate us here because we're a benefit to them, but remember, they have long been allies with the British!" Leopold looked around the quiet café, and whispered, "They're neutral because they're weak here in Africa . . . too much corruption and nepotism and all their commanders are from the decadent aristocracy. Not like Bismarck's army built on merit, competence, and discipline . . . Now, that's an army!"

They filled their glasses and nodded in agreement. Markus leaned back in his chair and was feeling the effects of the schnapps. He was thoughtful for a few minutes, then spoke, "Won't the British pick up my message and try an intercept?"

Leopold's eyes were red, and he slouched over the table. "No, no. First of all," his speech was slow and slightly slurred, "there are few, if any, British warships along this coast. *Mein Gott*, the Germans only have one in the entire Indian Ocean—far as I know." His hand flapped in the air.

"Besides if, *if*, there is a British warship around—highly, highly unlikely— and if they pick up that transmission of yours, they are going to think it's just another tramp steamer picking up freight." His head wagged back and forth.

"Remember, as a neutral, these Portuguese can trade with all the belligerents in this war—the Russians, the Austrians, the French, the Ottomans—all of them. See? See what I'm talking about?" He had exhausted himself and more or less collapsed onto the table, hitting his head with a bump. Herr Leopold was going to be out for the rest of the afternoon.

The rendezvous with the *Konigsberg* went off smoothly after Leopold arranged for one of his German fishing friends to transport Markus out into a misty night to the approximate coordinates. Their little boat was purposefully lit up with a half dozen lanterns so the war ship could easily spot them.

It slid out of the mists of a calm sea with hardly a sound. A massive steel wall, almost four hundred feet long, appeared fifty yards east of their little boat at the precise hour.

Only the rhythmic thumping of the engines was heard in the still night air as a rope ladder with wooden steps lowered over the side of the German cruiser to the waiting Bavarian captain.

Imperial German Navy

—— CHAPTER 33 ——

The SMS Konigsberg

W elcome aboard, Captain." Officer of the deck, Marine Lieutenant Alfred Mueller offered his hand to Markus as he reached the top rung of the rope ladder.

Markus stepped over the gunwale and onto the iron deck of the only German warship in the Indian Ocean. They both exchanged smart salutes as other sailors looked on.

"Welcome aboard the Kaiser's ship SMS *Konigsberg*," Mueller spoke with pride. Even in the dim light on deck, the marine lieutenant noted Mathias's ragged uniform.

"We were ordered to keep a lookout for you along the coast, but that was months ago. You officially were reported dead or captured." Markus, taken aback by the bluntness of Mueller's assertion, again realized how long it had been since he left Windhoek. *Could it really have been seven months ago?*

"Yes, it's been a very long journey, and it's not over. I must get to our colony up north as soon as possible . . . with your help."

"Yes, we know. Our commander, Captain Max Looff, ordered that you be brought to his cabin as soon as you came aboard. This way, Captain."

Markus was immediately impressed by the three-stack cruiser. It was the biggest warship he had ever been on, and he remembered it well from his voyage on her from Germany back in 1909. Although officially a light cruiser, it seemed immense to him.

After formal introductions in the captain's cabin, Captain Looff explained, "Before the wireless station at Windhoek was captured, your mission was communicated to us. We heard in British and Portuguese wireless intercepts that the wreckage of an aeroplane was found with no trace of the pilot. Since your aeroplane was one of the very few aircraft in all of Sub-Saharan Africa, we knew it was you." The ship's steward brought coffee for the two men and the other officers invited to the meeting.

"As far as the war in Europe is concerned, and you may have heard this from the Portuguese, there has developed somewhat of a stalemate on the western front in France and Belgium."

Captain Looff accepted the cup of coffee from the steward and gestured toward Markus as he continued. "However, General Hindenburg and General Ludendorff have pushed the Russians out of East Prussia and back into Poland. They encircled the Russian 2nd Army and captured 125,000 troops! Imagine!" The officers in the room grinned.

"It's being called the Battle of Tannenberg, and their general, General Samsonov, is reported to have committed suicide." Everyone sat easy and sipped their coffee in silence, anticipating their captain's next remarks.

"I met him once, in St. Petersburg, in '04, I think . . . a fine fellow, really." Again, a long stillness before the captain finished his thought: "It's not going to be a short war."

Captain Looff lit a cigarette and snapped the wooden match in two. "The Japanese invaded our colony in China. Tsingtao is holding on, but we can't resupply them, so . . ." he didn't have to finish the thought, as everyone understood the cause was lost in China.

"All our colonies are extremely vulnerable, including this one." He shuffled through wireless dispatches and added, "We've had considerable success off the coast of Chile. The *Konigsberg*'s sister ship, SMS *Nürnberg*, participated in the Battle of Coronel, sinking the British battle cruiser HMS *Monmouth* and another ship." The officers in the room looked at each other knowingly.

"Right now, Captain, we have to concern ourselves with Admiral King-Hall's Cape Squadron up from South Africa. He's got five capital ships: the *Astraea*, the *Hyacinth*, the *Chatham*, the *Dartmouth* and the *Weymouth*. They're searching for us as we speak. Fortunately, we're faster than any of the five, so we can out run them and be lost in the vastness of the sea . . . as long as we've got coal." He grinned and the other officers followed suit.

"Before you are shown to your quarters, Captain Mathias, you should know, our mission at the moment is to deliver you to Dar es Salaam."

Imperial German Cruiser SMS** Konigsberg, **Indian Ocean, 1915

Ostafrika

—— CHAPTER 34 ——

A Jungle Sanctuary

S everal days of sailing north from the Portuguese colony brought the SMS *Konigsberg* just south of the small island of Mafia. It was across from the mouth of the Rufiji River, both located in southeastern German East Africa on the Indian Ocean. Markus was on deck with a group of junior officers.

"The Captain says we must lay to for needed repairs," began the officer of the deck, "and here is where we will do it. We're heading up that river, out of sight of possible enemy ships before we sail north to Dar es Salaam. Clever, wouldn't you say?"

Markus scanned the far shoreline. For as far as he could see, there was jungle down to the beach. Mangroves as thick as giant birds' nests clustered around the mouth of a delta of channels emptying into the Indian Ocean.

"We're going to take this ship in there? Is it deep enough? Seems we'll run aground for sure."

"Captain Looff knows what he's doing . . . and we've got to service the boilers and wait for the coal tender. The bunkers are getting low." They both watched intently as the four-hundred-foot-long ship slowly maneuvered its way up one of the several channels of the Rufiji. A day of expert navigating eased the mighty German cruiser several miles upstream through shallow, winding bends in the jungle-shrouded river.

"It's surprising to me that a big ship like this could ever be brought this far inland from the sea," Markus stated in true amazement. "We can almost reach across the gunwales and touch the jungle." They both grinned as the turbines slowed and deck hands scurried around, securing lines and performing other duties.

Markus stayed busy onboard several days, making wireless contact with Doctor Schnee, governor of the colony, and Colonel von Vorbeck, overall military commander. He waited patiently for his escort.

For the last several months, the British had been making numerous, aggressive incursions into German territory, and it was vital that Markus have safe passage to the wireless station to complete his assignment. His precious cargo of advanced wireless instruments was always at his side.

While waiting for his escort to arrive at the *Konigsberg*'s isolated location, Markus noted the extensive efforts to camouflage the ship and conceal any trace of its hiding place. Vegetation was cut to cover the vessel, and shore batteries were placed at the mouth of the Rufiji, using several of the ship's guns, including two torpedo tubes.

I can't imagine the British ever finding her in this God-forsaken place, he thought with satisfaction.

On a bright, clear day in July, 1915, a detachment of Uhlans, a unit of German cavalry, appeared shipside. The small company of mounted riders, Markus's escort, was welcomed aboard for a generous midday meal. Both the sailors and the soldiers were glad to see each other, creating a sense of mutual camaraderie. Markus was sitting with the escort commander, Lieutenant Mueller, and Captain Looff, enjoying the conversation.

Suddenly the ship's alarm bell clanged furiously—a sound Markus was all too familiar with filled his ears. Over the din of the alarm bell and the clamor of dozens of running men, tipping over chairs and shouting orders, he could distinctly hear the roar of an aeroplane engine. And it was flying low, very low.

Obviously, the pilot had spotted the ship, and by the sound of the engine, Markus could tell it was circling around for a second look. As he passed through the iron doorway onto the deck, Markus jerked back involuntarily for a second at the sound of a volley of scattered rifle shots, banged out from the ship's sea marines, who were on deck. The riflemen swung their guns rapidly, trying to lead the aeroplane. It was over in seconds.

"That's it! They've spotted us now," someone shouted.

"Did you get a look at its marking? British, right? Was it British?" The marines looked at each other.

"It had no markings, nothing . . . nothing on the wings!" The questions came fast and furiously: "Where did it come from? How could an aeroplane be way out here?"

"This is German territory—Do we have aeroplanes here?"

Captain Looff, after ordering an armed watch, called an immediate meeting of his officers, with Markus in attendance. The heated discussion centered on what the implications were now that "someone"—probably the British or South Africans—had discovered their location. The captain turned to Markus, who had remained silent until then.

"What do you think, Captain Mathias? Where do you think—" he paused to rephrase his question. "How do you think the British, or whoever, could have flown an aeroplane over my ship?" There was dead silence from the others in the wardroom.

Markus looked up and hesitated a moment before stating, "There are three possibilities, sir. First of all, it was almost certainly British . . . or South African with British assistance. But I discount that, for a variety of reasons I'll skip for now."

He looked to the captain for approval. Looff nodded his head slightly, and Markus continued, "Second, the British are experimenting with ship-launched aeroplanes. They've created a floating airfield . . . a launching deck on one of their older ships. I've seen a photograph of that modified ship. The deck runs the full length of the ship and is long enough for an aeroplane to take off, with the right wind conditions. It's still very experimental, sir."

He looked around the wardroom table at the dozen or so men. He saw rapt attention and grave concern in their faces.

"Very good, Captain, and the third possibility?"

"*Ja*, I'm not sure, because I only caught a few seconds' view of the aeroplane, but it appeared to have either landing skis or pontoons." He stopped for a moment, as if working out his further explanation. "Many of the earlier-type aircraft used landing skis, as you probably know. Later skis with wheels were added. A lot of them are still flying." Again, Markus paused. "But I'm inclined to believe that what I saw were pontoons. It makes the most sense, logistics wise— for the British, I mean. They could tow or, more probably, carry the aeroplane on deck of any ship, then lower it into the water when they wanted to use it. And the ship could carry fuel and spare parts. That's probably what they did, sir. That's probably what it was."

"Yes, very good, Captain. That means there're enemy ships off shore. We're probably safe for the moment, but if they know our location up the Rufiji, we're bottled up. Their ships are deep draft, so they can't come up river, and with this jungle coverage, they can't see us to sight their cannon. But with that aeroplane used as a spotter and shallow draft vessels, they could walk their shells straight to my ship. We've got to destroy that aeroplane!"

Over the next two days, all haste was made to mount machine guns and cannon to bring down the aircraft, should it return.

These are challenges for the captain and his crew, Markus thought, *but not for me.* He saddled up with the Uhlans and headed out the next morning, after good luck salutations. Captain Looff gave Markus a salute, a hardy handshake, and a dispatch pouch for Colonel von Vorbeck.

—— CHAPTER 35 ——

Distant Thunder

Markus was glad when Lieutenant Martenn led the horsemen out of the steaming jungles of the pestilence-infested coastal region and toward the uplands of the Uluguru Mountains. They rode hard for most of the first day toward their goal: Vorbeck's military headquarters. The air seemed fresher and not so heavy with humidity that late July day of 1915, as the small mounted unit moved to higher elevations. Markus thought about the horses and how it was better for them to be out of the jungle. He reached down and patted his mount's neck.

For the first few seconds, Markus thought he heard thunder way off toward the coast. The lead horse pulled up, and the others followed. They all turned in their saddles and looked back toward the Indian Ocean.

"That's not—" he was interrupted.

"That's cannon fire . . . from a ship!" Martenn shouted.

"Sir, you think the *Konigsberg*'s shooting at that aeroplane?" one of the Uhlans asked.

"Hard to tell. Let's move to higher ground and see what we can see." Markus spurred his horse forward, and the small company was soon at a point that overlooked the long view to the coast six miles away. Several of the men with binoculars raised them to their eyes. Even at this great distance, faint puffs of smoke from the blasts of cordite-packed shells were seen. The low rumble of the big naval guns on the British ships swept over the group many seconds later, just faintly.

"Holy Mary! It's the British . . . That damned aeroplane did it. Now the Brits know where the *Konigsberg* is!"

The soldiers sat there with the bright sun to their backs, passing the binoculars back and forth, watching in silence. They waited for a long time, straining to see a response from the *Konigsberg*. Nothing.

"Captain Looff isn't going to give his exact position away by returning fire. Besides, he's got no way of telling the position of the enemy," Lieutenant Martenn offered. Nobody said a thing. Finally, he concluded, "Nothing we can do. Let's move out."

It was a hard, three-day ride to Vorbeck's headquarters. Early in the second day, one of the horses dropped in its tracks, breathing hard from the effects of the tsetse flies. The Uhlans stopped, dismounted, and began stripping the fallen horse of its saddle, bridle, and other gear. It seemed to be very perfunctory, the soldiers taking no particular interest in the downed animal. Markus remembered how their mounts in Bavaria and China were so kindly cared for, so valued.

As soon as the horse was stripped, a corporal drew his revolver and shot the horse in the head. The escort leader noted the frown on Markus's face.

"*JA*, I know what you're thinking. How could an Uhland shoot his mount like that? But this is Africa, not Germany. A good horse, a healthy horse, here in Africa, along the coast in these tsetse-fly-infested jungles, lasts about three months."

Markus looked incredulous.

"That's right, three months, but maybe only two months, or even one! One month for a splendid horse that back home would give good service for years. But, this is Africa . . . If you want to save horses, stay away from the coastal jungle."

They both stared at the horse for a few moments; then he shouted, "Mount up!"

Lieutenant Martenn knew Captain Mathias was new to German East Africa, so he offered to give a bit of information on the realities challenging Vorbeck's army. Markus assured him he was interested to hear it.

"Before the war, our patrols lived off the land. That is, we traded for killed game from scattered villages and for other assorted food. It was the way small military units survived in East Africa in normal times. It was of mutual benefit." He paused to take a compass reading. "Off to the right, you'll find an animal track," he ordered to the lead rider.

"Fortunately our colonial governor, Doctor Schnee, developed a good relationship with the indigenous people, insisting the military pay for any cattle or crops appropriated. He built trust, thank God, and it's proving extremely valuable to us now that hostilities have commenced."

Markus interrupted Martenn, "That is so different from the way the blacks were treated early on in Southwest Africa. The Herero people were practically wiped out after they revolted."

"Yes, I've heard about that disgraceful action. Doctor Schnee had a very different approach, and it's working well."

Martenn called a halt for a well-deserved break. As he and his troops sat in the shade, he continued, "You know, German East Africa is a huge colony of vast distances, inhospitable terrain, dangerous animals, and enemies all around. There are virtually no roads. These animal tracks," he pointed, "beaten down over centuries, serve as our only pathways through the landscape. Fortunately, before the war, we built an east-west railroad across the colony from Dar es Salaam to Lake Tanganyika. Across the lake is the Belgian Congo, our enemy. To the north lies British East Africa, and to the south, Portuguese East Africa, both also enemies. So you see the predicament we're in. *Ja*, so a second German rail line was built from the port of Tanga on the Indian Ocean, west to just south of Mount Kilimanjaro. Our rail lines are the only speedy way to move troops and supplies, so we are doing everything possible to protect them.

"You know, away from the rail lines, human porters, hundreds of them, and in some cases, thousands of them, have been recruited and paid to transport our military supplies. Some mules and horses are also used in upland savannah and mountain regions where the tsetse fly isn't so much of a threat. But only the indigenous people of our colony can resist the harsh conditions and the diseases. This war here in Africa is as much about staying alive as it is about fighting the enemy." Martenn stopped, looked over to Markus, chuckled and concluded, "Welcome to your final destination."

Colonel Von Vorbeck, Commander of
Imperial German Army in East Africa

—— CHAPTER 36 ——

Dar es Salaam: German East Africa

The capitol of German East Africa was bustling with Arab, Indian, Portuguese, and German traders and businessmen, compounded by hundreds of additional military personnel since war had been declared back in Europe. Many were packing to get out of the coastal city, fearing an eminent British attack. Markus had finally arrived at military command headquarters.

"So this is the airman who was lost and is finally found?" Colonel Paul Emil von Lettow-Vorbeck grinned as he sized up the captain standing at attention before him. "At ease, Captain. That was quite a trek you pursued. How long was your journey here?"

"Seven months, sir, close to eight." Markus hesitated before adding, "If I may, sir, I was never lost; I just kept heading toward the rising sun. However, I was found three times: first in a tree by the BaTonga people, then by a Portuguese Army patrol, and finally in the Indian Ocean by Captain Max von Looff of the SMS *Konigsberg*."

Markus could scarcely withhold a smile. When Vorbeck let out a hearty laugh, everyone in the commander's office joined in.

"Sit down, sit down, Captain Mathias." The colonel eyed him again for a long moment. *He looks like hell*, he thought. "*Ja*, I hear you landed your aircraft in a tree, and I suspect those deep scratches on your face have their own story."

"Yes, sir." Markus involuntarily touched his cheek.

"Later with that," the colonel said, growing decidedly more serious. "I've also been informed that the electrical apparatus you were transporting has survived. Is that true?"

"Yes, sir, except for several vacuum tubes that I'm sure our wireless station here can replace."

"Good. You probably know that our main relay transmitter in Tonga has ceased operations . . . as well as our wireless stations in Cameroon and, of course, German South West Africa. That's why it's essential that we expand our transmitting abilities here. We're the last operational station in Africa."

"Yes, sir, I know. I'll be upgrading our transmitter equipment and evaluating the communications system here in the colony over the next few weeks."

"Very good, Captain. One of the staff officers will brief you on accommodations and give you an overview of the colony. That will be all. Good to have you."

"Yes, sir." They exchanged salutes, and Vorbeck turned away. As Markus was about to leave, Vorbeck turned back around.

"Captain."

"Sir?"

"Make sure the transmitter is portable; we may have to move it out of Dar es Salaam." The colonel was staring at Markus, and then smiled slightly, "And by the way, a friend of yours has been asking about you: Captain Solomon Levi."

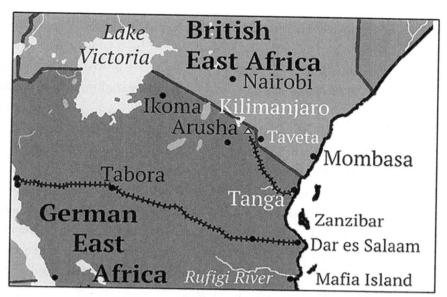

Map of Kilimanjaro/Tanga Area, German East Africa

―― CHAPTER 37 ――

A Tear in the Eye and the Massacre at Tanga

S ince restoring the railroad trestle bridge at Tabora just before war broke out, Levi was assigned to a position on Vorbeck's headquarters staff. His China experience in the field, fighting the Boxers at the same time that Colonel von Vorbeck served in China, created a bond between them, a sense of trust through mutual experience.

Markus, freshly arrived in the colony, made inquiries to find his lifelong friend, whom he had not seen in almost two years. After receiving permission for a brief visit, he traveled west fifty miles along the rail line to a sisal farm being used as a military supply depot. The farmhouse had been commandeered and the barns and outbuildings were piled high with military provisions. Dozens of German soldiers of all ranks and a company of *askari* were loading and unloading war material.

Markus looked around eagerly for that familiar face he longed to see. Levi was in among a small grove of linden trees the German farmer had planted several years earlier. He held in his hand a small branch of linden leaves and looked at them intently. Markus saw him from a distance and, at first, rushed toward his friend. He stopped short, out of sight, and was taken by the silhouette of a man he had shared most of his life with. There was something melancholy in his stance, in the way he bent to examine the leaves. As if, in the leaves of the linden tree, Levi was seeing, or possibly remembering, memories of a different time and place. Markus felt a rush of emotion as he slowly walked toward his friend.

Levi heard the footsteps, "Yes, yes, I know. I'll be right there, Sergeant. Give me a moment."

As he turned, still looking at the leaves, he said, almost to himself, "There appears to be a rust blight on the—" He stopped in mid-sentence and stared a long moment at the thin, gaunt man before him.

"Markus! Markus! *Mein Gott*, you're here. You've survived, and you're here!"

They rushed together in a bear hug of an embrace, each holding the other in a long, tight clutch. Levi was shocked to feel Markus's bones through his ill-fitting uniform.

"*Ja*, this is the best day I've had since arriving in this God-forsaken country," he managed to say.

"Oh, my dear friend, how are you?" Levi's look was one of concern as they stood there arm in arm.

He was shocked again when he saw Markus's face up close, with the deep, purple scars and his deeply tanned and weathered skin. Markus noticed his friend's subtly disturbed countenance.

"Oh, it's all right, Levi. Don't worry about me. I'm fine, really. I acquired a few souvenirs from a leopard in Portuguese East Africa on the way here. That's all."

They both half-smiled, but Levi was hard put to conceal his concern, a tear was in the corner of his eye.

"And you! Look at you, a captain!" Markus looked at Levi's insignia. "We should have saluted, sir!"

They laughed awkwardly and trailed off into silence. Both men were looking down, averting their eyes.

Finally, Levi spoke in a low voice: "I was so worried about you. Even more so than when you were missing in China. For months, we heard nothing. Most everyone thought you perished somewhere in the vastness." His arm made a sweeping gesture.

"Then, through a South African wireless intercept, we heard about a crashed aeroplane found in the bush. We figured it had to be you. But had you survived? That we didn't know."

Again, silence.

"Your Helena must have been so worried. When we got official confirmation from the *Konigsberg* that you were alive and on board, I insisted on sending a message through the neutral Portuguese to the British occupying our colony in the South West. They contacted your father-in-law at the ranch and then let us know of the contact. It was good of the Brits."

"Thanks so much for doing that . . . always looking out for me, just like old times."

They looked at each other and hugged a second time, with big grins on their faces. "I'm sure you've heard they sank the *Konigsberg* in the Rufiji River."

"*Ja*, I heard. I would have had a much tougher time getting here if it wasn't for Captain Looff and that ship. Did he and the crew survive?"

"Oh, that's a great story!" Levi livened up. "Not only did he and most of the crew survive, but they got off most of the big guns and ammunition before the British arrived. Now Vorbeck has the biggest artillery pieces in all of East Africa!"

The two long-lost friends laughed long and hard, as an involuntary release of emotion from the months of stress for both of them.

"*Ja*, so here we are in another war on another continent, my friend. How did this happen?" Levi asked.

"God only knows," Markus said, shaking his head and adding, "Helena and little Rupert and I were living a wonderful life at the ranch and in Windhoek. You should see the little fellow, Levi; he's going to be a fine German-African!"

They both burst into howls when Levi added, "Or African-German!"

After they composed themselves, Markus added, "And I got that wireless station running as smooth as a conductor's watch. Now it's all gone, and we've got this mess."

"Yes, I know. And I came from Baghdad to fix a bridge!"

"How is Katherina and Rebecca and your folks . . . Have you heard anything?"

"The last time I saw Katherina was in Baghdad. I haven't heard a thing since."

The two friends rode the train back to Vorbeck's headquarters in Dar es Salaam. During the ride, Levi filled Markus in on the military action to date in the colony. There was plenty to tell.

"At the outbreak of war, from the very beginning, Vorbeck pushed for swift engagement with the enemy. He felt, still feels, that the way to protect the colony is to threaten the enemy in his own territory. He contacted Captain Tom von Prince, a retired army officer who has lived in East Africa for years. Prince felt war was coming as early as 1913 and had raised his own private volunteer defense force made up of Usambara farmers. That's the tribe up around Mount Kilimanjaro—very disciplined whites, very loyal blacks."

Markus listened intently while Levi obviously enjoyed relating the news.

"On August 15, just two weeks after the outbreak of war in Europe, Vorbeck sent Colonel von Bock and Lieutenant Boell on raids across the border into British East Africa, using Prince's volunteers. They captured a garrison town called Traveta, but the British King's African Rifles stopped them from going farther. Since then, it's been a continuous series of small raids against the British and the Uganda Railroad; that's just over the northern border."

Markus was thoroughly engrossed in the history lesson, knowing that he and his friend would probably be engaged in other such actions in the near future.

"The British seemed as unprepared for war as we were, so things were fairly quiet for a while except for our raids. Then we discovered the British had an invasion fleet off our coastal town of Tanga, very close to our border with British East Africa. This was the first week of November, last."

The two were interrupted by a skinny native boy selling tea. "It's good, sirs. They grow it down south near Lake Tanganyika. Good German tea, sirs!"

They both chuckled at the unnatural idea of Germans growing tea and the young fellow's infectious smile. The boy poured two tin cups of the brown liquid from a large container on his back as the rail car swayed back and forth. Levi gave the boy twenty *pfennig*, and the boy's eyes lit up.

They handed back the empty cups as Markus said, "So, continue."

"*Ja*, last November, the British formed up this invasion force and—oh, we learned so much from the Brits and Indian soldiers we took as prisoners. What a sorry lot! Their ill-conceived invasion of our colony was made up of a couple of good British units, but mostly it consisted of poorly trained, poorly led British India units."

Levi was warming up to his storytelling, and Markus was taking it all in.

"It was called the Indian Expeditionary Force and consisted of the 27th Bangalore Brigade, the 63rd Palamcottah Light Infantry, the 13th Rajput's, the 2nd and 3rd Kashmir Rifles, and the 2nd Loyal North Lancashire Regiment and some others. Their intent was to sail into Tanga Bay, land eight thousand troops at three different landing beaches, and then take the town of Tanga." He paused.

"Their troops were then to roll west up our northern rail line and recapture Taveta and the town of Moshi at the end of the line . . . and apparently take the whole Mount Kilimanjaro region where most of our troops are concentrated. We know all this because we captured so many dispatch pouches. They intended to bring the whole of East Africa under British rule by this single action!" Levi stared at the floor, smiling. "Imagine, German East Africa, almost as big as the Fatherland and France combined! You know this, *ja*?"

"Of course, of course."

Levi was enjoying himself and sweating profusely. He got up for a moment, stepped outside their compartment, and looked both ways down the carriage aisle. "Where's that tea boy?" he said to no one.

Returning to his seat across from Markus, they both gazed out at the passing landscape before he continued. "Well, it was a disaster from the start. We learned that the Indian troops had been on the transports for three weeks sailing from India. Many were weak or sick, the poor bastards. And get this: several of these units didn't even speak the same language, and most units hadn't seen action in a generation! On top of all that, they had just been issued a new, different rifle two weeks earlier, with almost no hands-on training. Some units didn't even have their allotted two machine guns."

In response, Markus shook his head slightly, with a perplexed look on his face.

"So this is what happened. First of all Tanga is not a good town to invade from the sea because the bay is too shallow for transports, and there are a lot of coral reefs around. But the British thought the town was very lightly defended and would be easy to take . . . and you know what, Markus? It was! There were only fifty policemen in the town for the whole defense!" Levi let out a laugh, and Markus looked puzzled.

"But this is the important part. The night before the attack, the enemy sent in a few lighters, shallow enough to come in close to shore to reconnoiter the landing sites. We spotted them and realized what was up, so they lost the element of surprise."

Levi was gesticulating as he continued, "Vorbeck heard this and immediately dispatched the 7th, 8th, 13th, 16th and 17th field companies plus HQ from around Kilimanjaro, down the railroad to Tanga. I was with headquarters company." Levi smiled. "We arrived about four o'clock in the morning, in time to set up in-depth machine gun defenses between the town and the beaches."

Levi's smile disappeared and his voice changed to a lower and slower cadence. "It was a disaster for them . . . a massacre really. We cut down whole companies of Indian troops, whole companies wiped out, along with their British officers. We learned later that their commander, General Aitken, didn't even land any artillery or the sappers who had grenades and other explosives. And the Royal Navy Cruiser *Fox* was just off shore and didn't fire a shot to assist in the landing of troops . . . not a shot! It's hard to believe the level of incompetence among their general staff—apparently, too little planning and no coordination." He threw up his hands and pursed his lips in an expression of silent amazement.

Markus and Levi sat there discussing how an overwhelming force put together by the British High Command could have bungled such a comparatively easy target. The gross negligence in leadership, they agreed, could never occur in the Imperial German Army.

"Finish the story, my friend. How did it end?" Markus asked. Levi closed his eyes for a moment.

"The end was almost too painful for a professional military man to watch. It was pathetic, really. More Indian troops were landed, and as the earlier troops panicked and ran for the beaches, along with their black porters, through the ranks of the new arrivals, they must have demoralized the new troops! Only the 101st British Grenadiers and the Loyal North Lancasters fought bravely, but to no avail. By the end of the third day, a full retreat was called and an attempt was made for an orderly re-embarkation." Levi paused a moment to take a drag on his cigarette.

"At the end, it turned into a full panic . . . soldiers throwing away their new rifles and wading out into the sea, up to their necks, waiting to be picked up. Some Indian troops tried to swim to the transports and, I imagine, many drowned. Several of our men, using field glasses, actually observed these goings on. Later, we found out that orders were given that all supplies, ammunition, and even machine guns were to be left behind. It was mindless! Senseless!"

"What a story!" Markus said. "It seems the British learned a hard lesson about our ability to defend this colony."

"Yes, and we gained much-needed supplies, equipment, ammunition, and rifles for our *askari*. We'll need all we can get because they'll be back!"

The train slowed as it approached the town of Dar es Salaam. Levi continued to fill Markus in. "Since that failed invasion attempt at Tanga, things have been pretty quiet. We're busy recruiting the white farmers and other colonials, with training camps all over the colony, and we're enlisting large numbers of *askari*. We're going out to the various tribal chiefs and getting them to assist in recruiting porters."

"Five minutes. Dar es Salaam in five minutes," the conductor announced.

Levi ignored him. "Vorbeck is going to need lots of porters. When the enemy invade again, as they surely will, this war will be fought in the bush, inland most times, and far from our railroads. Victory and survival will depend on transport of troops and supplies. Porters are about the only way to carry food and ammunition in this road-less, trackless country."

Markus accepted a cigarette and lit it using Levi's.

"At headquarters, last week, the colonel spelled out how we're going to defend the colony. We'll fight a hit-and-run war—no frontal battles, if we can avoid them, because of the numbers disparity. We'll be outnumbered soon when they invade in force with the British to the north, the Belgians west, the South Africans to the South West, and the Portuguese to our south." Levi looked serious with deep furrows on his face. Before he concluding, "And no outside assistance from the sea, now that the *Konigsberg* is gone."

—— CHAPTER 38 ——

Kalvarianhof, August 1915

So much seemed the same as Katherina gazed out of their upstairs bedroom window at Kalvarianhof, the ancestral estate of the Levis. The lace curtains, freshly washed, were pulled back by her hand on which she wore her wedding ring. The same hand that had dug and scraped at ancient tombs and monuments in Mesopotamia a short twelve months ago, but now it had the slightest tremble when she looked out across the fields to the woods and thought of her husband far off in Africa. It had been a year since she saw him last in Baghdad.

Her precious Levi's last short telegram to her, now months old:

213

AM SAFE. STOP. ALL IS WELL. STOP. AWAITING WORD ON MARKUS. STOP. LOVES ALWAYS. STOP. LEVI. STOP.

She knew telegrams were kept short for military reasons and that, in fact, the relay stations in Togo, Cameroon, and German South West Africa had ceased broadcasting.

But she hoped a letter or a message of some kind, possibly through a neutral country, would arrive. She waited every day for the sound of the postman's bicycle on the gravel road ending at Kalvarianhof, but nothing came. Everything in her world was changing before her eyes it seemed.

How could all this be happening, this war and the deaths? They said thousands, tens of thousands, of soldiers killed in this one year. And Papa, who fled Russia to Uruguay to save his sons, my brothers, from the Tsar's army, now fears they'll be called to service in the Kaiser's army. What he and Mama must be going through!

"Ah, there you are," her father-in-law's voice sounded reassuring. Otto approached her and also pulled back the curtain and looked out.

"It's always beautiful in the summer like this . . . everything in full season."

He glanced sideways at her and knew she was thinking of his son. He put his hand on her arm. "I know, I know. We're all concerned about Levi and this war dragging on as it has."

She put her hand on top of his and forced a slight smile as he continued, "I truly believe he is safer in Africa than if he were fighting in France or Belgium or Poland. This trench fighting is terrible, a bloody hell for our boys. But East Africa is a wide-open country and with fewer people; surely the fighting doesn't amount to much there. You mustn't worry yourself so, Kathi."

He turned her from the window and added, "Let's go down to the kitchen and see what Mama is cooking."

She nodded and took his hand as they walked down the hall to the front staircase, the floor boards creaking in the old house as they went. She was silent the whole way down, and he knew his words helped only a little.

Otto Levi was right about the fighting in France and Belgium; it was hell. It was death and destruction for hundreds of miles along newly dug trenches that zigzagged across shell-cratered earth from the North Sea south to the Swiss border.

In one year of war, the number of casualties was staggering. Hundreds of thousands were dead and untold numbers wounded. Not even Napoleon's plundering of Europe all the way to Moscow, a hundred years earlier, had created such appalling numbers of casualties. It stunned civilians from Berlin to Paris, from St. Petersburg to London, and from Vienna to dozens of other cities.

Gone was the euphoria of the first months of war, with young men rushing to enlist and their sweethearts cheering them on. Now the casualty lists were the dreaded focus, with families scanning the names, hoping their trembling fingers did not stop at a name that would cause untold grief.

In many ways, life went on as before at Kalvarianhof. The fields were tilled; the cows were grazed in the pastures and woods;, timber was cut in the forest but each month, fewer and fewer men were available to work the land. Even Otto and Freidl helped Willie and the few other farmhands with the work, mostly in the barn, taking care of the animals. And there were plenty to feed: six draft horses, two carriage horses, several milk cows, and a sow with nine piglets. Even Otto, in his senior years now, drove the farm wagon out to the fields during haying or cabbage harvest time, something he had not done since his youth. And when the crops were ready, he let it be known in town that he wanted to hire young girls and women to help.

Enlistment posters were everywhere in the village, appealing to patriotic virtue but depleting farm workers. Military parades and recruitment drives stirred young men to do their duty. Chivalry was not dead, and the militarization of the country had gone on for a generation under Bismarck and Kaiser Wilhelm II. It had prepared the population to serve the Fatherland. No one, in late 1915, conceived of the war going badly for Germany.

"Anji is coming for dinner and bringing her new beau!" Frau Levi exclaimed as Otto swung open the door to the kitchen. She had a smile on her face as she busied herself helping the cook prepare fillet of carp with cucumber cream sauce. The cook chopped fruit for the apple carrot salad.

"We'll be served in the dining room. I laid the Meissen, the pattern with the roses; we haven't used it in ages." She hesitated and stopped work. "Not since Levi—since Levi . . ." her voice trailed off and ended with a sniffle.

Katherina came over and hugged Freidl from behind and said almost exactly what Otto had told her a few moments ago up in the bedroom.

"He's safe. I know it, Mama. Africa is big, with few people. How could there be much fighting there?" She looked down at Freidl's hands resting on the breadboard.

"Dinner smells so good and—"

"They're here! Anji and her young man!" Otto said on hearing the bell. He headed for the front door.

"Come, Mama, let's go take a look at this new young man."

Anji flowed through the door as lovely as a summer dream. Her pastel green, floor-length summer dress flowed gently around her body as her companion, Rolf, followed. The first image the Levis had was of the obviously new military uniform.

"Herr Levi, Frau Levi, Katherina, may I introduce Rolf Kepler, Lieutenant, North Bavarian Medical Corps, stationed in Nuremberg, and presently on a five-day leave." Anji was all smiles. "We met in medical school in Munich."

Iron Cross

—— CHAPTER 39 ——

1916: The Greater Peril

"Did you hear? Colonel von Vorbeck received the Iron Cross first class!" Markus, dripping wet, came huffing into the tent he shared with Levi.

"The Iron Cross given by the Kaiser, for the Tanga victory? What an honor!" Levi replied. He sat on his folding chair, examining the railroad maps of the colony next to several candles in the gloom of a rainy evening. "*Ja*, well, you have two Iron Crosses. And one of those is also first class." Smiling, he turned and looked up at Markus. "I suppose I should be grateful to be able to share a dry tent with you."

"A good point," Markus said, "and I suppose that means you'll wring out my wet clothes, right?"

They both had a good laugh.

Markus grew serious, "We just picked up several uncoded wireless messages. The Brits are bringing in native Nigerian and Gold Coast regiments from their colonies to beef up their ranks, now that Cameroon has fallen."

"That's General Smut's work," Levi added, "He's assembling a massive force for a serious invasion. Fortunately for us, the rainy season will last at least several more weeks, and nothing's going to move in these rains."

The rains did stop, and the invasion did come with full intensity. The British navy landed at four sites along the coast and occupied the capitol city Dar es Salaam without a fight. Colonel von Vorbeck evacuated his troops on the eve of the landings. It would have been futile to try to hold the city, see it destroyed, against overwhelming odds. Levi and Markus, having seen the British fleet off the coast, moved out with headquarters company.

"Don't blow the bridge till you hear from me directly, Sergeant. We have to make sure everyone's over, including the baggage train. Those supplies are vital," Captain Levi shouted over the thunder of battle as the rear guard of the German forces retreated toward the doomed bridge.

He was on the safe side of the gully the bridge traversed and could see the puffs of smoke shooting skyward as the coal- and wood-burning locomotive strained under an especially long string of boxcars crammed with military equipment and food from the abandoned city. The last several cars were flatbeds, piled high with sandbags and bristling with machine guns blasting away toward the invaders.

"Hold! Hold—now!" commanded Levi, who, with others, ducked for cover as the last railcars crossed safely. The gully was deep and narrow. The blast charges were set at the base of the train trestle, and when it blew, the blast geysered almost directly skyward. Timbers and rails, rocks and trees and dirt mushroomed into the humid air and began raining down in a surprisingly wide circle.

"Keep that train moving . . . Keep moving!" someone shouted. Several soldiers jumped over the sandbags of the end car and ran into the jungle for protection.

The deafening blast and dust-filled smoke mixed with the sounds of assorted pieces of the trestle slamming down onto the rail bed and surrounding jungle. There was no more shooting from across the gully, but the German soldiers moved quickly out of sight and range of enemy guns.

"Did you manage to collect the telegraph wire?" Levi asked Markus as they both crouched behind a thicket of dense, green foliage, staring across the gully.

"*Ja*, we spooled most of it. It'll be vital in maintaining communications when we're in the bush."

They were silent for a few moments, and then Levi said, "Don't you find it ironic that I came here to repair a bridge, and now I'm asked to blow them up?" He shook his head slightly in disgust. Markus said nothing.

Over the next several months, the combined South African, British, Belgian, and native troops from India, Nigeria, and the Gold Coast pushed Colonel von Vorbeck's army out of the northern half of the colony. But British and South Africans paid an enormous price in men killed, wounded, and, especially, sick.

Some British regiments lost 60-70 percent of their strength, making those units unable to function as a fighting force.

The war in German East Africa, for the invaders, became a war of survival, not from the war as much as against nature herself. Hundreds of troops were lost to lion attacks, elephant attacks, hippo attacks, and from snake bites, poisonous insects, and crocodiles. Nature took an appalling toll.

Diseases like malaria, cholera, swamp blindness, and yellow fever killed or disabled thousands of men, requiring, in many cases, their repatriation home. The logistics were a nightmare for the British, with military units far out beyond their supply and communication lines. It often took weeks for a local commander to send a message to headquarters hundreds of miles away. In some areas of the German colony, extreme dehydration, even starvation, among British troops, was not uncommon.

In addition, the British task of commanding a large army from several nations, many speaking obscure languages, was overwhelming. The fighting was over a vast, inhospitable geography of swamps, jungles, savannahs, and desert-like tracts, ranging in the thousands of square miles. There were numerous mountain ranges, with hundreds of rivers and streams. The two rainy seasons a year made it impossible to move supplies, equipment, and troops during these downpours. All this, while fighting a brilliantly led German colonial army on its own territory led by a guerrilla commander highly revered by both his white officers and his black *askari* soldiers.

All the hardships and expended resources of the British forces were exactly the goal and objective of Colonel von Vorbeck. To engage the enemy in hit-and-run attacks, to avoid entrenched battles where he was overwhelmingly outnumbered, and to tie up vast British resources in Africa for as long as possible was his only objective. British and South African troops and others could not be deployed to fight in France against the Fatherland—if they had to fight in Africa.

Levi had a blanket around his shoulders to ward off the night chill. It was mid-January, 1916, and the rains were slacking off, with day temperatures in the seventies, evenings in the low fifties. Whenever their duties allowed, Levi and Markus tented together

The dwindling numbers of able-bodied German troops continued in high spirits, even as the forced marches seldom eased up. It was a will of the wisp campaign, at least that's how the British saw the campaign.

Through good scouting, the Germans were able to choose when and how to attack, taking advantage of their knowledge of the terrain. In most cases, the strategy was simple: ambush, sustain attack until nightfall, then slip away, and be gone by dawn.

The British forces were constantly in the position of having to react to German maneuvers, not knowing when or where the next battle would be. This type of warfare was very hard on the morale of the British forces. Many of them called Vorbeck a ghost, an apparition never to be caught.

After one battle, a British soldier was captured, Lance Corporal Hopper of the 25th Royal Fusiliers. In his possession was his personal diary. Levi, one of the officers who questioned the young prisoner, "borrowed" the diary with the promise of returning it.

"Here, Markus," Levi ducked into their tent, "I just finished reading this. It's the diary of one of the prisoners." He handed it to his friend who rolled over in his cot.

"What?" Markus rubbed his eyes.

"It's a prisoner's diary. Very revealing, I think. The poor man just wants to go home . . . like the rest of us."

Markus sat up, took a drink of water from a tin cup, and flipped through the pages. "He's quite a writer."

"Read on."

Markus read the well-penciled lines in the fifty-page book, about half of them written on. He settled back on his cot. As he moved from page to page, line to line, the anonymous soldier's life unfolded.

"He enlisted in the heady autumn days of 1914, from the little village of Castle Comb. His two brothers did, too. One of them, Roger, was killed only a few weeks after joining up, during bayonet training. He was accidentally impaled by one of the other recruits. It was an appalling event for the two remaining brothers and had taken the high adventure out of their enlistment."

Markus read page after page and saw a version of himself in some of the writings. Near the end of the diary, with notations of only a week or so ago, Markus was startled to read a very forthright description of the morale of Lance Corporal Roger Hooper of the 25th Royal Fusiliers:

The officers are brutes and seem only to be interested in winning medals and glory. They got three or four porters each while we enlisted have to share one porter between the two of us. He's to carry our food, his food, water, ammunition, camp gear, and all. We end up having to carry most of it ourselves, and we have to pay the bloke out of our wages, and he only takes silver.

We've been on half-rations for over a week, while the officers got full rations. Our supply train is always late and seems half-plundered when it does get here.

We lost so many of our boys to disease, much more than from fighting. If I get too sick, maybe they'll send me home like the others.

Markus slowly closed the diary and handed it back to Levi, who was sitting, watching him, and asked, "What do you think of that?"

"I think he's a sorry 'bloke,' as the British say, probably like a thousand others on our side, too. It's hard to hate a soldier like that. For God's sake, we were allies in China! He's right, of course, illness among the British forces is a major reason for their failure to achieve greater success, thank God. You know, they use large contingents of white troops and native troops from far afield of East Africa. Those troops have little to no resistance to local varieties of diseases and pestilence."

Levi lit a cigarette and asked Markus if he wanted one. Markus shook his head. Levi continued, "On the other hand, we're making great use of a lot of native *askari* troops, with relatively few whites. And we give our black troops a lot of leadership positions in their ranks. It's good for their morale."

Markus finally spoke , "Colonel von Vorbeck told me that the most important advantage we have over the British forces, health wise, is that we've got a superior medical staff. Before the war, German medical teams were studying sleeping sickness and other diseases here and were even growing their own supply of quinine for malaria. So we have an unusually large number of doctors who can treat wounds and sickness in the field. I really never thought about that, but it's a big advantage."

"*Ja* and we know how to live off the land, make do, and improvise; that's for sure. Now it's time to get some rest."

When they needed supplies, ammunition, and medicine, Vorbeck found that raiding poorly defended Portuguese forts across the southern border in Portuguese East Africa was the easiest, richest source. Portuguese outposts were raided many times, and as it happened, the commander ordered a raiding party to again strike south.

In an unexpected move, the colonel ordered Markus to accompany the raiding party. It was on the strength of the fact that Captain Mathias had made contact with a German, Herr Leopold, who had a wireless in Portuguese East Africa.

Markus was to make contact, if possible, and assuming Leopold still had the wireless, to send a message to a neutral country to have it relayed to Berlin. The neutral country was the Kingdom of Abyssinia, in North Africa. Germans in Abyssinia would pass the message on to Berlin.

"Do you know what the message is about?" Levi asked on hearing Markus's order.

"Only the gist of it. It has to do with a supply ship disguised as a tramp freighter Berlin is sending; it's about a rendezvous site along the coast."

"That's going to be a clever trick!" Levi said in surprise. "The whole British navy is offshore!"

A messenger came up to them: "Sir, the raiding party will pull out in about an hour."

Markus nodded as Levi continued, "And the idea of finding Leopold . . . He could be anywhere, even interned. He's German! And him with a working wireless . . . what are the chances of that? You'll be searching like that Stanley character who went looking for Livingston. Remember how long that took!"

The rains had stopped, and they waited outside for breakfast to be prepared. "It's not like a few months ago," Levi continued in a moderate tone. "The Portuguese are getting better at defense, and who knows? The Brits might be down there, too . . . No, they *will* be down there! I know; I know; you don't have a say in this, but it doesn't make much sense to me, to send you. The supplies, yes; finding Leopold, no." The two shared a cigarette; one took a draw, then the other.

"I'll take every precaution, and I'll be with a company of cavalry."

"Well, I just want to get you home in one piece . . . to that lovely Helena of yours and your baby son."

"*Ja, natürlich. Danke*, but you're in just as much danger here as I'll be there. We've got the Belgians coming across Lake Tanganyika and the whole British army coming down from the north." Markus paused. "What do you think the colonel's up to now? We've been pushed out of three quarters of our colony!"

Levi appeared to be happy the conversation changed to something else. "The colonel will come up with a clever strategy; he's a masterful tactician. I predict we double back and head north while the Brits chase us south . . . something like that. It's a big country, and the dense cover is good for us. We'll pass them in the night!"

They both had a good laugh because that was a tactic they had used for the last year and a half. The laugher felt good. They both needed a break from the tension, but it didn't last long. Both men were in real danger—along with the whole German army in the colony. And now, after a month of being together again, they would be off in opposite directions.

During breakfast, they sat at a folding table in a tent. They wolfed down their tin plates of zebra steaks in thick gravy made from goat's milk. The friends washed it down with a rich African coffee grown fifty miles to the west. Markus didn't want to tell Levi the details of his mission. He knew he would not approve, but he felt he had to be honest with his old friend: "The raiding party is heading for the Newala garrison, just across the border. Vorbeck somehow got word that Leopold moved his trading office north to Palma, on the coast. The raiders will return here, and I'm riding on with five other volunteers." Markus looked at Levi, busy forking in his breakfast. "All five were German settlers before crossing over the border and enlisting here. They all speak Portuguese."

He paused, bit his lip, and continued, "We'll switch to British uniforms, after the raid, and head directly to Palma. The Portuguese troops will think we're British. We hope to find Leopold there with his wireless and the broadcast codes for our friends in Abyssinia. If all goes to plan, I'll be back in three weeks."

"British uniforms! What?" Levi sputtered. "If you're caught, you'll be shot! Three weeks? Are you kidding?" Levi was not upset; he was angry.

There was a long silence. Then Levi said, in a low voice, "You like this. Don't you? . . . The excitement of it, the thrill of going . . . the danger. It's like in China when you went to find Li Ling through a land full of murderous, imperial guards . . . or it's like your flying. You almost killed yourself!" He looked disgusted, turned in his chair, got up, and walked away. Markus got up and left to head south.

The raiding party was gone over a week. Late one evening, they were back. "What"? What's the commotion?" Levi rolled out of his cot and landed on his knees. He fumbled around for matches and lit a candle. *It must be near midnight,* he thought as he hurriedly pulled on his pants and boots, grabbed his shirt, and ducked out of his tent.

The raiding party was returning in disorder. Several low-ranking troopers who arrived first were gesturing wildly as they talked with Colonel von Vorbeck. More of the cavalry unit arrived, with some troopers leaning over in their saddles, obviously wounded. Three, four-horse wagons pulled up in a cloud of dust made visible by several dozen hastily lit lanterns. They were loaded with the stolen supplies, but several men were either sitting or lying on top. Their horses were nowhere in sight, although three riderless horses trotted in on their own and headed for the corral to feed. In the dim light, Levi recognized only a few of the troopers.

"Sergeant! Sergeant, over here!" Levi shouted. The soldier pulled his reins back and sideways and his mount responded.

"What's your situation?" Levi questioned.

"Yes, sir, we overran the fort all right. Gathered the best of what was there, mostly ammunition, guns, and food . . . some medical supplies." His horse wanted to go to the corral and tried to move off.

"Steady, boy, steady." The sergeant pulled back on the reins.

"What happened was, a scouting party of British cuirassiers intercepted us just before the border, which is no border at all, at this time, sir." He looked back at the rear guard just coming into camp.

"It was a running battle. We're lucky to have saved the wagons. We lost several *askari* and got some wounded." He nodded toward the soldiers being unloaded from the wagon.

"Our rear guard did a hell of a good job. Sir."

"Thank you, Sergeant. Carry on."

Levi's mind would not stop: I knew it! I knew the Brits would be over there. I told him they'd be there. And he in a British uniform, for God's sake. I can't talk any sense into him. He's always getting into trouble. He headed back to his tent through the dark to a night of fitful sleep.

Royal Portuguese Crest

—— CHAPTER 40 ——

Portuguese East Africa:
General Albuquerque

We found them several miles west of Palma, Commandante. We thought they looked suspicious, riding double like that. A British patrol would have fresh mounts. Their horses looked like they'd be dead in another day or two," the Portuguese corporal reported.

"Very good, Corporal. Where are they now?" asked General Albuquerque.

"We have them in the blockhouse storage room, the empty one, sir. They didn't put up a fight this time. Those Germans usually do."

"Fine, bring the five here, Corporal," the General commanded.

It had been almost a week since Markus and his volunteers left the cavalry unit at Newala. They hadn't participated in the raid, but immediately moved east toward Palma. The five of them knew they were in big trouble now, having been captured wearing British uniforms. They were all scared and nervous, but stoic.

General Joaquim Augusto Mouzinho de Albuquerque, regal in his uniform, sat behind his perfectly ordered desk. The five prisoners filed in and stood at attention, their British pith helmets low over their eyes. Silence.

The six guards with fixed bayonets stood behind the Germans. The general's eyes lingered on each prisoner. There was no noticeable recognition revealed by him.

"So, finally we have captured one of your raiding parties." His smooth voice in accented German was detached and distant, as if he had duties to perform that were not to his liking.

"Five German soldiers disguised as British." He looked at the five. "Why? What could five German soldiers be doing on this side of the border and in British uniforms? Lost? No. A raiding party? Too small. Assassins? Unlikely. Who is there to kill?" He chuckled to himself. The guards smiled.

After a few moments he said, "You must be looking for something . . . but what?" All these self-answered questions were spoken aloud, as Albuquerque watched carefully for any slight sign from the men before him.

"Yes, looking for something . . . or waiting for something or someone. Who or what could it be?" Another long pause. "And to risk your lives . . . wearing British uniforms. Most dangerous, don't you think? And for what? It's an interesting question."

He stopped talking, leaned back in his chair, and stared past his captives into empty space. *Spies*, he thought, *but for what?*

"You know, of course, our friends," he rephrased it, "our allies, the British, would see you as spies and have you shot immediately. I'm not so impulsive. I'm curious . . . I'm curious to know what you hoped to gain with this intrusion."

After a time, he said, "Dismissed. See they are fed."

Markus was in a dilemma. He was surprised, and in a way, glad to see General Albuquerque. He was sure he had not been recognized while in the general's office.

Should I reveal myself? What's to be gained? What lost? We're being treated well, he thought, as he shoveled the wild-meat stew down with a big spoon. At least we haven't been shot. Maybe I should approach the general. I wonder how he would react. I'd better act fast.

Early the next morning, Markus called out, "Guard, Guard." The sleepy Portuguese guard came to the heavy wooden door.

"It's early. What you want?"

Markus had to speak through a crack in the door. "Tell the general I need to speak to him. Tell him I'm the . . ." Markus almost said 'German.' "I'm the man from South West Africa who needed a horse to Quelimane. Please tell him that."

"All right, all right, German, but not now; it's too early."

Markus thought, *I'm not fooling anybody.*

He sat back down on the stone floor with the others in the blockhouse storage room. Several of his companions were already plotting an escape, searching the dark, near-empty room for weaknesses and weapons. One German mused, "We could probably pry the door open, but then what? We'd need horses . . . and time. At least these Portuguese are easy to overcome."

Markus spoke up, "Oh, really? Is that why we're here, and they have the guns and horses? We found out it's not so easy; it's not like a year ago." He startled himself in remembering that was exactly what Levi had warned him about.

Later, Markus was escorted to General Albuquerque's office. The general was busy signing papers and didn't look up when the captain was brought in. The general spoke with a dry, matter-of-fact tone: "I've just been informed a combined British-South African military unit will be arriving in the next day or two in preparation for the invasion of your colony. They will probably want to dispatch the five of you expeditiously. Tell me, why I shouldn't let—" he stopped in midsentence when he looked up.

He stared at the man in front of him. Finally, he spoke, "Captain Mathias, yes, yes of course, it is you."

"Yes, sir. I'm afraid it is."

"I assume you reached your intended destination months ago."

"Yes, sir, with your help, for which I am very grateful."

"And now you're back and under slightly different circumstances . . . dangerous circumstances. And what am I to do this time? Put you atop another supply wagon for the coast?" The general exhibited a wily smile. "At ease, Captain. Come; sit down."

Markus came round and sat in a wooden chair.

Albuquerque sat slumped in his chair across his desk from Markus. He stared at his captive a few moments before offering, "Life throws us into inexplicable circumstances; don't you think, Captain?"

Markus was about to reply when the general raised his hand slightly. Markus held his tongue.

"Do you think God is punishing you, consigning you to the end of the world—and to me?" His arm swung out, sweeping the room as if it were his entire world.

"Look at you, a young man in the prime of life . . . You're married. I see the ring. And yet, here you sit in another country's uniform, at the edge of death. Why? What are you doing here? Why are you not home with your wife in the hops-growing hills of Germany?" He laughed to himself at his little joke.

Markus sat in silence, perplexed at the strange conversation. *Is he drunk?* Markus thought.

"And I . . . to see again my estate in the hills of Lisbon. That was a different world, a different time . . . and gone." The general wasn't staring at the soldier in front of him but at lost visions of an earlier life.

Markus sat awkwardly, his eyes diverted but glancing back at the slumped figure behind the desk. Three light raps on the door broke the silence.

"Enter." The general snapped back to his real world and sat up in his chair. "Yes, Sergeant, what is it?"

"Should we prepare," he hesitated, looking at Markus, "the firing squad, sir?"
What? Oh, for God's sake! thought Markus, squirming in his chair.

"Not now, Sergeant. Leave us." The sergeant took a long look at the prisoner again and then at the general. "Yes, sir." The door clicked behind him.

"You see the situation you're in?" Albuquerque shuffled papers on his desk, picked them up, and slammed them down hard. "I can't save you and your men!" he shouted. "Those British bastards and their friends the South Africans are salivating over our colony. Any suggestion that we are in any way helping you Germans, and they'll invade us! Chop us up, just like they intend to do to your colony. All they want is more land, and they'll turn on anyone to get it."

He had risen out of his chair in his rage, then sat back down. Markus was white as a ghost on hearing such a fatalistic declaration.

"So, now you know your fate. Are you going to tell me what you could possibly gain from being here? You don't have to worry that I'll tell the bastards."

Markus shifted in his seat and cleared his throat, thinking if he should gamble everything and reveal his mission. *It may be my only chance to save my men*, he thought. *Can I trust General Albuquerque?* He decided in an instant to tell a much-altered version of the truth and hope it would appeal to the general's sympathies.

"General, we need medicine badly. Our troops—and particularly our civilians—are suffering from all manner of illness. We haven't been resupplied since before the war; that's . . ." he thought a moment, "over two years ago." He stopped to let that sink in.

"I was sent to try to find a supply ship flying a neutral Danish flag for cover that was, no, is, supposed to pull into one of your many small, secluded coves. We were going to steal a couple of wagons and hoped to pass as British troops. We didn't think Portuguese soldiers would challenge us. We didn't know the British were already here."

"You weren't captured by the British. You were captured by Portuguese troops. You didn't fool anybody!" The general shook his head. "What a foolish plan. You had ten-to-one odds of succeeding. And now you all will be charged with spying, and the price of spying is, well, you know what the price is. The British will probably be here tomorrow. As we are allies with the British and the British have overall command, they will convene a military court. It will take less than an hour. The sentence will be carried out immediately after. I wish there was something I could do." He crushed out a cigarette that had been smoldering in an ash-filled bowl.

"I'll end up in that blockhouse if I do anything," he continued, "and the whole colony will suffer."

They looked at each other, the general thinking what a fine soldier Markus was. *There will be thousands of fine young men that will die in this war, some from this colony. What is one more death? But I know this man, a fine man . . . and he will die for what, for wearing another nation's uniform? Or to get medicine, or whatever the true story is? I escaped death back home in Portugal. Now this captain hopes to escape death here.*

Markus sat patiently, watching. The general shook his head slightly. Markus noticed the moment.

Albuquerque called out, "Corporal!" The door opened. "Take the captain back with the others."

Back with his troops, Markus sat down on the dusty floor, and in a level voice, he said, "We've got to bust out of here, or it's over for us. When the British arrive here in a day or two, they'll try us as spies, and that will be it. Anyone have a plan?"

There was no reply.

"I really thought the general would be sympathetic." Markus thought about it for a moment and added, "Well, actually he was sympathetic, but he can't do anything on our behalf. It's up to us."

"We could jump the two guards who bring us food. That would get us at least through that door."

Markus looked at his companion who had spoken and countered, "Then what?"

"Then we take their guns and make a break for the horses." He was looking at Markus.

Markus replied, "Remember when they feed us? It's during the busiest time of the day; everyone's up and around. Getting horses out of this fort in daylight is impossible. There's got to be another way."

Everyone was silent, exchanging smokes, and resting as best each could on the hard floor. Rudy, one of the five, lying on his back trying to relax, was talking to one of his companions: "It would be nice to see the snow again in the Alps. That's what I think about a lot . . . hiking in summer and still seeing the snow way high in the mountains." He swung his arm up, "I'm saying way up in the—" He stopped. He was staring up at the ceiling.

"Look up there!" he said.

His companion looked up. "So?"

Rudy got to his feet and was straining his neck, looking up. No one else paid attention to him.

"It's made of wood . . . timbers and cross boards looks like. And there's light coming through over on the edge." The ceiling was at least eighteen feet off the floor. "If we could get up there, we could maybe knock some of them loose. What do you think?" His companions looked up also.

"*Ja*, but how are you going to get up there? Even the tallest two of us, standing on shoulders, couldn't come near reaching the ceiling." The others stirred on listening to the conversation.

Rudy spoke again, with an edge of excitement in his voice: "Rainer, remember our gymnasium classes when we built the pyramids? The human pyramids? Maybe we can do that here." Markus got up, and the other three followed.

"What's this pyramid talk?"

"Rudy's got this idea that we could build a human pyramid and bust through the ceiling." Everyone was looking at Rainer. One spoke up, "But we need more men to build one tall enough to reach the ceiling."

"No, no, wait," Rudy replied as he walked to the corner of the stock room with his back against the corner of the wall.

"We can use the two walls to substitute for the four men who'd normally be on the bottom of the pyramid. If we have just two men on the bottom and then one man on their shoulders, then another man on his shoulders, and then the lightest of us on his shoulders, we can reach the ceiling!" Rudy was pacing in a circle, looking up. Everyone else was looking up, too.

"I think you've got something there, Rudy!" Markus said.

Someone asked, "But will the guys on the bottom be able to support the three on the top?"

Another voice, "Let's try it!"

"First, who're the heaviest two men here? *Ja, Ja,* you two, into the corner, backs to the two walls. Plant your feet apart. That's right. Now, who's next?"

Everyone looked at each other.

"We're all pretty much the same," someone said.

Markus came forward. "I'll be the next one up, then you, and finally you, Rudy. You're the lightest one here."

The dimly lit room had no windows. The light from under the big wooden door and traces of light piercing down from cracks in the wooden ceiling were all the illumination they needed.

"Take your boots off."

"*Ja, ja.*"

All but the two bottom men took off their cavalry boots. Those two men cupped their hands in front of themselves as steps to their shoulders.

Markus came forward. "Steady, men, ready?"

He stepped into the cupped hands. They gave him a boost, and he was up. He gingerly turned around, one foot on each man.

"Good, good. Next!"

The fourth man of the five put his foot into the cupped hands. He had also to stand on the shoulders of the two bottom men. They held firm. Markus cupped his hands in front of himself and the fourth man slowly shifted his weight to one foot while lifting his leg to put his foot into Markus's entwined fingers.

"Wait, wait! Not yet! Is everyone ready?"

Every man in the pyramid let out a *Ja*.

The fourth man slowly shifted his weight into Markus's hands. "Easy now . . . Take your time," He rose as Markus lifted his cupped hands to chest height. Markus could feel him slowly step onto his shoulders, one foot at a time. The fourth man's legs were trembling as he pressed himself against the walls.

"I'm good. I'm good!" he said as sweat beaded on his forehead. Markus had his hands up, griping the two trembling legs of the man above him.

"OK, Rudy, your turn,"

The man who thought up the idea stepped toward the bottom of the human pyramid. "When I get to the top, I may have to push up. That's going to put pressure on all of you, so be ready," Rudy started his climb.

"Slowly, slowly . . . Slow down!" Everyone was tense and straining and sweating. Rudy was up, with his face inches away from Markus's. "Ease your foot in . . . a bit higher. That's it," Suddenly, the top man shouted, "Coming down!"

It was as if he had stepped back from the wall into space. He fell feet first, straight down, knocking Rudy off balance and out of Markus's cupped hands. Markus, destabilized, knew he was going to fall and pushed off from the shoulders he was standing on, in a leap that cleared him of the two others sprawled beneath him.

Rudy tumbled and rolled—just as he was taught in the gymnasium. Markus also broke his fall by rolling halfway across the blockhouse floor. The fourth man came straight down. It was a ten-foot drop onto a stone floor. The three fallen comrades got up quickly, with number four limping around the room.

"I'll be all right. I'll be all right. Just got to walk it off."

Everyone gathered around him. "Are you sure?"

"Yes, yes, it's nothing, really."

They all sat down with their backs to the wall, the smell of sweat permeating the still air. Number four rubbed his ankle.

Markus suggested, "Let's think this through. The pyramid collapse was just an accident. I still think this could work. We just have to be more careful. How was the load for you bottom guys?"

"We'll have sore shoulders, but we can handle the weight, right?" He was looking at his companion.

"*Ja, ja*, no problem."

Rudy raised an essential question: "How are we going to get everybody up there, if we actually break through the roof?"

They all looked at Rudy and then at Markus.

"We don't have a rope or anything to make one with," Markus concluded. "If we did have a rope, our top man, Rudy here, could tie it around that timber up there. Do you see it? There's some space between it and the roof. I saw it while I was climbing. We've got to figure out how to get us all up there before we risk our necks climbing again." Markus said in frustration.

"*Ja*, but how?"

Several men had stretched out and were dozing. The only real moveable object in the storage room was a slop bucket for the men to relieve themselves in. Several hours passed with a bit of small talk and a bit of sleep.

"Maybe we should go back to the idea of breaking through the door." The suggestion was met with silence.

The quiet was broken when the guards banged on the door. "Your food. The five of you stand against the far wall," ordered the corporal.

The captives complied, and the door opened slightly. One of the guards peered in.

"All clear!" The door swung open fully, revealing four rifles with bayonets pointing into the room. The soldiers came into the room slowly, followed by two others carrying a large basket with three bottles of wine, several loaves of bread, cheese, and boiled eggs. The other soldier spoke as he put down a covered soup pot and five spoons: "General Albuquerque insisted you get a nice meal."

The guard glanced around. "Why you have your boots off"?

"To rest our feet, why else?" someone said hastily. The guards backed out, and the sound of a heavy bolt and lock could be heard.

All five Germans descended on the basket, the wine, the bread, and the soup. Fortunately, someone had uncorked the wine, so it was easy for the five to pass the bottles around. They all sat down around the soup pot and dipped in with the extra-large serving spoons that came with the pot.

"Good, very good. These Portuguese eat well here." After everyone had his fill, not a crumb was left.

The soldiers were again stretched out on the floor, exchanging escape ideas. One of the group sat on the slop pot in the far corner of the room, doing his business. Army life had conditioned men to ignore the unpleasant bodily needs of each other. After only a casual glance by Markus, caused Markus to sit up and stare at his 'potted' companion.

"What are you looking' at? Christ!" the soldier muttered. The others looked at him and then at Markus.

"That's it! That's what we need. That'll be our rope!" Markus blurted out.

"What? What rope?" someone asked, looking back and forth between the two men.

"His pants!" Markus pointed toward his unfortunate companion. The pot sitter looked down between his legs at the crumpled up pants at his feet.

"What?"

"We take all our pants and tie them together, leg to leg . . . They should reach to the ceiling . . . or from the ceiling to the floor, I mean." Markus got up and turned to the group. "That's how we get everybody up!"

The pot sitter got up and pulled up his pants.

"No. Wait!" Markus exclaimed.

"*Ja*, so, everyone take off your pants. We have to test the strength of our breeches." Everyone got up and hesitated a moment and then started unfastening their belts. "You two, tie your pant legs together; we'll do the same." In short order, five cavalry breeches were strung together.

"Now what?" someone asked.

"Its tug-of-war time, gentlemen. Two on one side and three on the other." Both teams had to back into opposite corners to give them room to stretch their "rope."

"Now, start easy. No jerking." They all leaned into opposite directions.

"That's quite a strain on the seams, but they're holding," number four grunted.

"Good, that should do it. Now, it's back to pyramid building."

After several more attempts and another collapse, the group finally reached the ceiling. Rudy brought up one of the big spoons and was using it to pry loose the few rusty nails holding the overlapping boards together.

"I'm going to push now. Get ready." The four beneath him braced as best they could.

One of the bottom supporters blurted out between clenched teeth, "Hurry up!"

"How long can you hold?" Markus asked.

"Two minutes!"

"I got it! I got the board loose. Working on the second."

"Hurry up, for Christ's sake!"

"OK, Rudy, stop work. Come down." Coming down was as dangerous as going up, maybe more so. All the men were strained to the limit. Rudy made it down in seconds, almost sliding past his companions. All of them again sprawled out, sweating, on the cool stone floor.

"Good, very good," Markus gasped. "Next time, we take our 'rope' up."

After fifteen minutes of rest, Markus was about to order the men up for another try. They all heard it at the same time: The door bolt scraping, metal against metal.

"Everyone against the far wall!" The guard shouted. In a panic, everyone looked to Markus, but Rudy quickly said, "I'll play sick on the pile of pants!" He quickly gathered the tied-together breeches and lay on top of them, hiding as best he could the knotted parts.

The door opened far enough for one guard to peek in. "Why's he on the floor?"

Markus spoke up, "He's sick. I told him not to eat so much. You were too generous in giving so much food . . . He wouldn't stop eating. We told him."

The guard withdrew his head, and the five could hear the guards talking outside the door. The door creaked as it swung open. Bayonets again protruded into the supply room jail. The guards slowly entered the gloomy space, especially particularly alert.

"Why you have your pants off? Keep your backs to us!" One of the guards came over to Rudy and lightly kicked his leg.

"You sick?"

Rudy just mumbled and moaned.

"Why you have your pants off?" The lead guard shouted in anger.

"We were just having fun, grabbing each other, just horse play, till Rudy got sick. Then we let him lie on top of our pants till he feels better." Markus hoped the thin story would work.

"Horsy play? Grab each other?" The lead guard looked back and forth between Rudy and the four standing there in their briefs. "This is filthy game . . . You all going to hell tomorrow." He motioned for his troops to gather up the basket, bottles, and the pot. They left quickly, with disgusted looks on their faces.

Number four was the first to break out in deep, throaty laughter. The others joined in the hysterics. "He thought we were grabbing our privates!"

They all continued enjoying the deception till Markus motioned to quiet down, lest the guards return. "*Ja*, back to work now, while we still have some light."

The pyramid went up, and then Rudy went up, and before long, he was through the roof. An opening of two feet by about four feet let in the dimming light of dusk.

The plan was to tie the "rope" to the wooden beam next to the hole in the roof. After this was done, the pyramid came back down. The bottom breeches leg dangled five feet from the floor.

"Perfect!" exclaimed Rudy. All the men were pleased at their success and showed it with grins all around.

"What did you see outside when you stuck you head out, Rudy?"

"Nothing, except the walls of the fort and the distant landscape. This blockhouse is just about the height of the outer walls. No one was on the ramparts."

"Good. We don't want to stay here any longer then we have to. I suggest we wait another fifteen or twenty minutes for darkness before we go up." Everyone nodded in agreement. While waiting, each pair of boots was tied together with a short strip of cloth torn from shirts. The boots were swung around the neck, leaving hands free for climbing.

"It's time." Without a word, Rudy led the group to the rope. They formed the pyramid one last time, with the exception that Markus said he would be the last up.

Rudy shimmied up the last four feet of rope and was soon lying flat on the roof, looking down the hole. The next man on the pyramid had a longer climb up the rope but was soon lying next to Rudy. Markus had replaced one of the bottom men and tilted his head so he could see the third man scramble through the hole with the help of willing hands pulling him up.

Just two men remained on the blockhouse floor. Markus cupped his hands so his companion could step in, and with a boost, he was on Markus's shoulders.

"Up you go," Markus said. The man grabbed the rope and went hand over hand as he "walked" up the wall.

He reached the top and grabbed the timber holding the rope just as a sharp "bang" rang out. Markus immediately thought it was a gunshot. In a second, he realized the timber had snapped. The men on the roof lunged for their friend. Too late! He plunged backward toward the floor, bringing a cascade of roof boards behind him, trailed by the descending rope. He fell without a sound, his back arched, head first, toward the stone floor, just missing Markus.

He landed with a sickening smack as his skull split open, followed by a clatter of boards piling around and on top of him. The rope, pulled by the beam, fell into a pile on top of the grisly scene. The men on the roof, one of whom almost fell in, stared in disbelieve.

"Jesus, Mary and Joseph!"

"Christ Almighty!" another said. "How is he?"

"Are you all right, Captain?" The gasps and questions came one after another.

"I'm all right!" Markus frantically pulled several boards away from his companion soldier and looked down into his face. It was completely peaceful, but the rapidly growing pool of blood indicated his companion was dead.

"Lancer Helmut is dead!" he announced looking up.

Silence for a few moments, then from above, "Now what are we going to do?"

Royal Portuguese Flag

—— CHAPTER 41 ——

The Great Escape

L ay low; keep quiet; and give me a minute," Markus pleaded while his mind was racing. *There's no way I can get up through the hole in the roof. They're going to have to go on without me.*

"Listen up, men," he started. "You're going to have to go on without me. Make your way back across the border and join up with our troops. Tell Vorbeck that I'll try to—" He was interrupted by shouts in Portuguese and a great commotion.

"Go!" Markus shouted. The heads disappeared from the jagged opening as he heard scrambling on the roof. Garbled orders were shouted, and before Markus could imagine what was going on above him, he heard rifle fire that thundered in the night air. Twenty, thirty, maybe fifty shots Markus heard from above, like rain on a tin roof.

And then silence—except for a slight creeping noise from above. He looked up and squinted. Slowly, a head emerged in the hole. Rudy! His head, suspended for a moment, plopped down as rhythmic spurts of blood, pumped by his heart, showered his life away in a crimson mist floating to the floor.

For a moment, Markus was overcome by grief. "God in Heaven!" he exclaimed, stepping back to avoid being covered with the life-giving fluid. He wiped tears from his eyes. "They're gone. All of them!" he gasped aloud. "Now . . . now what?"

He pulled the rope to him and began untying the knot above and below his breeches. His eyes were so misted up he could hardly see.

"God, these knots are so tight!" He heard running. The last knot came loose just as he heard the scraping of the latch and lock on the big wooden door. He threw himself against the wall behind the door, just as it swung open. He clutched his pants to his chest and with the other, he reached up and allowed his fingertips to curl over the top of the door to keep it from swinging out from the wall.

Five or six guards scurried into the room, looked up at the huge hole in the roof, and then down at the body.

"He's dead! The rest are on the roof! Let's go!" the leader ordered. "Carlos, you stay here." They were gone in seconds. Markus held his breath and finally breathed a sigh of relief.

He peered around the corner of the door, saw the Portuguese soldier bending over the dead man and slowly swung the door away from the wall. A slight creak! He stopped, stepped sideways, stepped gingerly toward the guard and bent down.

The splintered board was three feet long. As Markus lifted it, he slightly dislodged others. The guard picked up on the slight movement and turned his head just as Markus gave a mighty swing of the board. It caught the soldier just below his nose. The bushy mustache was no help in cushioning the blow. He fell back onto the pile and slid to the side. Markus quickly closed the door, looked up to see if anyone was looking down, and grabbed the unconscious man, rolling him over. Rapidly he unbuttoned the shirt and pants and pulled off his boots.

In moments, Markus was standing in a Portuguese corporal's uniform. He had taken off his pants and shirt and put them on the still unconscious man. He looked around quickly and decided to pull the Portuguese closer to the debris pile and threw several boards on top of him.

Grabbing the rifle, he opened the door and looked out. No one was in the hall. He crept quickly down the short hall past the empty guardroom and peered outside.

Soldiers were milling around, looking up as several on the roof were dragging the dead Germans to the edge. One of the bodies was rolled off the roof and fell the two stories to the ground. Markus had to look away.

Act like one of them! Where to go? He worked his way away from the crowd to the side of a low, stone building that turned out to be the officers' quarters.

Several men, obviously officers, came out hurriedly, one buttoning his coat. They headed for the blockhouse. Someone yelled, "Three dead here!" Someone else yelled, "Are you sure? Look again. There should be four up there!" It was completely dark by now, with lanterns giving only weak light.

"One might be off the edge over here!" Markus heard from the roof.

He felt relatively safe in the shadows with little order to the troop's movements. Some soldiers drifted back to wherever they had been earlier. The stables, he thought, but how to get out the gate with a horse?

Someone again yelled up to the men on the roof: "There're two in the blockhouse . . . That makes your five."

So I fooled them so far, but for how long? I can't just stand here all night.

Most of the soldiers drifted indoors, with only a few hanging back, smoking and talking. There was only one guard on duty at the gate, as far as Markus could tell.

Suddenly from inside the blockhouse came a cry: "It's Carlos! It's Carlos! It's not the German! One of them got away!" This brought half the troops back into the plaza in front of the blockhouse. Most were bare-chested or in various stages of dress. Some were even barefoot. Several officers reappeared, went into the blockhouse, and returned shortly, leading Carlos out. He was bloodied but coherent.

"He came from behind the door, I guess, and hit me with a board. That's all I know—except I'm wearing his . . . his things." Markus's sense of relative safety vanished quickly.

"Call the garrison to general quarters! Assemble the men. Form search parties. Search every building and possible hiding place. Send out some mounted troops to patrol the immediate perimeter of the fort!"

"Si, Comandante!" The bugler sounded assembly. Soldiers were pouring out of the barrack, some dragging their rifles as they tucked in their shirts.

"And," General Albuquerque added, "I want to see the faces of the dead Germans. Clean them up immediately and bring several lanterns."

He paced back and forth as he waited for his orders to be carried out. Markus stepped way back into the deepest, darkest corner he could get to and watched.

They're going to find me for sure if I don't think of something fast.

The soldiers, directed in squads of six or eight, searched different locations within the fort.

None were coming in his direction at the moment. He scanned the roof. *No, they'll find me for sure up there.* He looked towards to stable. *That'll get searched down to the last straw. The barracks! Crazy! Back to the blockhouse? Where will that leave me? No. The officers' quarters—possibly.*

Suddenly several soldiers appeared right in front of him. "Did you find anything?" one of them said.

"No, nothing here," Markus replied as he made an exaggerated act of looking around.

"We haven't looked over there yet." He pointed. The two soldiers were young and weren't even carrying a lantern.

Do they even know what they're doing? The thought flashed through his mind. *No time for that now.*

He maneuvered over to the officers' quarters and found a back window. Very faint candle light barely illuminated the room.

Looks like it's the general's office. He moved sideways slightly to get a better view of different parts of the room. He tried to remember what it looked like when he was there just a day earlier. *Voices! A squad!*

"Which squad are you with, Soldier?" The question pierced the night.

"Which squad are you?" Returned Markus, in the best Portuguese he could muster. "We just finished this area."

"We're 'F' squad. And you?"

"A." As soon as "F" squad disappeared, Markus was back at the window.

Glancing in quickly and seeing no one, he tried the window. The sun-bleached frame slid up easily. He was in within seconds, but he banged the rifle on the floor and thought for sure he had given himself away. He froze. He waited. No sounds.

Walking gently, Markus looked for a hiding place. He leaned the rifle into a corner and examined a large chest along one wall. It had a long lid and was at least six feet long and three feet high. There was space behind it, but not quite enough for him to lie down, so he pulled the chest out from the wall an additional six inches.

I don't know what this is going to get me, but they probably won't find me tonight. I'll wait here a few hours till it quiets down outside.

With that, the German captain slid behind the chest and lay down. All was quiet for half an hour. It gave Markus time to reflect on the day's tragic events: it was pure chance that I wasn't killed with the rest of them.

His companions' faces formed in his mind, ending with a fine, red spray floating down into a pool of blood. Helena's face emerged out of the crimson pool, followed by a baby's face. Markus shook his head to stop the bad dream: I'm not going to allow bad visions of Rupert and Helena in my mind.

He lay there, thinking of Helena and the ranch in far-off German South West Africa. He fantasized about her body and their love making and their comfortable home at the ranch. *I wonder how everyone is faring—the boys, they must be prisoners of war, or maybe they let them return to the ranch? Who knows?*

He heard heavy footsteps in the outer hall. The door opened, "That will be all, Corporal. You are relieved." A faint reply, "Si, Commandante."

General Albuqueque closed the door behind him, walked to his desk, struck a match, and lit several more candles. The room brightened surprisingly from Markus's vantage point. He heard papers shuffling, liquid poured, a glass clinking, and an exhalation of satisfaction. Then silence, a long, long silence. Not a paper sound. Not a breath. Finally the clink of glass and bottle again and a question: "How long did you think you could stay there before you were detected?"

Markus was stunned.

"Well, you've already been detected, haven't you, Captain?"

Markus froze.

"Come out; I'm not going to shoot you now. I know it's you. I saw the bodies." The General blew out two candles. "And I saw the rifle in the corner. That wasn't very smart." He waited. "Well?"

Markus struggled to push the chest away a bit so he could get up. He stood, sheepishly, still behind the chest.

"I'm sorry for your comrades, truly. Come; sit down."

Markus came forward, looking at the candle in front of the general. Albuquerque noticed and snuffed it out with his fingers. Only one candle burned on a side table.

"Sit down; sit down." The general turned in his chair with his back to Markus and found another glass. Swinging around, he said nothing, but poured the second glass. He nodded to Markus, who sat and reached for the liquor.

"You've developed a habit of arriving in my office unannounced and always in desperate circumstances." He smiled and shook his head at the irony of it all. He took a drink, and Markus followed.

"There is no way you can sneak out of this fort. Every soldier in camp is looking for you and wants to earn a promotion doing it." Markus sat there in silence, trying to figure out what to do.

Albuquerque lit a cigarette, striking the match on the bottom of his boot. He offered one to Markus, but Markus shook his head slightly.

"That was a clever escape plan, up through the roof. Getting up there? Very resourceful."

"It was Rudy's idea. He's dead," Markus said bitterly.

"Yes, and you sitting here alive is . . . is what? Fate? A miracle? You had a guardian angel tonight." Markus looked down and turned his head aside, his shoulders slumped.

"Now what am I going to do with you?" The general stared at Markus with a perplexed and somewhat sad countenance. "You're like the condemned man who is hung but breaks the rope. Should he be hung again?"

"I was just trying to—" Markus was interrupted.

"I know; I know, just trying to do your job as a soldier. Aren't we all? Aren't all my soldiers? And some of them will die; many of them will die— like your soldiers."

Markus looked back up, listening to the general's words.

"But you and I, we don't die. We should have, but we didn't." He sucked on his cigarette deeply, the end of which glowed bright orange in the almost dark room. Smoke poured out of his nostrils.

"Back in Portugal, they think I'm dead . . . even my family. They think I killed myself or was murdered. But I'm here and good as dead. There are worse things than dying, Captain." He crushed out his cigarette and poured each of them another drink. They sat there together, in silence, in the dark, but far away in different worlds. Finally, General Albuquerque spoke, almost to himself, "I'm tired, I'm tired of all this." His arm swung out.

"For what? Huh? For what? Can you tell me? This war . . . The coming invasion of your colony . . . my soldiers. For what? More land? For God's sake, there's so much empty land already. For honor? Ask a soldier who's been shot or has malaria or cholera or swamp fever about honor. Huh?"

The general was mildly drunk, but obviously coherent. Markus was in a state of utter confusion. Finally, Albuquerque pushed himself away from his desk and stood up.

"You stay here," he said. He walked around the desk and headed for the door as Markus got up.

"Stay here. Sit down, and be quiet." Their eyes met and held for a moment. Markus backed up and sat down.

"What is going on here?" he said to himself. He heard the general outside the building. "Sergeant. Are the mounted guards outside the walls still out there?"

"Yes, sir."

"Fetch me two horses."

"Yes, sir."

The general returned to his office. "Come with me, Captain. Don't say a word. Pull down your hat. No, no, leave the rifle." He looked around his office. "Here, take this map case."

He handed Markus a leather pouch with shoulder straps that had an elaborate bronze cipher of the Portuguese Royal Coat of Arms on its flap. Markus swung it over his shoulder so it crossed his chest diagonally.

"Good, let's go." The general put on his hat, and the two of them left the office. A black stable boy was waiting with two saddled horses.

"Mount up," Albuquerque said. They walked their horses across the almost-deserted plaza, only several squads of men were still searching. The two horsemen headed toward the gate.

"Open the gate for the Commandante," the sergeant of the guard commanded. No one questioned the general and his aide as they passed into the night.

I can't believe I'm outside the walls, Markus thought. Should I make a run for it?

"Don't even think of galloping off, Captain. My mounted troops know this area well and would hunt you down before dawn."

He must be reading my mind!

They rode along the wall on a well-worn path through the cool, damp air, finally coming face to face with a troop of mounted guards. They all reined in.

"That will be all for tonight, Sergeant. Take your men back to the barracks. We'll continue the search in the morning. He couldn't have gotten far."

"Yes, sir." After the guards moved off, Markus asked quietly, "Now what?"

"You wanted to go to the coast, didn't you? So go. Take this trail. Ride hard all night. When the sun comes up, just keep heading east. If you're lucky, and you are lucky, you should hit the Indian Ocean in two days."

Markus was flabbergasted. "You're just letting me go? Just like that?"

The general circled his horse around Markus. "You're an interesting man," Albuquerque began. "You're like a cat with nine lives. How many have you used up so far? Maybe you'll have just enough to survive this war."

"And you, General?"

"It's too late for me. I've outlived all my lives already. As I said earlier, most people who mean anything to me think I'm dead. For God's sake, there's a tomb in Lisbon that proclaims my demise!" He let out a brief chuckle.

"Why don't you come with me, General? There's surely a way for you . . ." he hesitated, "a life for you, somewhere out of Africa. Spain or—"

"Stop! Stop with such nonsense. I'm going to stay here and try to keep my troops out of the battles that are sure to come, and for as long as possible . . . filthy war that it is."

They both stopped talking and reined in their restless horses. Finally Albuquerque spoke, "So, Captain Mathias, time to depart."

Markus was moved by the extraordinary events of the day and by this extraordinary man beside him. "General Albuquerque, sir. I don't know how to thank you, how to express my gratitude. You've saved my life and risked your position here. What can—?"

"Stop, Captain, stop. Just make it worth my while. Stay alive and return to your family." The two closed the distance of their horses and hands extended in a long and hearty handshake.

Markus saluted the general crisply. Albuquerque returned it in a softer salute, more a salutation of farewell. Markus eased the reins, clicked, and his mount moved away. He turned back after a few moments and saw the general sitting in his saddle watching him. The German gave a wave and spurred his horse down the trail toward the Indian Ocean.

Markus rode hard and made it to Palma without being detected. There were so many South African and British troops in the crowded port that he easily passed unnoticed, and in fact, he was asked for directions twice by British officers.

"Sorry, sir, I'm new in town myself," was his reply. He smiled as he rode on.

He also had little trouble finding Herr Leopold's trading company down on the waterfront. Leopold was amazed and happy to see the captain he'd helped months earlier. They sat in his shabby office, drinking and smoking, as Markus related the news from up north and about his recent experiences.

"He's a good man, that General Albuquerque," Leopold commented as he poured more schnapps. Markus sat drinking with the German trader for several hours and was thankful that the old man still had his wireless transmitter.

"I can put you up, but we have to get rid of your horse. Portuguese patrols might see it and get suspicious. I think I know who I can sell it to, and we can split the—" He was interrupted by a great commotion and cheering from the foreign troops in the street outside his window.

"What the . . . What's going on out there?" He got up, went to the door, and shouted to a very young looking nearby British soldier. "What's this?"

"Didn't you hear? Germany just declared war on Portugal! That means the invasion is on—any day now. We're going to kick those German asses!"

Windhoek, German South West Africa, 1916

— CHAPTER 42 —

Iron Wheels of Pain and Sorrow

The wireless station Captain Markus Mathias had so meticulously upgraded lay in ruins, blown up by the very people who helped construct it. No one paid much attention to the pile of wreckage anymore. The British and South African military now occupied the garrison and all other military bases and towns in the country. They also requisitioned many of the better homes and estates.

Fortunately, Tomas Conrad's ranch was told to accommodate only two South African officers because the ranch was so far out of town. It was unpleasant but manageable to have strangers, and the enemy, living so close. Helena, with baby Rupert, made a point of avoiding the two soldiers; however, since it was required to feed these military men, contact was unavoidable.

Of greater concern were the two boys, now young men, Wolfgang and Arnold, held in a prisoner of war camp—which camp was unknown. Tomas Conrad heard stories of the Boer camps that the South Africans had established, including for the families of fighters. They were brutal, savage places with starvation and other deprivations. Back then, the camps were used as a military tactic by the South Africans to demoralize the Boer fighters in the field. It worked but at a ghastly cost of starving women and children, with thousands of deaths.

Now every effort was made to find the two Conrad boys and petition for their release. The British and South African authorities, having subdued the German colonial militarily, now had to administer the colony. A strategy of benevolence was instituted for the purpose of pacifying the civilian population, so as to free up occupying troops to fight in France and German East Africa.

To the surprise and relief of Tomas and Helena, one of the officers billeted at their ranch, a Captain Llewellyn, one day announced the pending release of the two young Conrad men.

"It's our new policy," he began. "Captured German colonial troops are to be paroled to their families with a pledge not to provoke or support any insurrection."

He smiled, looking at Helena. She was in riding breeches, sitting there with her father in the front parlor. "After all, before the war, we were good neighbors. Is that not true?" He radiated a broad grin.

"*Ja, ja*, of course, Captain. This is very good news. Do you know when we will see our boys?"

Several weeks passed with no word from the South African authorities as to when Arnold and Wolfgang would be released from the POW camp. One day Helena rode into town for mail and was elated at seeing Wolfgang's handwriting on a *pfennig* postcard:

DEAR PAPA AND HELENA AND EVERYONE.
ARRIVING WINDHOEK BY TRAIN, MAY 15. WE ARE BOTH
A BIT BETTER NOW. SO HAPPY TO BE COMING HOME.
LOVE WOLF AND ARN

Tears rose in her eyes as a mix of emotions swept over her.

"Thank you, *mein Gott*, for delivering them home," she said in a low voice, making the sign of the cross and touching the crucifix around her neck.

She read and reread the short passage, noting Wolfgang's steady script: "a bit better." A bit better from what? Were they injured, sick? Papa must see this right away. She hurried to her horse.

She unhitched the reins from the hitching post and was about to mount up when Captain Llewellyn came up behind her and said, "Here, Frau Mathias, let me help you up."

"Oh, Captain Llewellyn. I'm fine, really."

"Nonsense, I'll give you a boost." And with that, he moved in close, offering her his cupped hands. She reluctantly stepped in, and he lifted her up as she swung her other leg over the horse.

He lingered a moment with his hand on her boot. "Fine boots for a fine rider," he said softly with a grin.

"Yes, Captain. They were made in Berlin." With that, she pulled her reins to the side and gave her horse a little kick and rode off. Captain Llewellyn, still grinning, watched her, sitting high in the saddle, the sun shining on her stiffened back, depart.

She was riding her best horse, and it was lathered up by the time she got to the ranch. She dropped the reins as she slid down from the saddle. Sambolo ran up to take the horse.

"Hi, Sam. Papa, Papa, good news!" She shouted with enthusiasm as she entered the house. "Are you here?"

Her sister, Christiana, came into the parlor, wiping her hands with a towel. "He's out . . . be back for supper. What's got you so?"

"Look, look, Christiana. We just got a postcard from Wolfgang and Arnold! They'll be arriving May 15 by train. Isn't that wonderful?" Christiana came close and read the card herself, as Michael and Norbert came running in.

"That's wonderful news! Wait till Papa sees this," Christiana bubbled.

"What is it?" Humboldt exclaimed, craning his neck to see the postcard. At dinner, everyone wanted to talk at once and had an opinion as to what "a bit better" meant. Tomas offered, "Now, now, whatever their condition, we can thank *Gott* they are coming home alive, and if Wolf and Arn are traveling by train, they must be reasonably fit."

Early the morning of May 15, the entire Conrad clan was at the train station in Windhoek. "When is the train due?" The same question was asked several times by first one and then another of Tomas's sons.

"You know it's a slow train, making stops along the line, loading, unloading. It'll be along shortly, any time now," Helena spoke hopefully.

"Look! Smoke!" one of the boys exclaimed. "Here she comes!" The snorting, coal-burning locomotive could be seen in the far distance, swaying back and forth on the long ribbon of track.

A surprisingly large crowd of civilians edged closer to the station platform, all eyes peering down the rails. Tomas Conrad glanced around at the familiar faces and strangers near his family. Several black-veiled women were dabbing their eyes and holding handkerchiefs to their faces. A nearby woman sobbed softly. He heard her husband say quietly, "Now, now, Mother. He's at peace now."

Helena also heard the man, and a shudder rippled down her spine. She met her father's eyes for a long moment and gripped his arm tightly. He squeezed her hand in reassurance. Helena quickly wiped away a tear.

She and her father realized, in that moment, what was being delivered to the vanquished families of the defeated and fallen warriors. The brave young men had answered the call of their Kaiser, to a cause, to a fight, most knew was lost before it even began. And now the iron wheels rolled ever forward with their cargo of pain, anguish, and sorrow.

Not everyone was aware of the pending grief for some families. The Conrad boys were laughing and at horseplay with several others of their own age, off to the side of the station. Christiana was with two young ladies, chatting merrily and looking lovely in their long dresses. Most everyone was dressed as if going to church on Sunday. The return of their soldiers was a major patriotic event for the people of the town and surrounding farmers and ranchers.

The occupying South African and British military authorities turned a blind eye to the many Imperial German flags flying and the German colonial flag for South West Africa, with its symbolic long-horned Cape buffalo head in the center.

As the train grew closer, the station master and several other railroad men ordered the crowd back: "Make room, please. Make room for the disembarking passengers. Make room." The crowd reluctantly but obediently backed away, as the hissing, steaming engine clanged its bell and let out a long, deafening blast from its horn.

The screeching steel-on-steel brakes brought the black, sooty machine to a halt. There was an eerie silence in the crowd as everyone waited for some word, some order, from some authority to tell them what was next. Nothing happened.

The stillness was finally broken by the sound of the heavy wooden doors sliding open on the nearest baggage car. All eyes were fixed on the dark opening as a large luggage cart was pulled up parallel to the opening by two workers. They hopped up onto the cart and faced inward. Slowly, a white form appeared and was slid out onto the cart.

A fresh, raw wooden coffin sat there in the bright sun. A gasp was heard. Soft murmurs passed through the onlookers. Another white box appeared, then another, and another. The cart pulled away with eight stacked coffins. Another cart appeared and pulled away with seven more stacked coffins. A small group of black veils melted out of the crowd and followed the carts.

Unbeknownst to the people at the station, the passengers were asked not to disembark until the dead and wounded were offloaded. Next, a second baggage car's doors slid open. This time, a dozen men in German uniforms with red crosses on their arms hopped onto the platform. They formed a line, and as stretchers were brought out, four men took the ends of the stretchers and carried them a short distance to a shaded overhang. The stretchers were lined up with several attendants overseeing them.

Each soldier had a cardboard name tag and other pertinent information pinned to his covering. Most were smiling. Some were bandaged, and some sat up and waved to their families who scurried to greet them. Soon the shaded station platform was crowded with stretchers. Another baggage door slid open and the process continued.

"Papa, I'm going over and check the stretchers," Helena said. Christiana saw Helena moving through the crowd and broke off from her friends and followed her.

"Are they here?" Christiana's voice sounded concerned.

"I don't know. I'll check this row of stretchers. You check that one." The two women moved swiftly down the lines of soldiers, trying not to stare at the outstretched men. The women didn't pause to read names, but they scanned the faces of the five dozen or so casualties in the two rows.

"Neither of them are here, thank God," said Christiana as the two women met at the end of the lines.

"Now what shall we do?"

"Let's go back through, just to be sure. You take my row this time, and pay particular attention to the quiet ones. Wolf and Arn are probably on the train, but let's just be sure about the ones here."

Half-way down the line, Christiana stopped and stared intently at one stretcher. She slowly backed up, almost toppling over. Helena noticed and came over quickly.

"What? What is it?"

"That bandaged man . . . all bandaged. I couldn't see his face, but the hair; it looks like Arnold's." She whimpered.

"Hush, Sister, hush. You'll alarm the men," she said in a forced whisper.

"Let's see." The two women approached the bandaged man, one on each side of the stretcher. They both gathered their long skirts and swept them behind so they could kneel.

Helena reached for the tag attached to a wide, white bandage wrapped around the upper arm of the still man. She looked intently at the tag for longer than necessary. She leaned over and spoke gently, "Arn, Arn, it's me, Helena." She made a heroic effort to control the quiver in her voice. "You're home . . . We're here to take you home . . . Can you hear me?"

Christiana's hand went to her throat. Her other hand, the back of it, covered her mouth. There was a long, silent pause. Helena leaned in closer, to within inches of the bandaged head. Flies buzzed around the bandages.

Helena could smell the dreadful smell of soaked bandages where the swaying, bumpy train had broken scabs and opened stitched, half-healed wounds. Her eyes focused on the chin and corner of mouth visible to her. She saw it move. The lips quivered.

She moved even closer. Waited. Finally a lone word, half-spoken. She waited another moment, touching the tips of her fingers to the exposed chin. His head responded and moved ever so lightly toward the touch. Again the word, just audible now, was spoken. "Home" is all he said.

―― CHAPTER 43 ――

A Trail of Falling Wild Flowers

W e were caught in an artillery barrage from their navel guns. Well, we found out later it was their naval guns. We'd heard a distant thunder, and five or ten seconds later, the earth around us just exploded." Wolfgang was propped up in an overstuffed chair in the front parlor, with his injured leg outstretched on an ottoman. He was talking to his father and brothers. He and Arnold were finally back at the ranch. The week since they arrived home held a mixture of powerful emotions.

"This cursed war! What has it got us? What were they thinking back in Europe?" a disheveled Tomas stammered.

The original shock of Arnold's wounds lingered in the house. His body and head received and still contained dozens of small shards of steel, some very tiny, others up to an inch long, and most resembling splinters of wood, small and jagged. The larger pieces of the exploded naval shell were removed by doctors at the aid station and later in hospital. But the small fragments, some unknown, some too deep or too dangerous to remove, remained. All that could be done had been done. He was sent home to free up the doctors' time. His fate rested in his body's ability to fight off the countless, small infections.

A nurse hired to change dressings also medicated the wounds. All the family attended Arn as best they could, at least one by his side at all times.

Wolfgang was the lucky one. He was not out in the open when the shell exploded. His broken leg was the result of being hit by the head and neck of a cavalry horse, torn apart and flung in all directions. The rider of the horse simply disappeared in the blast.

True resentment grew with two injured boys home and the South Africa officers still residing at the Conrad ranch. They gave token acknowledgement of the terrible effects of the short war on the colony. Tomas Conrad and Helena felt obliged to continue attending most meals with the South Africans. The other family members refused.

"Now don't be disrespectful toward them," Tomas counseled his family. "They could cause real trouble. Just stay away from them as much as possible. They won't stay here forever." He hoped silently that it was true.

As the days passed, high fever and delirium plagued Arnold. He accepted little food. Even water was hard for him to get down. He wasted away slowly, but no one wanted to confront the truth. On a bright afternoon in early June, Christiana happened by to look in on her brother. The nurse and her father were giving a sponge bath to Arnold. He lay there in silence, with only a towel covering his abdomen. The poor young man was a mere skeleton, and it was the first time Christiana had seen her brother unclothed.

She stared in wide-eyed disbelief. Her shock at seeing Arn's rib bones and skinny, withered arms and legs was too much to endure. She let out a gasp that turned her father's head. He saw the fright and pain in his daughter's face and came to her, stepping to block her view. He spoke gently, "Now, now, steady girl, steady. He's resting quietly. Come, and sit awhile."

He signaled the nurse to cover Arnold and leave for a few minutes. The two of them sat together on chairs close to Arnold.

"Arnold spoke to me last night for a few moments, Christiana dear. He told me he knew he was dying." Tomas stopped to clear his throat, then continued, "He said he had talked to *Gott*, and when he told me that, he seemed in a beautiful place in his mind. It is we who feel this great pain . . . our helplessness . . . and . . ." Tomas wiped a tear from his cheek and sniffled. Christiana leaned in toward her father, their heads touching. Tears dripped in silence.

Unexpectedly and almost shockingly, they heard a distant, familiar voice whisper in half- breaths, "Ah . . . it's all right . . . I'm home."

They both looked up. As Christiana clutched her rosary and sobbed gently, she held her brother's cold, bony hand and kissed it.

Arnold coughed and gagged, and his body stiffened. The nurse, just outside the door, came in, and with a rubber, bulbous device, she suctioned Arnold's mouth and throat. He sank back into a calmer state. The nurse silently took his pulse and listened to his heart with a stethoscope. After taking her readings, she signaled Tomas, and the two of them quietly left the room. The nurse gently explained, "He'll be going soon, sir. There is very low blood pressure and almost no heartbeat. I'm so very sorry, Herr Conrad."

Tomas nodded his head. "Thank you, Frau Bruin. I'll tell the others. Best you go back in and keep Christiana company."

"*Ja, ja,* of course."

Tomas encountered Michael in the kitchen. "Michael, go get your brothers and go to Arnold's room. Where is Helena?"

"In the garden, Papa. What's the matter?"

"Just do it, son."

Tomas found her sitting in the shade with a bunch of wild flowers in her hand. She saw him coming. She knew from the expression on her father's face and by his urgent pace what he was going to say. She said it first, saving her father the pain.

"I know, Papa. I know. It's time." She stood up as her father approached, and they hugged for a long moment. As they hurried back to the house, a trail of falling wild flowers cascaded from her hand.

Bavaria

CHAPTER 44

Kalvarianhof, Bavaria, 1916

How are they going to continue to enforce these new rationing laws, Papa? Did you read of the food riots in Munich and dozens of cities—even Berlin?" Katherina spoke without looking up from the newspaper. She was sitting in the front parlor with Otto and Freidl Levi at Kalvarianhof.

"The Kaiser says this, and the Kaiser says that, but there's no progress in this awful war, and the blockade has cut off all our food imports." She sat up and peered intently at the open newspaper.

"Mama, did you see the new list of rationed foods? Meat, bacon, ham, sugar, butter, cooking fats, coffee, cheese, and they say here, maybe milk and eggs! There are quantities for each item per adult—oh, you'll have to read it."

Otto could hear the frustration and anger in his daughter-in-law's voice. "*Ja,* it's going to be a very difficult time for the government to enforce rationing of food fairly, especially here in the country . . . Well, that is a challenge. Farmers like us are always the last to go hungry, as it should be. We do the work and grow the crops."

"But, Papa, the people in the cities, the workers, like it says in the paper, they don't have our advantage, the land and the animals." She trailed off into silence.

Otto was also reading part of the paper.

"Look at these prices, Mama. At Opalstein's shoe store in Munich . . . Why, I bought a pair of shoes just last year for a third of this price, and—"

"You bought those shoes before the war, dear. Now, as for the Kaiser, Kathi, you mustn't be heard speaking out like that . . . even if we feel that something must be done to end this, this carnage. The Kaiser was right in feeling Germany was threatened by Russia on the east and France on the west, after all—"

"*Ja, ja,* I know the story, but he should have settled it diplomatically, not with the army!" Katherina's voice rose in anger. "The army has my husband in East Africa . . . Africa!"

Freidl was disturbed by the tone of Kathi's voice and put down her sewing. "Kathi, dear, I'm sure Levi is all right and Markus, too. When they're together, they take care of each other. And we can make due here on the farm. Isn't that right, Papa?"

"*Ja,* of course." He knew it was best to reassure both women, even though he had heard the casualty numbers. Almost one million German troops killed or injured in two years of war. He continued, "And as I've said before, I think it's best that the two of them are in Africa. The Brits and French have taken our other colonies in Africa, and from what I've read from the neutrals, our people are being humanely treated."

Otto put down his newspaper as he had the women's attention. "It's hard to say if our last colony in Africa can hold out. We'll have to wait and see."

It was a depressing thought for everyone, but it was interrupted by a knock on the front door.

"I thought I heard someone on the gravel," Katherina said as she jumped up. The two elder Levis waited and listened. They heard exaggerated welcomes and knew it was Markus's sister, Anji. The two women walked arm in arm into the room in their light, summer dresses.

"Greetings, greetings, Anji, you're just on time. Where is your mother, Frau Mathias?" Frau Levi inquired.

She gestured with her hand toward the door. "Mama is coming. She stopped to chat with your man, Willie. He's quite a huntsman, always has a rabbit or two to sell. It's awful in town . . . the lines, and then when you get to the butcher, he is either entirely out or the portion allowed is pitiful. And you, Frau Levi, you've always been so kind. Might you have any eggs to spare?" Anji asked in a slightly embarrassed tone.

"Of course, dear, we can spare a few. Ah, here is Frau Mathias now."

"Fanny, do come in," Otto spoke as he got up, smiling as she entered the parlor.

"Come sit by me," Freidl offered.

"Thank you. My, the walk out here from the village train station seems to get longer every year, but it's so beautiful and quiet in the woods." Everyone smiled.

"The shopping in town is dreadful, and if you want a bargain, they want gold marks, gold!" She let out a cackle. "Ever since last year when the Kaiser asked everyone to trade in their gold coins for paper money, why, nobody's got any gold left—well, mostly nobody." Frau Mathias spoke in a low, conspiratorial voice. "I've kept some, for special purchases, but at this rate, my few gold marks will be gone in no time." She settled into the soft chair. "Then what am I going to do?"

Katherina was watching, as was Anji, and they loved the way Frau Mathias dramatized on occasion. They both smiled at her endearing ways.

The group moved to the kitchen alcove table for an informal dinner of cold fish in jellied brine; several salads of tomatoes, cucumbers, and cabbage; potato salad; and freshly baked bread. Most all the talk related to the war and food.

"Have you seen the airfield in the village? So many new aeroplanes and so big!" exclaimed Anji.

"Markus would be surprised and delighted and eager to pilot them. That one he was flying when he landed here at Kalvarianhof was so little and shaky!" Everyone smiled and nodded in agreement, particularly Otto, remembering that day vividly.

"And so many young, handsome men at the airfield," Katherina laughingly joked, looking at Anji.

"Oh, don't get me started," began Frau Mathias. "She could have married that nice, young doctor, but—"

"Mama, please!" Anji declared. "Besides, I wasn't in love with him."

There was an awkward few moments of silence. Fanny changed the subject. "Anji is working in the Prince Ruperich Hospital in Munich."

"Yes, yes, and its important work," Anji. began. "There are so many wounded . . . hundreds! We get dozens every day. All the hospitals are over capacity. Wounded soldiers are in cots in the halls and even the waiting room."

Her enthusiastic descriptions were infectious. "It's so very tragic, but it's important work . . . to help the ones we can. Everyone is bone tired, but each keeps going. Our boys appreciate every little thing we do for them. This war is so ghastly awful." She was silent, as was everyone else, lost in thoughts of Markus and Levi. Everyone merely poked at the food.

Suddenly, the dinner was interrupted by the sound of a fusillade of pistol shots. With the guns ringing in their ears, Anji and her mother jerked up and stopped eating, their eyes wide with fear. They looked apprehensively to Otto.

"Now don't be frightened. The shooting club across the meadow has a target range. The pilots come over for pistol practice."

"Heavens! I was nearly scared to death," Freidl said, sinking her teeth into a fork full of potato salad.

"I thought the French army was coming through the forest!" Everyone had to laugh at that absurd comment, and it broke the gloomy mood. Anji simply smiled and rolled her eyes at her mother.

"What? What?" Fanny asked.

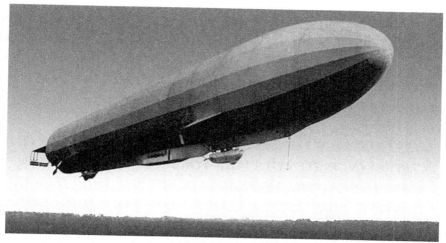

German Airship L59

―― CHAPTER 45 ――

Summer 1916: Riding with the Enemy

Since hearing Germany had declared war on Portugal last month, colonist noted the invasion of German East Africa from the south had begun. Using the same strategy as in the last two years, Vorbeck evaded the bulk of the invading British, South African, and Portuguese armies. The tactic: ambush unprepared enemy units, fight till nightfall, and then slip into the bush or jungle before dawn to avoid organized enemy counterattacks.

Markus had sent Vorbeck's wireless message to Berlin through neutral Abyssinia, from Leopold's trading company in Portuguese East Africa. He impatiently waited for a reply as weeks passed. Finally, also through Abyssinia, a coded reply arrived. He was sitting in Herr Leopold's office in the port city of Palma, still in a Portuguese corporal's uniform.

"Here's the wireless you've been waiting for!" Leopold exclaimed, swinging around in his chair in front of his wireless set. "Intriguing, to say the least . . . I've never seen a more interesting message!"

He was genuinely taken aback by the remarkable contents in the brief Berlin note. He handed it to Markus.

FIRST MESSAGE TOP SECRET. STOP. BY MOST IMMEDIATE CONVEYANCE TO COL. VON VORBECK. STOP. GERMAN EAST AFRICA DANISH FLAGGED SUPPLY SHIP JELICO ARRIVING PORTUGUESE COAST LATE MAY. STOP. CODE NAME DANJEL. STOP. SECOND MESSAGE TOP SECRET. STOP. RESUPPLY ZEPPELIN #L59 ARRIVING SPRING 1917 ALONG CENTRAL RAIL LINE TABORA. STOP. DETAILS TO FOLLOW. STOP.

"The supply ship should be here in a month! The colonel has to see this!" Can you send it to him, Leo? I'll give you the call sign. I'll put it in code. Here, let me write it down for you." He took the pencil offered by Leopold.

The merchant offered a warning: "I'll send it, but I have to be very careful. You know the British can pick up every message sent by wireless. The air is free, no?" He chuckled at his own little joke. "But truly, the British, if they catch me . . ." he made a slitting sound and drew his finger across his neck.

"Yes, I know. You're risking much just having me here. But I must inform the colonel about the supply ship, and I must inform Berlin that Tabora and the northern two-thirds of the colony are under British occupation, including most of the central railroad. That zeppelin would be in grave danger at Tabora."

Leopold grunted, sent the messages, and repeated to himself, "A zeppelin!" He smiled and shook his head. "This calls for a drink."

"*Ja*, I'll drink to that as my mission is accomplished here!" Markus exclaimed with a big smile. "Now, I have to decide if I should return to my unit up north, or stay here till the supply ship arrives."

Herr Leopold looked at his guest and grinned. "You leave here, for there? Ho, ho! You've been drinking too much of my poor schnapps! You'll never find your colonel, and besides, the invasion is on! Don't be stupid, my young friend. Stay here . . . at least for your supply ship."

The next day, Markus rolled out of the makeshift bunk Leopold had made for him in an upper storage room. His host was brewing coffee, real coffee, one of the advantages of being in the trading business. Markus followed the pleasant aroma to Leo's coffee pot and sat down.

"Business is booming for my little business," Leopold announced. "The Arabs in Madagascar are selling everything they can get their hands on to the British—mostly food—and they need an importer. That's me! Here, have some dates, or oranges, or a nice slice of melon." He was jolly in his playfulness. "Wash it down with Turkish coffee. Yes, real Turkish coffee! From the enemy of the British! Ha!"

Markus was thoroughly content to share in Herr Leopold's happiness. The shabby old man in his shabby office felt he was on top of the world.

What a wonderful place to be—what a wonderful mind set, Markus thought.

"I will, indeed, indulge in your 'royal' breakfast offerings," Markus responded. They both sat there, melon juice dripping off their chins, enjoying the sweetness of life.

Markus finally returned to the reality of his present circumstances. He had made the decision late last night, staring into the future. "My dear friend, can you do something for me? One last thing?"

Leo looked sideways at his companion. "Ah oh, I don't like it when someone says 'one last thing.'"

"I need a horse . . . with a Portuguese military saddle, and your advice on the best place to ford the river."

"You're going back?" Leo sat up and threw a melon rind into an already overflowing basket. "What is it with you military men, so eager to be in harm's way? Do they need you up there? No! Do they want you up there? Well, *ja,* your friend wants to see you again, but who else? Your colonel is too busy running from the invasion to care where you are. So why risk your life in the enemy's uniform? You know what that means!"

He was silent for a few moments, as was Markus.

Leo finally began, "That horse is going to cost three times what we sold your other one for. It's probably right off the boat and will be dead in six weeks, maybe sooner."

"I only need it for a few weeks at most, till I get back to my unit."

"Only a few weeks? Your colony is about one twenty-fifth of the entire African continent. You think you can find your unit in a few weeks?"

"Yes, I do."

"How are you going to do that, Lieutenant?"

"I'm going to ride with the enemy."

—— CHAPTER 46 ——

Corporal Carlos Verdi

The horse took great leaps as he forged his way across the stirrup-deep Ruvuma River at a very wide and shallow spot. Markus studied the surface of the slow-streaming river, looking for any dark shapes or forms, the evidence of crocodiles lying in wait. He had seen these primeval beasts, some twenty feet long, snatch zebras, wildebeests, and other animals, dragging their prey to a watery death—and they had killed scores of soldiers too.

The newly washed and pressed Portuguese corporal's uniform Herr Leopold prepared for Markus got a second washing in the muddy water. Leopold also secured for the German captain all the military equipment a Portuguese mounted dispatch rider would possess, including a map-dispatch pouch. It all came at considerable expense for the merchant, including the horse and saddle, but as he grandly stated, "It's for the Fatherland, a place I shall never see again in my lifetime!"

Markus knew the invading army would pursue Vorbeck's army. It was only a matter of time before he would be close enough to slip away and rejoin his German unit. He also knew two other things: soldiers get separated from their assigned units all the time. And, in a major military engagement like this one, individual soldiers are absorbed into whatever units they're near. They all get sorted out later. This, Markus felt, gave him sufficient cover for his deception.

He did have to get his facts straight, however. Herr Leopold, warming to the intrigue, helped Markus create a cover story. Now, Markus was Corporal Carlos Verdi, attached to the brigade of General Joaquim Augusto Mouzinho de Albuquerque, stationed at the Newala garrison town.

As he reached the opposite bank of the Ruvuma River, he had accomplished one of his goals. He was back in German East Africa. Two days of hard riding since leaving Leopold brought Markus across the river and up to the rear guard of the enemy.

Portuguese, British, and South African army units were scattered miles apart in separate columns on a wide arc in front of him, looking for their German quarry.

Markus tried to stay away from the Portuguese units. He figured the British and South Africans would not be as apt to question a lone Portuguese dispatch rider.

One evening Markus attached himself to a British encampment for the night.

"We got several other Portuguese men in camp, lost as you are. You don't want to join your own people?" The British soldier spoke with a strong Irish accent.

"I'm happy right here by your fire," Markus answered. "I'll see them later, and thanks for the food and blanket."

"They call this food?" the Brit grumbled. "My old mother would feed this to our hogs back home."

"And where is that?" Markus, alias Corporal Carlos Verdi, asked. Several more soldiers joined them. They all greeted each other and sat down around the fire. One of them, Sergeant William Gregory of the Royal Marines, stared for a long time at "Carlos Verdi" but said nothing. The troops ate their dinners in silence, out of the tin plates from their mess kits.

Finally, Sergeant Gregory said, "Hey, Portuguese, you look vaguely familiar. I know I've seen you some place before. I just can't place it. Have you always been here in Africa?" Several other soldiers in the group casually looked over to Markus.

"You ever been to York or Plymouth, England?" he continued. Markus gave a chuckle and shook his head and concentrated on his food.

"Where'd you get those scars on your face?"

Markus was willing to tell that true story. "*Ja*, a leopard jumped out of a tree as I rode by." As soon as he said that, he bit his tongue and thought, *Christ, be careful with the language.*

Gregory was silent for a while. "I never forget a face; I know I've seen you somewhere. It's a game with me. I challenge myself. I'll figure it out."

Markus thought to himself, I'd better move on to a South African unit tomorrow.

The invasion troops roused early the next morning. By six o'clock, breakfast was boiling in large pots, and the latrines were in full use. Markus returned from there and was rolling up his bedroll, being conscious to do it the Portuguese military way, not the German army way. Sergeant Gregory was back and had a disturbing question for Markus.

"What did you say your name was?" The Royal Marine was smiling a sly smile.

Markus looked up and said casually, "Carl—that is, in English. Carlos Verdi." He turned away and the thought raced through his mind, *Christ! How could I make such a dumb mistake?*

"So you're Carl, Carlos Verdi, *huh*?" Gregory was eyeing Markus intently.

"You ever been to China? No, no there weren't any Portuguese in Peking, as I recall." He answered his own question, walking away toward the chow line.

Markus had to make a quick decision: Do I get fed this morning, or do I saddle up and get out of here right away? That British guy is way too interested in me.

He decided to get all his gear packed and on his horse, then make a quick trip to grab some food, and be gone.

"Hey, Portuguese!" Markus froze. He was standing third man in line for food when he got a rough slap on his shoulder. He slowly turned toward the voice.

He vaguely recognized the face of one of the men around the fire from the night before. The man was smiling.

"That Sergeant Gregory! Ha! He's saying he thinks he saw you in China! China!" The man laughed in a jolly way and shook his head. "I think I'd rather be in China than in this hell hole." He laughed again. "How about you, Portuguese? You rather be in China?"

Markus's face must have revealed some unpleasant sign because the man stopped smiling. They both were looking at each other, only several feet apart. Markus quickly gathered his wits.

"China? I don't speak Chinese. I'd rather go home to Lisbon," he added, "for some home cooking! Not this." He gestured toward the food pots. The other man seemed to understand that idea completely.

"Yes, right you are. I could go for a good Irish stew right now myself, instead of this crap!" They both got a blob of what looked like oatmeal on their tins and a cup of very black, very over-brewed coffee. Markus and the man ate together, standing up. When they were finished, both knelt down and rubbed sand in their tins to clean them.

"Good talking with you; now, I've got to go find my unit." With that, Markus headed straight to his horse, shoved his tin and cup into his pack, and mounted up.

As he swung into the saddle, he saw Sergeant Gregory talking to an officer. Their eyes met, and Gregory's face lit up, and he pointed directly at Markus. Just as he turned his horse's head, he saw his nemesis gesturing wildly, raising his voice.

Markus tried to control the feeling of panic and the urge to flee. As he clicked his horse into a fast walk, he thought he heard the word "German." He was moving through lines of cavalry men and horses in various stages of preparation. There were probably two hundred mounts, and Markus had to try to weave his way northwest, toward the outer edge of the encampment.

He glanced back to see the officer and the sergeant walking briskly in his direction, each with a raised arm. Markus broke his horse into a trot. When space opened up, he was in a canter. And when clear of the encampment and obscured by vegetation, he was in full gallop.

German *Askari* **Troops**

—— CHAPTER 47 ——

Smoke in the Sky

A lthough he had not been to all the vast regions of German East Africa, Markus had studied the *Kriegskarte von Deutsch-Ostafrica*, 1904, the war maps prepared for the German colonies at that time. He also knew the location of most of the major German units, at least as of the time he had left on his mission south. Now it was a guessing game, where to intercept his HQ company.

In his mind's eye, he could see the maps of the southern part of the colony: the mountain ranges, valleys, woodlands, and vast savannas.

"As long as this horse holds up, I'll be all right," he said aloud to himself. It was a sort of entertainment in his solitude. He had been riding at a steady pace for three days, remembering that the German forces had been pushed to the southern quarter of the colony. Along the way, he shot and roasted a peahen for food.

Of course, Vorbeck's strategy was not to hold any particular bit of land but to tie up as many enemy forces for as long as possible. It was a vast cat and mouse game, over thousands of miles of roadless, trackless land. Now in the last quarter of 1916, Vorbeck continued his brilliant strategy of attack, retreat, double back, fade into the vastness of the landscape, regroup, move on, and attack again. His ever shrinking forces were bolstered by his loyal *askari*.

Through years of fighting a white man's war, his black troops remained firm and loyal soldiers. Vorbeck and the other German officers and men were loyal to them as well. They ate the same food, were treated by the same doctors, endured the same hardships, and shared the joy of infrequent triumphs.

One afternoon Markus sat on a rock, chewing on the carcass of the bird he had shot. His horse grazed nearby. He was on an endless slope that descended for miles into a plain that stretched to the horizon. As he looked out at the shimmering scene before him, he saw thousands of black dots scattered across the landscape, each representing a wildebeest, Cape buffalo, zebra, antelope, or some other animal.

It was an awesome sight that he never got tired of watching. This land, in its vastness, had beauty, limitless beyond belief—nothing at all like back home.

As he sat there reflecting on the grandeur of it all, his eyes focused on a vertical column of dust or smoke, visible only because a cloud blocked the sun on the land behind the smoky column, allowing its lightness to stand out against the shadow. On focusing his binoculars, he realized he was looking at, not a column of smoke or dust, but the end view of a line or wall of smoke.

"That sure looks like a firing line," he said out loud. Getting up, he continued, "That's not natural; it's what I've been looking for. Let's ride toward the enemy!"

It was a full day's ride to the vicinity of the fire fight. Both sides had moved on, one fading away, the other in pursuit, probably. Markus didn't know who was where when he first arrived. He cautiously dismounted and started a thorough search of the area, kicking at dust as he went along. A number of newly dug, unmarked graves were nearby.

Did we bury them, or did they bury us?

"*Ja*, so this was our line here," he said aloud as he stooped to pick up a German *askari* cap.

"Blood." He picked up spent cartridges. "Hard to tell who fired these."

Remounting, he walked his horse slowly down the firing line to follow tracks in the sand. "They went off that way." He guided his horse slowly through the high grass and thorn trees, keeping his noise down and his peripheral vision up, ever conscious of the threat of lions, other predators, or the enemy.

The encounter was the following day. October was always the driest month of the year in this part of Africa, so when the first of the rains started, Markus was thankful. Now, drinking water would be plentiful for him and his horse. He guided his mount at a walk through the rough, muddy land of dead grass and scrubby trees called Whistling Thorn, with branches down to the ground. The thorn spikes were three inches long and sharp as pins. He stopped to unsnag a thorn from his pant leg.

Bang! The bullet just grazed his horse's rump, caused it to bolt, lose balance, and fall sideways. Markus had just enough time to instinctively slide his boot out of the down-side stirrup. The sound of the single shot echoed off the low clouds, as he rolled clear of his horse and clung to the ground. He was on his stomach, arms outstretched, his face inches above the mud. He saw boots, the tip of a rifle barrel, and heard voices.

"Portuguese!" he heard, in a native German accent.

"No, no, I'm German. Captain Markus Mathias, attached to Vorbeck's headquarters company."

He looked up into several black faces staring down. The German *askari* were skeptical of the mud-coated white man, but did not tie his hands. He was

able to ride his "grazed" horse. He had, indeed, stumbled into the rear guard unit of one of the retreating German battalions. And their commander was none other than Captain Max Looff, late of the SMS *Konigsberg* and now commander of his sea marines and naval crew, newly made German infantry.

Markus arrived at the battalion headquarters several hours later.

"We meet again, Captain. This time in altogether different circumstances," Captain Looff said, returning Markus's salute. "Sit down; sit down." They were in the commander's field headquarters tent.

"I much prefer a ship under me, but circumstances . . ." he made a gesture of "such is life." "We did manage to get off several of the big cannon, and I'm told I'm now the commander of the largest artillery guns in East Africa!" They both enjoyed the thought and the military reality of it.

Markus changed the subject, "Sir, I'm trying to return to my duty station with headquarters company. Do you know where they are? How far off?"

Looff shuffled through several maps on a small, square wooden table. He concentrated on a sector map from the 1904 War Charts.

"*Ja*, to the east and north. The last we've heard is that Colonel von Vorbeck was south of the Rufiji River . . . See, hereabouts." He was pointing to the river that held the sunken wreck of the *Konigsberg*.

"I suspect he's heading south. That was six days ago. He's probably seventy-five, maybe a hundred miles out from here."

Markus exhaled audibly, studying the map. "I'd like permission to rejoin them—my unit—sir. If I could have a fresh horse, I'm sure I could find headquarters company. Their porters can do about fifteen miles a day, assuming they're on the move. With a good horse, I could do thirty or more." He hesitated to see the reaction of the captain. It appeared Looff was skeptical and about to speak.

Markus quickly added, "My duties are to maintain our wireless system and the telegraph; perhaps I could find a wireless transceiver and a generator for your battalion, sir."

Captain Looff appeared to change his mind about what he was going to say. He smiled broadly, "You are a clever fellow, Captain. How can I refuse a bribe like that, however unrealistic?"

Markus broke into a similar grin as the captain added, "You're a survivor; that's for sure. Now, get cleaned up, get some food and sleep, and—" He called out, "Orderly, see that Lieutenant Mathias has one fresh horse tomorrow morning, first light!"

Markus did ride his horse hard, but not too hard, for his long journey. The days lengthened into a week, but finally he detected and approached Vorbeck's rear guard. Now in German officer uniform, he had less trouble being recognized and was soon escorted to Vorbeck's tent.

After formal greetings and a two-hour report of his experiences, including the supply ship and the possible arrival of a zeppelin in 1917, Markus had one other important story to tell. He related how General Albuquerque had assisted him in his escape from certain death.

"I felt—feel—that it's a personal relationship I share with the general. He is strongly against the war and will do whatever he can to keep his Portuguese troops out of harm's way."

"Very interesting, Captain. I'd like to hear more about this general, but right now, I've got more important tasks. We'll talk later. Dismissed." Markus got up, saluted, and turned to leave as the colonel added, "Glad you're back, Captain."

It wasn't long before Markus found Levi. He was sitting on a folding chair in front of his tent. He was busy doing something to his leg, which was out of his boot and stocking, with his breeches rolled up to his knee.

Markus came striding up with a big smile on his face and started, "So this is what you do while I'm gone? You preen yourself!"

Levi looked up with a start. "Markus! *Mein Gott*, I'm glad to see you." He tried to get up, but winced and sat back down as blood streamed down his leg. Markus saw Levi's condition.

"Have you been shot? That looks serious. Why isn't it bandaged up? Did it break the bone?" He knelt down and examined the one-inch hole in Levi's calf. "What? What happened?"

"They won't even give me a medal for this!" Levi, grinning, looked at his friend.

"Give me your hand; come sit by me." They shook hands vigorously, and Markus sat down. It was then he noticed that Levi had a bayonet out, unsheathed.

"What are you doing with that? What happened?" He gestured toward Levi's calf.

"No heroics here," he began. "We were in a firing line north of here, lying in tall grass, and somehow a poisonous spider got down my boot. It bit me. I didn't feel a thing at the time, but then it swelled up, but good." He looked down at the wound.

"My calf was twice as big as it is now. Of course, I couldn't put my boot on, and it was very painful. Fortunately, Captain Herr Doctor Spencer saw it and knew what it was. Thank God, because these damned little bugs are dangerous. The doc put me in sick bay. There was another fellow in there that was in the field, got bit like me, but didn't get treated right away. They had to cut his leg off just below the knee!"

"What? Why? Just for a spider bite?"

"Because these damnable little spiders are not only poisonous, but when they bite you, they also lay their eggs in the wound. If the wound is not kept open and a scab grows over it, the little devils can't get out. So guess what they do?" He hesitated a moment. Markus gestured an unknowing shrug.

"They begin to eat their way out . . . all of them, in different directions, till finally you end up like that poor fellow who lost his leg." Levi brought his injured calf up and rested that leg on his other knee and went on. "So that explains the bayonet. Doctor Spencer says I have to scrape this wound at least once a day so a scab doesn't form. I've been doing this since just a couple of days after you left."

Markus had a repulsed look on his face and said, "Well, you can thank God the doctor caught it in time." They were both silent for a few moments. "Got any room in your tent for a returning man-at-arms?"

"Of course, I could use an additional *aide-de-camp*!" They both laughed. "So tell me all about your mission with the Portuguese. Much danger?"

The two went to the mess tent, and over dinner, Markus told his friend the whole story. It was a sobering tale for Levi to hear: the loss of Rudy and the others, how close his friend came to a firing squad, and the strange tale of General Albuquerque. It was all an amazing tale.

"So the Kaiser might send a zeppelin all this way to resupply us? Remarkable! You're the flyer; do you think that's possible, an airship all the way to Africa?"

The Danish Supply Ship

—— CHAPTER 48 ——

Sunken Treasure

Months went by, with the Germans evading their enemy in the vast wilds of their colony, striking when they could, fleeing when they had to. And the number of able-bodied German troops of all ranks slowly but inexorably declined as sickness, injury, and death took their toll.

Now, late summer of 1917, Vorbeck had been engaged in the defense of the colony for over three years. It had become a way of life, separate from that world of long ago, of home, families, and houses, with real beds and regular meals set on porcelain china and silverware on lace table cloths.

It became a game of survival, for both the Germans and their foes. The colonel hastened to intercept wild herds of roaming animals for food. He guided his troops to the few, known watering holes and wells in the desert-like parts of the colony in the dry seasons. He knew when the native crops were due for harvest and led his troops to them.

The supply ship did arrive off the coast of Portuguese East Africa, but it was spotted by a British cruiser and shelled. The smart-thinking captain ran it aground, and it sank in shallow water. The British saw the ship aflame and left. Vorbeck's troops found the wreck, burned to the water line, but realized most of the vital supplies of guns, ammunition, medicine, and other items were under water and salvageable. They spent several weeks, undetected by the enemy, diving and retrieving most of the valuable cargo.

And remarkably, only after the war did the East African Germans learn that the L59 Zeppelin did make it to Africa. It had flown south, high above the White Nile and Anglo-Egyptian Sudan, and onward south above ancient Nubia to the western edge of British East Africa. Through a tragic series of miscommunications and over vast distances, with garbled relays along the way, it was thought in Berlin that the troops in German East Africa had sufficient supplies and equipment. The giant airship, so close to its goal, was ordered to turn around and head back. The vast stores of guns, ammunition, medicine, and other provisions—so desperately needed—were never delivered.

On its long, remarkable journey to the center of Africa and back to Europe, Zeppelin L59 met a tragic fate April 7, 1918, when it accidentally caught fire, exploded, and sank off the eastern coast of Southern Italy near Brindisi in the Adriatic Sea. Its valuable cargo and all eighty-three crew members perished.

Captured enemy prisoners and British and South African newspapers were the German colonists' main source of European war news. Captain Levi spent most of his energy advising German sappers on how best to blow up or otherwise disable installations in enemy hands.

He also became an expert, with others, in maintaining the dwindling supply of fighting equipment, including machines guns, light mountain cannon, and the big guns off the SMS *Konigsberg*. Vorbeck's troops were inventive in replacing their worn out uniforms with mended, captured clothing and refilling spent cartridges with gunpowder for their assorted small arms.

Markus had finally given up on maintaining a wireless capability because of the frequent moves of headquarters company. He still helped maintain sporadic telegraph connections between near units when not on the march. But for both

Levi and Markus, leading infantry troops was their main assignment. It reminded Markus of the intense fighting in China during the Boxer Rebellion.

Now, in their shared tent, both men stretched out on their cots, mosquito netting shrouding them both. Markus asked his friend, "I was just thinking about Captain Olivieri and his Italian soldiers when we were fighting our way to the Peitang Cathedral in Peking. Do you remember him, Levi?"

"*Ja*, vaguely, remember, I was never at the cathedral. It was a chaotic time." Levi wiped the sweat from his forehead as he continued, "I spent most of my time up on the Tartar Wall with the others. It sure was nice to see that American flag and the Japanese troops coming over the eastern wall." He lay there, staring at the flies, trying to find a hole through the netting. "Now the Japanese are fighting us—at least the Americans are staying out of it."

"*Ja*," Markus responded and was silent for a while "How do you think this is going to end?" He rolled on his side, looking across to Levi through the gauze screening. Levi did the same.

"Badly," Levi replied, looking directly at his friend. "Oh, I think we can out fox our 'friends,' the British, pretty much indefinitely, since we're led by one of the most brilliant military tacticians since Napoleon. I mean, the colonel has a sixth sense for strategy, for what the enemy will do, and what we can get away with."

"But what about the war . . . I mean, in Europe?" Markus asked the question in an almost naive tone of voice, like the way he used to ask Levi for answers, as a younger brother would an older one.

"The European War?" Levi almost said it as a statement. "You've seen the South African and British papers we've found. Even if they're exaggerating their victories and our defeats, it can't be going well for us. Have you seen the articles about supposed food riots in German cities . . . and those political strikes by workers on half-rations . . . Sounds a lot like us."

They both had to laugh at the irony as Markus finished the thought, "Except we're not rioting."

"*Ja*, it surprises me how morale has held up, given these deplorable conditions . . . especially among the *askari*. They're an amazing lot." With that, Levi ended with, "Let's get some sleep; we're moving out tomorrow."

In the morning, at a nearby, friendly village, the sick, wounded, and diseased, whose conditions were too serious to travel, were left with food, water, medicine, and a military doctor who volunteered to stay behind. They were left for the enemy to find and intern as prisoners of war. They would probably be better cared for than what would happen in the wild. It was the only way Vorbeck could keep up his hit-and-run strategy. The number of porters was rapidly diminishing, and there were not enough to be stretcher bearers for all the sick. The exception: white officers whose wounds would heal rapidly so they could be back on the line.

—— CHAPTER 49 ——

Shakespeare

By November 1917, Vorbeck and his intrepid army escaped to Portuguese territory again, as the Allied Army of Belgians, British, South Africans, Portuguese, Indians, Nigerians, and Rhodesian troops forced the Germans south. Portuguese East Africa was in such inept political turmoil and general military incompetence that the Germans found little resistance, except from the British and South African troops in coastal towns like Port Amelia and Mozambique.

The Germans were moving south toward the Portuguese town of Chiruinba. The skies were gray and threatening. It was the beginning of the fall rains. They rode three abreast.

"Levi, did you read that newspaper being passed around about a revolution in Russia? That could only benefit us . . . I mean, if we won't have to fight on two fronts in Europe, it would—" Markus was interrupted by a returning scout who galloped up and brought his horse to a jarring stop in front of them.

"Enemy troops a half mile to the east, moving this way!" he shouted.

Colonel von Vorbeck, who was riding in the lead group, responded, "Pass the word along the file. Captain Levi, bring up two companies of *askari* and reinforce them with four additional machine gun units. Form a firing line along that small rise. You'll have a good field of fire. Strengthen your flanks; we don't want to be outflanked. Captain Mathias, withdraw the porters and supply train back up the trail a quarter mile and rest them. Keep them ready to move out."

The colonel was always quick and decisive when immediate action was needed: "Sergeant, send out scouts to the enemy's farthest flanks, but absolutely no contact. We don't want to lose the element of surprise. Quiet; be absolutely quiet."

"Yes sir, Colonel." With that, the sergeant, Levi, and Mathias turned their horses to task.

The German *askari* were superb soldiers. After more than three years of hit-and-run fighting, they moved swiftly and knowingly into position for yet another ambush. It wasn't long before the scouts returned, leading their horses on foot. One scout communicated, in a loud whisper, "Three hundred yards." He pointed.

The first enemy troops were spotted coming through the tall grass. Through hand signals, the Germans relayed that fact back to Colonel von Vorbeck. The *askari* were as disciplined as any Berlin-trained soldier. They kept low and silent. The grass tucked into the front of their headgear allowed them to see but not be seen. More forward contingents of the enemy appeared, moving slowly to within less than one hundred yards of a lethal confrontation.

The machine guns opened up in unison, mowing down the tall grass and vegetation like a scythe through wheat. The enemy in that field of fire were sliced through with a stream of bullets and died without a sound. It was another successful ambush that sent the enemy South Africans reeling in retreat. The expected counterattack came and was resisted until dark settled over the bloodied ground and the guns fell silent. Only the moans of the wounded were heard as the Germans slipped away into the darkness.

Two days of marching brought the intrepid band of three thousand hardy souls to a relatively safe region near the ramparts of the upland plateau that spread out for a hundred miles towards the Indian Ocean in northern Portuguese East Africa.

A tented encampment was set up on the high plateau with the expectation that it would exist for at least several weeks and maybe until the beginning of the New Year, 1918. The colonel ordered scouting parties out in all directions to a distance of five miles and was repeated every few days. Outer sentries encircling the camp were a half mile out and still others were closer in.

Markus and Levi returned from the mess tent on the run but were still pretty well soaked when they dashed into their tent.

"Ooh, there's a chill in the air tonight," Markus observed as he peeled off his shirt. The strange carved figure of Nyaminyami given to him by Sisibeco dangled from a leather strap.

"You still wearing that thing?" Levi asked, with a smile.

"Oh, *ja*. This brings me luck. Powerful magic!" They both were smiling.

"Well, I guess it's worked for you so far. Maybe I should get one of those."

"You'll have to go to the BaTonga people along the Zambezi. I wonder how far we are from them," Markus replied but paused in thought as he put on a dry shirt.

"Levi, you remember I told you about that beautiful black woman at the village who took me in? Her name was Sisibeco. What a woman! Her skin! Oiled and smooth as silk—and naked. When she leaned over me, it was all I could do not to reach up to those lovely—"

"Hold on, friend. Save it for your dreams, will you? I'm horny enough without you conjuring up visions of a pretty black." Levi was also getting out of his wet clothes.

"She was more than just beautiful," Markus continued. "She and I had something . . . a connection, even though we couldn't talk. We had a special—"

"You didn't!"

"No, no! Not that I didn't want to," Markus's voice trailed off.

"All you need is to bring a couple of light-skinned black kids home to Helena," Levi laughed. "She'll love that!"

"But haven't you wanted to . . . ?"

"Of course, but wanting and doing are two different things. It's not like Samoa. We're both married and with a kid each," Levi spoke while wringing out his shirt, the water dripping onto the damp earth.

"Well," Markus began, "there're a number of women among our blacks—wives, widows, daughters, and what not, of some of the porters. They make themselves available for a little silver. You've seen it. I've seen it . . . And we've heard them at night, right?"

"*Ja*, it's tempting, but . . ." Levi didn't finish.

A bit later, Markus was on his bunk, staring at the tent ceiling and listening to the rain beat down. Levi was at the small, wooden table, only eighteen inches square, writing in his diary by candle light. "I don't believe it," he mumbled to himself. "I don't agree."

"What?"

"Shakespeare." "What? Who?"

"Shakespeare . . . you know, the English writer."

Levi finished writing in his diary, looked up, and went on, "I don't agree with him about life 'signifying nothing.'

"Shakespeare? What are you talking about?"

"Shakespeare, from *Macbeth*, I think. It goes something like 'life is a walking shadow that struts on a stage,' and something and something, 'and then we hear him no more, a tale told by a fool, full of fury, signifying nothing.' Well, that's not exactly right, but it's the idea. I was just thinking about that quote."

He looked over to his friend as Markus swung his legs over the edge of his cot.

"Why?" Markus asked. "What made you start thinking about Shakespeare, of all people?" A crack of lightning and a few seconds later a long, thundering clap interrupted their conversation.

"I don't know what made me think of that verse . . . I guess it's this endless war, endless fighting and running. What the hell are we doing, making these sacrifices day in and day out for years?" He looked across at his friend.

"When did you arrive in East Africa?" Markus asked.

"Ah, I don't recall the date . . . early 1915, before the *Konigsberg* was sunk."

"Well I've been here since a few weeks before the war started August 1914!" They both were silent as the endless rains hammered their tent.

Levi couldn't suppress his frustration: "It's almost 1918, for God's sake! How much longer are we supposed to continue this bloody, ridiculous campaign?"

"Better not let Vorbeck hear you talking like that, he'll—"

"I'm just talking." Another long silence. "What I was really thinking about was that Shakespeare line about life having no meaning. As I see it, this war drives home for me just the opposite. I mean, what I treasure most: Kathi, Rebecca, Kalvarianhof, Mama and Papa—you—and our life before the war. It was a wonderful life, wasn't it, Markus?" He was waiting for an affirmative.

"*Ja*, of course—except for several *situations.*"

"Yes, yes, of course." Levi immediately recalled his sister's letter and the reason that brought Markus to Africa in the first place. "If we just had news from back home," he said as he blew out the candle.

Royal Portuguese Crest

—— CHAPTER 50 ——

Tragedy

They hadn't been asleep for more than two hours when a corporal carrying a lantern called out, "Captain Levi, wake up, sir." He was outside the tent.

"What? Oh, come in, Corporal. What is it?"

"One of our patrols detected a column of several companies of enemy nearby. They appear to be heading in the direction of the coast. The colonel ordered you to report to him; I think for some action tonight, sir."

"Right. Thank you, Corporal." Levi struck a light.

"For God's sake, I have to go out in this?" he mumbled to himself.

Markus was awake and asked, "You want me to come along? You'll need several officers if we have action."

"Kind of you to offer. I know how much you love getting soaked!" They both smirked at the joke.

"Heading for the coast? Doesn't sound like the British to me. What do you think, Levi?

"I haven't a clue."

They dressed, strapped on their side arms, and left the tent. Their horses were already saddled with rifles in their saddle holsters. Two companies of *askari* had formed up in double marching lines. They were up to their ankles in the powdery soil turned to soupy mud. The intensity of the downpour muffled sound. The darkness of a moonless night made communication difficult. The troops were used to it and pretty much knew what was expected of them without receiving direct orders.

The scouts rode beside Captain Levi, with Captain Mathias farther back, leading one of the two companies. They guided their mounts at a walk, on a course estimated to intercept the enemy column. Their plan was to arrive and establish a firing line for the ambush before their adversaries arrived.

Soon after arriving at the ambush site, the first volley of rifle fire, with their flashes of flame, lit up the night and completely surprised the enemy. Markus was down the line, fifty feet from Levi, when he realized who they had ambushed. He was shocked and appalled.

"Good God! Cease fire! Cease fire!" He screamed at the top of his voice. His company stopped firing almost instantly. Half of Levi's company continued firing, having not heard the order. Markus jumped up and ran toward Levi's troops shouting, "Cease firing!" The enemy troops not dead or wounded ran into the darkness of the night.

"What? What is it? Are they some of ours?" Levi shouted at Markus.

Markus came running up in a very agitated state. "No, no!" he gasped. "They're not ours; they're Portuguese! Didn't you see their uniforms? They're Portuguese."

"Have you lost your mind? They're the enemy!" Levi blurted out. "Sergeant, send out scouting parties. Double them, and prepare for an enemy counterattack."

"Yes, Captain."

"There won't be a counterattack!" Markus shouted, "They don't want to fight. They don't want to have anything to do with this war! Didn't I tell you General Albuquerque said so? He told me—"

"You're crazy . . . and insubordinate!" Levi yelled in anger. "Now get back to your men and prepare them for the counterattack. *Verdammt*, Markus! Now they know we're here, and we hardly dented their strength."

"But—"

Levi stepped up to Markus, grabbed him roughly, swung him around, and pushed him in the direction of his company. "Go!"

Markus was in a daze as he stumbled back to his company and slumped down behind cover. His sergeant had seen and heard the exchange and realized Markus was in no shape to command. He heard Captain Levi's order, so he directed the *askari* to prepare for a counterattack. All was in place as the Germans waited for the enemy's first shots.

"Sergeant, double-check our flanks. Go wide. A flank attack is what I'd do." Levi ordered.

The rains continued in the almost pitch-black night. Every ear was turned to detect the slightest sound that could be the enemy. Was that the sliding bolt of a gun or the sound of an animal finding its prey? They waited several hours, with nothing, nothing but the spatter of falling water. Dawn broke slowly with just a hint of light tinting the dark gray clouds.

The sergeant in Mathias's company was at one end of the firing line, and Markus was at the other. As daylight slowly crept over the ranks, the sergeant came up the line to inquire about further orders. Markus was not at the far end.

The sergeant said something to the highest ranking *askari*, and then he went to find Captain Levi, assuming Captain Mathias was with him. Levi was crouched down talking to his sergeant. Both were soaking wet, as were all the other troops.

"Yes, Sergeant, what is it?"

"Sir, I thought Captain Mathias was with you. He's not with the company."

"What?" Levi rose quickly. "What do you mean not with the company? Did you check down the line?"

"Yes, sir, I spent the night at the far end, and the captain was at the other, nearest your company, sir."

"Maybe he's—the captain may be relieving himself. Did you look around?"

"Yes, sir, I sent out a couple of *askari* to search for him, sir."

"*Verdammt*, now what?" Levi muttered under his breath. "Sergeant, take over the company while I go see what's up." He moved off quickly, his pace strident. He suddenly turned to ask, "Where did you last see him, Sergeant?"

"Last night, sir, just after he returned from your meeting with him. Just about here, sir. He was out of sorts, so to speak. Then I left to resume my position on the line."

"Very good, Sergeant." Levi looked around, thinking about what to do. He squinted into a misty rain as the day brightened to a lighter gray.

"*Ja*, so form up several search parties, Sergeant. Squad strength. Is the captain's horse still here?"

"I believe it is, sir."

"Have a mounted *askari* go back the way we came last night, see if the captain has returned to camp . . . and send out a squad to search the battle field for any enemy wounded. Have the men be especially alert; we still may be attacked."

"Yes, sir."

What in hell's name has gotten into Markus? Levi thought. This could be big trouble for him with Coronel von Vorbeck. Come on, Markus, turn up and get back in ranks.

It was only a short time after the search squads went out that an *askari* came jogging up to Levi. "Captain, sir, you come quick. We find da captain."

"What's that?"

"In da mud, sir, with the dead Porta-guese. He . . ."

Levi's throat tightened, and his heart raced. "You found the Captain with the dead Portuguese?"

"*Ja*, sir. He talking to da dead."

"He's talking? Take me to him. Now!" Levi started running in the direction the *askari* had come as the black soldier caught up with him. With the mist and dense foliage, it was hard to see which way to go without guidance.

"This way, Captain."

They soon were at the ambush site, with several dead Portuguese soldiers half-buried in the mud. Levi could see Markus before he got to him. He only saw his back as Markus was half-sitting, half-kneeling over a prostrate body.

Levi could only tell it was Markus by his left shoulder epaulet that was not covered in mud.

"Markus, Markus! Are you all right?" Levi's voice hung heavy with anxiety as he approached is friend. "Markus?" Levi looked around, scanning the dense vegetation. "You, Soldier. Get some more *askari* and form a perimeter around us, fifty feet out, all sides."

"*Ja*, sir."

"Markus, what . . . who is—" He stopped his question after a closer look at the soldier Markus was cradling in his arms. General Albuquerque? Is it? Oh, for God's sake, why did it have to be him?

He put his hand on Markus' shoulder. "I'm sor—"

"Go away! Look what you've done . . . we've done." Markus's voice was breaking.

"He only wanted to get to the coast to save his troops. He wanted none of this . . . this killing, killing, killing. Now look what we've done."

Markus was rocking back and forth, holding the general. "He saved me twice. He saved my life. He was like a father, and this is what he gets. I did this . . . *I* did this."

Levi was at a loss as to what to do. He held back, squatting down near Markus. Only the rain drops hitting the mud and Markus's choked breathing could be heard. Levi shook his head back and forth, thinking, What a mess! What a God damn mess!

Suddenly, General Albuquerque coughed several times and let out a long moan.

Levi drew close and bent over the old soldier. Markus and Levi's faces were so close to the general's, they could see his eyes flicker. He coughed again and spat out blood. Markus wiped it away from his lips.

"General, General, I'm sorry . . . I'm so sorry for this," Markus whispered. "You saved me . . . I owe you so much, my friend."

Albuquerque tried to make the sound for quiet, "Shhhhh."

"It's nothing," he stammered and coughed again. More blood.

"I'm already dead . . . Don't you remember? I've been dead for a long . . ." He stopped to try to clear his throat with a grinding, gurgling sound, "for a long time." He moved his trembling hand up to his chest.

"Here, in here." He patted his chest. "Letters . . . for my daughter . . . in Lisbon."

His hand grabbed Markus's tunic, and with the last of his strength, he whispered, "Captain, promise me . . . ." again the coughing and blood. "Deliver . . . them." Gurgling and coughing and more moans. He tried to say something else.

"What? What was that, General?" Both Levi and Markus leaned to within inches of the old man's lips.

"Don't . . . don't . . ."

"Yes, what?" Both said in unison. Markus tried to force the last words: "Don't?"

Albuquerque's lips moved, mumbling a few words.

"Did you get it, Levi? Did you get it?" Levi lowered his ear to the general's mouth. He heard the last words of General Joaquim Augusto Mouzinho de Albuquerque.

"What? What did he say?" Markus pressed. Levi looked up into Markus's face and put his hand on his friends shoulder.

"His last words were," Levi spoke in a broken voice, "don't kill my soldiers."

Markus's lips quivered and his tears mingled with raindrops. He asked Levi the General's last words again, already sure of the answer.

Levi repeated: "Don't kill my soldiers." They both looked down on the general.

"He didn't want to fight. He did whatever he could to keep his troops safe, but in the end," Markus paused, "in the end . . ."

Levi was at a complete loss as to what to do. He knew Markus spoke the truth.

Later, through a lengthy searching, with white flags flying, contact was made with General Albuquerque's troops. A truce was agreed upon for the Portuguese soldiers to retrieve the general's body and their other casualties.

Captain Levi met with the commander of the remaining Portuguese soldiers, a Lieutenant Nunos. The Portuguese practice was to bury the dead immediately. With Markus's intervention and insistence, Levi reluctantly agreed to have an honor guard at the burial. Captain Mathias led the eight-man honor guard.

Later, Markus said to Levi, "It's the least we could do for a soldier who probably saved countless German lives by staying out of the fights. Whatever happens, Levi, I'm going to deliver these letters to his daughter in Lisbon."

Imperial German Eagle

—— CHAPTER 51 ——

Honor, Loss, and the Zimmermann Telegram

I t was two days later that Captain Levi's forces returned to camp. Levi spent hours mulling over in his mind how he was going to explain what had transpired in contact with the "enemy" troops. Markus had insisted Levi tell the truth, both to protect his own military career and because it was the honorable, forthright thing to do.

"I owe it to the general, to his memory," Markus said. "I'll take whatever happens."

"Don't be so noble, Markus. I can leave out certain 'parts' of the encounter."

"No. Give your report as you would if I was a complete stranger. Just do it."

In the end, Levi did pretty much what Markus said to do. Colonel von Vorbeck called Markus into his headquarters tent, with Levi also present. He and Levi were sitting at a small table. Markus saluted the colonel and was put "at ease." He stood there in silence as the colonel sat staring at him. Finally, he spoke, "Captain Mathias, I've just been given a very disturbing account of your conduct, by Captain Levi, during and after an engagement with the enemy two days ago." Markus's eyes darted to Levi, who sat expressionless, his eyes averted.

"You have proven to be a remarkable soldier as your two Iron Crosses testify. That is why your most recent behavior is mystifying, to say the least. Let me get this straight, and correct me if I'm wrong. First, you volunteered to go on a dangerous night mission. Then, in the heat of battle, during an ambush operation with the enemy, you called a 'cease fire' order to the troops under your command."

"Yes sir, that's—"

"Silence! You gave a cease fire order that disrupted the surprise attack on the enemy, allowing the enemy to escape. You endangered your troops by giving up the element of surprise, and you've probably endangered this entire camp by allowing the enemy to regroup."

Levi shut his eyes and involuntarily shook his head.

The colonel continued, "You think the Portuguese are not the enemy? Who do you think we were fighting back at Newala?"

"They weren't Albuquerque's forces, sir—"

"Silence!" Colonel von Vorbeck shouted, getting up from his chair and pacing back and forth in front of Markus. He stopped and wagged his finger, inches away from Markus's face. "I could have you shot!" Colonel von Vorbeck took a step back, recovered his composure, and stepped behind the small table.

"All this because you were friends with this, this, General Albuquerque? An enemy general!" His voice rose again, "And then you initiated, on your own, an unauthorized truce during which you gave an Imperial German honor guard for the burial of a Portuguese general! That's more than fraternizing with the enemy, Captain."

Vorbeck returned to his seat as Levi moved uncomfortably in his chair with a sickened expression on his face. The colonel picked up on the body language and looked over to Captain Levi. "Do you have something to say, Captain, in addition to what you told me earlier?"

Levi took a deep breath, took a few seconds to formulate his ideas, and began, "Colonel, everything you have said is factually true. But there is much more that has not been said . . . or considered. First of all, I don't believe Captain Mathias would ever do anything to endanger his men or compromise with the enemy. Markus, that is, Captain Mathias, truly believes that the troops under General Albuquerque's command would never engage in combat with us. He believes that because he has experienced the general's actions toward him and toward our military."

He had started out looking first at the colonel and then at Markus, but now he looked Vorbeck straight in the eye. "You will recall, sir, General Albuquerque gave assistance to the captain after his grueling trek from South West Africa. He gave him food and sustenance and a ride to the coast on a Portuguese military wagon with those valuable wireless parts."

Levi cleared his throat and continued, "And again, when we raided the Portuguese fort and you sent Mathias to find Leopold and his wireless, again he helped Captain Mathias. Markus was captured by Portuguese troops, but Albuquerque allowed him to hide in his office and later furnished him a horse to reach the coast. During these extended encounters, the general made clear his hatred of the war and, as he expressed it, 'I'm not sacrificing a single Portuguese soldier for a piece of that German colony.' Sir, I believe we had a friend—almost an ally—in General Albuquerque."

Colonel von Vorbeck raised an eyebrow as he pushed back from his table and looked up at Markus. His anger had subsided.

"May I continue, Colonel?"

Vorbeck signaled approval with his hand, and Levi went on: "As regards what transpired on the two evenings last, I too was initially angry with Captain Mathias's actions. It wasn't until I was with the dying general, and later in conversation with Captain Nunos, that I realized Markus was right about him . . . er, them."

Again, Levi stopped for a moment. "I must add, sir, that I supported the truce for the purpose of burial details, and I engaged in our honor guard at the burial ceremony for the general."

Vorbeck waited a moment, looked at Levi and then at Mathias. "What have you to say for yourself, Captain? Is all this true?" Levi and the Colonel looked intently at Markus.

"Yes, sir, it was the way Captain Levi said. I don't have anything to add, sir, except that General Albuquerque and the troops under his command were not, in my opinion, the enemy."

The colonel sat a long moment in silence, staring at this unusual man before him. "You have placed this command in a very awkward position. Both of you, to a greater or lesser extent, have not followed official military regulations when engaging the enemy." He emphasized the word *enemy*. "However, there are extenuating circumstances in both cases."

He turned to Levi. "Captain Levi, an honor guard for an enemy general in war time is probably unprecedented. However, because, and only because, of General Albuquerque's service to Captain Mathias, I will overlook your questionable judgment. In other circumstances, you would have been demoted. However, under these circumstances, with our officer attrition rate, I need all my officers at rank."

"Yes, sir."

"Captain Mathias, your charges are more serious. I will not repeat them all here. But I must consider your long, devoted, and brilliant service to the Kaiser's army. In the past, you would have received a very severe punishment." Again the commander paused. "I do understand your position and why you took the actions you did based on those beliefs, but it is not for you to decide who the enemy is and is not. Since you continue to hold that 'some' Portuguese forces are not the enemy, I have no choice but to relieve you of your officer rank and duties. From now and until we are out of Portuguese territory, you, Lancer Mathias, are confined to the camp until further notice."

"Yes, sir."

"That concludes this inquiry."

Levi rose from his chair and waited to be dismissed. Markus stayed in his position also and waited. The colonel turned in his chair and opened a field chest. The sliding latch scraped and clattered. He took out several papers and a small box. Levi and Markus looked at each other while the colonel's back was turned. They waited. The commander turned back around and looked up at the two men.

"Captain, sit down. Lancer, pull up that crate, and sit." Both did what they were told.

"I have something to tell you that only a single courier and I know." He interrupted himself to shout, "Corporal, three glasses and some Portuguese Madeira."

From the attached adjoining tent a faint reply, "Yes, Colonel."

Again, Levi and Markus looked at each other.

"Two weeks ago, one of our submarines landed along the coast south of the Rufiji River. An extraordinary trip all the way from Helgoland, wouldn't you say?"

He didn't wait for an answer, but continued, "It brought medicine, ammunition, some guns, and repair parts. The submarine was met by some of our troops still operating independently of my command. It also brought dispatches from Berlin and news of the war in Europe. Things are not going well for us in France, but Russia is out of the war."

"That's very good news, sir. It's no longer a two-front war, right?" Markus said.

"We'll have to wait and see, Lancer." There was a slight smile on the colonel's face when his emphasized "lancer." Both men picked up on it.

"Was any mail on board, sir?" Levi asked.

"I wish I could say it brought mail, but it didn't."

The corporal interrupted Vorbeck. "Ah, good. Thank you, Corporal." The colonel poured three full glasses of the deep-red wine.

"To your health and our success," Vorbeck declared. The two friends were hesitant, but then took up the glasses and drank. Both men were thinking the same thing: First we're disciplined, then in a moment, we're toasting with wine! What's going on?

"I mentioned there were dispatches from Berlin. There is one for each of us, as a matter of fact. First, Captain Levi." Vorbeck shuffled through the papers he pulled from the chest.

"You have been awarded the Iron Cross, Second Class, for your military leadership under fire, and in addition, for your outstanding efforts throughout this campaign, in the repair and maintenance of His Majesty's military structures in arduous conditions. Congratulations, Captain, and here it is." He opened the small box from the chest.

"Stand up, Captain." They all stood while the Colonel pinned the heavy, metal Iron Cross onto Levi's uniform. After a shake of the hands and formal salute, they all sat down again.

"Next, we have Lancer Mathias. Let me read, in part, from this citation: 'for gallantry and fortitude in overcoming great hardship and danger in executing a singular mission across vast tracks of Africa through enemy territory, this award is given in the name of Kaiser Wilhelm II, September 14, 1917.' You are awarded the Iron Cross First Class for your service to date in Africa."

Everyone again stood, and Vorbeck placed the ribboned military award around Mathias's neck and shook his hand, as did Levi. Markus blinked in amazement.

"You are in an exceptionally small group of superior military men who have earned the distinction of three Iron Crosses. And you, Captain Levi, you have two awards, an admirable achievement." He was smiling broadly.

"I myself, while commander of all forces in our colony, have only one Iron Cross, until now! The Kaiser has generously bestowed on me an Iron Cross First Class." He exaggerated for humorous affect and all three men burst into prolonged laughter and shook their commander's hand.

After they settled down and had an additional glass of wine, the colonel spoke up: "Given the recognition you have received from Berlin, your reduced rank to lancer will be brief and remain off the official company logs. You may resume your rank of captain."

Markus was taken aback by the sudden turn of events, to have received two surprises after such discipline. Levi was beaming with delight for his friend.

"And, now, to the final surprise. I, myself, have been promoted to general, as of some time ago. It will have no effect on our continued mission, of course, but it is gratifying that Berlin appreciates our efforts here in East Africa."

Both Captain Levi and newly elevated Captain Mathias stood up, saluted the general, and gave a hearty congratulation to their new commanding general.

"Now sit back down, gentlemen; we are not finished." He poured a new round of Madeira, and they all took up their glasses.

"The news is not good for us in the war in Europe. Military and political events among our allies are also grim." The two captains sat sober faced as the mood in the tent changed abruptly. The new general continued, "The dispatches include an up-to-date, as of mid-September 1917, account of our war efforts and those of the enemy."

He turned back to the open field chest. Out came a shift of papers. He studied several in silence as Levi and Markus dragged their chairs closer to the table.

"Yes, well, you know of the massive losses on both sides. It's pretty much a continuing stalemate on the Western Front . . . completely different from our situation. By the way, we'll be heading north again, very soon." He sipped his wine.

"High Command believes we've been very successful in keeping enemy troops here in Africa and out of Europe. That's the good news. The bad news is there are food riots in several major cities and mutinies in isolated army and navel units. That's bad, very bad. If we start losing discipline in the army . . ." He didn't need to finish the thought.

"Apparently the Kaiser has made numerous attempts to call for negotiations—both with the British and with Wilson over there in America. They've been rejected. Worse yet, it appears the Americans may get into the war. It's all that submarine sinking of neutral shipping, including several passenger liners." He paused and mused, "How did the High Command allow that to happen?" General von Vorbeck rustled his papers and exclaimed, "America, in the war! Christ! All that industrial power . . . and unlimited fresh troops. That's what our forces may be facing back home, gentlemen."

He eased back in his chair. "Well, we've got our own work cut out for us here. Any questions?" There were none.

"Then that will be all for now."

"Yes, General, and congratulations, sir," they said in unison. Levi and Markus stood up, saluted, gave their salutations, and turned to leave.

"By the way, gentlemen, here are several German newspapers and a British one, too. They're old but nevertheless interesting. Don't share them. No need to distract the men."

The rain had stopped. It was early evening with a heavy, gun-metal gray sky. The two newly bemedaled officers walked side by side in silence toward their tent.

Finally, Levi spoke up: "He knew all along what was in the dispatches, our medals and honors. It was all a show of sorts. He wanted to discipline you—and me—first, on principle. He couldn't just let us get away with . . . with what happened. But he more or less absolved us of everything with the wine and awards. It was the strangest meeting, really bizarre, and a true insight into his personality. Don't you think, Markus?"

"*Ja*, it was. He's hard as horseshoes in a fight, but that was a different side of him. I thought I'd had it there for a while, early on. Then there was this complete change . . . He's a hell of a commander, er, general."

Back in their tent, reading the newspapers, both men had their noses buried in the pages. Levi arranged the only candle so that he could hold a single sheet of newsprint so that it was backlit. He moved the paper back and forth in front of the flame, illuminating the lines as he read. It worked out quite well, and it allowed Markus to sit opposite for candle reading, too.

"*Mein Gott*, did you read this . . . about this, this secret Zimmerman proposal? I can't believe our diplomats tried this!" Markus said in consternation.

"What? What's that?"

"According to this British paper, German Foreign Minister Zimmerman sent a secret proposal to Mexico via the transatlantic cable; it was intercepted by the British. Anyway, this outlandish proposal was an offer from the Kaiser, that if Mexico would declare war on the United States, Germany would help her with arms and money. And that's not all!"

Markus almost set his newspaper on fire in his agitation. He went on, "It says here that Germany would help Mexico get back their lost territories of Texas, New Mexico, and Arizona after the war!" He shook his head as Levi sat up and grabbed the paper.

"What?" Levi had to read it for himself.

"It says . . . that the Kaiser tried to buy part of some place called Baja California as a new colony . . . *Verdammt*!" Levi sputtered. "This is just too crazy to believe! It goes on to say the Japanese also tried to buy it, this Baja place, and that . . . let's see, Germany wants an alliance with Japan against America!" He collapsed back into his chair.

"This is a damned . . . This'll bring the Americans into the war for sure! How old is this paper? They're probably already in the war. How could Berlin think this would not leak out . . . that it wouldn't infuriate the Americans? If there ever was going to be a mortal blow for us in this war, this is it."

Silence for a moment and then, in almost a whisper, Levi declared, "This'll bring them in—the Americans." He let the month-old paper slip out of his hands in an unconscious gesture of hopelessness.

Markus just looked at his friend in silence.

Finally, Levi spoke, "It's lost, you know; it's hopeless." He eased over to his cot, lay down, and turned his face to the tent wall. "Markus?"

"Yes, Levi."

"Now we just have to stay alive to go home."

CHAPTER 52

East To The End, Northern Rhodesia: November 11, 1918

The worn and weary Germans trudged on. Like the migrating wildebeest, their single-file line of white officers and men, with their *aAskari*, porters and camp followers, stretched out for almost two miles as they followed a narrow animal track that wove its curvaceous way north like a long snake in the short grass of the Serengeti.

Onward, the battle-hardened warriors marched, determined to go another day, another week, another month, defending as they could the staggering Fatherland back home. They were still a dangerous fighting force. They still maintained a solid morale among the dwindling ranks, now numbering fewer than three thousand souls, fewer than two thousand of them fighters, 130 prisoners, and the rest porters and their families.

Northward into their own colony they marched, into familiar territory, with familiar villages of Massai and other friendly natives. These were the kin of many of General von Vorbeck's *askari,* and all were happy to see the other, in spite of the plundering and ravages of a war they had no stake in.

Even as their numbers grew, the British and their allies were stymied, out foxed, and out fought. Like lions in tall grass, the Germans pounced at every chance. As the months of 1918 slipped past—the fourth year of war— the dry September days found the German colony officially occupied by the British and her assorted allies. But, because of the great distances, the rugged, sometimes impassable terrain, and the diseases, deaths, and injuries plaguing the British and South African armies, General von Vorbeck continued to elude capture.

"Sir, we intercepted a courier with a dispatch pouch," Sergeant Koln exclaimed as he rode up to the head of the column. He handed the leather satchel to the general, as Vorbeck guided his horse off to the side to let the column continue. Markus and Levi happened to be there with several other officers.

"It seems, gentlemen, the Kaiser has asked for an armistice with the British, but it's been rejected," He looked at his officers, "We continue the fight."

In late autumn, the German colonial forces marched six hundred miles from southern Portuguese East Africa back north to the western edge of their colony, near the shores of Lake Nyasa. There, General von Vorbeck devised the most daring and audacious battle plan of the entire war. In his tent that night, at his regular officers' staff meeting, he announced the plan.

"Gentlemen, we are going to execute a surprise invasion of Northern Rhodesia. That British territory is just north and west of our present position." The officers, as one, expressed surprise and enthusiasm on hearing the plan: "Rhodesia! Brilliant! That'll shock the British right out of their—"

"Yes," the general interrupted, "Rhodesia hasn't seen any of our troops in their territory the entire war."

Levi spoke up, "I hope food supplies and other provisions are as we think they will be over there. It was a welcome few days we had, a week ago at Songea, with the fat cattle and all the fresh farm produce. Our men needed that." The officers nodded in the affirmative. Vorbeck, continued, "I believe we'll find what we need and surprise the English in doing it."

The short rainy season of late November and December was about to start, but the still-dry, powdery dust swirled up and clung to the sweat of every man. In camp that night, sitting around one of the many camp fires, Vorbeck,

Levi, Markus, and a half dozen other officers talked over their dwindling options as the British forces grew stronger and stronger. In addition, a new threat appeared.

"A new illness is hitting the men . . . some kind of flu with inflammation of the lungs," said one of the six doctors still serving the soldiers.

"Our choices are limited. We'll have to leave the severely sick behind again for the British to tend. We simply don't have the medicine or porters to carry them."

The animated discussion about military strategy and options continued into the night as sparks sputtered from the burning logs and rose to join the millions of dazzling stars above the vastness of the African sky.

One officer asked, "Why don't we head straight north, fight our way through British East Africa, all the way to Abyssinia? It's a neutral country and friendly to us Germans . . . and the British wouldn't be expecting such a daring attack."

"That'll never work. We're exhausted, and our porters would desert as soon as we left the colony," one officer ventured.

Another officer added, "If we could get to the Indian Ocean and commandeer a ship, we could sail to some part of the Ottoman Empire, our ally on the Arabian Peninsula!"

Someone else chimed in, "That's crazy! The whole British Navy is in the Indian Ocean. We wouldn't get far."

More eccentric ideas passed among the men: "Let's march west through Northern Rhodesia to Portuguese Angola on the Atlantic and then commandeer a ship."

General von Vorbeck remained silent through the discussion of these fanciful options, but now spoke up: "British General Deventer, I'm sure, thinks we are heading toward the center of our colony, north and east, toward Tabora. That's why we're going west into Northern Rhodesia."

The raid, indeed, came as a complete surprise to the British and Rhodesians. It was early November, 1918, when Vorbeck's soldiers overran the small town of Fife just across the border in Northern Rhodesia. Further on, in what became a major battle against the Ugandan 2nd and 4th King's African Rifles, Rhodesian police units, and British *askari*, the defenders became exhausted from months of fighting elsewhere without relief. The surprise German onslaught led to the Rhodesian units finally collapsing in panic. The British *askari* deserted, and the Northern Rhodesian police mutinied.

It was the last big battle of what was to be called the Great War and the last battle led by General von Vorbeck in defense of the German East African colony.

Unbeknownst to all the combatants that day, November 12, 1918, an armistice was agreed to by Imperial Germany and her allies and Great Britain and her allies. The armistice began the previous day at the eleventh hour of the eleventh day of the eleventh month.

Just outside of the Rhodesian town of Chambeshi, General Vorbeck again prepared for battle, not knowing of the armistice. Captain Markus Mathias, in the scouting party surveying the best attack approaches, heard from one of his officers, "Captain, look southeast!"

Markus raised his binoculars to his eyes and yelled, "White flag of truce. Hold your fire! Maybe they'll surrender the town without a fight. Let the truce party through."

The Rhodesian officer spurred his horse forward while his escorts waited farther off. He saluted. Markus returned it, and the officer began, "I have a wireless for General Paul von Vorbeck, Commander of the Imperial German East African Army. It is from General van Deventer, Commander of all Allied Forces in East Africa." He handed a leather-bound map case to Markus.

"Is that all?" Markus asked the Rhodesian.

"Yes, sir, that is all." He saluted again and turned his horse. Markus watched him ride off with his two escorts, the white flag fluttering from an Uhlan spear. He looked at the case, then spurred his horse to Vorbeck's position.

Markus reined in, slid out of the saddle, and walked briskly to the general. Vorbeck was standing with a group of officers, including Levi, studying a hand-drawn map.

"General, under a white flag, a Rhodesian courier delivered this." Vorbeck turned and looked at the leather pouch. He handed the map to a subordinate.

"What have we here?" he said, taking the case. He slipped the stiff paper out of the pouch.

He read through the long message—twice.

"Gentleman, I want to read part of this telegram to you out loud." His officers closed in around him.

"It's a telegram from General Deventer to me, from the British War Office in London, dated 11/13/1918. It reads, as follows:

ARMISTICE SIGNED BETWEEN BRITISH ALLIED FORCES AND IMPERIAL GERMANY AS OF 11/11/18 CLAUSE 17 REQUIRES UNCONDITIONAL SURRENDER ALL GERMAN FORCES OPERATING IN EAST AFRICA WITHIN ONE MONTH. CONDITIONS ARE: FIRST: HAND OVER ALL ALLIED PRISONERS. SECOND: DELIVER ALL GERMAN FORCES TO TOWN OF ABERCORN WITHOUT DELAY. THIRD: DELIVER ALL ARMS AND AMMUNITION AT ABERCORN. SIGNED: BRITISH WAR OFFICE, LONDON

A silence fell over the tightly drawn cluster of officers on that cool, sunny day. Most were stunned by the suddenness and finality of the message.

"Over? Could it really be over?" someone said. "Is it a trick?"

"After all this . . . four years of hardship, death, and destruction, can it be? Is it true?"

"Well, gentlemen, if this is, in fact, true, and I believe it is, then the war is over for us here in East Africa. Remember, this is an armistice, not a surrender. This dreadful war has finally ground to a halt. Our hard-fought battles have come to an end. We accomplished what we set out to do. No one could have asked us to do more. Now, it is our duty to carry out these instructions, safeguard our men, and see everyone home." Most of the men standing there were too stunned to speak.

Vorbeck continued, "We must assume enemy forces in the field have not heard about the armistice, so we must be vigilant. We will have time to discuss this at length later. I have further news to share this evening, but for now, pass the word." He looked at his men and solemnly said, "This war is over, gentlemen. Thank you for your service."

Finally, when most everyone believed the news, there were congratulations all around the small group of German officers standing in the rolling lands of Northern Rhodesia—so far from home, so far in time and miles from their families and loved ones.

Word of the armistice passed quickly through the ranks. First it was a buzz, then a hum, and soon a crescendo of voices. Handshakes, hugs, cheers, tears, laughter, jokes, cursing, and shouting ensued. Everyone wanted to share something, something intangible but real and needed. Some were simply stunned, looking nowhere, with blank faces; others sobbed in pain and joy.

Questions flew from man to man: "Why did we have to have this fight? For what? What was it for? It's an armistice, right? That means nobody won, right? We just stop fighting, right—us and the enemy?"

So much pain, so much death over the years, and so much overwhelming fatigue wore on the men. Some soldiers collapsed to the ground, laughing and shouting. Others just looked bewildered. "Could it be true? Is it a trick? Is it really the end of fighting?" It went on for hours, with the officers reassuring the men of this profound truth: the war was over.

Camp was set up on the spot, and pickets were placed, mainly out of regulations and for animal watch. The Allied troops a short distance away did not come near.

They too were celebrating. Markus and Levi both were in a kind of shock. They hugged each other in a long, long grip, mumbling almost incoherent words to each other. Near the camp, among the fires that evening, the blazing wood lit up happy, animated faces late into the night.

"I can't seem to comprehend this—to accept it," Markus said, looking to Levi. "This is such a way of life for us . . . for me. We've grown hard like this land, like those thousand year old Baobab trees up on the Serengeti. We're as skinny as the Massai warriors and almost as tanned, dark, and leathery as they are."

Levi and the others around the camp fire had a good and knowing laugh. Levi countered with, "Wait till Helena sees your scratched, chewed-up, and blackened hide. She'll think she married a Cape buffalo!" More laughs.

"*Ja*, and you? You're as dark as a wildebeest!" Markus exclaimed. The one-up-man-ship finally petered out and the two friends and their companions retired, emotionally and physically exhausted, to their bedrolls.

Deep sleep swept over them on this first night of peace. Each slipped into his separate dream of home and family and the woman he left behind, four long years ago. It was four bitter years of fighting in an Africa, a land of immense scale, beauty, hardship, and danger.

Each of these men who managed to survive the travails of countless battles had seared into his soul memories of fallen friends, brave deeds, sacrifice, heartbreak, triumph, and tragedy. For the two friends, Levi and Markus, sleeping side by side that night, a future awaited them full of love, hope, and promise.

The month-long trek to Abercorn, done in short, leisurely stages, seemed almost surreal. There was no need for apprehensive surveillance of the terrain on all sides—no feeling for the gun constantly, gripping it for reassurance. General von Vorbeck informed the officers and European men that the conditions agreed upon included the right to retain their firearms, in British recognition of their gallantry over the past four years.

Arriving in Abercorn, the formal surrender of arms ceremony took place on November 25, 1918, with General Edwards accepting the surrender in the name of King George V. The German troops were transported to Morogoro and thence Dar es Salaam on the Indian Ocean to await ships bound for home.

"This whole process is taking an exasperatingly long time," Levi said. But finally, in late January, 1919, Markus and Levi boarded one of the ships leaving German East Africa for the Fatherland, with several ports of call in between, including German South West Africa.

During the wait for embarkation, the pandemic flu swept across Europe and America and also hit hard the survivors in Africa. Many died. It was heartbreaking to see some of their comrades die of the new disease after surviving the limitless dangers of war. It was dreadful to see fear creep through the remaining troops, now facing a new danger.

Markus and Levi shared a cabin on board their ship with two other officers. Both were on deck as the last lines were heaved off the wharf dockside in Dar es

Salaam. British flags were flapping in the wind where once the Imperial German Insignia flew. It was a bittersweet sight, charged with so many mixed emotions.

"*Ja*, there she goes, German East Africa," Levi said as he jostled for space on the railing. The ship was packed with returning soldiers, including hundreds of South African troops to be dropped off in Cape Town.

Markus spoke into the wind, "I'm just glad this ship stops at Walis Bay, nearest port to Windhoek. They let me send a telegram to Helena, so she knows we're both OK. She and the family will be waiting. God, I'm anxious to see her . . . and little Rupert. He'll be close to five now. And you, Levi, your little one is about seven "

The two friends stayed by the ship's rail till well past sundown, till well past the time when Imperial German East Africa slipped out of sight and into history.

List of Historic and Fictional Characters

Historic Characters:

Admiral King-Hall: commander of British East African and South African forces

Archduke Franz Ferdinand of Austria-Hungary; Wife, Sofie, Duchess of Hohenberg

Bismarck: chancellor of Germany

British Lord Northecliffe

Captain Max Looff: commander of German light cruiser SMS *Konigsberg*

Captain Tom Von Prince, German South West Africa officer

Colonel Von Bock, German East Africa officer

Count Eiffel, architect, designer of the Eiffel Tower

Franz Josef: emperor of Austria-Hungary

General Diventer: commander of British forces in German East Africa

General von Hindenburg, Supreme German Commander during WW I

General Joagusto Monzinho De Albuquerque, Portuguese general

General Ludendorff, German General

General Samsonov, Russian General

General Smuts, English General

General Von Heyebreck: commander, military forces, German South
    West Africa

German Foreign Minister Zimmermann

Governor Seitz, German East Africa

Governor Theodor Leutwein, German South West Africa

Gugliermo Marconi, Italian, inventor of wireless radio

Herero, Hadzas, and BeTongan peoples of Sub-Saharan Africa

Kaiser Wilhelm II: King of Prussia and Emperor of Germany

King Albert I of Belgium

King Carlos of Portugal

Lance Corporal Hopper, British 25th Royal Fusiliers

Lieutenant Boell, German East Africa officer

Lieutenant Colonel Paul Von Lettow Vorbeck: Army commander,
    German East Africa

Napoleon I: emperor of France

Nyaminyami: Zambezi river mythical monster

Premier Stolypin of Russia

President Woodrow Wilson, USA

Prince Ferdinand of Belgium

Robert Koleweg: archaeologist, German Oriental Society

Robert Von Liebon: Austrian electrical engineer

Sergeant William Gregory: British Royal Marines

Fictional Characters:

Anji Mathais: Markus's sister, medical student

Arnold Conrad: son of Tomas Conrad

Gunther and Heiner: old army friends of Levi and Markus

Helena Conrad: eldest daughter of Tomas

Captain Becker: purser on the SMS *Konigsberg*

Captain Llewellyn: South African officer

Captain Spencer: chief medical officer on the German cruiser SMS *Konigsberg*

Christina Conrad: daughter of Tomas

Corporal Ubanga: German *askari* (black soldier) German Southwest Africa

Diana Lange: Warner Lange's daughter

Doctor Rungi: village doctor in Bavaria

Dorothy Lange: Warner Lange's wife

Father Lorraine: Catholic priest in Windhoek, South West Africa

Frau Hoftein: shop owner in Windhoek

Frau Mathais: Markus's mother

Freidl Levi: Levi's mother

Herr Leopold: German trading company owner in Portuguese East Africa

Horst Dorfmann: railway worker in German East Africa

Humboldt Conrad: son of Tomas Conrad

Ilsa Levi: Levi's sister

Joseph Schrager: German businessman and exporter, Tabora, German East Africa

Katherina Levi: Levi's wife

Le Ling: Markus's former love interest in China

Lieutenant Andre Rosenbloom: German officer of train, German East Africa

Lieutenant Markus Mathais: electrical unit officer of the 1st Battalion, for Lower Bavaria, headquartered in Munich

Lieutenant Rolf Kepler: North Bavarian medical corps, Anji's boyfriend

Lieutenant Siegfried Schleiffer: pilot, German Southwest Africa

Michael and Norbert Conrad: twin sons of Tomas Conrad

Mina Schrager: Joseph's wife

Otto Levi: Levi's father

Petre: black housekeeper and cook at Conrad ranch

Portuguese Corporal Carlos Verdi

Portuguese Lieutenant Nunos

Professor Dr. Schellenberger: University Of Munich historian and archeologist

Professor Warner Lange: American electrical engineer

Rashid: Indian manservant to Joseph Schrager There is no last name

Rebecca Levi: Levi's daughter

Rudy, Helmut, and Rainer: military comrades of Markus

Sambolo: black stable boy at Conrad ranch

Sidney Lancaster: big game hunter in German East Africa,
   employed by Schrager
Sisibeco: young, black African woman of the BoTonga people
Solomon Levi: engineer, called Levi (later, Captain),
Tomas Conrad: widowed German rancher in German South West Africa
Wan Ling: Le Ling's father
Willie: orphan, stable boy, and farm hand at Kalvarianhof
Wolfgang Conrad: eldest son of Tomas Conrad

Bibliography

Abbot, W. *The Nations at War*. New York: Leslie-Judge Co., 1918.

Abbot, W. J. (1915). *The Nations at War*. London: Syndicate Pub. Co.

Anderson, R. (2004). *The Forgotten Front, East Africa*. Gloucestershire: Tempus.
Barraclough, G. (1982). *Concise Atlas of World History*. New Jersey: Hammond Inc.

Clark, A. (1971). *Suicide of the Empires*. New York.: American Heritage Press.

Craig, G. A. (1982). *The Germans*. New York: G. P. Putnam's Sons.

Critchler, S. (2008). *The Book of Dead Philosophers*. New York.: Random House. Daniel, C. E. (1975). *Chronicle of the 20th Century*. New York.: Dorling Kindersley.

Dendooven, C. &. (2008). *World War I, Five Continents in Flanders*. Belgium: Lannoo.

Diamond, J. (2005). *Africa*. Washington, D.C.: National Geographic Mag.

Dooly, J. W. (1970). *Great Weapons of W.W. One*. New York: Bonanza Books.

Editors, T. (1915). *The Times History of the War, Europe*. New York.: Woodward & Van Slyke Inc.

Editors. (2004 to 2015). *Auktion, Hermann Historica*. Munchen, Bavaria, Germany: Hermann Historica

Editors, C. (1916). *Collier's Photographic History of the European War*. New York: Collier and Son. Editors, T. (1915*). The Times History of the War, Land & Sea*. New York: Woodward & Van Slyke Inc.

FitzLyon, B. &. (1978). *Before the Revolution*. Woodstock, New York: Overlook Press.

Fromkin, D. (2004). *Europe's Last Summer*. New York: Alfred Knopf.

Funcken, F. &. (1974). *Arms and Uniforms, WW1*. London: Ward Lock.

Gilbertert, M. (1970). *Atlas of the First World War*. New York: Oxford Univ.

Giles, F. &. (2005). *Mini and Toutou's Big Adventure*. New York: Alfred Knopf.

Gliddon, G. (2005*). The Sideshows*. Gloucestershire, Eng.: Sutton Pub.

Keegan, J. (1998). *The First World War*. New York: Alfred Knopf.

Keegan, L. (1971). *Opening Moves*, August 1914. New York: Ballantine.

Krebs, C. B. (2011). *A Most Dangerous Book, Tacitus's Germania*. New York: W. W. Norton & Co.

Laffin, J. (1965). *Jackboot, Hist. of the German Soldier 1713-1945*. New York: Barnes & Noble.

Lobsenz, N. (1960). *Africa*. New York: Golden Press.

Lyford, G. &. (2005). *Germany*. New York: Dorling Kindersley. Grun, B. (1979). *The Timetables of History*. New York: Simon & Schuster.

Hadenberger, W. (1915). *Deutschland's Croberung Der Luft*. Berlin: Berlag Hermann Montanus. Haupt, W. (1984). *Deutschland's Schutzgebiete in Ubersee 1884-1918*. Friedberg, Ger,: Podzum.

Hill-Norton. (1915). *Official Navel Dispatches*. Dewsbury, England: Fernmoor Pub.

Hochschild, A. (1998). *King Leopold's Ghost*. New York: Houghton Mifflin.

Inman & Macdonald, E. (2000). *Jerusalem & the Holy Land*. New York: Dorling Kindersley. Madddocks, S. &. (1975*). The Imperial German Army 1900-1918*. London: Almark Pub.

Marshall, S. (1964). *American Heritage Hist. Of World War One*. New York: American Heritage Pub.

Martel, G. (2003). *The Origins of the First World War*. Essex, Eng.: Person Edu. Limited. Mason, D. (1972). *Churchill 1914-1918*. New York: Ballantine.

Messenger, C. (1972). *Trench Fighting 1914-1918*. New York: Ballantine.

Muller, K. &. (2009*). German Colonial Troops 1889-1918*. Vienna, Austria Verlag Militaria Pub.*Nicholas II, the Imperial Family*. (1998). St. Petersburg, Rus.: Abris Pub.

Perkins, J. (1981). *To The Ends of the Earth*. New York: Pantheon Books.

Persico, J. (2004). *Eleventh Month, Eleventh Day, Eleventh Hour*. New York: Random House. Postman, F. (1979). *The Yiddish Alphabet Book*. Palo Alto, Ca: P'Nye Press.

Reimer, Dietrich, *Kriegskarte von Deutsch-Sudwestafrika 1904*. (War maps)

Reynolds, E. &. (2000). *Kingdom of the Soul*. New York: Prestel.

Robinson, J. &. (2009). *Handbook of Imperial Germany*. Bloomington, Ind.: Author House. Semenov, N. (1998). *Nicholas Romanov, Life and Death*. St. Petersburg, Russia: Liki Rossii Pub.

Sibley, J. R. (1971*). Tanganyikan Guerrilla, E. Africa Campaign 1914-18*. New York.: Ballantine. Smith, W. (2010). *Assegai*. London: Pan Macmillan.

Solzhenitsyn, A. (1983*). August, 1914*. New York: Farrar, Straus and Giroux.

Strachen, H. (2004). *The First World War in Africa*. New York: Oxford Univ. Press

Sleicher, John A. (1918*). Leslie's Illustrated Weekly Newspaper, August 17, 1918* edition, London.

Sturmer, M. (2000). *The German Empire 1870-1918*. New York: Random House.

Tantum, H. &. (1968). *German Army, Navy Uniforms 1871-1918*. Greenwich, Conn.: We, Inc. Taylor, A. (1963). *Illus. History First World War*. London: George Rainbird.

Thoeny, E. (1899). *Der Leutnant. Muenchen*, Ger.: Albert Langen

Tuchman, B. W. (1958). *The Zimmermann Telegram*. New York: Ballantine.

White, W. E. (1967). *By-Line: Ernest Hemingway*. New York: Charles Scribner's & Sons.

Williamson, G. (1994*). The Iron Cross*. Denison, Texas: Reddick.

Willmott, H. (2003). *World War One*. New York: Dorling Kindersley.

Winter, B. &. (1996). *The Great War*. New Yor: Penguin Books.

Woolley, C. (2009). *Uniforms of the German Colonial Troops*. Atglen, Pa.:
Schiffer Military History.

.

Descendants of Abraham Levi

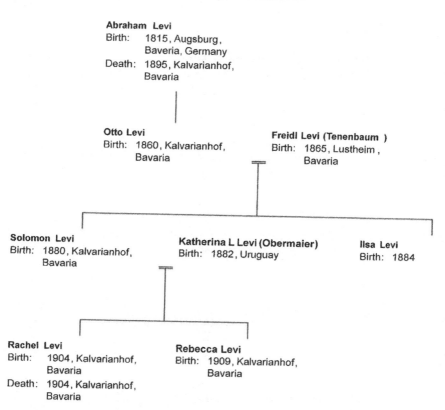

Abraham Levi
Birth: 1815, Augsburg,
Baveria, Germany
Death: 1895, Kalvarianhof,
Bavaria

Otto Levi
Birth: 1860, Kalvarianhof,
Bavaria

Freidl Levi (Tenenbaum)
Birth: 1865, Lustheim ,
Bavaria

Solomon Levi
Birth: 1880, Kalvarianhof,
Bavaria

Katherina L Levi (Obermaier)
Birth: 1882, Uruguay

Ilsa Levi
Birth: 1884

Rachel Levi
Birth: 1904, Kalvarianhof,
Bavaria
Death: 1904, Kalvarianhof,
Bavaria

Rebecca Levi
Birth: 1909, Kalvarianhof,
Bavaria

Descendants of Captain George Mathias

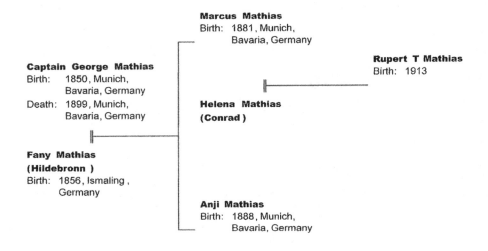

Descendants of Wolfgang Conrad

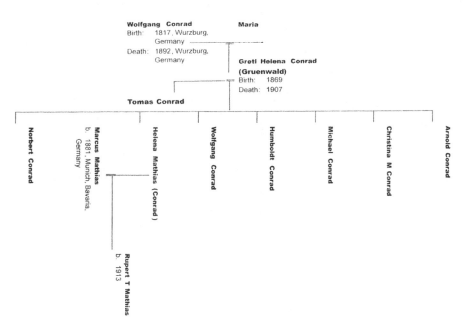

For your pleasure, here are the first 7 Chapters of

The Long Way Home

Book III of the Kalvarianhof Series

Kalvarianhof, February, 1919

—— CHAPTER 1 ——

Bavaria, Winter 1919

K alvarianhof, the grand manor house and farm of the Levi family in the forests near Munich in Bavaria, Germany, was a white wonderland to the eye in February.

It was 1919. Foot-thick snow, untouched in its purity, blanketed the house, the out buildings, and surrounding landscape. The only tracks in the icy, white powder led from the barn to the woods where timber harvesting continued through the winter.

The horse-drawn sled dragged the cut logs easily to the clearing where they would lie, stacked for drying, for a year. Wood smoke rose from two Kalvarianhof chimneys, creating a blue haze in the cold air.

In earlier years, before the Great War, the Levis burned mostly coal. But now, with the country bled dry of resources by the carnage of the war, inflation, and the miners' strikes for higher wages, even coal had become a luxury. Otto Levi, always wise where his Imperial marks were concerned, switched to the unlimited supply of free wood fuel on the estate.

They had weathered the war better than most, with the rich resources of the farm and forest. Paper money was less valuable by the day, so Otto and Freidl had taken to bartering, like so many other Germans. Otto, early on, sensing the economic dangers of the war, had gathered a considerable amount of Imperial gold coin and hidden it away in the undercroft of the old manor house, before the Kaiser converted gold marks to paper money. Otto made it a point not to reveal his precious secret, feeling secure in the knowledge that it was there when needed.

Now they waited for word from their son Levi, away for over five years serving as an officer in Kaiser Wilhelm II's East African Colonial Forces. Five long years had passed, and the world had changed forever. Rebecca, Levi's daughter, was now seven-years-old, and while Katherina, his wife, spoke constantly of Levi, he remained an unknown stranger to the little girl.

For months, the newspapers had articles about homeward-bound soldiers, lists of names of those returning and those who were never to be seen again. The telegram only stated that Levi was safe and would be arriving by ship from Africa sometime in early 1919.

One snowy afternoon, the telephone rang in the front parlor at Kalvarianhof and was picked up by Freidl, Levi's mother. "Ja, good day . . . What, operator? I can't hear you . . . long distance? Where?"

Her heart beat faster as little Rebecca ran up to her grandmama. "I want to talk too!" she shouted. "Who is it? . . . Is it for me?"

"Berlin? Oh, my! Otto, Otto! It's a call from Berlin! Hurry, dear, hurry!"

Otto came scurrying in, favoring a sprained ankle. "Who is it, Freidl? From Berlin?"

Rebecca, sensing the excitement, started jumping up and down. "Me too!" she shouted.

"Oh, my God!" Freidl burst into tears. "Levi, Levi, it's really you! Oh, my son, my son . . . your voice." She couldn't talk through her sobs.

Otto grabbed the receiver, but Freidl was reluctant to let it go. "Go get Kathi, quick, quick!" he urged as he put the receiver to his ear and heard a storm of static.

"Hello? Hello? Operator, I can't hear a thing." Through the crackle of the copper wires swaying in winter storms between Berlin and the family estate in Bavaria, Otto finally heard his son's voice for the first time in five years.

"Papa, Papa!" Levi blurted out. "It's so good to hear your voice."

"Levi, my boy, you're safe again in Germany? Thank God! Where are you? When are you coming home? Should we come up to Berlin?"

The Brandenburg Gate, Berlin, 1919

"No, no, Papa, I'm still in the army. I have to be processed, and there's a big welcoming ceremony for General von Vorbeck, a parade up Unter der Linden and through the Brandenburg Gate. All of us from East Africa will participate . . . but is Katherina there?"

"Yes, yes, here she is." Katherina rushed down the front stairs, almost tripping on the last step, and ran into the parlor. Otto held out the telephone earpiece to the full extent of the black cord. She took it and moved her lips to almost touch the wooden boxed telephone speaker on the wall. "Levi, darling, is it really you at last? I've missed you so, darling . . . Yes, yes, I love you too . . . I'm so sorry; I can't stop crying. Oh, darling, I've waited so long for you, to hear your voice, to be sure of your safe return. What? Yes, I understand . . . How soon, my darling? Several days then . . . Yes, I understand."

The operator interrupted the conversation: "Your time is up. Each soldier gets three minutes. You have fifteen seconds."

"My dearest Kathi, I love you so . . . I'll call again and let you know when the troop train leaves Berlin. Yes, yes, me too. *Auf wiedersehen*, my love."

Everyone had tears streaming down his or her face and was hugging each other. "Why is everybody crying?" pouted Rebecca, who commenced to sniffle.

Freidl, wiping tears with a soggy handkerchief, said, "We have to call Ilsa and her husband; she'll be thrilled to hear her brother is coming home soon. And Katherina's parents, the Obermaiers. I'm sure Levi will call them, of course, but we must call too . . . and Frau Mathais and Anji. Oh, we have to get the house ready—and my baking . . . Isn't it wonderful, Papa? Levi's coming home at last."

— CHAPTER 2 —

Soldiers All and Fighting Too

T he troop train finally pulled out of the snowbound Berlin station near the end of February, 1919 crammed with soldiers, sailors, sea marines, and assorted other men, mostly from Germany's African colonies. Most were able bodied, but some were still on stretchers and others, sadly, missing limbs. Levi thought the saddest of all were the blind and the ones with terribly disfiguring face wounds.

"God, I'm lucky," he mumbled to himself as he shifted his thin frame on the wooden railcar bench.

"There you are, Captain Levi. We've got a compartment. Come on, before it fills up." It was Captain Kohl, who fought in German Cameroon. He reached up and got Levi's carrying bag down from the net shelf.

"And we've got schnapps to smooth the rails!" Both men smiled broadly.

As Levi and Captain Kohl settled into the soft, cushioned seating in the eight-man compartment, someone exclaimed, "We seem to be slowing down!" Several soldiers looked out the window as the southern suburbs of Berlin slipped by. With a screech of steel brakes on steel rails, the train came to a jerking stop.

"Now what?" someone said. Moments later, the conductor came hurrying down the narrow passage. Levi slid open the windowed compartment door and took the train man's arm. "Why are we stopping?"

"It's the Communists and the Socialists and the Monarchists, all fighting it out right across our tracks! Can't you hear the gun fire?" He pulled away and hurried on.

"What? Who's fighting?" He turned back to see several men hanging out the window and looking toward the engine. "Did you hear that . . . what the conductor said?"

"Ja, well, they don't like the present government. All those soldiers of different stripes, that is, with different ideas of what the government should be. They seem to all be against the Weimar Republic."

Captain Kohl looked at Levi, smiled, and said, "You really are out of it, aren't you? At least I got to read British newspapers while in the prisoner of war camp in Cameroon." He shook his head in exasperation and looked at his companion.

Kohl explained, "It's like this. The Monarchists want the Kaiser's son, August Wilhelm, to assume the throne, to be king of Germany. The Communists, that is, the Spartacus Bolsheviks, want a revolution like the Russian Revolution, where they killed the Tsar and his whole rojal family. The Socialists want a strong Labor government, where they control big industry. Now the Weimar government is just trying to create a working, duly elected democratic state. But it seems these other groups don't want to cooperate with Weimar, so we've got all these veterans fighting in the streets."

Levi slumped into the cushions and stared at the floor. "More fighting? I've just spent four and a half years fighting in Africa. Now I come home to find fighting in the streets? Damn! Will it never end?"

The train did move on eventually, and the sounds of civil unrest moved on with it. The schnapps helped Levi slip into a dreamless sleep as rousing army drinking songs rolled down the aisles of the train.

Beer and liquor were easy to come by for these men, thrown together in a bond of comradeship by the war. They, who saw slaughter and mayhem for four long years, we're the lucky ones, still in one piece—or almost so. They were heading home, most to an unknown future.

None of these soldiers were the same men who had left their civilian lives in what seemed a lifetime ago. Fear, pain, and deprivation had altered them and had altered the people they left behind: wives, lovers, mothers, fathers—all were affected by the Great War, as it was now being called.

The troop train stopped north of Munich in the town of Nuremberg. Levi had just enough time to jump off and hurry to the line forming at the telephone booth.

"Kathi, my love, it's me. I'm in Nuremberg. We stopped to let off some of the men. You have no idea what it means to me to be back in Germany, to see the landscape and the towns . . . But there is so much fighting up in Berlin . . . You can't imagine what's going on up there."

"Yes, yes, my darling, it's like that here in Munich. Will you be on the next scheduled train from Nuremberg, or—"

"No. They're letting the troop train go straight on through."

"Levi, darling, be careful in Munich, at the station, when you transfer. They're fighting here in Munich too. The Soldiers and Workers Council is trying to set up a Communist government in Bavaria, but it's quiet in the village, thank God. We'll meet you at the train station in Munich."

"No, my love, it will be too dangerous. I'll go straight through and see you at the village depot . . . in a few hours, my love."

And so, after four and a half years apart, Levi and Katherina were in each other's arms at last. Of course, everyone was at the village train station. They hugged and kissed and laughed and cried and touched him to believe their eyes.

Otto drove the seven-year-old Benz through the snow, and Willie, the farm hand, brought the one-horse carriage to accommodate the rest of the family.

As they passed familiar landmarks, Levi heard the "clink, clink" he knew from his earliest childhood. The blacksmith's shop and stables were lit with several bare bulbs and from the glow of the coal forge fire. Two men were busy shoeing a farm horse. The sweet smell of coal smoke was like a warm greeting to him. The two vehicles passed the last of the village houses and entered the darkly forested lane to Kalvarianhof.

Finally at home and in the kitchen alcove, the Levi family enjoyed coffee and cake while little Rebecca asked one question after another.

"You look different from your picture." She stared at her father, a man she did not know, for a long moment. "You're so brown. Does everyone turn brown when they go to Africa?" The innocent eye and the innocent question brought laughs.

Later, in their own bed in their old bedroom and in a private, emotional meeting of their bodies and minds, the years of separation slipped away in the rhythm of their lovemaking. Katherina held her husband's lean, hardened body in a tight embrace, until the power of sleep loosened her firm hold. The young family, with Rebecca asleep nearby, finally commenced their new life together.

"By the way, my dearest," Katherina began soon after Levi's return, "I have the most exciting development to share with you. Professor Adelman has secured a lectureship for me at the University in Munich. I've been teaching in the archeology department for the last four sessions. I'm so thrilled; imagine, me teaching at the University of Munich!"

She was bubbling with delight in telling how her hard work in the dig in Palestine before the war had paid off, when so many men were called away to duty. "I was genuinely shocked and saddened to hear several of our finest young professors died in the conflict. It left holes in the teaching staff, and I was offered a job. I love what I'm doing. And now I couldn't be happier, with you coming home safely and Rebecca taking to you so. Thank you, my dear husband."

She kissed him, as he said, "But I didn't do anything."

"You survived."

Days passed into weeks as Levi walked the woods and fields of the snowbound estate, clearing his mind and planning his future. He also reflected on how everyone had aged—how the war had imposed pain and suffering on everyone, soldier and civilian alike. Even the buildings at Kalvarianhof needed serious maintenance. He made a note to himself that when spring came he would bring the estate up to the beautiful vision of it he had known before the war.

Former German East Africa

—— CHAPTER 3 ——

Tales of Beauty and Valor

I n the evenings around the wooden table in the alcove, Levi regaled everyone
with stories of the grandeur and mysteries East Africa: the tens of thousands
of wild animals in endless savannahs; the deserts and jungles; the strange
exotic tribes of people. "It's a magnificent, other world. The endless vistas of the
Serengeti plains stretch to the horizon . . . We crossed that vastness time and time
again, Markus and I and all our comrades." He reflected on some visual memory
and then continued, "Swamps and mountain ranges . . . *Ja*, we have the Alps, but
our mountains are different, steeper and higher, with so much snow."

He stopped for a moment and then laughed, "And Queen Victoria's gift, you
know she 'gave' Kaiser Wilhelm Kilimanjaro, that lone mountain rising out of
the landscape with its snowcapped peak. That's something I'll never forget. Can
you imagine? She gave the Kaiser a mountain!"

He was interrupted by his mother, Freidl. "Here we are, your favorite potato
soup with Maggi. You always loved Maggie in your soup."

"He always loved Maggi in everything, Mama," Ilsa said, smiling.

"And I still do! We never had it in Africa after the first few months."

"Oh, my rye bread, still in the oven!" Freidl exclaimed as she scurried to open the wood-fired oven door. "Here, pass this to Levi . . . and the butter," she commanded.

Bread dumplings followed, in a clear, golden-brown broth that almost floated the slab of goose breast. "Mama, you're spoiling me!" Levi looked across to Kathi and winked. "How will my wife ever keep up with your cooking?"

"Do you want to hear about our friend Markus, in Africa?" he asked, knowing the answer. "Well, first I must tell you about my commanding officer and the amazing stories of Colonel von Vorbeck's brilliant leadership. He led us, his hardy band of soldiers, pursuing and being pursued by the British, Belgians, Portuguese, and South Africans for the entire four and a half years of war."

It was twenty minutes of a thrilling monologue of near disasters, brilliant victories, and clever escapes—many clever escapes from the enemy. Otto brought a pitcher of beer and refilled the glasses all around the table.

"A toast to our brave men who served: prost!" It was bittersweet for Levi, reflecting back to the many, many comrades, both white and black, buried out in the vastness of Africa, mostly in unmarked graves. Only a pile of rocks marked their final resting place—to keep the animals from digging.

"*Ja*, so that leads me to the exploits of Markus Mathais. Did I tell you he was awarded another Iron Cross?" Levi was enjoying the telling.

"He flew from South West Africa almost all the way to German East Africa on a dangerous, secret mission before he crashed in a rain storm. I've forgotten the name of the tribe of those natives who found him and took him in. They were kind, caring, gentle blacks; that's for sure. They saved his life, nursing him back to health for almost two months, with their folk medicine. I won't even begin to tell you what some of that medicine was made from . . . another time maybe." They laughed as he took a long draft of his beer; his daughter, Rebecca, slept on the wooden bench.

"And Markus also had encounters with leopards and hyenas and other wild animals." Levi stopped and shook his head. "He got himself pretty scratched up; I can tell you!" His little family audience, spellbound, asked, "And you, Levi?"

"*Ja*, well, I didn't do much. I was with headquarters company."

Munich

—— CHAPTER 4 ——

Shock, Peace, and a November Surprise

With a bit of luck and Otto's village contacts, Levi got a temporary job helping to finish the large aerodrome started during the war. It was at the same, grassy air field where his friend Markus had made his first solo flight. It was also the airfield where old Bavarian King Leopold III started the first Royale Bavarian Military Air Corp in 1913. *This is a lucky break for me*, he thought, as he trudged the mile or so back through the snowbound woods to Kalvarianhof. *Most days I can walk to work!*

Kalvarianhof, with its isolated location in a clearing, in former hunting grounds of royalty, seemed far away from the turmoil in the cities. Of course, the newspapers were full of the clashes of the opposing political groups, but the visceral effects of an unstable society didn't reach to their forest home.

Civil unrest continued in most German cities, including Munich, with gangs of soldiers of one faction or another fighting each other. Surprisingly, civilian life seemed to go on as usual, with city dwellers flowing around and through the armed skirmishes.

Finally, on a spring day, April 5, 1919, the Congress of Soldiers' and Workers' Councils proclaimed a Communist Republic in Bavaria to great protests. Sporadic fighting still continued, even as most citizens waited to see what exactly this new form of governing would be like.

Katherina took the train into the city several days a week for her lectures at the university, and one day Levi accompanied her. His intent was to meet a former colleague from the Berlin to Bagdad company he had worked with before the war. The construction and architectural firm was located near the main train station.

"I take a street car to the university, or I walk on nice days if there are no troubles in the area," Katherina said as the two stepped down from the train.

"So, I go this way and you that," she pointed. "I can get away for lunch. Shall we meet at Dolmaiers?"

"Yes, noon would be fine, but be careful. Who knows what lurks around the next corner?"

"I'll be ever alert, dearest. Don't worry." They came together for a hug and parted. Levi knew well the city of his youth, but the address was new to him.

It was located in a poorer neighborhood, near the converging rail lines. As he moved along the crowded sidewalks, bustling with peddler carts selling roasted chestnuts, vegetables, pots and pans, and all manner of household goods, he also saw a disturbing sight: soldiers and civilians with guns, milling around casually. Obviously, the military men had no officer in charge and no apparent leadership. And there on the street were his other comrades: soldiers of the Great War, veterans all, sitting on the pavement, alone or in groups of two or three, selling pencils or cigarettes from tin cups. Most wore their dress uniforms with military decorations on their chests, proving their valor.

Most disturbing of all, Levi noted, the sight of missing limbs. There were stumps of legs, empty sleeves folded up and pinned neatly, vacant stares from damaged eyes, and facial wounds that repelled. Many soldiers appeared to be shivering, shaking at times, cowering against dark memories of the war.

I've seen all this on the battlefield, he thought, but in Munich, on the streets? He was appalled and embarrassed. How could the government abandon these brave men and the others? What are they waiting for? His mind was reeling. *Why are they reduced to begging, for God's sake?* He dug into his pocket and pulled out what he had in paper and coin. He gave it all to the men along the street.

"Thank you, my friend, for serving . . . for your sacrifice," he said to each of them. *My God, it's the least I can do. Something has to be done.*

He finally arrived at a coal-dust-covered building, the results of being near the rail lines. The construction and architectural company was on the second floor, and to his surprise, his old boss Herr Gustoff Liebermann met him at the door.

"Greetings, old friend, I see you survived the war!" They exchanged a hearty handshake as Liebermann ushered Levi into a small suite of offices. Piles of blueprints and hand-drawn plans for buildings, bridges, factories, and other assorted projects littered the desks and tables.

Looking around, Levi commented, "You seem to be busy enough, Herr Liebermann."

"*Ja*, it looks so, but most projects are on hold because of politics . . . And please, drop the Herr Liebermann. It's Gustoff to you."

A half-empty schnapps bottle drained into two glasses as the men settled into cracked, leather chairs. After talking the war, Gustoff asked, "What have you been doing since you got home, my friend?"

"Working on the big aerodrome at the village air field. I was lucky to get the job. Now it's done, and I'm looking for a new opportunity. I was hoping you might have something I could put my skills to."

Gustoff swung his arm out in an arc. Only a one-armed draftsman was working, head down, at a drafting table across the room. "My nephew . . . he does good work, but I pay him very little. He's also missing half a leg." They stared a few moments at the veteran.

"There just isn't any business for an additional man, at least not full time." Both men looked at each other.

"Tell you what. I can hire you with half-time pay, and the other half time you spend looking for business for this company. You bring in business, you go full-time salary. What do you think?" Levi was silent a moment as Gustoff added, "With your contacts and reputation, I'll bet you can find us a contract or two." He was grinning broadly.

"You've got a deal, Gustoff." Lunch at Dolmaier's with Katherina became a celebration as Levi told about his new position. Levi also was animated as he told his wife about how Otto told him of a large, new estate planned beyond the woods of Kalvarianhof. "It's for a big industrialist . . . one of those men who made a fortune during the war." He was watching Katherina's reaction.

"I know; I know. I don't like it either, but it possibly means work." Over the next few weeks, Levi beat the pavement in Munich, approaching companies and corporations he felt might need architectural work. No one seemed to be expanding their facilities.

"Try the government agencies," Gustoff suggested. "They're the only ones with real money. *Ja*, or the war profiteers!"

— CHAPTER 5 —

The Coldest Hearts of the Vastly Unjust

On January 10, 1920, he Treaty of Versailles was ratified in Paris, officially ending the most dreadfully bloody war in history. News came by telephone from Levi, who was in Berlin exploring a possible government contract to rebuild several bridges across the Rhine damaged during the war.

"Ja, ja, it seems the same to me. What's to change? that's right, Papa; the war is finally, officially over." Otto got to the phone first and listened intently as Levi continued. "The Reichstag has just voted on the treaty, and it passed, though many denounced it as vastly unjust and a betrayal . . . It puts all the blame for the war on us, and we lose our colonies . . . all of them, and the reparations are extreme!" Otto could hear the anguish in his son's voice. "It's going to bankrupt the country, Papa. It's going to create inflation and injure almost everybody. I think there's going to be trouble, big trouble, over this." He reflected a moment and added, "Well, at least it ends the armistice, and the war is officially over, so we can get on with our lives."

"Ja, but we were expecting Germany would get a fair shake, a reasonable treaty like what Wilson proposed . . . Even the British supported most of Wilson's ideas. But those French, they just wanted revenge. Those exorbitant reparations!" Otto exclaimed. "How can Germany recover if it gives all its limited resources to France and Belgium and England and America?"

"You're right. That treaty is going to cause a lot of trouble." Silence on the line, and finally, "Ja, well, I'll be home on the train tomorrow, till then . . ."

Levi did secure a contract to repair two bridges, with, surprisingly, help from the French. They wanted the bridges over the Rhine repaired for their trade ambitions, not as a gesture of friendship after the Great War. Nevertheless, it was work for Levi's skills and good news for the family and for Gustoff.

The political unrest in Bavaria and greater Germany continued when the Prussian Monarchists seized power in a coup in March in Berlin. It lasted a short week or so, with fighting in the streets of many cities.

The national government in Weimar regained control of the old imperial capital and, at the same time, fended off the Communists, who had controlled half of Berlin at one time. In April, the extreme-right German Workers Party changed its name to the National Socialist Workers' Party and continued its national rights agitation. All this turmoil stressed the greater portion of the German people, but at Kalvarianhof, there was happy news.

Katherina had a special surprise. "We're going to have an addition to the family in November, darling."

Levi was ecstatic. "With my bridge construction work on the Rhine and a new baby," he laughed, "life is good again at Kalvarianhof!" Sweeping Kathi off her feet, he and she both smiled gaily as they swirled around in pure joy.

Former German Southwest Africa

—— CHAPTER 6 ——

Violence and Silence in Africa

Meanwhile, in far off Africa, Levi's childhood friend Captain Markus Mathais, battle scared from four long years of fighting, was soon to reunite with his family.

He served in the army with Levi in East Africa and was now on a troop ship full of vanquished veterans, all heading home.

The Conrad ranch was northeast of the capitol Windhoek. Under Allied occupation, German South West Africa was unusually quiet that day in February 1919. The armistice had been signed a few short months ago between Germany and her allies and France, Britain, Belgium, and America. His ship was due in port in two weeks.

Markus had lived in the South West Africa colony since 1909. He married Helena Conrad and had a son, Rupert, now waiting for him at their isolated ranch home northeast of Windhoek, the capitol.

Two weeks or so before Markus's ship was to dock, his father-in-law, Tomas Conrad, was in town with two of his sons, Wolfgang and Norbert, and their house man, Petre. His other son and daughter, Michael and Christina, were on horseback out in the bush, looking for stray cattle.

Helena, his wife, still startlingly lovely with her long, light-brown hair, was home alone except for their boy, Rupert, now almost six. Their stable boy, Sambolo, was in the barn. Helena stepped back into the kitchen, having just placed flowers on the graves of her mother, Frau Conrad, dead many years, and the graves of Arnold, killed in the war, and Humboldt, taken by influenza a year ago.

She heard the horse ride up to the house and knew it was Captain Llewellyn. The war was over but the occupation by the victors continued. She felt the occupation keenly, with the presence of one South African officer who still billeted in her home. They had all tolerated him for over three years, he with his prying eyes and arrogant way.

He strolled into the ranch house, his riding boots loud on the wood floor. "Good afternoon, Helena. You look as lovely as ever today in that lavender blouse. Is there any gin left in that bottle?" He gestured toward the buffet.

"Help yourself, as you always do," she said coldly.

"I want you to pour one for me this time," he said. "I have something very important to tell . . . to offer you. Sit down."

She was startled by his bluntness, but complied, sitting in one of the overstuffed chairs in the front parlor. He took a long draft from his gin glass and looked at her.

"I've been assigned the task of recommending which German individuals and families are to be deported from this district, that is, repatriated back to Germany."

A cold chill crept over Helena.

"We're looking for troublemakers and those who don't cooperate with the order in this new South African Protectorate. Those who do cooperate, who are 'friendly,' will be given every consideration. Do you understand, Helena?"

She despised his stare.

"Will you cooperate?" he pressed.

"But we have," she began. "We took into our home four of your soldiers. We fed and cleaned and housed you and the three others. What more could we do?" She paused to collect her thoughts. "We accepted the results of the war here in Southwest Africa. I lost my brother Arnold to this terrible war." She rose from the chair, her voice strained. "What more could we have done?" He closed the distance between them. She pulled back slightly.

"It's not what your family did; it's what you can do now for them." He smiled at her as his eyes roamed across her like caressing hands. He stepped closer. She crossed her arms tightly in front of her.

"You could—no—you should be more friendly to someone who holds the fate of this ranch and your family in his hands. He reached out as if to brush some unseen object off her shoulder. His hand lingered on her upper arm, stroking it gently. "We should be more friendly to each other," he whispered, gazing at her intently. "After all, I've lived here with you for quite some time-in your home, just down the hall from your bedroom."

She looked away, saying, "Please, we've done all you've asked. I have a husband and my child is sleeping in the—" He cut her off.

"And I have a wife back in Johannesburg, whom I haven't seen in months. And you, Frau Mathais, Helena," he emphasized "Helena," "you haven't seen your husband in, what, four years? That's a long time for a married woman to be alone."

He paused for emphasis and repeated, "A long time to be . . . well, alone."

He took a short step closer to her, and his hand went around her arm. He pulled her in closer. She could smell him. "I can help your family in all of this." His eyes darted away from her as his arm swept the air. "I can save this, but I need you, your cooperation, because . . . I have needs too." His face was close to hers. He could smell her hair. It inflamed him.

"Please!" she said. His lips brushed her cheek. His other hand touched her chin and turned her head toward him. He kissed her, first most gently, then with greater passion. She tried to pull back but she was in his grip. His hands slid around her back and pressed her to him. He could feel her body against him. She squirmed loose and turned her back to him.

"No! I have a husband and child," she repeated. He came up behind her, drawing her to him.

"I have the papers right here," he groaned in a low voice. "I can sign them right now. I just need you to—" He spun her around and kissed her as his hands pulled her blouse out of her skirt. His hands plunged inside the back of her skirt. He could feel her warm, smooth skin.

She let out a plaintive sound and, breaking away, she hissed, "No!"

He let her go. "All right; have it your way. I'll just turn your names in to headquarters, but I'll give you a little while to think about it before I do."

He walked to the center of the room, straightened his uniform, and ran his hands through his hair. He looked at her as she stared away from him. "I have to put my horse in the stable. I'll be back. Think about it." With that, he strolled out, his boots again pounding on the wooden floor.

—— CHAPTER 7 ——

The Incident

H elena stood there alone, thoughts racing through her mind. *I knew he would try something like this, but to threaten the ranch . . . and our very right to live here. God in heaven! Can he really throw us out, deport us, to Germany or who knows where else? I've never even lived in Germany, just one short visit. We're Africans!* Out loud she exclaimed, "Mother of God, what shall I do?"

Pacing back and forth, she clutched the small gold cross on her chest. She stopped and looked in to see young Rupert, sound asleep.

I've got to do something. I'll go talk to that brute; maybe he will be reasonable

————

I hope you enjoyed these first chapters of 'The Long Way Home', the third historic fiction book in the Kalvrianhof series. The fourth book in the series is in process.

Please visit the author on facebook: Walter Soellner and on his Web Site: waltersoellner.com

I invite you to read and enjoy my first book in this series of four entitled: *Kalvarianhof, The Perilous Journey.*